I0650174

Wildest Wish

by

Alex Gordon

Darkest Wishes, Book Two

Copyright Notice

This is a work of fiction. Names, characters, places, and incidents are either the product of the author's imagination or are used fictitiously, and any resemblance to actual persons living or dead, business establishments, events, or locales, is entirely coincidental.

Wildest Wish

COPYRIGHT © 2024 by Alex Gordon

All rights reserved. No part of this book may be used or reproduced in any manner whatsoever without written permission of the author or The Wild Rose Press, Inc. except in the case of brief quotations embodied in critical articles or reviews.

Contact Information: info@thewildrosepress.com

Cover Art by *Kristian Norris*

The Wild Rose Press, Inc.
PO Box 708
Adams Basin, NY 14410-0708
Visit us at www.thewildrosepress.com

Publishing History
First Edition, 2024
Trade Paperback ISBN 978-1-5092-5906-9
Digital ISBN 978-1-5092-5907-6

Darkest Wishes, Book Two
Published in the United States of America

Dedication

To Jesse--Thank you for the strangest birthday gift I've ever received. Who could've predicted that a psychic reading would change the course of my life? Only you!

Chapter 1: Regan

June 15th
They deserve to die was the last thing I said before I killed them.

"I know you say you're ready, but you don't have to do this, Regan," Gin said. He threw an arm around my shoulder as we strolled along the sidewalk in downtown Anchorage, Alaska. Thankfully, it wasn't the same street corner where I'd killed my father. All the same, I could feel him staring—wondering how I was handling the pressure.

Gin's brown hair caught the salty breeze coming off the ocean. It flopped over his forehead covering the concern in his deep-set eyes. Since their emerald green color was so distinctive, he wore brown contacts as part of our cover. I was surprised to find he was as good-looking even with the muted hue. It allowed his other features to be seen.

I glanced away, as he was particularly preceptive and I didn't want him to see my building apprehension. My face wasn't always cooperative when it came to hiding emotions.

With my elbow, I gently jabbed his ribs.

"Gin, shut your cake hole. I've got this." Though I wasn't sure that I did. It was one thing to humiliate a tyrannical cheerleader, today's mission was . . . slightly more advanced.

The golem living inside my mind danced with anticipation behind the glass walls of its prison. *Why glass?* Because that way I could keep an eye on it. Wisps of black smoke swirled and crept along the edges of the clear box testing the security. But it didn't have to wait much longer. Soon, its wildest wish would be granted. I prayed that once it was released, I could rein it back in.

"Feisty this evening, are we?" He squeezed my arm harder.

I snarled my lip and pushed him away. He didn't need to think his support was warranted right before I murdered two people. If successful, it would bring my body count to three. Officially, I'd be labeled a serial killer. But that's only if I counted my dad in the tally. Technically, killing him was an accident, my greatest sin. And here I was trying to atone for it by killing more people. The irony was not lost.

But these guys—these villains in my crosshairs— they were bad news. The worst. After I'd graduated from high school, I'd accepted a job with Global Security Systems, and because of my training with Gin, my golem and I had become stronger.

We stopped in front of a towering condo with lush flower baskets hanging outside the entryway. Gin opened the door and motioned for me to go first. Dust swirled as we stepped into the reception area of the newly constructed building.

"Welcome. Can I help you?" A gentleman with a full head of silver hair stood behind the front desk wearing a wide smile and a suit.

Gin glanced at the man's name tag. "Hi, Tomas. I'm a real estate agent with Summer and Sons," he lied in a very convincing Midwestern accent. I muffled my laughter behind a fake cough. The boy was as southern as Tennessee Whiskey. All those acting skills he'd acquired while singing professionally for the opera had definitely paid off.

Gin shook Tomas's hand and gave him a realtor card. It's not like GSS had moral concerns about faking a document or two. In the big picture, as far as I could tell, we were doing good things for the world. And if I succeeded in this assignment, I'd officially become part of the team.

"Ah, yes. Which apartment? So, I can sign you in." Tomas's fingers hovered over a keyboard.

A droll grin curled Gin's lips as if he knew what the man's reaction was about to be. "Penthouse, please."

Tomas's eyes widened, his bushy eyebrows touching his forehead, while he paused and took in all five feet of my stature and my youth. He blinked a couple of times and cleared his throat to cover his disbelief that I was able to afford a luxury apartment.

"My parents asked me to look at it for them," I clarified with a lie.

"Oh, yes. I understand." Tomas pressed a button and the elevator to his right silently slid open. "All set," he said.

I swallowed hard before stepping inside and settling against the back corner. My sweating hands were slick against the stainless-steel railing. As each floor lit up, my anxiety and the golem's eagerness mingled together, making it hard to differentiate my emotions from the monster's. *I* was not excited about the prospect of killing someone. The golem, however, was sharpening its imaginary claws in preparation. Our combative reactions made me feel as if I were standing on the side of a bridge in bungee gear and about to step off the edge. Adrenaline fueled by fear.

The elevator dinged and came to a smooth halt. Gin poked his head out to look around.

"Clear." He stepped onto the laminate wood flooring.

I shook out my hands next to my thighs trying to release excess tension. I'd been training at GSS for only a couple of weeks, but my initiation—or what I considered my final exam—had been bumped forward thanks to our overzealous criminals' intent on expanding their sex trafficking operation.

When Mr. LaCroix, Gin's uncle and my boss, approached me with this mission I'd insisted that I was ready. But the closer we got to the apartment, the worse my guts wound into a nervous knot.

"Breathe," Gin gently reminded me. He rested the palm of his hand on the small of my back while guiding me down the hall.

I inhaled slowly through my nose and out my mouth. The smell of new construction lingered in the air.

We paused in front of the entrance of the desired apartment and Gin typed in the passcode. The lock buzzed and he opened the door. Though inside smelled homey, like freshly baked cookies, it wasn't. It was an open-concept bachelor pad with dark wood floors, light gray walls, and black stainless-steel appliances.

My stomach growled loudly in the quiet space. I slapped a hand over it as if that would muffle the sound and stop the grumbling. Gin grinned and cocked an eyebrow. I twitched one shoulder. I'd been too queasy to eat breakfast or lunch. And despite my body's response to the delicious scent of baked goods, the thought of actually eating made my mouth water. Not in anticipation—more like right before you puke.

I strode around the dining room table, careful not to knock over a vase of white roses, toward the expansive view of Cook Inlet. I placed a hand on the floor-to-ceiling window and leaned close, my breath fogging up the glass.

The evening sun wouldn't set until after midnight this far north. It reflected on the mirrored windows of the surrounding buildings and gilded the pockets of landscaped greenery.

"We'll spend twenty minutes in here." Gin checked his watch. "Then we'll go across the hall. If we've timed this right, they'll be meeting in his office soon."

My heart lurched behind my ribs as bile crept up the back of my throat.

I meandered over to the kitchen and ran my hand over the cool slab of black granite atop the white cabinets. The desire to press my face onto the cold stone to stop me from sweating was tempting, but I was doing my best to hide my nerves from Gin.

Though he wasn't paying any attention to me, he was busy fiddling with the fireplace remote. With a whoosh, flames emerged from the crystals behind the hearth.

"Sit," he said. He made himself comfortable on the white leather couch and glanced at his watch again.

I shook my head. I needed to keep moving. Anything to keep my mind off the task at hand. I snooped through the cabinet drawers only to find them empty.

"Does anyone live here?" I asked.

"No. But it's nice." His gaze swept around the space. "And the view? I'm thinking about buying it myself."

My forehead wrinkled. "Can you afford it?"

A look of irritated humor painted his features. "Darlin', I could buy this entire floor."

I plopped down on the edge of a chair and stared out over the ocean as the sun scooted behind some wispy clouds. Ribbons of yellow, orange, and pink streaked the horizon until they faded into a pale blue sky. After what felt like only a few minutes, he looked at his watch again. "Are you ready?" He stood and clasped his hands behind his back.

With my teeth clenched and my nostrils flared, I inhaled deeply and nodded, afraid that if I spoke the answer would come out—No. His lips pressed into a firm line, and he returned my nod with a brief one of his own.

Reluctantly, I rose from the chair and stood behind Gin as he peered out the door to check if the coast was clear. We needed to make sure no one saw us enter or exit the apartment across the way. For safety measures, the I.T. department at GSS had temporarily disabled the security cameras on every floor of this and the surrounding complexes.

Gin took my hand and pulled me across the hall. The lock on the door popped open of its own accord and we rushed inside.

The apartment was identical except there was no furniture to make it seem welcoming. Just a large, cold, open space with a peek-a-boo view of the Chugach mountains instead of the ocean. When the door clicked shut, I stepped backward. Sweat beaded on my upper lip and under my long bangs. I swept them aside and tucked them behind my ear. Instead of maintaining my pixie, I'd let it grow out to a short bob.

With his hands resting in his pant pockets, Gin strode over to the colossal windows as if we were here to check out this view. In a way, I supposed we were. Again, he checked his watch. "Anytime now," he said.

I wiped my clammy hands on my jeans and forced my jittery legs to carry me across the floor.

The golem pressed against the side of its glass prison in anticipation, like a drooling dog about to receive a bone. So long as I kept my anger in check, the golem mostly did my bidding. But I'd never killed anyone on purpose.

In the condo across the street, on the floor level to ours, a light flipped on causing my pulse to race. My hand trembled as I pulled a small set of binoculars out of my jacket and peered through the lenses.

Two guys in their late twenties—one short and portly, the other tall, blonde, and handsome—walked into the office decorated with wood walls, built-in bookcases, and leather furniture. I could practically smell the cigars and whiskey from here.

The chubby one sat down behind the desk while the blonde took a seat on the other side and casually crossed his legs.

Because of GSS's intel, we were able to piece together their story of criminal activity. These two scum bags were childhood friends who'd attended college together. After graduation, they formed a bogus start-up company here in Alaska as a cover for their nefarious activities. Over the last three years, they'd both profited greatly from dealing drugs and sex trafficking. My jaw twitched at the mere thought. I'd seen the proof with my own eyes.

A few nights ago, Gin had taken me out to a seedy

bar that lacked basic security—no cameras—no bouncers. He wanted me to witness the good-looking one in action. I think he was trying to keep my first job easier by making it personal.

Intending to use me as bait on our reconnaissance mission, he insisted I dress up.

"Catch his eye," Gin said as we sat at a bar table. He stirred his martini with the green olives on a toothpick. His hair was artfully messy and his outfit was on point. More so than normal.

"What?" I paused with my soda in hand. I was here to observe and report—not get involved.

"I want you to see how charming he is with his SoCal good looks and surfer boy persona. I want you to see how easily he preys on innocent women."

I wrinkled my nose. "Uh, I'm not equipped to flirt." He was well aware of my social graces. Or lack thereof.

He let his gaze wander down my frame and back up. "Trust me, you'll be fine."

I scowled. I was uncomfortable in the low-cut black dress with a ridiculously short hemline.

He chuckled. "Just follow my lead." He cocked his head ever so slightly and smiled at a guy sitting alone at the bar. He licked his bottom lip before he nibbled on the corner of his mouth.

"Are you gay?" I blurted, shocked because, minus that moment, I'd never gotten that vibe from him. Quite the opposite really.

He winked at me. "No, but I don't want SoCal to think you're here on a date."

"Are you for real?" I grumbled as the guy from the bar strolled over to our table holding two martinis.

Shaking my head at Gin's audacity, I slid off the tall

stool. *"I have to pee."* I yanked on the dress making sure it was covering my butt.

Gin gently grabbed my arm holding me back for a second as he whispered in my ear, *"Don't drink anything SoCal buys you. Okay? He likes to drug his dates."*

I narrowed my eyes before I hiked my purse higher on my shoulder and nodded in agreement.

On my way to the restroom, I caught SoCal's eye and did my best to smile at him. I was not debasing myself with the rest of Gin's techniques.

After I came out, SoCal was waiting for me at the end of the hallway. He flashed his perfect grin, dimples creasing his cheeks giving him a boyish air. He was gorgeous. But often deadly predators were.

His eyes didn't even flash to the practically full exposure of my boobs.

"Can I buy you a drink? I see your friend is otherwise occupied for the moment and thought you might like some company." He hesitated and held a hand up like a white flag. *"If I read the situation wrong and you don't, I'm sorry for bothering you. It's just that sometimes, ya know, I like to meet people in person and not on the other end of the phone. But I . . . I understand if you're not interested."* His tone and the expression behind his warm brown eyes bordered on a lost puppy in need of rescue.

I wasn't falling for it. With his looks, he could have anyone in the room but I could see how someone could be charmed. Good looking—confident enough to approach me—and a dash of insecurity. He was the perfect combination. It made him seem warm and safe.

He was neither.

I did have a drink with him, but somewhere along

the way, I might've made him switch with me. Gin's laughter rang from across the room. Shortly after I made SoCal down my drink in one big swallow, he started flirting openly with me.

"So gorgeous, how do I get you to come home with me?" he asked, his words loosening. His self-control from earlier vanished as his eyes traveled down my face and paused on my cleavage for a long beat. A hungry— or horny—smile lifted his lips revealing his dimples.

"You don't," I said flatly. I shook my head. Dang, he was gorgeous. What a waste.

He met my eyes, and his smile grew larger as if he liked the challenge of someone who told him no. "Oh, come on." He touched the end of my nose with his finger. I brushed his hand away. The golem nudged at its prison.

"I think I'd like to take you for a ride before I sell you at the auction." He chuckled at his inside joke—one that I understood perfectly. Just as the golem and I were about to get creative, Gin grabbed me from behind to pull me off the bar stool before I made the guy choke on a maraschino cherry and suffocate right there. Gin firmly escorted me to the car. I pouted the entire ride back to our hotel.

But the last laugh was mine. Here I was, about to introduce SoCal to Karma in an epic way. Well, not epic, but I was here to arrange their final meeting.

"Regan, are you ready?" Gin startled me out of my musings.

"Uh, yeah," I answered with very little conviction. I tucked the binoculars back in my pocket and stared out the window. I blinked hard adjusting my eyes to the change in distance.

Gin came up behind me and laid a hand on my

shoulder. "You don't have to do this. We've talked about it and I don't think you're ready. Regan, it's okay to walk away."

My nostrils flared and I forced my reluctance aside. "No, it's not."

If I could save one innocent person, my actions would be worth it. These villains had destroyed hundreds of lives. There was no way I was letting them walk free on this planet another minute.

I moved away from Gin's comforting touch, positioned my feet firmly, folded my arms, and said, "They deserve to die."

A tingle spread from my chest to the ends of my fingers and the tips of my toes—*I wish.*

Chapter 2: Jude

Memorial Day Weekend—two weeks prior

Regan sat next to me, her leg touching mine and our feet dangling in the clear mountain creek. Fool's gold glittered under the water, sparkling in the afternoon sun. A gentle breeze wafted through the trees bringing with it the scent of pine needles and spring flowers.

I reached out and grabbed her hand. It was chilly despite the warm air. My skin had deepened with the sun and hers, despite how much time we spent outside, stayed pale. She liked to compare her tone to the underbelly of a halibut fish. I very much disagreed. Colors were my strength. Not only in my art, but in my daily life of witnessing auras, and Regan's skin was the exact shade of a fresh water pearl. Exquisitely porcelain, yet in certain lights flashed with rose undertones. But it was the black smoke that cloaked her shoulders and head like a rolling fog that had initially caught my interest. Her aura was like nothing I'd ever witnessed. Inside the thick haze, tiny shards of light twinkled like crystals of fresh fallen snow under the midnight moon.

I squeezed her hand. "You know, you don't have to go," I said, referring to her plane flight for the next morning. Despite my protests, she'd accepted a tentative job offer with Global Security Systems. They had a location in Alaska where Regan, and the other new hires, would be training for the next three months to see if they were a good fit for the company.

Her shoulders dropped with resignation. It wasn't the first time we'd had this conversation, but I was like a hound dog on a scent trail and I couldn't let it go.

She sighed. "You know that I do. They're never going to give up. Besides, maybe I can learn how to control this thing. Gin said—"

"Uh," I groaned. There was something about the guy that bothered me. The way that he looked at my girlfriend as if she were his new pet, his new project, rankled on my nerves. Regan insisted it wasn't like that, and for her it wasn't. All I could feel coming through our connection was curiosity and hope. Hope that he could help her learn to live a normal life. Though her version of normal and mine seemed to be on different trajectories, giving me another set of worries.

She shrugged. "What? He's the only one who has abilities that are as powerful as mine."

My jaw clenched and I took a deep breath in order to harness my attitude. "And has he admitted to what these special powers are yet?"

She could be walking into a dangerous situation. Matter of fact, I was sure she was and she wasn't concerned in the least. She believed that she was untouchable. And to most humans, she was. But what if she wasn't the biggest badass around? What about all of GSS's other recruits?

She lifted our hands and bumped me lightly with her elbow. "No. But I'm sure he'll tell me eventually. I can be charming when I want to."

That's what I was afraid of.

"How are you going to manage without me?" I asked. For some reason, I had the ability to minimize the darkness inside of her. When I touched her, the emotions feeding her golem subsided. Unfortunately, they often fueled my anger. By the time they funneled through her and made their way to me, they were manageable for the most part. I'd yet to tell Regan how her darkness affected me, and currently, I had no plans to ever tell her. Because if I did, she would insist we break our connection. I knew her. If she could save someone she loved by jumping off a bridge, she'd do it.

Funny how she was so twisted up inside, yet had a heart of gold. She was Yin and Yang. I guess all of us were to a certain extent. But my grandpa said that Regan's battle was a constant fight between good and evil. The dark wolf versus the light wolf. Only she could choose which wolf to feed. I threw a silent prayer into the wind that she would hold strong in the face of temptation.

She shrugged. "I'll figure it out. Plus, I can't imagine anyone making me *that mad* between here and Alaska. It takes something significant for the golem to break free nowadays."

"Well, let's just hope nobody irritates you before you've had coffee." I released her hand and wrapped my arm around her shoulder, pulling her close. The perfume I'd bought her for Christmas wafted around me. I reveled in the scent of vanilla and the undercurrent of a darker spice. She smelled good enough to eat.

"If they do succeed, I promise to just make them toss their phone in the toilet. Harmless, really."

We both laughed, knowing that to some people, it might be the worst punishment possible.

In order to keep her darkness on a leash, she had to do bad things to people. But because she was a good person, she chose only to torment those who deserved it. I was okay with her tactics as long as she didn't physically hurt anyone. I was afraid that physical violence was exactly what GSS had planned for her. They had a notorious reputation for undertaking off-the-books operations. And I most certainly hated her new boss, George LaCroix. He was Gabby LaCroix's father and, after what she'd done to me, I didn't trust anyone in that family. Especially, his nephew Gin—Regan's new instructor.

Besides, why else would GSS want someone like Regan? She could make anyone do anything at any time. She was the ultimate assassin. She could kill you without ever touching you, leaving behind no trace that she'd even been there. I often fretted what her abilities could be capable of if she didn't have the filter of her kind soul.

Again, I pressed. "Well, the job orientation is only for the summer. If you don't like it, or you don't think their morals fit yours, you can always come home. You don't have to accept their offer once the probation period is over."

"You're right. So, let's not worry about it." She kicked her foot in the creek, splashing water high in the air creating a momentary rainbow.

I couldn't help but worry. But mostly because *she* wasn't actually concerned with the situation she was walking into. She was excited. It made me feel like I was losing her, even though we had a bond that could never be broken.

My thoughts reluctantly bounced back to my grandpa and his wisdom. Though he liked Regan, he didn't trust her because of the entity residing within her. He was even more upset when I finally admitted that—

to keep her from dying— I'd tied my essence, my soul, my whatever, to hers. When he learned what I'd done, he gave me the address of a local medicine man. First, I'd crumpled it and tossed it in the garbage. Later that night, after I'd woken up from a nightmare, I pulled it from the trash and smoothed it out. I stared at it, the white paper glowing eerily in my night light, before I'd stuffed it between the pages of a book about Norse Mythology. Strangely, it opened to the chapter on Loki the Norse God of Mischief. Probably because I'd read it a million times.

Not ready to lose the battle just yet, I said, "You can always enroll at the community college in Powell, if you want."

She had forgone her college dreams when she decided to accept GSS's job offer but I didn't want her to forget her original goals. She was incredibly smart and had a bright future. I just wanted to make sure I was in it.

She tucked a strand of hair behind her ear. It was an unusual color of tawny brown mixed with silvery blonde highlights. "You know I can't do that until I'm sure I won't hurt anyone again."

"Okay," I conceded. *Sort of.* "And say that you figure it out by the end of summer? We've talked about this. You would make a fantastic architect. You're brilliant, you love numbers and art. It's a win-win. Once we're both finished with our education, we'll start a construction company." Over the summer, I'd enrolled in some contracting classes and in the fall, I had plans to get an associate in business. "We'll be set for the future."

Hesitation, and what felt like irritation, that flashed through our connection found me holding my breath for a few seconds. Thankfully, while I could feel Regan's emotions, for some reason, she couldn't pick up on mine unless they were intense. For that I was grateful. I didn't want her to know of my insecurities, the imaginary voice inside my head telling me I wasn't good enough. And though I'd poured my heart out to her—told her things I'd never said aloud—she couldn't reach inside and touch my pain like I could hers.

She turned her head and looked up at me. Golden rays of sun spread across her face and lightened her steel-blue eyes to a bright cerulean. She smiled and, though she appeared happy, a pinch of sadness swirled under the surface. "Nothing is possible until I get this monster under control. And the only option I have is GSS."

Chapter 3: Regan

I tossed my backpack over one shoulder, nearly knocking myself off my feet from the weight and stepped off the plane into the airport. I texted Jude letting him know that I'd arrived safely. He was worried. I could feel it.

Like me, he had unusual powers. He could see auras and track them by their colors. A few months ago, to keep me from dying, Jude had created a unique bond between the two of us. I wasn't a huge fan of the connection, but we couldn't break it without endangering our lives.

He responded with a thumbs-up emoji and a heart. What he really wanted to say without actually saying it was: *Be careful. Trust no one. I love you.*

I responded with a kiss emoji and shoved my phone back in my pocket. I missed him already and it hadn't even been a full twenty-four hours. With my heart lodged in my throat, I hurried to the baggage claim. The flight had landed late, and I didn't want to keep Gin waiting long. He'd already texted he was outside.

I wish.

A tingle spread from the ends of my fingers to the tips of my toes. The crowd of people gathered around the carousel parted like the Red Sea giving me a clear path to my suitcases. I heaved both bags from the conveyer, tossed the lighter one over the top of the other, and rolled them out the door to meet Gin.

Immediately, the smell of the ocean and the heaviness of the air wrapped me in a big Alaskan hug. Tears swam in my eyes and burned the back of my nose. Pressure in my chest, one that I didn't know was there, loosened. I was home.

Part of the reason I'd agreed to work for Global Security was that they had an office in Anchorage and their remote training facility was here as well. But the main part was to keep my family safe and protect them from further harassment. Not only from GSS but from other security companies as well.

The downside was that the head of the corporation was George LaCroix. Gabby LaCroix's father. She had been the head cheerleader of the Three Musketcheers and my nemesis for the last year. Our feud hadn't ended well and being around him made both me and the golem edgy and suspicious.

Upon our initial meeting in Seattle Washington, my mom practically had a stroke when introduced to Mr. LaCroix. Though he wasn't the one who'd bullied me in school, my mom was convinced like father, like daughter. Up until that point, our only contact had been with Ron Stevens, the COO. None of us had known for sure that Mr. Lacroix was the CEO of GSS. The company originated in one of those states that allow the information to stay secret. Though, since Gin worked for them, we all had an inkling that Mr. LaCroix might be involved. After all, there were rumors abounded that he owned a high-tech security company that did dirty deeds for the Federal Government.

When we had arrived back home in Wyoming after the meeting, Jude and my mom had argued with my decision to accept their employment offer. Honestly, the money was too good to pass up. And now that my dad was gone (thanks to me), we could really use it. It was the least I could do. And you know what they say about keeping your enemies close.

Barry, my mom's boyfriend and a local cop, had been on the fence about the company. He'd done a deep-dive on GSS but he came back empty handed. Even without evidence, once my mom and Jude had found out who was in charge, they were firmly against me working there.

Standing up from the kitchen table, I propped my hands on my hips and addressed Jude. "So let me get this right. You think because he's Gabby's dad, that makes him a bad person?"

My gaze snapped toward my mom, who was picking at her bright pink nail polish. As if she could feel my glare, she looked up and sighed with what I had hoped was resignation. It's hard to argue with logic.

"I think it's a fair assumption," Jude grumbled, his emotions swirling with mine.

Over the last few months, I'd learned to separate the two most of the time, but occasionally his strong feelings managed to bleed through.

My lips pursed and then I pulled out the devil's advocate card. "Is that true about you and *your* father?" Jude's dad wasn't a very good guy according to—well, everyone.

Jude's eyes slivered and he crossed his arms, his well-defined biceps bulging over his muscular chest. He threw me an angry look that said I'd hit below the belt.

After that, I won the argument. The only true advantage that the other companies had over GSS was that Mr. LaCroix wouldn't be my boss. And I really missed home.

I thought that the Land of the Midnight Sun, where it all began, would make the transition easier for me.

Strange logic, I know. Most people would want to avoid the place where they killed their father. But Alaska made me feel closer to him. All of our great adventures happened here.

I stepped out of the automatic doors of the airport onto the sidewalk where a line of cars waited. The tears won and they spilled in hot rivulets over my cheeks. Before anyone could witness it, I swiped them away with the sleeve of my hoodie.

The sharp blast of a horn made me jump, and I glanced its way. Gin climbed out of the cab of a black SUV, looking as if he'd come from a photo shoot for a men's magazine. Dressed in expensive jeans, a button-down shirt, and brown leather shoes that matched a bracelet wrapped around his wrist, he was even hotter now than when he pretended to go to high school. He had been there in order to ferret out my talents. Looking back, I should've known he wasn't a student. He had carried himself with much more confidence than a normal teenager, though he was only twenty-two.

He grunted as he lifted my suitcases into the trunk next to his. "What did you pack in this thing? Rocks?" His southern accent always made him sound polite, even when he was being sarcastic.

Laughter bubbled from my chest. I'd inherited my dad's ability to fit a lot of things into a small space.

Always the gentleman, he opened the passenger door. I slid down into the leather seat and leaned my head against the headrest. The interior smelled divine, like a tobacco leaf, a hint of vanilla, and something spicy and sexy.

"Welcome home," Gin said as he crawled behind the wheel.

The knot in my throat contracted and I squeezed my eyes shut. "Thanks," I said quietly.

In silence, we drove outside of the airport gates to Campbell Lake where we unloaded our belongings from the trunk and loaded them into the small compartment of the red and white float plane.

"Go ahead and get in," Gin said.

After finishing his final inspection of the aircraft, he climbed up and handed me a headset. I'd been excited, though apprehensive, since signing my contract with the company. This was the exciting part.

Gin motored the plane into the middle of the lake. He said a few things over his headset before we picked up speed. He pulled back on the yoke and the aircraft rose heavily, almost as if we were traveling in slow motion.

A huge smile bloomed until unwanted tears prickled my eyes. I clenched my fists. Maybe this wasn't a good idea. Every sight, sound, and smell triggered a joyful memory that bled into pain.

"It was brave of you to choose our company. I know this can't be easy for you."

I nodded tightly, my vocal cords paralyzed, and stared out the side window at the snowcapped mountains. Even today, ancient glaciers lazily carved their way through the granite leaving behind green valleys, huge boulders, and the meandering rivers below.

"If you need to talk, I'm here. I realize we don't know each other well. And I don't know what it's like to lose a parent, but I have felt alone. Like you, my gift is a blessing and a curse."

I'd not only lost a parent—I'd killed him myself. Here, I hoped I would have the opportunity to finally feel the pain that I'd bottled up for so long in fear of hurting anyone else. But I wasn't ready to share, especially two thousand feet in the air. What if Gin wasn't as formidable as he hinted?

"What kind of powers do you have?"

He looked away and paused for a beat before turning toward me. His aviators reflected my image. "With skin-to-skin contact, I'm able to kill. I have a unique connection between the body and brain." One shoulder twitched as if his powers weren't a big deal. "I can interrupt the synapses and short out whatever I choose. It's kind of like pulling a fuse."

"Why wouldn't you tell me earlier?" Until today, he'd been evasive about his capabilities.

He raised a brow over the frame of his sunglasses. "Because now we're on the same team."

Curiosity begged me to ask how he discovered his gift, but I didn't want to be rude. I massaged the back of my neck to loosen my muscles.

After half an hour of comfortable silence with me absorbing the magnificent scenery, he pointed ahead. "There it is."

My breath hitched. I'd heard about it and even seen pictures. Beyond the shores of a large dark lake was GSS's remote training facility. An Alaskan lodge with peaked roofs of green metal sitting atop massive logs, angled windows, and a stone chimney. Smaller buildings of the same materials were scattered throughout the trees and along the edges of the murky lake.

Gin set the plane down flawlessly—and having high standards—I'd know. I'd spent every summer in a float plane with my dad. The lump in my throat constricted again. I bit the inside of my cheek hoping the discomfort would distract me from the upheaval of emotions.

We eased alongside a dock and slid into the empty spot next to another plane. On the other side were three aluminum boats. Silver lures, hanging from fishing poles, glittered in the sun as the boat rocked from the wakes. My fingers itched to pick one up and cast it into the waters.

We jumped out, and Gin tied the plane down.

I went to grab my things and he said with a wave, "No need. Someone will put them in your cabin. Come on." He gestured with his hand for me to follow.

Along the trail to the lodge, my fingers brushed over the fireweed. None of the magenta flowers were yet in bloom. The smell of campfire, spruce trees, and flora lingered in the air.

We walked up a few steps onto a considerable deck overlooking the water with the mountains beyond.

I settled in front of the railing with the palm of my hand pressed against my heart. "You know, no matter how many times I see these views, they always get to me."

"Yeah, I've been all over the world, and still nothing quite compares to the last frontier. I think it's the amalgamation of beauty and danger. And lucky me," his drawl dripped with sarcasm, "you're the only one I don't need to lecture about the wildlife."

"Don't forget to warn them about the cow parsnip," I reminded. Nobody needed to witness the aftermath of brushing up against one of those plants. Painful, gushing blisters formed upon contact, but only if the sun was out. In the shade, they weren't dangerous.

"Please help me keep an eye on the others, will you? This isn't my normal gig." A ray of golden sunlight peeked out from behind a puffy cloud and flooded his face with light. He removed his sunglasses and his green eyes flashed like faceted emeralds. They were quite hypnotizing.

I glanced away. "You're normally not an instructor." I wasn't asking a question, but rather confirming what I already knew.

"No."

"Why this time?"

"You."

My instinct was to look at him, but I defied the impulse. "Yeah, you've said that before." The all-too-familiar feeling of guilt cloaked my shoulders. As if just being me was trouble with a capital T.

"You and I—well, we're kind of like Alaska, beautiful and dangerous."

My cheeks warmed under the compliment. Or at least what sounded like a compliment. He was definitely good-looking, but it was those eyes with thick dark lashes that made him borderline breathtaking.

"Most of the other people that'll be training alongside you—well, they have gifts but nothing as deadly as ours. Their abilities are more . . . subtle. Like your father's."

I gripped the deck railing, my knuckles whitened under my skin.

"If it bothers you that I talk about your dad, I will refrain."

"No," I responded immediately, "I actually like it.

My family spends too much time tip-toeing around the past. And even though it still hurts, I'm afraid if I don't talk about him, parts of my memory will fade." I tried swallowing but my mouth was parched.

"You know I was there that day to discuss the terms of his employment."

That day was the day I killed my father. Moments before I got angry and accidentally made him walk in front of a speeding bus, he'd told me that the military had rejected his retirement. *They can do that you know.* That's why I got mad. We were moving again. But I'd later found out my dad lied. He had a friend who worked for GSS, and my dad was considering them for employment. My parents had decided to tell me he'd been retained by the Air Force so they could blame our move on the government.

One of the reasons they wanted to leave was because of the trouble I'd gotten into in Anchorage. They thought a fresh start would do me some good. To think, if they would've told me the truth then we might've been living in Prague. Or wherever, for that matter. The important part was we would be living, not merely surviving.

Gin took a step closer to me, the sleeve of his coat touching mine. "I didn't know Craig well, what I did know impressed me. And it isn't his powers that I'm referring to, he was a good man. A true leader without being a bully. It's a rare gift. I know you've lost him, but you were lucky to have had him."

My vision blurred out of focus, and I let out a deep breath. If only my dad's footsteps were that easy to follow. My path seemed to be leading me away from the straight and narrow, down a long winding road obscured by darkness.

Chapter 4: Gin

After getting Regan settled in her cabin, I wandered toward the dining hall to grab a snack. My stomach was off, not queasy, or hungry really, just amped up. Never having trained anyone before, I chalked it up to trepidation. Years ago, I'd learned to control my emotions, but regardless, this new feeling was bleeding through. My phone buzzed in my pocket. "Uncle," I answered.

"Yeah, Gin. Did you get Regan situated comfortably?" He asked rapidly, as if there was something he wanted to say yet he needed to get the niceties out of the way first. It was a Southern thing, and it was a hard habit to break.

"Yes, sir. She's settled in."

"Dr. Gloria's having some issues. Do you mind flying back to Anchorage tonight?"

I started to say, *sure thing, no problem* since I enjoyed flying, but the words froze on my tongue. A familiar sensation started humming inside my chest. Normally, I was the one to initiate my powers, but it seemed as if my alter ego didn't like the idea of us leaving. Knowing better than to allow it too much freedom, I mentally snapped at it to back down. It obeyed. After five years of studying with the Tibetan Monks—it always did. Usually, it only stepped out of line when I was distressed. Which wasn't often. Years of meditation allowed me to keep my emotions tranquil. I had complete control over my alter, but its current state was concerning. Like a petulant child, it pouted. It hadn't acted that way in eons.

Regan, who hadn't been trained how to leash her powers, had somehow learned to confine them inside a cage. At least, that's how she'd explained it to my uncle and me during her interview in Seattle. It was impressive that she'd figured out a way to control the darkness of her own volition.

Mine was free to roam about—but I was its master. "Yes, of course, Uncle, I'll be there soon."

After the quick flight, I drove to our building located in the Anchorage Medical Park in midtown and pulled into a parking spot near the front door.

"Christian, Gin—hi!" The young woman sitting behind the reception desk stuttered my name as I walked inside. She stood up and the two buns piled on top of her head wobbled precariously in her excitement.

"Good afternoon, Mable Ann." I nodded politely.

She chewed on her lower lip—not as an invitation, she was nervous. My presence seemed to garner that reaction from most people. "Can I get you anything?" she asked.

"No, thank you. I'm here to see Dr. Gloria."

"Of course. Go right on back. If you need anything at any time let me know." Her wide brown eyes blinked.

"Thank you." I tapped the countertop with a knuckle on my way to the elevator and pressed the button. Once inside, I turned around to find Mable Ann waving at me. A smirk rose on my lips and after the door slid shut, I shook my head and chuckled. I drew the key out of my pocket and inserted it into the slot that allowed me access to the basement.

When I stepped out, everything was quiet except for the lights buzzing overhead and my footsteps as they echoed in the hall. It smelled the same as any other hospital, like caustic cleaning chemicals and sorrow.

Our facility wasn't large and most of the employees didn't know this level existed. It was used only when someone was considered dangerous.

I peeked in the door window before knocking lightly on the bullet-proof glass. Dr. Gloria looked up. The patient sitting on the corner of the bed wearing handcuffs glared my way. His steel-blue eyes flashed.

Dr. Gloria stepped out into the hall, firmly closing the door behind her. She adjusted her white doctor coat. "I'm glad you're here." She dabbed the sweat from her brow with a handkerchief she pulled from her pocket. "He's incredibly strong. And seems to be getting stronger every day. I don't like it."

Dr. Gloria's newest patient had only recently woken up from his coma. According to her medical opinion, one that she'd shared at our last meeting, he'd suffered complete amnesia from the accident. Her plan was to slowly introduce him to his past in order to trigger his memory recall without overwhelming him. Or endangering any of us.

After he had woke up, Dr. Gloria informed us that he was different. Which according to her was perfectly normal. Her medical recommendation was time. She said the brain was a funny creature and often had a way of healing itself.

I'd hoped she was correct, but over the last couple of weeks, even with treatment, his demeanor had remained the same. Cold, detached, withdrawn. And dangerous. He'd recently tried to convince one of the orderlies to commit suicide. Thankfully, his antics weren't successful. With distance, his suggestion weakened. Once the orderly realized what was going on, he went straight to Dr. Gloria with the information.

Yesterday he forced a nurse to take his anti-psychotic medication.

Dr. Gloria had tried a number of prescriptions to keep him calm, but as of yet, my powers presented our best solution. With my ability to delve inside the brain, I was able to release significant amounts of his own serotonin and dopamine into his system. It allowed Dr. Gloria to continue working with him without fearing for her safety.

The last time I was here, she and I had discussed other options. This new plan was like nothing we'd ever attempted before. But if there was a chance of helping him, no matter how slim, I was willing to try.

"Are you ready?" Dr. Gloria asked.

I filled my lungs with air, held it in for a count of three, and slowly exhaled while I prepared. "Yes, ma'am."

As Dr. Gloria lifted her invisible shield, the energy in the vicinity rushed to her in a strong gust of wind. She had the ability to block out other people's powers. That was her only gift, but seeing that she was our head psychiatrist, it came in handy.

Once she was prepared, she glanced up at the overhead camera and gave a curt nod. The door clicked and she opened it before stepping inside with me behind her.

He was sitting on the corner of his bed wearing sweats, a T-shirt, slippers, a pair of shackles on his feet, and handcuffs on his wrists. His eyes flashed an eerie silver, and he snarled as we approached. Though I hadn't known him well, this was not the same man.

"Do your thing," Dr. Gloria said, her voice strained.

I reached out quickly and laid my hand on the back of his neck. Even with what little of my body was exposed behind Dr. Gloria's invisible armor, the hairs on my arm prickled and I could feel his power wash over me. It was like nothing I'd experienced before. My hand instantly tightened as if it had a mind of its own. It wanted to snap back and grab Dr. Gloria by the neck and squeeze. With clenched teeth, I pushed past the impulse and closed my eyes, concentrating on calming my mind while invading his. Quickly, I located his brain stem. Once there, I found the needed pathways and released a heavy dose of serotonin. Immediately, he relaxed.

During my extended stay with the monks, I'd learned how to control my gift, keep my body and mind fit, and received a top-notch education that would compete with any Ivy League college. Most of my advanced studies were of a medical nature focusing on anatomy and neurology.

My powers pulsed their way through his hypothalamus and rewarded him with a healthy amount of dopamine. Then I found his pineal gland and hit him with a wave of melatonin. Within ten seconds his head drooped, and he was asleep.

After a few tense moments, Dr. Gloria let down her shield and the temperature in the room cooled instantaneously. Sweat trickled over her temples.

We laid him back on the bed, and I pulled up a chair. With my hand resting on his arm, I began to search his hippocampus. Most of the time, people's memories were easy to access. But here, inside his mind, my senses could find only darkness. It was as if everything was cloaked in a roiling cloud of black smoke. When I pushed beyond the veil, there was nothing. No memories at all. Only smoke. Even people with extensive brain damage still had their memories, but they didn't have the key to access them. I'd never come across a case where someone's life had truly been erased. I probed deeper, into where trauma liked to hide away in the deep recesses of one's mind. I opened the door to where his worst memories should be hiding and again was met with nothing but thick black smoke. A long icy shiver crawled across my skin. No wonder he was cold, detached, and dangerous. Craig Braaten, Regan's father, was an empty, hollow shell.

Determined to help him, I thought back to every memory I had of Regan. My abilities allowed me to effectively erase people's memories, but it also gave me the option to replace them, or in this case, replace them with my recollections. If he could connect with his daughter, there might be hope.

I relaxed my mind and delved into the very first memory I had of Regan, though it wasn't a particularly happy one for any of us.

I yanked the hood of my rain jacket over my head as I walked along the city sidewalk in downtown Anchorage. From a distance, I could see Regan and Craig. It appeared as if they were arguing. Having heard about her temper, I wasn't surprised.

Even from this distance, I recognized the anger flashing silver in her eyes. Craig's entire body drooped as if he'd been unplugged from his grid. Then, before I had a chance to run toward them, he stepped off the curb into the path of a speeding bus.

The driver hit the brakes and the tires squealed over the wet asphalt. The back end of the bus shifted sideways, and a few other cars veered trying to miss it. One succeeded, but the others didn't. Glass shattered and metal crunched. Then the bus hit Craig's body with a sickening thump.

Screams erupted.

Elbowing my way through the growing crowd, I knelt beside his body. Blood pooled on the road and ran down the drain in bright red streaks.

I pushed up the sleeve of his jacket and laid my hand on his arm. I closed my eyes and prayed out loud—I was wearing a priest collar and it seemed appropriate. Inside my mind, I found the corner of his brain that controlled the electrical impulses of the heart and his breathing. Because both were strong, but his bleeding was heavy and his brain was swelling, I slowed them to a dangerous pace hoping my gamble would pay off.

A scream shattered the air as Regan busted through. Her eyes were wide with horror and fear. Her short hair was wet from the rain, and it dripped down her face. She landed hard on her knees and flung herself over her father, screaming the whole time. "I didn't mean it! I'm sorry! Please don't die. This is my fault! I killed my dad. I killed my dad . . ."

The ambulance arrived moments later. They took one look at Regan and started to pull her away. She twisted and kicked and tried to bite.

Not wanting them to hurt her, I motioned for them to stop. I laid my hand on her back, and a flash of energy shot up my arm. Startled by the transfer, I almost shied away but managed to keep my composure. I whispered in her ear that if she didn't calm down, they were going to take her away from him. And then I pushed a small dose of dopamine, serotonin, and melatonin into her system. She collapsed into my arms. The EMTs laid her on the gurney and strapped her down. As they rolled her away, I pulled out my phone and called my uncle.

Not wanting to overwhelm Craig's mind I gave him only one more memory. This one happened after my uncle had sent me to Regan's high school to spy on her. At the time, he wasn't convinced she had powers. I was. My instincts were solidified the day Regan and Layne, my cousin Gabby's current boy toy, stopped by the house so he could break up with her. Gabby had mentioned Regan was a nasty piece of work and was trying to steal her man. She laughed it off as an impossibility. I wasn't sure why, even at the time I thought Regan was far more interesting than Gabby could ever hope to be.

I focused on the memory and slowly wove it into the neurons in his brain.

Regan was wandering around the sitting room looking at my aunt's questionable taste in art and décor.

"Well, Regan," I said from behind her. She twitched like I'd surprised her and turned around. "You're the last person I expected to be here."

Her brows rose. "You and me both."

She stared hard at my face, and I was curious as to how long it would take her to solve that puzzle.

"And you are?" she asked as her eyes narrowed.

I stepped forward and held out my hand. "Pardon me, I'm Gabriella's cousin, Christian LaCroix. Most people call me Gin." When her skin touched mine, the hairs on my arm rose. I could only assume it was my alter ego recognizing one of its own. Curiously, it only happened with her and no one else, even if they had powers. It was the first clue that I might've found someone as gifted as I was.

She yanked her hand away, practically yelling, "Why are you here?"

I could tell I unsettled her as much as she unsettled me. "I see you get right to the point. My parents are in France on business," I lied. My parents had abandoned me to my uncle when they realized what I was capable of. "So instead of staying home alone, I thought I'd finish out my senior year with my favorite cousin."

Her eyes widened in horror as her lips parted.

I chuckled. "I hear you're a right nasty piece of work."

"Me?"

"Yes, ma'am. According to Gabby, you're trying to steal her man." A loud crash came from upstairs. "I believe that's my cue to depart." But I didn't leave, not really. I faded into the shadows and watched. That was my job after all.

I snuck out of the room and around the hallway where I could see Gabby standing at the top of the stairs. She looked as if she were about to say something but had been frozen in place like a snapshot in time.

Regan pointed to the room I'd just vacated. Gabby, not arguing, bounced down the stairs and disappeared into the sitting room. I crept back to hide behind a bushy potted plant just as she made herself comfortable on the pink tufted chair. Regan sat down across from her. "You're going to listen to me. When I'm done, I'll let you speak. You're going to let Layne go. You're going to tell the peasants that you got tired of him."

I almost barked out a laugh—she had my cousin

pegged all right.

"He bored you. If you decide to retaliate, I'll take measures into my own hands. And I promise you that you won't like my tactics. I have nothing to lose. The question is: Do you?" Regan waited a moment. "Cat got your tongue?"

Gabby snarled, "You—" She stopped as if the words stuck in her throat. Her mouth was frozen in a pucker as if she were about to say bitch—but something, or someone, prevented her from voicing her opinion.

"No, no, no." Regan ticked a finger in front of Gabby's face. "We're going to be civil. Okay? Try again."

"What are you doing to me?" Gabby hissed.

"Whatever do you mean?" Regan stood up and propped her hands on her hips. She blinked her blue eyes intentionally as if to seem harmless.

Again, I almost laughed. She was a predator. I had no doubt.

"You need to leave," my cousin said, sounding frightened. I couldn't blame her.

"Gladly, but remember what I said. If you hurt him in any way, I'll destroy you in ways you cannot even imagine."

With the memories in place, I pulled away my hand from Craig and stood up to move out of Dr. Gloria's way.

She stepped forward, her shield ready but not at full capacity, and said, "Can you hear me?" She picked up his wrist to check his pulse and then lifted each eyelid shining a bright light into his eyes.

A sigh that sounded suspiciously like relief moved past her lips as she drew the blanket over him. With her hands on her hips, she turned to me. "I think he's going to be out for a while. I'll give you a call when I know if the memories were accepted or rejected."

I smiled tightly and hoped for everyone's sake, especially Regan's, that my efforts would help. I dreaded the day I had to tell her he was alive. Would she accept my reasons for keeping him a secret? Or would she strike again?

Chapter 5: Regan

I hung my rain jacket over a wooden dowel inside the foyer next to another coat that was dripping water on the concrete floor. I worried at my bottom lip. Behind that door was a mystery. All I knew was this was a probationary period for GSS to see if we were a good fit. At the end of the training, we would be offered a full-time position with the company or let go. When I asked Gin what to expect from the new employee orientation/training camp, he said he had no clue since he had never attended one. He did mention that all of the other people were close to my age and had some pretty interesting gifts.

Squaring my shoulders, I grabbed the knob and pulled.

The room was cozily decorated with five loveseats flanking the log walls. Green and blue throw pillows and knitted blankets matched the plaid carpet in the middle of the floor.

A woman, somewhere in her late thirties with dark hair cut shorter than mine, sat behind a desk reading something on her phone. She glanced up and anger or frustration crinkled her forehead.

I started to smile, ready to say *good morning* but she glimpsed at her watch and snapped, "What are you doing here so early?"

I stepped back, my smile faltering while the golem

perked up at her rudeness. "I didn't want to be late." *Not really.* Not knowing what to expect, I'd hoped to be the first one there—I'd certainly arrived early enough.

She huffed. "No danger of that."

"Whatever," I muttered under my breath. *Somebody woke up on the wrong side of the bed.* With both hands, I grabbed the hood of my sweatshirt and jerked it up before storming outside, forgetting my jacket.

Coming toward me on the boardwalk was a kid wearing a thick pair of glasses fogged up and spattered with raindrops. In each hand, he was carrying two paper cups, steam swirling from the tiny drinking holes in the lid.

I backtracked and opened the entryway door to let him in.

"Thanks," he said, searching the small space for somewhere to set the cups.

As I stood on the threshold, I held out my hands to hold them so he could remove his jacket.

"Again, thanks."

I couldn't pinpoint his accent, but my best guess was Australian.

"Why are you leaving?" he asked, wiping down his glasses with the edge of his silk shirt. The buttons, precariously low, revealed a scrawny tan chest adorned with several gold chains. I couldn't tell if he was going for New Jersey thug or something earlier like 1970s disco.

"Because being early is frowned upon."

"Really?" His voice cracked.

I nodded.

"But I brought the instructor chia tea," he said as if that would help her unpleasant mood. He adjusted his glasses over his large nose and behind his protruding ears.

"Good luck," I wished him over my shoulder as I left.

"You're going to be late," he hollered.

That was the plan.

Since I'd missed breakfast in order to get to class ultra-early, I was hungry. I snuck around the back side of the dining hall to swipe a doughnut and another cup of coffee.

Taking my sweet time, I meandered back intent on being fashionably late. Tossing the paper cup in the trash inside the entryway, I licked the last of the glaze off my fingers, opened the door, and sauntered in.

A veritable gaggle of misfits, all somewhere in their teens or slightly beyond, sat one person on each loveseat.

"You're late," the rude woman barked.

I gritted my teeth. "Technically, I was early." I didn't say more as I crossed the room.

"Can I sit here?" I pointed to the empty spot next to the kid with glasses.

A grin lit up his face exposing a set of braces. "Absolutely. My pleasure."

"Now that we are all here . . ." The lady got up and wrote her name on the dry-erase board behind the desk. "My name is Pamela Guthrie. You can call me Pamela. And for the next three months, we'll be getting to know each other. Exploring your gifts. And creating bonds and friendship along the way." Her voice, high pitched and nasally, contained such zeal that it made me mentally roll my eyes considering my first impression of her wasn't one of enthusiasm.

She patted her chest. "I'm originally from the

Oregon coast but now I work most of the year out of our Seattle office. It's my third summer training new recruits. I love my job and this," she swirled her hand toward us, "is like my summer vacation."

The kid next to me raised his hand.

"Umm," Pam looked down at the piece of paper on her desk, "Yes, Tim, no need to raise your hand. This isn't a classroom. This is a relaxed atmosphere. Put your feet up, drink your tea, and let's have a conversation." Her large teeth and overly exaggerated gestures were cartoonish. I'd bet she'd been a kindergarten teacher before landing this gig.

"What powers do you have?" He sat back and spread his long gangly arms out over the length of the sofa, nearly touching my shoulder.

She chuckled. "I have the ability to tell if someone is lying. It helps me track down people like us. But enough about me, let's hear from you."

Tim's face brightened as if he were pleased she'd asked about him but as he started to speak, Pam firmly raised her hand in the air to cut him off. A blush spread from his semi-exposed chest to his neck. His shoulders drooped and he stared at his lap like a cowering dog. Pam didn't even notice his distress.

"Rory, why don't you go first?" Pam aimed her horsey smile at the redhead with a massive mane of curly hair.

The girl tucked a stockinged foot up underneath her and said in a Celtic brogue, "My name is Rory, I'm twenty and I grew up on a farm outside of Dublin, Ireland. I was five when we discovered I had the ability to control the elements. Probably comes from my Pagan ancestry." She turned her gaze systematically to everyone in the room, her voice heavy with what sounded like false humility. "My grandmother has been training me—but there's only so much she can do without having these incredible gifts herself. I was recruited by Pamela." Rory's long narrow fingers curled into a heart symbol in front of her chest as if being picked by Pam was a badge of honor.

And to think, I thought I was going to be the most arrogant person in the room.

"Yes, Rory," Pam said, "what a rare and incredible gift you have. I can't wait to see how you develop with training." She pressed her hands into a prayer position and bowed her head like she was the freaking Dalai Lama. "So, why don't you give us a demonstration?"

Rory's face paled, which was impressive since her skin—minus the freckles spattered across her nose—was already the color of milk.

She tossed her curls behind her shoulders. "Uh, okay. Can someone please open the window?"

Tim jumped up and cranked open the window behind us. The pattering of the rain clinked on the metal roof and a cold breeze blew down the back of my neck.

Rory closed her eyes.

One minute passed by. Then another. Soon we all started glancing around. *Was this a joke?*

Rory, with her squinted eyes and face puckered, appeared to be constipated. Her skin flushed bright pink and glistened with sweat. One of her curls stuck to her forehead.

Just as I was about to say something to break the tension, the fireweed outside began to magically grow taller and creep over the window sill. The tiny magenta flowers bloomed one by one.

Pam clapped her hands. "Well, done!"

I expected everyone to start laughing. They didn't. Two of the new recruits looked impressed. The other two seemed bored.

Rory's spine slumped and she was breathing heavily as if she'd birthed that plant herself.

Pam motioned to the guy sitting directly across the room from me. "And Benjamin, why don't you go next?"

He had red hair too, but it was a dark auburn and pulled back into a short ponytail. Unlike Rory, who had an ivory complexion, Benjamin had a perfect tan. Although he was slight in stature, with his smoldering dark eyes and unusual coloring, he was quite attractive.

"Just Ben. I'm nineteen. I can create illusions of dead people. For the last five years, I've been doing psychic readings out of my mom's boutique in Sedona, Arizona."

With her brows furrowed, Pam glanced at her phone and checked something before she looked back at Ben and asked, "So, you're psychic too?" Wonder danced over her face. She propped her elbows on the desk and rested her chin on her closed fists.

"No. When people make their appointments, I research their phone numbers. Find out who they are and do a little social media investigating. It's cake really."

I bit down hard on my cheek to mask my smile. *And here I was thinking I was going to be the biggest jerk in the room.*

"Mom and I make quite a good living," Ben said without a hint of remorse. He leaned back in his seat, pushed his cowboy boots out in front of him, and crossed his legs.

Pam's backbone straightened like a rod had been

shoved up her butt and her wonder faded to distaste. "And how did you end up here?" Her perky tone turned cold and was wrapped with a hint of displeasure.

A one-sided smirk curled Ben's lips as if he enjoyed the weight of Pam's judgment. "I suppose I did a reading for the wrong person," he said drily.

"Care to demonstrate?" she asked.

He shrugged. "Know anyone who has died recently?"

I didn't volunteer.

Tim raised his hand again, though he kept it low and close to his chest as if he were afraid to be embarrassed a second time. "We lost our family dog a month ago."

"That'll work," Ben said. "Got any pictures?"

Tim got up and handed his phone to Ben.

Ben scrolled through for a minute. "Looks like you have a way with the ladies," Ben said as he gave him his phone back.

Tim popped the collar of his silk shirt like he was *all that and a snack* and sat back down.

At that point, I couldn't hide my smile any longer without drawing blood from the inside of my cheek. This was getting interesting.

Ben closed his eyes and pressed the tips of his fingers to his temple. He wore rings of gold, silver, and turquoise on almost every digit. "Hmmm, someone— no—yes, hmm . . . oh, I think I have a pet coming through? A cocker spaniel." Ben tilted his head. "No," he said firmly. "An English setter. Sparrow?" He opened his eyes. At the foot of our couch, a hazy image of a dog with feathery white fur and small russet spots began to form at Tim's feet. It wasn't solid, but see-through like a ghost.

"Crikey," Tim said as his eyes rounded. He scrunched his nose trying to keep his glasses from sliding further down.

The image slowly vanished.

"That's a beaut," Tim said, admiration coating his tone.

Ben raised a brow and nodded once.

Pam huffed and her lips thinned leaching out all the color. "And you have no problem deceiving people when they're at the lowest point of their lives?"

Ben yanked the ponytail holder out of his hair and ran his fingers through his locks before tying it back again. "I don't really consider it to be deceiving people. I'm giving them comfort in their time of need."

Pam tipped her chin in the air and turned her attention to the tiny girl dressed in all black. She was wearing heavy eyeliner and had small piercings above each corner of her lip like two beauty marks.

She had her elbow propped on the arm of the loveseat and the palm of her hand holding up her head. "Yeah, I'm Mae. Eighteen. I was adopted by a couple of hippies in California. When I was fourteen I ran away to Montana. I'm telekinetic. And because of that, I was able to survive as a pick-pocket. It's not like anyone in Bozeman expects to be robbed by an Asian girl sitting on the street corner making a living playing the guitar."

Before Pam could ask for a demonstration, Mae held up the watch Pam had been wearing earlier and jingled it in the air. Pam reached frantically for her wrist to grasp at the empty spot.

With a devious smile, Mae chucked the watch through the air. Pam brought her hands up to protect her face and flinched. The watch stopped shortly before it hit her in the head. It paused, floating in the air, until it dropped unceremoniously on her desk with a thunk.

Ben and I busted out laughing. Tim's eyes darted around the room, and he chuckled nervously. Rory and the other girl seemed horrified with their mouths agape.

"Navi," Pam said calmly, ignoring Mae's little trick, but her flaring nostrils and the angry set of her jaw gave away her ire.

In a blink of an eye, Navi was sitting next to Ben. He shunned sideways and jumped. "What the!" he yelled

"My name is Navi. I'm nineteen." She waved causing her bracelets to jingle. A tiny nose ring glinted in the overhead light. "I'm from Houston. And as you can see, I can teleport."

"Amazing!" Pam praised and clapped with the tips of her fingers. Navi fiddled with a chunk of dark hair that had escaped from behind her ear.

"Sorry for startling you," Navi apologized to Ben before she returned—like a normal person—to her seat.

"And Tim?"

"Queensland. I'm fourteen. And I can make people fall in love with me."

Pam interrupted him again. "So, I've heard. Usually, we don't allow anyone under the age of seventeen to attend training, but in this case, you were causing too much trouble, and your parents needed our help."

"Trouble's my middle name," Tim said. He leaned back and latched his hands behind his head.

Yeah. I was definitely going to like it here. The golem, in agreement, seemed to relax. I could imagine it lounging on a settee with its smoky legs crossed and a cigar in one hand and a glass of whiskey in the other.

The classroom door opened slowly, and we all

stared at the newcomer entering the room. She held her hands in front of her and gave us a tiny wave. A shy smile rounded her blushing cheeks.

"This is Cammy. She's Ron Steven's daughter," Pam introduced. "She's volunteered so Tim and Regan can demonstrate their talents."

Tim cleared his throat. Cammy's head snapped sideways. Her eyes locked onto him. She chewed on the corner of her full bottom lip and reached up to twirl the end of her blonde braid.

Tim smiled.

Cammy hurried across the room. She removed his glasses and stroked the side of his face with the back of her fingers before she sat down on his lap. She was practically panting. As she moved in for the kiss, Pam said, "Tim stop, that's enough."

He chuckled and stopped whatever he was doing.

Cammy scuttled off his lap, her cheeks flaming red. She backed over to Navi and sat down on the corner of the couch looking as if she were ready to flee the scene. Her round blue eyes met mine. She was probably wondering what form of torture I had planned for her.

In a dismissive tone, Pam said, "All right, Regan. Your turn."

Having thought Cammy had been through enough embarrassment for the day, my focus spun to Pam.

Yeah—I realized I was about to get myself in trouble. The golem trembled with joy.

I opened the corner of its cage and slowly let out a tendril of smoke.

A mischievous smirk directed at Pam rose on my lips before I said out loud, "*I wish.*"

Tingles spread from the tips of my fingers to the tips

of my toes.

Pam's eyes flared in a wild panic. She resisted my wishes, so I opened the glass prison wider. A coil of smoke flowed lazily down the side of the box infusing me with more power. Delight swelled in my chest. When they resisted—the high was so much purer.

I pressed play on my phone and soon the beat picked up.

I wish.

Pam stood up and hip-popped her way out from behind the desk. *Beat. Pop. Beat. Pop.* Her long peasant skirt swished with every move.

Varying expressions traveled around the room.

With a dash of joy and a pinch of revenge for her earlier rudeness, I made Pam turn around and crouch in front of us with her hand on her knees. Then I made that woman twerk to some fierce opera music. *They say there's a first time for everything, right?*

Ben and Mae yelped with hilarity, grabbing their stomachs as their howls echoed off the log walls. Tim looked at me with his brows raised well above his glasses. Navi and Cammy giggled nervously as if they weren't sure it was okay to laugh.

Rory narrowed her eyes and said, "Stop it!" She stood up and stomped her unusually large feet.

I reined in my power, leaving Pam's memory intact. A big sigh of pleasure escaped as the high traveled like electricity through my bloodstream. It was a fusion of mind-numbing carbonation that carried a drug only I could create. I stood up to stretch my arms over my head and strode leisurely toward the door knowing *exactly* how Pam was about to react. The boiling red flush swooping up her neck, over her face to the tips of her ears was a dead giveaway.

"Get out," she screamed and stabbed her finger toward the door. "All of you—out now!"

Chapter 6: Jude

Wood dust from sanding the walnut slab stuck to my sweaty forehead and tarnished my safety goggles. I ran the tips of my fingers over the wood surface searching for signs of roughness and imperfection. Once satisfied that the tabletop was finished to my standards, I pulled off my eye protection and cleaned them with the inside of my shirt before setting them aside.

To clear the dust from my throat, I took a swig of water as I tried to ignore Regan's emotions bleeding through our connection. It had been more difficult since she'd left.

No matter how badly I wanted to go with her, we'd all decided it was wiser for me to stay home and keep my gifts a secret. If anything should happen to Regan, I could always find her because of the bond I'd created between the two of us. It was like a rubber band that stretched between her heart and mine. It pulled me toward her no matter where she was. To be honest, it wasn't her safety that troubled me, that girl wasn't defenseless.

It was the way Gin, her so-called instructor, looked at her. He didn't even hide his fascination with my girlfriend, and it irritated me.

It didn't surprise me. She was unique. I knew it the second she stepped foot into our homeroom class last year. The color of her aura alone was cautionary. The fact that it moved, screamed danger.

During her first week at high school, I watched her and waited for her to strike. Her aura suggested she was evil. But she didn't retaliate even when she should have, thus defying all of my expectations.

And then, when I learned that she had powers beyond my imagination, I was caught hook, line, and sinker.

To this day, I believe that was my first mistake. She could tell that I was charmed by her darkness, and it scared her. Since then, she'd admitted that's why she chose to date Layne instead of me. She thought he would keep her on a path of goodness, and because I liked her—all of her—I wouldn't.

She was wrong. Though I couldn't deny I had been fascinated with her abilities from the get-go. After having a conversation with my grandfather, I earned a healthy respect for them.

Early on, before we even dated, he'd warned me to be careful.

"It isn't that you can't trust her per se," my grandfather said, "you can't trust whatever lingers inside of her. Chaos, mischief, and destruction are buried deep in her DNA. Whatever your choice, you must proceed with caution."

Once I decided that I wanted Regan no matter the cost, I jumped in with both feet.

Now that I could read her emotions, I often worried that her darkness would win in the end and the girl I loved would disappear. To compound the problem, I also had to worry about the green-eyed monster that had his sights set on my girlfriend.

Often my insecurities whispered inside my head and

filled me with what ifs. What if someone like Gin was a better fit for Regan? Or what about anyone else that worked at GSS? Regan was an extraordinary person. Was I enough when all I wanted was ordinary?

I thought that we'd talked about the life we longed for, but looking back, had we? I'd told her what I yearned for; a fulfilling career that allowed me to provide for my future family, a home close to my grandparents since they were getting older, and Regan by my side. She'd always smiled and nodded but was that her confirmation or a conciliation? I'd just assumed she was scared to commit because she was afraid she might hurt someone. When she signed on with GSS, some of her fear abated. And though I could gage her feelings, I couldn't decipher the reason behind them. Was her fear lessened because she'd found someone who could help her? Or was she relieved because she had an excuse to leave?

I dragged my fingers through my hair and groaned, trying to drown out my self-doubts. Our abilities to sense each other's feelings often intensified them—or at least I thought so. I loved her beyond reason. And because of that, she had the power to destroy me. How was I going to manage our separation?

We texted but the service in remote Alaska was spotty.

I shook my head, knowing I should've gone with her, if for nothing else than my sanity. Maybe then my subconscious would finally shut up. I kicked a piece of discarded two by four. It sailed across the room, stopping when it hit the wall.

I'd plead my case again when I got to Sara and Barry's house to install their kitchen cabinets. The project was coming along, and was a welcome distraction from my inner monologue. Plus, I'd learned a lot from Barry. Though he was a cop, his family owned a construction company and he'd grown up around the business. With twelve siblings, there was no need for him to take over and he got to follow his dream. He'd worked the first ten years of his career in Salt Lake City, Utah before coming home when his mom got sick. When she recovered, he decided he'd had enough of the city and stayed on at the sheriff's department.

Every day I thanked my lucky stars for his decision. From the very beginning, he didn't believe my ex-girlfriend's accusations of sexual assault. Gabriella LaCroix—Mr. LaCroix's daughter— said I'd be sorry for breaking up with her and that she'd make me pay. Barry was one of the only people who stood by me when friends I'd had for years vanished. It made trusting people difficult.

I looked at the time on my phone and decided to stop in town for a burger before heading out to their place. I texted Barry and asked if they wanted anything, since they didn't have a working kitchen.

I growled while reading Barry's text.

—Sara wants to know if you would pick her up a salad at the bar. Ranch dressing on the side. I'd take a burger and fries if that's ok. If not, just grab us some fast food. Thanks.—

I texted back a thumbs-up emoji because I didn't want to disappoint them, even though the notion of going to the restaurant where Regan used to work made me nervous. There was a high probability of running into people I didn't want to see.

I ordered ahead to make it a quick stop. I parked my pick-up next to an old beat-up car that looked suspiciously like Layne's.

That meant his mom was here too, and perhaps Gabby. Layne had started dating her again almost immediately after he and Regan broke up. Nobody was surprised. Layne had a type and didn't seem to learn from his mistakes.

I opened the door to the restaurant and the smell of fries wafted past my nose. I'd put the order under Barry's name—he was well-respected in the area. Even after my name had been cleared and Gabby admitted that she was lying about me, some people in the town still treated me poorly.

Layne was sitting at the bar eating but thankfully, Gabby was nowhere to be seen.

I stepped up next to him, drawing his attention.

His nostrils flared slightly before he glanced down at his plate. "Is she okay?" he asked without looking at me.

"As far as I know she's doing fine."

How would you know? She hasn't even called. My insecurity mocked me.

I ignored it, Regan had only been gone a few days. She'd texted me when she arrived in Anchorage so I knew she got there safely.

"Good." Layne's lips pressed together as he nodded.

"Hey, man, in case I haven't said it yet, congratulations. You earned it."

As talented as Layne was, he was destined to play for the NFL. So long as he didn't get injured or his girlfriend didn't sabotage him. It wasn't beneath her. But Regan had warned Gabby that if she did anything to hurt Layne, she'd pay for it. Regan wasn't joking. Though she was no longer in love with Layne, she still loved him.

And I respected that even if at times it made me jealous.

"Thanks," he said, rubbing his hand over his mouth.

The waitress slammed through the bar doors carrying a to-go bag of food for me. She set it on the counter, and I handed her a wad of cash. "Keep the change," I said as I left.

I turned up the music in my truck hoping to escape my soured mood. It took about twenty minutes to arrive at Regan's house. Dust followed me up the driveway and swirled around the truck when I stopped and got out.

Sara hurried over and grabbed the bag out of my hand so I could gather the tools from the bed of my truck.

"I'm going to take this out back. Do you want anything to drink?" she asked over her shoulder.

"Some iced tea?" Though she wasn't southern, she made the best sweet tea.

I dropped my tools off in the living room and opened the sliding glass doors to the back porch.

"Thanks, Jude," Barry said, offering me money.

"No, it's my treat. You bought the last two times."

He looked as if he was about to argue with me when Sara set a hand on his arm forcing him to sit at the picnic table.

"How's she doing?" Sara asked while passing out our food.

"Good as far as I know."

"Uh, it's a constant worry being a parent. Especially because . . ." Sara paused with a fork full of salad. She didn't need to say it out loud. "Though I love them, it's not for the faint of heart."

I'd mentioned to Regan that someday I wanted kids, and she freaked out. She said she would *never* be willing to pass her curse on to someone else. Then she vocally imagined how horrible it would be if our talents collided inside another human being. I didn't bring it up again.

"Have you talked to her lately?" Sara blinked, her big blue eyes holding sadness and concern.

"Not really, the service sucks." I knew Regan was enjoying herself, but not because I'd spoken with her. This morning she was anxious, then angry, then irritated, and a short while ago amused. But because they didn't know about our connection, I couldn't tell them. The only adult who was aware was my grandfather. Both Regan and I had decided that, for the time being, it was better that way. "I still think I should join her."

"Why is that?" Barry asked. He cocked his head and dipped a fry in Sara's ranch dressing. She playfully slapped his hand away.

"Because I miss her." It was true but not the whole truth.

"It's only been a few days," Barry said.

"Your point is?" I knew that if Barry was away from Sara, he'd be struggling too. He attempted to put up a strong front, but the dude was totally hooked. The eyes never lied.

That's how I knew Gin had a thing for Regan. During her interview in Seattle, which we were allowed to sit in on, not once did his eyes stray. He was hyper-focused on her, but I seemed to be the only one who noticed. After it was over, Barry and Sara decided they liked Gin, but both were still concerned about Mr. LaCroix and GSS's shady reputation.

Sara set her fork down on a napkin. "Jude, you have to stay here. It's the only way. If something should happen to her, you're my only way to find her. If you're there . . ."

I huffed. She was right. Though they didn't know of mine and Regan's bond, they did know I could track auras and they were counting on those abilities if Regan should go missing. If I was there and anything should happen to me too—Regan might be lost forever.

Though I was concerned, and the feelings of jealousy were overwhelming at times, I knew that I had to stay here in order to protect her. But I didn't have to like it.

Chapter 7: Regan

All of the cabins along the lakeshore were surrounded by greenery, giving each one ample privacy and glorious views. I was right at home.

Since we were going to be here for three months, I decided it was time to finish unpacking my clothes. With a hanger in one hand and a sweatshirt in the other, a knock on my door startled me but it didn't surprise me. After my earlier demonstration, I was expecting a reprimand. Pam seemed like the type to hold a grudge.

I opened the door to find Gin standing there with a cocked eyebrow and a smirk. "Trying to get fired on your first day?"

"No." I knew Pam would be mad, but she couldn't possibly be mad enough to have me booted from the program.

Gin blinked slowly and held my gaze until I looked away. With a sweeping motion, I beckoned him to enter my messy abode.

He stepped inside and glanced at the clothes littering my bed before he pulled the chair out from the small table. He sat down and picked up a small vase of flowers before placing them on the window sill. The breeze coming through the open window fluttered the bouquet.

"What?" I propped my hands on my hips. "She was the one who said we needed to demonstrate our powers. She didn't specify how."

"Yeah, about that . . ." Gin rubbed the back of his neck and pointed for me to sit. "Your powers actually worked on her?"

I slid the chair over the wood floor, turned it around, and straddled it. "Yeah, no problem. I mean she gave me a little resistance," my thumb and finger created a space two inches apart, "but nothing I couldn't handle. Heck, I've had people who aren't *special* give me more trouble."

Gin took a deep breath. "Our powers don't normally work on one another."

My lips dipped into a quick frown. "How was I supposed to know that? Mine obviously worked on my dad."

"Yes, they did, but that was an extreme situation. I wasn't sure if it would translate. I guess now we know. Anyway, it's not your fault. But from now on, if you're asked to demonstrate, use the person without powers. Okay? Most of us in this organization don't like to be reminded that we aren't at the top of the food chain."

Though he was scolding me, I didn't get the feeling he was angry. "That wasn't my goal."

He stayed silent.

"Okay. Maybe a little. She was being rude. And not just to me. She was rude to others also." Which meant there was no need for me to feel guilty about screwing with her.

"Here's the thing. So far as we know, your powers and mine are the only ones that work on people like us."

I laid my arms on the back of the chair, leaned forward, and propped my chin on my arms.

Not true. Jude's powers worked on me—though mine didn't work on him. He could see everyone's aura's

59

whether they had gifts or not.

Out of curiosity, I once asked Jude what Gin's aura looked like. He said it was green—I imagined it matched his eyes—and trembled like an earthquake. Since then, Jude had started to notice that strange auras corresponded with extraordinary gifts.

"Then how does Pam's gift help her track down others if her powers don't work on us?"

"She has the tedious job of questioning friends and family. Old school." He folded his hands together over the table and took a deep breath as if he knew I'd found a scab and I planned on picking it.

"Then why didn't you just have her question my mom?" I asked. Though Gin had told me his version of the day my dad died and how GSS was keeping tabs on my family afterward, I had a hunch he was leaving out some of the important details.

He shrugged. "We tried. She wasn't particularly cooperative. Either your mom has powers or she didn't know she was lying at the time."

I lifted my head off the backs of my arms and stared out the window, thick fog covered the mountain peaks. "Well, as far as I know, she doesn't have any. But can I be trusted? I didn't know my dad had them either."

Or my twin brothers. Kennedy got tiny glimpses of multiple futures. It was impossible to beat him at any game. Lincoln was superhuman fast. If given the opportunity, he could've smashed Olympic records. But my parents refused to let either of them use their gifts for fear of discovery. My mom had confessed that my dad's powers didn't work well on her so I had to assume Pam and her lie-detecting abilities might not have worked either. *Add it to the list of secrets.*

It wasn't that I didn't like Gin, but I wasn't sure I could trust him or the company he worked for. While they'd offered me a job, they'd yet to give me a job description. In our initial meetings, they'd been vague. They said those of us who stayed after the training program was completed would be offered positions that complemented our skill sets.

Gin rubbed his chin. "I don't believe your mom has powers. And by the time she realized you had them—I'd already figured you out." A ghost of a smile quirked his lips.

"Oh, do tell," I teased curious about his thoughts. I tossed a wadded-up napkin at his head.

He dodged it and pinned me down with an amused stare. "I'm still learning. Speaking of learning, the next few days, you'll be with me. Pack some gear. We're going an adventure."

I held his gaze for a few seconds before he gestured with a flutter of his hand and said, "Hurry up. I think you're going to enjoy our outing."

I huffed, pretending to be irritated. While he waited, I threw some clothes and other basic necessities together.

As we walked out the door, I tossed my backpack over my shoulders and Gin grabbed his bag off the front deck. We headed down the path toward the lake. Breaking past the tree line, my feet stopped dead in their tracks.

"Whoa," Gin said, almost running into me. "Give a guy some warning." He was so close I could feel his breath brush my cheek.

"What's he doing here?" I pointed at George LaCroix sitting in one of the aluminum boats visiting with the other new employees.

"He's taking Pamela's place for the next few days. She threatened to quit if you weren't fired."

Drama Queen. "A bit extreme don't ya think?"

"He said he was happy to accept her resignation. But thought perhaps she would come to regret it. He told her to take a few days to think it over. She was welcome to keep her job but you—you were going nowhere."

"Ouch."

"My uncle does not take kindly to idle threats."
Noted.

As we walked down the dock, Mr. LaCroix stood up and smiled. His eyes, though green, were nowhere near the brilliance of his nephew's, but I could see the family resemblance.

"Regan. It's so good to see you again," he said, sounding sincere. He held out his hand and helped me onto his boat. Gin climbed aboard the other vessel with Rory, Navi, Mae, Cammy, and a middle-aged guy I didn't recognize.

"I'm Cammy's brother, Casey," the only stranger on our boat introduced himself. He gestured with a chin thrust toward the other group. "You know my dad, Ron. We're here to be your wilderness guides—though I hear you may not need one."

"It's always nice to have another set of eyes and ears out here." I snaked my arms through a red life vest, buckled it, then fist-bumped Ben and Tim. I sat down at the front with my legs straddling the metal bench, allowing me to see everyone.

"Ain't that the truth," Casey said. He started the engine and hit the throttle before following Ron across the murky lake. The rain had finally stopped, but a fine mist of humidity dampened my skin. The wind blew my hair over my face, sticking it to my lip gloss.

"Ron's actually one of us," George said above the noisy hum of the propeller. "His gift is a bit like yours. Though he can control animals, not humans."

"Oh," I said with a slight whine. It was the first time I was jealous of someone else's gift. "I might've preferred that."

"And missed all the fun?" Ben said. By the mischievous look on his face, I could only assume he was talking about Pam with her mad dancing skills.

I grinned and ticked my head to the side. "True."

In the distance, white swans floated in a group at the edge of the lake. High on the ridge, the head of a bald eagle gave away its position atop the dark background of the spruce tree. I sighed, happy to be home.

Too soon we pulled up on a small sandy beach. Since I was the only person besides Casey wearing rubber boots, I hopped into the water and helped him drag the boat onto the shore.

Together, we hauled the camping gear up a small hill and set it next to a rustic log cabin with solar panels on the roof and a firepit out front.

Not needing any help, I picked a spot at the edge of the clearing and set up my tent in record time.

"Anyone need a hand?" I asked, wandering about.

Mae was almost finished. Having been a runaway, she'd probably been there, done that.

Rory glared at me. Her lack of progress told me she needed help—just not mine.

"Please," Navi said. She blew her heavy dark bangs out of her face with a puff of air. "I've never been camping. Heck, I've never even been out of the city."

I couldn't hide the horror on my face. "Seriously?

That sounds like a nightmare."

"Yeah, well my parents are both doctors, and this," she gazed up at the tall spruce trees swaying gently, "is not in their wheelhouse. Though I'm kind of enjoying it, I do find it hard to sleep with it so quiet."

The breeze picked up and the yellow pollen, thick on the branches, visibly drifted in the air. Navi sneezed violently. Before I could say *bless you*, she vanished and reappeared across the campsite splayed out on her rear end.

"What the!!!" Ben and I yelled in tandem.

"Sorry," she hollered. Ben hurried over to offer her a hand up. She brushed the dirt off her pants as she walked back to me. "That happens sometimes when I sneeze." Red flushed up her neck and cheeks. "Or fart," she whispered to me.

I snorted and we laughed.

"What's so funny?" Tim hollered.

"Ya had to be there," I said. Once we stopped giggling, we assembled her tent in no time.

I ambled over to Tim. "Need help?"

He threw down the extra poles he was holding. "Fine." It wasn't only his clothing that led me to believe that he was a newbie. Even out here, he was wearing a silk shirt and jewelry under his jacket. At least he had on sneakers and not dress shoes today.

"Yeah, cause those," I pointed at the rods on the ground, "go in there." I pointed at his tent which was listing precariously sideways.

"So how did you end up here?" I asked him as we ripped his shelter apart and started to reassemble it correctly.

"Funny story," he said and proceeded to tell me that

a year ago, he fell in love with his middle school English teacher. Apparently, she was freshly out of the university. One day she wore a V-neck shirt and when she leaned down to help him with his homework, he caught a glimpse of—*his words, not mine*—her pretty titties and he was in love. His parents, his mother a film actress (I use that term lightly), and his father—a producer of said films—were quite amused by their son's ambitious dating goals. Soon they began to worry when the teacher started paying too much attention to Tim. Way too much attention—like convincing him to run away with her.

Tim's large Adam's apple bobbed as he spoke, "I really thought she loved me at the time." He took a deep breath, but he couldn't hide the anguish on his face. "Anyway, my parents went to the principal and told them what was going on. They'd gotten a hold of my phone." He stopped what he was doing and laced his hands together. "She was fired. I haven't seen her since. I feel bad, you know." He sniffed and wiped his nose with a tissue he pulled from his pocket. "I didn't even get in trouble. Because of course, who in their right mind blames the child?" he said, lacking conviction. "After she left, I was heartbroken, and to make myself feel better, I—in a sense—moved on. I had girls dropping like flies at my feet, begging for a piece of this." He gestured down his frame, however, his expression contradicted his words.

"After that, it was only a matter of time before my parents figured out something was *really* wrong with me."

Though I felt sorry for the teacher—she had no control over her feelings at the time— my heart broke for poor Tim. "Pfuttt," I huffed. I knew all about carrying around soul-crushing guilt. Tim had loved her. And he blamed himself for destroying her career and maybe her life. I couldn't let him think he was the worst person here. "Tim, nothing's wrong with you. Well, not any worse than the rest of us. I killed my father straight out of the gate."

"What!?" He pushed up his fallen glasses.

"Yeah, it's been fourteen months, and . . ." I paused and counted the days in my head, "five days since I'd wished for my dad to walk in front of that bus." It took all of my control to keep from giving away the pain it still caused. The longing I had to see my dad's face, to hear his voice, was a constant companion.

"Yo, Regan, way to make me feel better, mate."

I brushed off my melancholy and shrugged. They were all going to find out one way or another.

"And to think, once you get older and get those braces removed," I used my hand and circled in front of his face, "you're going to be so hot, you won't even need those powers to get the girl. And then you'll know it's for real."

The tips of his ears flushed pink, "Ya think so?"

"Trust me, Tim, we've all been there. Start working out and in a couple of years, boy, you're gonna so be handsome."

I wasn't lying to him. All he needed was to grow into his parts and pieces. And to take a teenager shopping with him and not his parents. I would work on that later. For the time being, baby steps would have to suffice.

Chapter 8: Regan

Ron stuck his fingers in his mouth and whistled loudly to gain everyone's attention. Once we crowded around the campfire he said, "Okay, now that everyone's finished, we need to gather some wood to keep this fire going. Split up into groups of two and bring back what you can."

Gin leaned over and grabbed a beer out of the cooler before he sat down on a foldable chair.

"What? You're not helping?" I stepped between him and the flames to warm my behind.

Humor rumbled silently in his chest. "No. You're the peasant. Not me."

I snarled a lip and stuck out my tongue. "Prima Donna." My eyes tracked a deliberate path to his cabin.

He pressed his free hand to his chest. "You meant Prince Charming, right?"

I rolled my eyes before I turned away to go scour the beach for driftwood. "Hey—" I was about to say *"Tim"* when I was interrupted by Rory.

"I'll come with you," Rory said.

My eyes darted to Gin, hoping he'd save me. It was obvious Rory didn't care for me.

"Why?" I asked her, as Gin shooed me out of the way with a hand. Presumably so he could have access to the fire.

She pushed a loose tendril of kinky hair behind her

ear. "Because you're the only one who's familiar with the territory."

Sound reasoning. I couldn't blame her.

Shrugging, I grabbed a can of bear spray and headed down the beach. Rory fell into step next to me, our feet crunching over the rocks.

"You know Gin's not into you." She grabbed a small log and tucked it under her arm.

"W-What?" I stuttered.

"Gin. He doesn't like you like that."

I stopped. "What are you talking about? Gin and I are—" *What were we really?* I paused. "Friends. Co-workers. And right now, he's my . . . instructor, I guess." It was the best explanation I had. "Besides, for your clarification, I have a serious boyfriend. Like serious with a capital S."

Rory didn't deserve an explanation, but I didn't want to be in the same situation that landed me here in the first place. If I could fix this riff with her, now was the time to do it.

"And not to brag, but the boy is hot." Not that Gin wasn't, but she didn't need to think my intentions were to upgrade because she thought I was hot for the teacher. I yanked my phone out of my pocket.

I held up a picture of Jude so she could witness him in all his glory. The guy was gorgeous with his perfect lips, almost black-colored eyes, bronze skin, and a body that spent hours in a gym. With the fierce cheekbones he got from his Native American heritage, he photographed like a model. I scrolled through a few more of us together. "See."

She huffed and tossed her hair over her shoulder as if she wasn't convinced.

"Anything else you wish to clear up while we're alone?" I stopped walking and shoved my phone into my pocket.

"You're just not very nice." Her lips pursed with disapproval.

Perceptive. Everyone here knew that I could control people, but most of them didn't know I had to do something bad or I'd get sick. Because I didn't want to get off on the wrong foot with another person, I decided to plead my case.

"Why? Because of Pam? You do realize nobody told me that we couldn't demonstrate on each other, right? I was trying to save Cammy more embarrassment after she almost kissed Tim. Don't get me wrong, Tim's cool, but come on, the poor girl was fifty shades of red."

Rory snorted and quickly covered her nose. "I suppose you're right."

"Yeah. And I figured it was best to use Pam since she's in charge. Plus, I didn't know our powers weren't supposed to work on each other."

"They're not?" Shock widened her already large doe eyes as she glanced down at me.

I shook my head.

Her gaze narrowed. "Then why do yours?"

"Your guess is as good as mine." Truthfully, it probably wasn't. If I were a betting person, I'd say my powers were stronger than hers. But after bragging about my ultra-hot boyfriend, I planned to keep the strength of my gift on the down-low. "So, can we start over?" I asked. I was enjoying myself and didn't want to spoil this experience with another mean-girl moment.

She held out her free hand. "Deal."

Crisis averted. Soon, we were talking like new

friends.

Her grandparents owned a farm, just like mine. They raised sheep though, my grandparents raised cattle. Her parents ran the local pub, so her stories about Ireland were entertaining. It sounded like drinking was their national sport.

By the time we got back to camp, hot dogs and condiments were spread over a checkered tablecloth waiting for us to roast our own dinner.

After we all finished eating, Casey brought out the fixings for s'mores and Ron handed Mae a guitar. I'd hoped Gin would start singing, but he didn't.

Hunger sated, exhaustion began to set in, and soon multiple sets of eyes started to drift close. Camping was my happy place, but to the other kids, this was quite the excursion. Eventually, everyone but me, Gin, and Mr. Lacroix excused themselves and went to bed even though the sun was still out and wouldn't go down for a few hours. And even then, there would be a hazy glow on the horizon.

"So," Gin side-eyed me. "It looks as if you and Rory are now getting along. After the way she was glaring at you by the docks this morning, I thought we were about to have another incident on our hands."

I reached out and lightly smacked his arm. "Most of the *issue* revolved around you."

He turned his head and threw me a look of *say what?*

"She told me you weren't interested in me that way."

"*What way?*"

"Exactly. I showed her a picture of Jude and told her that you," I swirled a hand toward him, "were still on the market." I blinked innocently and smiled as if I hadn't thrown him under the bus.

His bottom lip gaped in protest. "Christ, you couldn't have just lied?"

"Did you—a good southern boy—just use the Lord's name in vain?" I heard Mr. LaCroix sputter a laugh from the other side of the campfire. "Besides, I don't want another incident any more than you do," I mumbled quietly, hoping Mr. LaCroix couldn't hear me.

Gin swallowed the rest of his beer and gave me a dirty look. "I'm going to bed." The steps leading up to the cabin creaked under his weight.

After a few minutes of listening to the crackling fire and the lonely call of the loons, my hopes that Mr. LaCroix was going to follow Gin's lead were dashed.

He took a long sip of his beer. "I've never known Gin to get along with someone so well. He usually avoids people. But you—he seems comfortable with you. It makes me happy to see it. You have something in common. With great power," he started the famous quote. We both finished together, "Comes great responsibility."

Deep laughter shook his chest, and I couldn't help it, I joined in.

I stuffed my hands into the pockets of my puffy jacket. "Mr. LaCroix, can I ask you a question?"

"Absolutely, Regan. Anything." He fiddled with a large ring, the blue stone glittering in the firelight. It reminded me of the one my dad wore from West Point but my dad's was a ruby surrounded by diamonds and a couple of sapphires.

"I don't understand, if my dad was going to work for GSS, why was my mom so determined to keep me away from you?"

He crossed his legs and nodded as if I'd asked an interesting question. "Did you ask her?"

"I did. She said she didn't trust you and was trying to keep me safe." Yes, her answer was that vague.

He nodded again. "That seems reasonable. I know your father planned on working for us, but he insisted you and your brothers had no abilities. I'm sure it was to protect you. Regan, your powers, in the wrong hands, could topple governments. Destroy worlds even."

I cringed. Hearing it spoken out loud was jarring. "And that's not the plan?" I hurled him a glare that said he was full of it.

"No," he said as his brows creased. He seemed genuinely taken aback by the idea. He pushed up his glasses. "Besides, I don't believe you'd do something like that."

My eyes narrowed and I folded my arms. "You don't?"

"No. You don't give yourself enough credit. With your abilities and the limitations around them, you have more restraint than anyone I know, except for Gin."

He referred to the fact that when my powers were unleashed in great amounts, I had to do bad things. Hence the whole vigilante justice angle. If they were used for good, I got sick and often ended up in the hospital, if they were ignored, I ended up in the other hospital—the kind with straitjackets.

He sat forward, his forearms resting on his thighs with his beer still in his hands. "Regan, you could've destroyed my daughter. But instead, you taught her a lesson on what it was like to be bullied."

"How are you okay with me after what I did to her?"

He tapped the top of his bottle with his thumb. "Do

I like what you did? Or approve? No. But you could have done *so* much worse."

Perhaps, but the girl tried to kill herself after what I'd done. I still hadn't completely gotten over the guilt. Though I suspected that she'd only done it to get her boyfriend back.

He inhaled and stared at the fire for a few seconds. "But knowing what I know now, I understand why you did it. You have to understand," he raised a hand like a white flag, "I didn't know the extent of her actions until after." He pinched the bridge of his nose as he paused for a few seconds. "I thought most of her behavior was normal for a teenage girl. And everything with Jude, well, let's just say, my daughter is a very convincing actress. The point I'm trying to make is, I believe if the situations were reversed and Gabby had your powers, she would've squashed you and not suffered a moment of remorse."

I couldn't disagree.

He stood up and said, "You, Regan, could be a monster if you chose. But time and time again, you chose not to."

I huffed as I watched him walk toward his cabin. There had to be an angle that I was missing. And though I liked Gin, and Mr. LaCroix seemed okay so far, they were hiding something. I could feel it. "I still don't trust you," I said.

Mr. LaCroix stopped and looked over his shoulder. "Well, Regan, you're far more dangerous than I am, and I trust you."

Chapter 9: Regan

A beam of muted sunlight skimmed over the sexy scruff along Gin's jawline as he unzipped my tent and stepped through the opening. He wore a stocking cap and a plaid shirt under his down vest, all he was missing was an ax and an ox.

I gripped my pillow, threatening to throw it at his head for waking me up, but he held a cup of coffee out in front of him like a peace offering. Not wanting to waste it, I glared instead.

He winked—knowing exactly my quandary. "We're going for a hike. You have ten minutes to get ready. May I suggest you wet down your hair? You look like you were breakdancing in your sleep last night. On your head." He handed me the steaming hot mug.

After he turned around, I threw my pillow and hit him in the back.

"That's dirty. You'll pay for it later," he teasingly threatened over his shoulder.

"Don't make promises you can't keep!" I hollered as he disappeared.

Slipping out of my warm sleeping bag, I threw on some clothes before the morning air chilled my skin. Eagerness swirled inside my stomach as I packed the necessities. Hiking was my favorite.

I met Gin in front of the trailhead. He motioned for me to cross the boardwalk over the creek and followed behind. Wooden planks creaked quietly under our feet. Water bubbled over the rocks and wind rustled through the leaves. The smell of damp, decaying earth and fresh mountain air brought momentary peace to my soul.

A quarter of the journey was bliss. Then we came to a fork in the trail and Gin chose the one going up the side of the mountain. After an hour on the incline, the thick bramble of trees, ferns, and moss changed to slate rocks, scrub brushes, and marmot holes.

Sweat ran down my back and soaked into the waistband of my leggings.

Finally, we stopped at the top near the edge of the precipice to catch our breath and admire the view. The snowcapped peaks and cloudless blue sky reflected on the glasslike surface of the lake below. I snapped a photo with my phone. The images so perfectly mirrored each other that it was hard to decipher which way was up.

"What are we doing here?" I asked, when my lungs finished heaving for air. Not that I didn't enjoy the hike. It had been too long since I'd stretched my legs in this fashion.

Thinking my emotions were solid, I swiped through my pictures to find the one I was looking for—me and my dad on our last adventure. He had one arm wrapped around my shoulder and in his other hand, he held our fishing poles. We stood in front of his float plane, wearing identical smiles as Mom snapped the photo. I missed him. At times it was unbearable.

My bottom lip trembled. "Damn," I whispered between clenched teeth.

Gin peeked at the picture and gave my bicep a gentle squeeze, "Regan, I'm so sorry. I can't imagine how difficult all of this is."

"But why all of the sudden? I've had more than a year to deal with my grief."

"But have you?" Gin said quietly. "I think you've been dealing with much more than grief for the last year."

He was right. I hadn't had the opportunity to mourn my dad's death. Because every time my anger and sadness collided, the golem seized the upper hand. I'd spent the last year trying to contain the golem living inside of me. My greatest fear was hurting someone else I loved. So, to keep that from happening I imprisoned my sorrow in a separate box alongside the monster.

He held out his hand. "I think I can help you."

I side-eyed him suspiciously and blinked slowly— *like yeah right.*

"Really." He glanced at his outreached hand encouraging me to take it. "But you're going to have to trust me. Can you do that?"

Could I? What choice did I have? According to Gin, he was the only one capable of handling me and my pet.

Decision made, I nodded and placed my hand in his. His skin was warm and soft. Holding it gave me a small measure of comfort. If anyone could help, it was Gin.

One side of his lip arched gently as if he were pleased by my faith in him. Though we hadn't known each other long, I felt as if we shared a connection. One created by circumstance and a cruel twist of fate.

He pulled me away from the edge of the cliff until we found a large clearing. He let go of my hand and removed his stocking cap. He tossed it to the ground and scrubbed his fingers through his hair which, as always, fell perfectly into place.

He said, "Now, I need you to show me what you can

do. Darlin' hit me with your wildest wish."

My heart stumbled, then kicked double time. I backed away from him, shaking my head rapidly. I'd changed my mind. The last person who'd faced my wrath was dead. And Jude wasn't here to stop me.

"Regan, as your mentor—I'm not asking you. I'm telling you. I'm ready for whatever you throw at me."

My fists clenched and unclenched. Sweat dampened my forehead. I shook my head again.

Gin's glare slivered to razor precision. "Don't be a coward and disappoint me."

My mouth dropped open. I cocked my head, not sure if I'd heard him right.

He quirked an eyebrow as if to answer my question. Yes, I'd heard him correctly.

Black smoke curled inside the glass box manically grinning. *Fine. Have it your way.* A shiver tumbled down my spine. With a deep inhale, I lifted the corner of the golem's prison. Tingles spread from my chest to the tips of my fingers and the tips of my toes.

I wish.

Gin lifted his hand with his palm raised up and flicked two fingers daring me to bring it on.

Knowing he wasn't going to break easily, I cracked my neck to one side, then released more power.

I wish.

Deviousness bloomed on his handsome face, and he buried his hands into his jacket pockets as if he were on a Sunday stroll in the park. "Oh, come on Regan, you're going to have to do better than that. I'm not Pamela."

I snorted a laugh. So, he didn't want to twerk for me then. All right. He was a cultured guy who sang opera, he probably preferred ballet.

Knocking the lid off of the golem's glass prison, smoke gushed over the edges like water spilling out of a broken dam. The numbness of hedonism flowed lazily through my veins as if it were blood seeping into a bandage. Blue webs of electricity sparked over my skin. My hair rose from my head. I concentrated harder.

I wish.

Gin stiffened as strands of his brown hair began to float in the air like he'd rubbed his head with a balloon. A bead of sweat rolled from his hairline down his temples. He wiped his upper lip with the back of his hand. Still, he didn't perform. But the fire in his eyes, and roguish grin—said he might be enjoying it as much as I was.

Not one for dancing? How about something else even more humiliating?

With my eyes closed, I mentally visualized his every move. Him walking over to the nearest birch tree, stopping in front of it and caressing its pure white bark like a lover's skin. Then gently, with some tongue for good measure, I commanded him to *kiss the tree.* I cracked open my eyes. He wasn't moving.

The muscles in Gin's jaw flexed and his irises glowed like emeralds basking in the sunlight. From the forward-leaning of his posture to the tenseness flexing his muscles, I could tell his body was demanding that he obey.

He picked up one foot and set it down, followed by the other. But he wasn't headed to the tree. With heavy robotic movements, he methodically walked toward me. His smile of victory grew larger and larger with every stride.

Panic fluttered inside my chest.

I wish.

The electricity dancing over my skin dove deeper and vibrated through my flesh. It was as if my cells had been injected with volatile carbonation and yearned for release, else they would explode. They buzzed, they bounced, and they raced around. It was intoxicating—borderline orgasmic. I'd never been able to use my power fully without fear of the repercussions. It was new for me—and it was magic.

Gin stopped in front of me and slowly studied the curves of my face, pausing at my mouth.

I desperately wanted to reach out and touch the sexy freckle, or what my mom would call a beauty mark, high on his cheekbone. I licked my bottom lip and then nipped it between my teeth trying to contain my impulse.

His eyelids drooped and the smile of victory vanished unmasking a hunger that made my breath hitch in my chest.

I wish.

Standing there, staring at his gorgeous face, my body was doused with desire. My pulse raced, my core tightened, my nipples hardened.

I wish.

Chapter 10: Gin

Not having to use much of my own power to resist Regan's first two commands, I was almost caught off guard by the third. The initial sensation was that of pleasure swathing my skin. Then a hint of pain prickled deeper as if tiny electrical impulses were burrowing themselves inside my flesh. The signals sunk deeper and deeper until they connected to the core of my nervous system. My teeth clamped together to keep me from growling. My body demanded I obey, pleading with my mind to relinquish control and act. Her command wasn't *exactly* what I craved though; the subject matter differed.

When I'd agreed to this assignment, I'd made it clear to my uncle that I had a thing for her. He had chuckled and said not to worry. Both Regan and I were consenting adults, and if something were to happen, he wouldn't fire me.

At the moment, with sweat running down my face and the fly of my pants uncomfortably tight, I wasn't worried about my job, I was worried about maintaining control. She was commanding me to make out with a tree. It wasn't going to happen. I sought something else. Or someone else.

Instead of heading toward the birch as she'd ordered, I picked up my foot—even though it felt as if it were weighted down with lead—and took one grueling step toward her. Then another. Her powers wavered with uncertainty. My smile grew bigger with each gain until I was looming above her, gazing down at her beautiful face.

My eyes traced the lines of her blushing cheeks, to her lips, then down her throat to where her pulse was hammering under the cut of her jaw. She slid her lower lip between her teeth, she often did when she was nervous, drawing my attention back to the rosy red curves of her mouth.

Desire, so dark, so demanding pummeled my soul. In my twenty-two years, I'd never wanted anyone or needed anything so fiercely. It was as if my alter ego recognized its soul mate and was insisting I claim her as mine.

I drew my gaze away from her lips to the blue of her eyes. They burned lighter in color matching the clear sky above.

Completely of my own volition, I reached out to her face with a trembling hand and swept her long bangs behind her ear. Her skin was soft and warm. I had to taste her. My fingers wove into the back of her hair, and I pulled her close. I hesitated for a moment, giving her time to deny me if she chose. Not wanting to accidentally hurt her with my own powers, I kissed her lightly, my lips feathering over hers. Desire was the only emotion I tended to struggle with, probably because I didn't have much practice.

She obviously wasn't satisfied with my method and gripped the back of my skull forcing me to kiss her harder. Our tongues met and sensations that I'd never experienced quaked through my body. Happiness, so intense, so foreign, settled inside my soul causing all reason to vacate. With my palm splayed over her back, I yanked her to me, her breasts smashing against my chest. She moaned into my mouth. The notion that I could harm her snapped me into focus. I froze. "Are you okay," I asked with our lips still touching. I couldn't bear to separate myself from her.

"Better than okay," her sweet voice whispered.

"Are you positive?" The last girl I'd kissed ended up in the hospital. She was one of us—but even that didn't buffer her against my powers. As things began to heat up, I'd let down my guard and my alter-ego took it upon himself to galivant inside her brain and erase big chunks of her memory. I didn't realize what was happening until I let go of her to take off my jeans. She passed out and fell on the floor. Between my unattended alter-ego and her bashing her head on the concrete, it was enough to put her in a coma for an entire month. When she finally woke up, her powers were gone along with many of her memories. Dr. Gloria and I did what we could to help heal her brain and the damage I'd caused. But no matter how hard I tried, I couldn't restore her memories or her powers.

There was no way I'd allow that to happen to Regan even if it meant locking up my hunger for her and throwing away the key. I could only pray that her abilities were truly a match for mine.

"Absolutely," she said breathlessly.

Something inside of me cracked. All the years I'd spent hiding who I really was from everyone, except a few monks and my uncle, fractured leaving space for pure bliss to seep inside. It felt curiously like hope. Possibilities. A future not spent alone.

Optimism lifted my lips before I kissed her again. Following my earlier desires, I devoured her lips with plans to explore her entire body should she allow it.

I inhaled the spicy vanilla perfume wafting from her heated skin. "God, you smell so good."

She stiffened as if I'd done something, or said something, wrong, and then a cry of distress warbled from her chest.

She let go of me and bolted backward with her hands gripping her hair. "What have I done?" she gasped, looking up at me, her eyes fraught with pain.

I didn't know what to say. It was as if a bucket of cold water had been dumped over my head. "Regan, what's going on?" I asked.

"Jude." Her chin trembled. "I just cheated on Jude."

To be honest, I almost started crying myself. Her rejection smothered my earlier joy. "Regan, I'm so sorry. This is all my fault." And it was. I was acting upon my desires. With her weakened state, I should've known better. I quickly stifled the impulse to punch the nearest tree. Instead, I mentally talked to myself to keep calm. I hadn't had to use that technique in years, it was second nature, yet this tiny woman seemed to be testing my skills.

She crouched to the ground to tie her shoe—I assumed so she could avoid my gaze.

"This isn't all your fault," she said. "I wanted you to kiss me. Why do you have to be so freaking hot and nice?" she asked, though she didn't sound happy at the idea. "You exude power but you're not arrogant." She stood up with her head turned away and cussed under her breath. "It's intoxicating."

Her rejection was kicked aside by—again—hope. "Darlin' the only reason you wanted to kiss me was because your defenses were down. This is my fault. I know better. Forgive me?"

"Bull," she snapped. "Even with my defenses down, I should've been able to resist. The problem is, I didn't want to. Nor did my pet."

"Yes, but with your pet loose, you were busy with other things. You would've never allowed it to happen otherwise."

"You're wrong." She broke down into heavy sobs as she slid to the ground.

I rushed over to her side and set my hand on her quaking shoulder. Her pain wove through me as if it were my own co-mingling with my guilt and stupidity. And since it was my fault, I offered her the one thing I didn't want to give her. "Regan, do you want me to make you forget this ever happened?" The notion that only I would retain this idyllic memory was torture but seeing her like this was infinitely worse.

She looked up at me, her black lashes wet with tears, and said between breaths, "You can do that?"

My voice was strangled as if my alter ego was trying to prevent me from uttering those dreadful words. "Yes, Darlin', I can. If you ask it of me."

"Yes. Please. Make me forget."

With a clutched fist, I closed my eyes momentarily, forcing away frustration and sorrow. Inhaling deeply, I laid my hand on the top of her head, caressing her soft hair while weaving my way into her memories. Because she asked, I used my powers to erase the sweetest kiss I'd ever beheld.

I supported her as she slumped forward from the aftermath of my abilities. Knowing she'd be out for a few minutes, I used the time to set up the picnic.

I picked her up and laid her down on the plaid

blanket. It didn't take her long to wake up. "What the?" she sputtered, scrambling onto her feet. She listed sideways into a tree and grabbed onto it to keep from falling. Pale bark flaked to the ground.

I chuckled lightly as if my heart hadn't just been shattered, leaving the remnants withered and broken. It was my fault, but it didn't diminish the pain. "Welcome back. I know that feeling all too well. Need some help?" I offered.

She shook her head and exhaled as she gazed in wonder at her surroundings. "Wow, the colors—the greens, the blue, the purples—they're practically shimmering as if they're alive." She pointed above her head. "And I can see the aurora."

Most people thought they only shined in the winter. That wasn't true, they existed with every solar flare. Being this far north, the auroras should have been only visible during the winter when it was dark. But because of our intense practice session, we could both see the northern lights dance in the bright summer sky.

She spun in a circle with her arms twirling away from her sides. "The earth's energy is humming with mine. I feel like I'm floating, flying, free as the eagle riding the thermal waves above."

I looked away from her afraid my composure would fail. My alter ego was screaming at me to capture her in my arms and kiss her again. It hadn't been this unreasonable for years. But between its desires and my feelings for Regan, I was having a hard time containing it.

In order to squash my urge, I focused on her earlier distress; the anguish in her eyes when she realized what I'd done. My throat constricted with remorse as I offered her a sandwich.

She rushed over and snatched it from my hand. She sniffed it with a long inhale and sighed as she took a large bite. "Mmmmm, this is amazing!"

I patted the ground next to me, feelings of disappointment coagulating in my stomach. A small part of me had wanted my powers to have failed.

With unsteady legs, she plopped down. I reached out and braced her by her shoulder until she was stable. I had to force myself to let go.

She shoved another huge bite in her mouth and groaned with pleasure. "This is the best sandwich I've ever tasted."

Damn it all. I shut my eyes and turned my head away. Only minutes ago, she'd made a similar sound with my lips on hers.

After she finished chewing, she tapped my arm, forcing me to look her way, and asked, "What happened?"

"You passed out." I took a bite of my sandwich to keep quiet. I had to admit it was rather tasty for a regular PB and J.

"Yeah, I caught that," she said through another mouthful.

I heaved out a breath, the gust ruffled her hair. "Darlin', you're amazing. I knew you were strong—but wow!"

"Not strong enough to make you dance." Her cheeks began to flush. She spun away and grabbed a bottle of water from her bag.

"Not strong enough for me to make out with a tree either, though I must admit, I've kissed worse." I elbowed her lightly in the ribs.

She threw back her head and laughed. The sound shivered up my spine. I clenched my teeth and looked away to keep it from affecting other parts of my anatomy. *What was wrong with me?* I'd spent years controlling my impulses. Even though I really, *really*, liked her, it shouldn't be causing this much grief.

"I don't doubt it. I mean as girls go—a tree is practically harmless," she said.

It was—but she wasn't. I'd *only* erased the memory of the kiss. Intentionally, I'd left in the moments that led up to it. I was no saint. I wanted her to know. With time, I hoped she would realize I was worth considering.

It's not that I didn't like her boyfriend. Jude seemed like a good guy, but I certainly wasn't going to go down without a fight. If, in the end, she chose to stay with him, so be it. But I'd be dammed if I was going to sit this one out. She was my perfect match, and I intended to show her.

After she ate what amounted to a small feast, she asked, "So, do you want to see if your powers work on me?"

I didn't doubt that my powers worked on her. It would have its limits, just as hers did with me. She was strong enough to deflect anything I could throw at her that would be life-threatening. I leaned back onto the blanket, clasped my hands behind my head, and released a deep sigh. "Not today, Darlin', one of us has to get us off this mountain eventually."

Chapter 11: Jude

Grandma placed hamburgers with homemade French fries on the kitchen table in front of my grandpa and me. I waited for her to sit down with her meal before I squirted a large puddle of catsup on my plate and more over the beef patty. Melted cheese oozed onto the toasted bun.

My stomach growled and Grandma smirked. She knew how much I enjoyed her cooking. My mom hadn't inherited her talents so I took it upon myself to learn all that I could from my grandma. At home, I did most of the cooking.

Piled high with fresh tomatoes, lettuce, and Grandma's famous canned pickles, I squished it together and took a huge bite. I groaned with satisfaction and swallowed. "Nobody knows how to make a burger like you do. What's your secret?"

"Love, good beef, and vine ripened tomatoes."

Having grown up in Wyoming, all were must have ingredients. It also helped that my grandparents had a greenhouse and a summer garden providing us with fresh vegetables most of the year.

As I finished savoring my last bite, Regan's emotions, that had varied this morning from trepidation to excitement, veered off the reservation to intense sorrow. Tears, that weren't my own burned the back of my nose. I swallowed quickly to keep from choking.

"You okay, son?" my grandpa asked. Concern and a deeper knowing were etched into his weathered face. Though he'd promised not to tell anyone about Regan's powers or our bond—that meant everyone except for Grandma.

Nonetheless, she pretended nothing interesting was happening and cleared the table giving us some privacy.

"It's nothing. I think. She's just sad. I'm sure she's fine," I rambled in an attempt to convince myself otherwise but the intensity behind the feelings were starting to concern me.

Grandpa sat in silence studying my face.

I threw him an exasperated look and held up my hands. "Really. I'm fine. She's fine. Do you mind?" I didn't mean to sound so disrespectful but I didn't like that he could read my emotions so easily.

It's unwelcome isn't it? My insecurity whispered. *Now imagine how she feels knowing that you're there all the time spying, creeping around, waiting for her to mess up.*

I buried my head into my hands hiding my face.

Grandpa got up from the table and patted the pack of cigarettes in his shirt pocket. I could hear them crinkle under the tap of his hand. "Well, then, if you need anything, I'll be on the porch."

I nodded.

As quickly as the sorrow had hit me, a stab of fear penetrated my lungs taking my breath away momentarily. Whatever was going on, Regan's emotions were on high alert. Sometimes I questioned needing a service dog just to warn me about her and *her feelings.*

Not wanting any witnesses to the impending roller coaster I was about to experience, I excused myself from the table and headed to the bedroom. As an only grandchild, my grandparents kept a room in both of their houses, this one and the one on the reservation, for me and my mom to share when we stayed over. But mostly I used it.

I opened the door and closed it behind me. I slipped off my shoes and laid back on the bed while rubbing the tenderness along my sternum. Most of the time Regan's emotions hit me purely in a mental state, but when she was unprepared for the impact they often manifested physically as well. Thankfully, that didn't happen often.

With my hands clasped behind my head, I prepared for the ride. Her fear morphed into what felt like a dare mingling with excitement. Should she jump off the fictitious cliff or back away?

I guessed her decision before she did. After knowing her for almost a year, I was getting good at predicting her reactions. In the beginning, that wasn't the case. It was her response to situations that got me romantically interested in the first place.

With that cloud of smoke surrounding her like a warning, I expected her to be wicked. She surprised me. Which doesn't often happen. Humans, if nothing else, are predictable. But even when people were cruel to Regan, she responded with indifference. Then when I learned what she was dealing with and how she had to handle the monster living inside of her, my respect skyrocketed. It didn't take my heart long to follow.

Sweat began to bead on my forehead and upper lip. Something or someone was forcing her to work extra hard. I wondered if this would get easier for her with practice, subsequently making it easier on me.

What wasn't getting easier, or going away, was the

tingling sensation awakening down under. I shifted uncomfortably and grabbed my book off the bedside table hoping to take my mind off the events playing out.

When Regan unleashed her powers in quantity, they were often accompanied by sexual urges. Normally, I was the one who benefited and if she was here, I would've embraced the adventure. Even if I were alone. I had a good imagination and she'd given me plenty to work with before she left. But with her away. . .

"Gin will come out to play."

I caught my breath and listened carefully while scanning my room. But nobody was there. My insecurity, normally just a whisper of my own subconscious, seemed as if it had spoken out loud.

"Fuck! Fuck! Fuck!" I grabbed my pillow, pulling it up over my ears.

A faint cackle echoed in my brain as the front of my pants tightened with the pressure. The physical sensations were amazing, except for the heaving of my stomach and the apprehension in my heart. It was like having someone give you blow job while punching you in the face. Not my idea of a good time.

For the next five minutes or so, my fear and pleasure traveled to dizzying heights then crashed to the ground leaving me mangled in the wreckage. My hearts blood drained from my veins as did my trust.

Who? Who was she with? I sat up with my legs over the side of the bed, gripping my hands together.

"You know who." I could hear the voice clearly, like a low rumbling growl, as if someone was speaking directly into my ear.

What are they doing?

The voice chuckled as if it didn't need to answer, but

it did anyway. *"Don't be naïve. You know what they're doing."*

Why? Why would she cheat on me? I ran my fingers through my hair, and squeezed.

"Because she's a cheating, lying, whore. And it's only going to get worse."

My guts kicked. I jumped off bed and rushed to the toilet just in time to vomit my lunch. I wiped my mouth on the bottom of my shirt before I took it off and tossed it in the laundry pile.

And just when I thought the worst was over—I was disappointed. Sorrow and shame traveled the length of our connection when she realized what she'd done, finishing with an oily sheen of guilt because she'd enjoyed it.

The final blow was her fear slicing through my ribs, puncturing my barely beating heart. Because she would know that I knew. The voice in my head was right. She was a cheating, lying, whore. She'd done it before, not on me, but she cheated with me when she was dating Layne. Why did I think I'd be any different?

After I rinsed out my mouth in the bathroom sink, I looked up at mirror to see silent tears streaming down my face. And then, in an instant, her emotions fizzled out and disappeared. Poof. Gone. Taking with it sorrow, shame, and guilt as if they were never there to begin with.

But she couldn't fool me no matter what kind of tricks he'd taught her. You can't hide from the person who has a direct line to your soul.

I walked back into the bedroom, the hole in my chest a gaping wound, and stared at the book still on the bed. *A Complete Guide to Norse Mythology.* I opened to the chapter of Loki, the God of Mischief and pulled out the address my grandpa had given me just in case of emergency.

Chapter 12: Regan

We all stood around the campfire, side-stepping in one direction and then the other to avoid the billowing smoke. It had rained during the night, leaving the wood damp.

I clasped my hands together behind my back and stretched my arms. After yesterday's training with Gin, I felt stronger and more in control of my pet. A tiny flower of hope bloomed inside, perhaps training would actually help and I could be released back into the wild someday without the fear of hurting someone.

"Here's how this is going to work, people." Gin swept his brown hair away from his forehead, addressing our group and a bunch of newcomers. He had the uncanny knack of looking perpetually bored. His face, unless he wanted it to, gave away very little of what he was thinking. It was irritating.

I shifted restlessly and stared at the group of teenage castaways—five guys and one girl—huddled in their own cluster. They'd washed up on shore shortly after breakfast. *Okay, so Ron had brought them over by boat.* But with their ratty sneakers, saggy pants, and mean mugs, they looked as if they'd been out to sea for a few weeks or living on the streets doing who knows what.

Gin swiveled his feet away and faced them. "On your right; the juvenile delinquents."

They spread out, forming a line, shoulder to

shoulder, arms crossed, and feet spread.

Called it. Though with their tattoos, partially shaved heads, and multiple piercings it wasn't that impressive of a guess.

Gin tilted his head as if waiting for them to take offense. Not one of them seemed insulted by the label.

"And over here," Gin turned back to us, "we have our group of . . . well, to be determined." With a quick scan, he took our measure. His air, amused and arrogant, suggested he doubted our capabilities. I folded my arms at the slight.

"Anyway," he continued, pacing between us with his thumbs hooked in the pockets of his jeans, "your objective is to capture the other team's flag and get it back here first. Your reward," Gin acknowledged to the other kids, "as you know, is a free pass out of the juvenile detention center. And to sweeten the pot, $1000. Each."

They smiled, exchanged glances, and did some kind of chest pounding with finger signs.

Gin's head snapped back to us, his eyes deadly serious. "Your reward is to win." His scrutiny landed on each one of us individually and then he nodded once as if to say—*don't disappoint me.*

The opposition chuckled as if our chance was less than zero. They relaxed their postures and started joking amongst themselves indicating we were no threat.

My pet perked and slithered to the edges of the box. If it could have rubbed its tiny non-existent hands together, it would've.

I took a second to openly study our opponents. By the way that they'd behaved, they were familiar with one another. How familiar? Were they family? Or *family*—as in an established gang of sorts. Their clothes all had a similar theme: old, except for identical black rain jackets, which from the sheen and saturated color appeared to be brand new. My intent wasn't to judge them for being poor, it was simply another bit of information used to assess their skills. These kids looked as if they knew how to survive on the streets and they'd be willing to do whatever was necessary to win.

I glanced at our motley crew and repressed the urge to throw in the towel. Rory was braiding her hair, Tim was staring longingly at the pretty girl on the other team, Ben was also staring—though I wasn't sure who'd captured his attention, and Navi was chewing on her cuticles around her nails like a mouse with a cracker.

Mae slid next to me and mimicked my body language as she scowled at our enemy. I'm sure we were as intimidating as a pair of rabid Chihuahuas.

"What are the rules?" I asked. The excitement started to build inside my chest like little bubbles of pressure. Or was that my pet? Either way, this was going to be fun.

"Patience, we're getting there," Gin said. "This one, ladies and gentlemen," he tapped my cheek with his hand a couple of times, "is the one you have to watch out for."

Laughter thundered from the guys. One hit the girl lightly on her arm. Her sharp eyes gave me a quick once over and blew me off with a snort.

"Well, Darlin'." Gin gently gripped the back of my neck. Sparks leached into my skin and made my stomach flitter with nervous energy. "Give them a demonstration."

I stepped away. The weird effect he was having on me was confusing at best. "What?"

Mae pushed my shoulder and encouraged me. "Do

it," she whispered.

"Why must I always repeat myself?" Gin raised a brow in challenge.

"Fine." I flung my hands in the air. Tingles spread from the tips of my fingers to the tips of my toes.

I wish.

The five guys immediately capitulated to my will and struck a pose even the savviest cheerleader could appreciate. Their eyes registered confusion, fear, and then anger. The girl resisted.

I opened the box further. Sweat sheened her forehead and she managed to wipe it away before she fashioned a Y with her arms and joined the rest of her crew. After that, I didn't even need to spell the rest of the song.

"What is it with you and making people dance?" Gin tossed an arm over my shoulder. That same spark blanketed my skin, but I didn't move away this time. He smelled nice, familiar, and comforting like clean laundry, a campfire, and coffee. It reminded me of my past life. Now my world was fractured into two categories—before I killed my father and after.

Ben, Tim, and Mae laughed and a smile tugged at Navi's lips. Rory on the other hand didn't seem to like Gin's familiarity with me. She propped her hands on her hips and glared. I wasn't sure if she was irritated because I'd been cruel to the other team or because Gin had his arm around me. The latter was undoubtedly a solid bet.

"What?" I mouthed at her and shrugged. It wasn't my fault he was comfortable with me. Then I answered Gin's question. "Dancing is fun and harmless. And most people don't like to make fools of themselves in front of other people." I smiled and shot a knowing look at Gin.

"The high is *so* nice."

He pushed me gently out of his grasp. "You're such a junkie."

"Takes one to know one."

He swiped my long bangs out of my eyes leaving behind a sensation that refused to diminish. It dove deep into my heart and took up residence inside. I refused to acknowledge it. This was a stupid, embarrassing, simple crush, and nothing more.

As the dancers finished their performance, Gin said, "Y'all believe me now?"

Raising my hands high in the air, I gave them a polite round of applause. Ben, Tim, and Mae joined me.

None of the opposing team looked scared, they looked more angry than anything.

"She can teleport." Gin pointed at Navi. Her eyes popped open and she covered her mouth with her hand. Her collection of bracelets clinked on her wrist.

Then he went down the line naming our gifts. "Absolute control." I glared. Giving away my secret wasn't something I did willingly.

"Illusions," Gin said. Ben bowed, one hand on his stomach, the other up in the air. "This one here," he gestured to Tim, "can make you fall in love with him."

A couple of the guys on the other team snickered and the biggest one muttered, "Ya sure, I'd like to see him try."

Tim and I exchanged Machiavellian grins. Goosebumps peppered my arms. This had potential.

"She can control plants." Gin pointed at Rory keeping his distance. The skin between her perfectly sculpted brows puckered as Gin passed her by to stop in front of Mae. With a big sweep of his hand, he said, "And this one, she's telekinetic."

"What does that mean?" a guy asked while tugging up his sagging pants.

"It means she can make objects move, stupid," the girl said, snapping her head sideways to glare at him. Her hoop earrings bounced, and her long ponytail slapped the guy standing next to her. He brushed a lock of hair out of his mouth but didn't say anything.

"I can manage those," she said to Gin, dismissing my other teammate's gift with a wave of her hand. "But she," she said, scrutinizing me, "has an unfair advantage."

"You're right, she does." Gin gazed at me fondly as if I were his favorite pet.

A half smirk, half sneer, lifted the side of my lip. It's not like I could argue with her.

"So, to make this fair—" Gin started, only to be interrupted.

"Fair! There's no way this can be fair!" The guy, built like a redwood, barked. He crossed his large arms over the huge expanse of his chest. The girl reached up and rested her hand on his shoulder.

Gin stepped in front of the guy and stared up at him without blinking, not intimidated in the least. With a gift like his, who could blame him? "Didn't your momma ever tell you, life ain't fair?" Gin said in a quiet but hard tone. After a beat, he continued, "To *balance* the odds— Regan, you can choose one person to control. Only one. If that person is taken out of the game, by you, or their own team . . ." He pushed his hands into his pockets and shrugged.

I turned my half smirk, half sneer on him. For all intents and purposes, he'd neutered me.

Knowing that he'd cut me off at the knees, he blew me an infuriating kiss before moving closer to the leader. He looked down at her and blessed her with his charming Southern smile. One that I had no doubt melted even the coldest of hearts. "I never said this was going to be easy, but your reward—should you win—is substantial."

The girl licked her full red lips and purred, "Oh, we'll win."

Chapter 13: Regan

Ben held up the flap on the canvas tent for the rest of to us duck inside. The other team had a separate tent to plan their attack. We gathered around a card table and I picked up one of the small maps laying on the surface. The rules were simple: the red X was the location of the opponents' flag, the blue X was our flag, and the black X was our current position. We were to capture the red flag and get it back here before the other team.

I tapped my finger over the paper and asked if they had any ideas on how to win.

We all threw out our best strategies but eventually we settled on mine. My brothers and I had spent hours playing a military tactic game with my dad. Plus, we often competed in paintball tournaments. Only Rory was resistant to my plan. The others tried to explain why my tactics were solid, but Rory spent half of our allotted planning time nit-picking.

Finally, Mae had enough and tossed her arms in the air. "Do you have any military training?" She stepped up to Rory's face, and though Mae was a foot shorter, Rory was the one who retreated. I didn't blame her, Mae was a force of nature. Her parents had raised her on a hippy commune in rural California, though it sounded like a cult. The leader took a shine to cute little Mae when he found out what she could do. For years, he exploited her gifts for the benefit of the "community". When she turned fourteen, he upped his game and declared she was to be his bride. She ran away with only the clothes on her back and not a penny to her name. According to Mae, they were still searching for her. Nobody, especially a narcissistic cult leader, likes to lose their greatest asset.

Rory flipped her hand toward me. "No, but the *chosen one* doesn't have any military training either. Correct me if I'm wrong."

My dander flared at her choice of words. I wasn't the chosen one, we all had gifts, and hers, though I hated to admit it, could be pretty cool if she'd put in some effort. Her problem was that she didn't like it when other people stole her spotlight. Gin said that I could only control one person. At that moment, Rory was topping my list. It might have been worth it, but Mae was doing a fine job defending me.

"Seriously, Rory?" Ben rubbed the back of his neck. She scowled, the skin around her hazel eyes tightening.

"The only way we're going to win is if we come up with a plan." I glanced at my phone to check the time and huffed. "If you have something better, we're willing to listen."

Everyone nodded.

Rory's frown deepened. She didn't have a better idea—she just didn't like me. *Here we go again. And I hadn't even stolen this one's boyfriend.*

Within five minutes, Mae and I concocted a basic strategy. Everyone had a partner and their mission. I chose Rory because I knew without a doubt, she'd throw the game just to make me look bad.

"You realize if we lose, they're going to blame you, right?" I said to Rory as we ducked under the tent door, zipping it behind me to keep out the mosquitos.

I pulled the goggles down over my eyes using my free hand and then adjusted my grip on the paintball gun. I scanned the perimeter listening for snapping twigs, angry squirrels, or the hushing of the forest.

"I don't care," she spat. "We're supposed to be learning to use our powers, not *this*."

I bit my tongue. I didn't have the inclination to explain what we were doing out here or what we were supposed to be learning. Did she think GSS was going to hire her as a gardener? Besides, the only one who'd been hog-tied was me. The rest of them got to use their gifts as they saw fit.

With a light step, I led the way down a trail. Our job was to ambush the other team. Mine in particular was to take control of one of our opponents and make them shoot their own teammates.

Rory trudged behind. Her paintball gun was tossed over her shoulder like a purse, not out in front of her like a weapon. She created quite the racket as she hummed a happy tune while slapping the bushes with a broken tree branch.

Stopping behind a twisted grove of shrubs, I pulled the map out of my pocket and glanced down to make sure we were headed in the correct direction. We assumed the other team was going to leave their flag unguarded. They'd capture ours, then eliminate whoever had captured theirs. That's what I would've done if I thought my opposition wasn't worthy. Ben and Tim, experts at first-person shooter video games, agreed with me.

Rory and I headed to the spot where I believed we would intercept the enemy.

Along the way, she bent down to inspect some kind of fungus growing at the base of a tree instead of paying attention.

"Are you planning on helping at all? If not, just go back to camp and stay out of my way." It irritated me that she wasn't taking the exercise seriously. It wouldn't have bothered me if she lacked experience. Or if she was scared because she'd never fired a gun before, but she'd told me she'd been deer hunting most of her life. That was the reason she was paired with me—she knew how to shoot, and she knew how to be quiet in the woods. Not that she was utilizing said skills.

Ben and Tim, having no actual field experience, were assigned to protect our flag.

Mae and Navi, with their gifts conducive to stealing, were to capture the other team's flag. And yet it seemed as if Rory was trying to make us lose on purpose, though I couldn't figure out why.

She stood up and propped her hands on her hips. "You know, Regan, you're not my boss." She flipped her hair over her shoulder in what I was beginning to think of as her signature move.

My fists tightened. "Didn't say I was. But if you're not going to help. Leave. Get out of the way. You're making too much noise." I pointed toward our campsite.

Pink stained her neck and cheeks. "No." She smacked a tree trunk hard with her broken branch. Bark crumbled to the ground and a few green leaves flitted to the forest floor.

I pressed my lips together concentrating on controlling my temper. I hiked the paintball gun over my shoulder so I wouldn't be tempted to use it on her and grabbed the water bottle out of my backpack. It crinkled as I twisted off the cap. "For a person who has the gift of the elements, you treat them like crap." My mercurial attitude bled into my comment as I glanced at the tree she'd assaulted. "No wonder your powers aren't very strong. The elements don't like you."

Her face morphed from pink to bright red. I caught the decision in her eyes a split second before she pulled her weapon and shot me point-blank in the chest.

The bottle fell and water spilled onto the ground. My lungs grunted under the force of the paintball, and I slapped my chest with my hand. I pulled it away and stared in shock at the blue paint. With a snarl bowing my lips, I dragged my gaze from my stained palm to her smiling Irish eyes.

The glass box inside my head fractured and tiny cracks jerkily spread over the surface. Black smoke curled like horns and the golem butted at its prison. White spots peppered the corners of my vision. Forest noises disappeared as if they had been swallowed by a black hole.

Through clenched teeth, I growled. "Run." It sounded as if my voice had escaped from the bowels of hell.

Her smiling eyes switched to terror as she stumbled backward and crashed on her butt.

My body shook as the golem repeatedly rammed against the compromised glass. It was as if someone was inside my head beating my skull with a hammer.

With her stomach toward the sky, she crab-walked away. With some distance between us, she scrambled to her feet and stood up straight. Before she could turn to run, something hit her in the back. She hurtled headfirst onto the ground. Her eyes bugged out and her head snapped forward from the force of the blow, sending a rush of wild curls around her face before she faceplanted in the mud. Four splotches of red paint stained the back of her jacket where she'd been shot by the enemy.

She pushed up from the mud puddle she'd been launched into. Filth dripped from her hair and the whites of her eyes contrasted with the muck.

My anger quickly faded to malicious amusement. The white spots dimmed and the forest sounds slowly returned. I bent over holding my stomach as I cackled. *Ain't karma a bitch?*

Standing some yards away, hidden behind the trees with their guns aimed at me, was the opposing team.

Victory highlighted their leader's face. She bobbed her head side to side, her hoop earrings swinging, like *sucka, told you we'd win.* I gritted my teeth and shook my head slightly. The golem, having had its fun ripped away, was more than ready to finish this game. It didn't care who my target was.

The girl must've read something in my eyes because her grin vanished, replaced with unease. She motioned to her teammates to leave. "Thanks," she quipped to Rory before they disappeared.

Rory's chin trembled and an outpouring of tears washed tracks down both cheeks.

I stabbed my finger in the air for her to leave. My voice, now that my pet was back under control, sounded normal though livid when I ordered, "Go. Before you find out why I'm the chosen one."

Chapter 14: Regan

My pet eddied inside its cage in frustration. I wasn't sure if it was irritated because all we could do was watch our team fail or if it was mad because it was denied a snack.

I kicked the ground, sending clumps of mud, leaves, and dirt in the air. As furious as I was with Rory, I was quite proud of myself. When I'd signed on with GSS, they'd appointed me a therapist. Each of us newbies had one. Dr. Gloria's main objective was to teach me how to control my negative emotions.

A smile brightened my face. Rory was going to be my guinea pig. Oh, how she would fume if she knew.

I couldn't wait to tell Dr. Gloria that the counseling sessions seemed to be helping. When I used my powers with clarity and control, the high I got was amazing. All the guilt I carried from killing my father was momentarily vanquished. That was the best part. For a few minutes in time, I didn't hate myself. However, when the golem was in complete control, I tended to short-circuit and someone was bound to get hurt. Often, I ended up in the hospital though I'd yet to figure out why. I assumed it was because the golem zapped all of my energy and sucked my life force dry. So, it was in my best interest, as well as everyone else's, to keep my pet on a leash.

I sulked down the short trail back to camp and

succeeded in keeping my cool even as the earlier events replayed in my head.

Before I could change out of my dirty clothes, Mr. Lacroix's head popped out of the cabin door. With a wave of his hand, he said, "Regan, come in here for a minute."

I stepped inside and he shut the door behind me.

The air smelled faintly of mildew and wood smoke. Ron was standing in the middle of the room in front of a computer monitor, rubbing his chin. The setup seemed quite sophisticated in the rustic cabin.

"Come watch," Mr. Lacroix urged.

On the split screen, images from multiple cameras played live. The picture was ultra-sharp and in color. It didn't come as a surprise that they were watching us nor that their equipment was state of the art. How else were they going to know what was happening out there?

With my hands cozy in my hoodie pouch, I watched as Tim and Ben attempted to protect our flag. The delinquents used the bound and overwatch technique to get closer to their target.

Tim and Ben, sheltered behind a wooden barrier, jumped up at the same time to pelt the incoming ambush. Red paint splashed trees and the ground, but hit no one.

Seconds later, Ben slid down behind the shelter and a ghostly figure materialized out of thin air. The entity floated toward the enemy. Her long skirt and dark hair whipped in the nonexistent wind.

Their eyes widened with alarm, a couple of them stumbled and one made the sign of the cross over his chest before he dodged behind a mess of bushes. Their fearless leader yelled something and they seemed to snap out of their fright.

I glanced at the other screen as Navi and Mae snatched the enemy's flag with no resistance.

Mae stopped, looked around, then pulled the map from her pocket and traced the direction back to camp with her finger.

If Ben and Tim could keep the opposition busy long enough, Navi and Mae could capture the win.

My eyes darted to the other screen just in time to see Tim stand up with his weapon aimed. He stared hard at the big guy who'd poked his head out from behind a tree, giving Tim the perfect opportunity to utilize his gift. He smirked deviously as the big guy stepped away from his cover.

With a meaty hand, the big guy flipped his paintball gun over his shoulder and sauntered past his teammates. They yelled at him to stop. It was easy to read their lips. He ignored their warnings and stopped ten feet away from Tim and Ben's shelter.

He grinned as he pushed his hands casually into the pockets of his drooping jeans. He tipped his chin up in greeting and said, "Hey." Or at least that's what it looked like he said. His tongue darted out to wet his bottom lip.

Tim winked and returned the gesture.

I snorted.

Both Mr. Lacroix and Ron glanced at me with matching expressions of mirth.

As the rest of the enemy crept from their positions, Ben popped up like a windup toy and shot the big guy in the chest. Tim took a shot at the others, but his aim was lacking since he was still trying to flirt with his target. He wasn't having much success doing both things at once. The big guy's expression turned from a sexy *hey hey* to a savage *hell no*. His eyes widened then lasered on

Tim. His skin turned an angry shade of purple and he rapidly closed the distance between them in two large strides. He grabbed Tim by the front of the jacket and lifted him effortlessly over the wooden barrier, Tim's legs dangling in the air.

"That's not fair," I said. My head swiveled between Ron and Mr. LaCroix. "He's out!"

Mr. Lacroix patted my shoulder. "Tim can figure it out. He might get roughed up a bit, but the others were warned that if they injured any of you, they'd get life in prison. All of you are going to have to learn to think on your feet."

The big guy put Tim on the ground, wound up his fist, and clocked him in the face. I gasped.

Tim flopped backward into the shelter and slid down like a rag doll. I had to give the kid credit, he scrambled right back up. His lips moved—I don't know what he said— and the big guy's eyes bulged, and he raised his hands in the air surrendering as he stomped away.

Ben stood up and reached over to hand Tim a rag for his bleeding nose. As he leaned forward, he was shot from behind. He slammed into the barrier and the cloth, outstretched in his hand, dropped to the ground. An obvious curse tore from his lips.

Tim ducked, blood running freely from his nose, and grabbed the hanky before attempting to retreat to safety. The big guy had punched him, but he hadn't shot him, so officially, he was still in play. To solve that issue, the girl stepped out from behind a tree with her paintball gun aimed at Tim's chest. He lifted his free hand and gave her the easy shot. She pelted him with one paintball before she winked and darted away.

A lopsided grin bent Tim's lips as he watched her

leave.

With only one of their teammates down, it was now a five-to-two battle. A few cameras picked up the opposition's mad dash to intercept Mae and Navi. Once they caught sight of the girls, they fanned out for the ambush.

Mae's head cocked to the side, and she held up a finger for Navi to stop when she figured out that they were surrounded. Then she ordered, "Go."

Navi, her dark eyes glistening like wet onyx, looked as if she were about to cry. She gripped the flag to her chest and started to run, her gun bouncing on her back.

I shook my head and sighed. It was over.

Mae hunkered down. She used her powers to rip the paintball gun out of the hands of one of the other team members. It flew in the air and dropped to the forest floor. But before she had a chance to do it again, Navi was shot from all sides at the same time. She flashed in and out of focus, then appeared ten feet ahead of where she was. But it didn't matter. Red paint dripped down the back of her black rain jacket and the flag was stained with enemy colors.

I muttered under my breath.

"Did that go how you expected?" Mr. LaCroix didn't seem disappointed or angry, just curious.

I shrugged. It kind of did.

He rubbed his nose. "And about Rory, I'll have her sent home this afternoon."

"No," I said firmly. "Sorry." I shook my head realizing I was addressing the boss. On my walk back to camp, I'd decided to give her another shot. Though I wasn't sure she deserved it. "What I mean is—Rory's good practice for me to keep my anger under control.

That's all. If you have to send her home, I understand. But don't do it on my account."

With a small nod and an expression that resembled approval, he said, "Yeah, I can see that. You did well out there after she shot you. I wasn't worried for a second."

"I was," I said, laughing nervously.

"Nah." Ron patted me on the shoulder. "You got this, kid."

My heart reveled in the praise.

"Go on," Ron motioned a hand toward the cabin door, "go, have some fun."

Rushing down the stairs, I searched the area for Gin. Though I couldn't see him, I could hear him singing. His voice was amazing—as soothing and sexy as his accent. Goosebumps showered my arms, after all, opera was my favorite.

I found him sitting by the campfire. "Hey," I said.

The afternoon sun peeked out from behind some passing clouds and highlighted his brown hair with streaks of dark gold.

When he didn't acknowledge me, I stepped next to him. He pulled out his earbuds. His eyes shot to my torso, then found my face. A look of disappointment flashed.

"Don't ask." I hung my jacket over a tree branch.

Gin tipped his chin at the empty chair next to him and we sat quietly waiting for the others. One after another, they slunk out of the trees covered in splashes of red paint and stood across the fire. They shifted uneasily as if Gin's disapproval was a physical discomfort.

Rory came out of her tent wearing clean clothes, though her curls were twisted in dirty ropes.

"Welcome back losers," Gin said, in a friendly

upbeat way as only a true Southerner can. "Anyone care to tell me what went wrong?" He leaned forward with his elbows on his knees.

Rory's eyes rounded, I think she was surprised that I hadn't ratted her out.

Tim scooted closer to the fire and filled Gin in on the events. He pulled a tissue from his pocket to dab at the blood still dripping from his nose. He had a black eye to match.

I wanted to ask Tim what he'd said to make the guy back off, but I'd have to wait until we had some privacy or the others would know I'd been watching.

"Regan, what happened to you?" Tim asked. "Nobody was around when you got shot."

I glanced at Rory and shrugged. "I didn't get a good look at who it was either."

"Uggg," Tim groaned. "Even with the big bloke out of commission, with you gone, we didn't stand a chance."

"You mean the guy who returned to camp with hearts in his eyes?" I teased, batting my lashes.

His cheeks blushed. "Ya do whatcha gotta do," he said, faking a New York accent.

I glanced at Rory again. "That you do." She swallowed and stared into the trees.

Ron ambled out of the cabin with a coffee cup in his hands and asked, "And what have you all learned from this experience?"

Trust no one? "That even with powers, other people can outsmart and outmaneuver us," I said.

"Good," Ron said.

Ben ripped off his ruined rain jacket and hung it on a tree branch next to mine. His eyes paused over the splotched blue paint then darted to the others wearing matching red stains. His jaw flexed and he shook his head before he flopped down in the chair next to me. "Well, if Regan wouldn't have been cut off at the knees, we would've won," Ben grumbled.

"Possibly," Ron said. "But what happens if you don't have her around or she's busy fulfilling her end of the mission? Here you need to work together as a team. And from what I've observed, thus far, some of you have a problem with that." His eyes lingered on Rory.

I glanced at the ground to hide the smile trying to form. I didn't need to tattle on her, I was pretty sure Ben had figured out we had a traitor in our midst, and obviously, the instructors had watched the whole thing behind closed doors.

"You guys are a mess. Anyone care to go for a swim?" Gin said, pushing himself out of his chair.

Rory's face lit up, then fell. "I didn't bring a bathing suit with me."

Gin ignored her.

Thankfully, he'd told me to bring mine.

I ran to my tent and changed into a pair of board shorts, a bikini top, and a ribbed tank. I tied a clean sweatshirt around my waist and grabbed a towel.

We followed Gin down a narrow trail lined with ferns, devil club, and trees until we came to a small cove protected from the wind. A weathered dock with a square platform at the end jutted into the dark green lake. The direct afternoon sunlight had warmed the air until it was almost hot. At least by Alaskan standards.

Once on the beach, Mae and Navi pulled off their sweatpants and T-shirts.

Navi wore a sensible one-piece suit in solid black.

Mae had on a tiny bikini in red, white, and blue like the American flag.

Tim swallowed, his prominent Adam's apple bobbing hard before he took off running down the dock. Navi and Mae followed. Their laughter echoed in the wind. Ben strolled beside me, still looking sour.

"Don't worry Ben," I reassured him, "we'll win next time."

He glared at the back of Rory's head and said unnaturally loud but not yelling, "Maybe if we can get rid of some dead weight."

He'd definitely suspected that she was the one who shot me.

Her shoulders went rigid and she scuttled down the boardwalk instead of hanging back with us.

I reached out to push Ben's arm teasingly.

"What? I can't help it. I don't like her."

"She's not that bad," I said.

Ben threw me a dirty look that said I was lying. "Really? Obviously, you're a lost cause, I'm going to go save Navi and Mae from the Celt." Ben trotted down the docks leaving Gin and me alone.

Gin stopped me with a warm hand on my shoulder. "What? Is there something you're not telling me?"

"I'm sure Ron and your uncle will fill you in." I blinked deliberately as if daring him to lie to me about the cameras. He didn't know they had pulled me into the cabin earlier. But he did now.

A sly smile grew, sharpening his already strong jawline, and making the small cleft in his chin more prominent. "But I'd rather hear it from you, Darlin'."

Chapter 15: Gin

It had been a good day, even though Regan and the other recruits had lost the game. Despite their advantage, I hadn't expected them to win. The other kids had been working together for years. Our recruits met a week ago. The exercise was about building relationships, not about winning. After it was over, I'd used my powers to erase the other kids' memories and replace them with a paintball competition which they'd won. Hence the reason each of them carried a thousand dollars in their pockets.

My abilities helped keep GSS safe from discovery, but now that my job was done for the day, I could enjoy the rest of the afternoon in Regan's company.

In one tug, I yanked my T-shirt over my head and tossed it on a piece of driftwood. The sun rays shining directly on my skin were uncomfortably hot and I was looking forward to cooling off in the lake.

Regan inhaled sharply. She slapped her hand over her chest, which momentarily drew my eye to the pale skin of her breasts peeking out from under her tank top. As if clutching her pearls, she teased in a pretty convincing drawl, "Why Christian LaCroix, I do declare. Where have you been hiding all of this?" She fanned her forehead with her free hand.

A crooked grin built, and a flush warmed my cheeks. Being in top physical shape was as important as my mental health when it came to controlling my alter ego.

The look of admiration on Regan's face implied that my workouts had multiple benefits.

My self-consciousness grew deeper with the passing seconds, and I was almost thankful when she reached out to turn me around. My breath hitched, and I couldn't hide the shiver as she traced the tattoo of a snow leopard covering half of my back. I wasn't used to physical contact.

"Wow," she whispered. "It's beautiful. There's meaning there." Her hand trailed downward until she pulled away. Immediately, I missed the warmth of her fingers. Having no desire to embarrass myself further, I clenched my teeth trying to control my body's reaction to her. It had been years since I allowed someone to touch my bare skin for any length of time for fear of hurting them.

"Hey, no need to share if you don't want to. We're all entitled to our secrets, Gin."

I spun around before she had a chance to move too far away and grabbed her hand. "No." I wanted to tell her my story without making her feel sorry for me. Deciding that wasn't a possibility, I relinquished my grip. "I accidentally killed someone too."

Her lovely lips parted, and I craved to taste them. Delving from temptation, I looked away and scrubbed my hand over my jaw. "I was six. She was four and she broke my favorite toy dump truck. I was still mad when my mom made us hug and make up. My sister dropped dead in my arms. Later it was determined she had a brain aneurysm."

Tears pooled in Regan's blue eyes making them shimmer like the deepest parts of a tropical sea.

I heaved a breath and stared out over the lake. "Nobody blamed me. At that age, even I wasn't aware of my abilities. Though my mom changed that day. She became standoffish. It was like she sensed something wrong with me. Over time, a pattern started to develop. When I got angry, sad, or excited, strange things would happen to the person who brought forth those emotions. Usually, they'd pass out or fall asleep. Often, they'd get a migraine and then forget things. If I hugged someone I loved, they'd get all goofy like they were intoxicated. Soon my parents and my uncle put two and two together. Back then I wasn't strong enough to kill an adult, but when I was thirteen my mom got pregnant again. She didn't even try to hide that she was relieved to get rid of me. She told me she was right about me all along and then my parents sent me to live with my Uncle George."

Regan reached out like she wanted to comfort me, then pulled away at the last moment. "I'm so sorry," she said.

Disappointment swirled. "Yeah, well he was single at the time, and I didn't pose as much of a danger to him."

Her cute nose wrinkled. "He wasn't married yet? Gabby isn't his biological daughter?"

"No. Long story short, George helped me the best that he could. He'd been out of the military for about five years and GSS was starting to prosper. Once we figured out what exactly was going on with me, he contacted some Tibetan monks he'd had the opportunity to work with when he'd been a Navy SEAL."

I laughed at her shock and raked my fingers through my hair. "You didn't know that either?"

She shook her head.

"They welcomed me like family and trained me for

five years. One of the monks said that I reminded him of a snow leopard. I thought it was the color of my eyes, but he said no, it was the intensity behind them and my single-minded ability to focus." I shifted my feet debating whether to divulge my most precious memory. I'd never told anyone before, not my uncle or the monks. Not because it was bad, quite the opposite, but because it was transcendent in a way that still couldn't be explained. It was the day I decided to accept myself for who I was and what I could do. And though I'd met people who had abilities, I'd never once had the desire to share my secret.

A shadow of a smile rounded her cheeks, and she shuffled a tiny step closer to me. I didn't care that she had a boyfriend—I wanted her body, heart, and soul. Realizing how serious I was about making *us* happen, I lowered my defenses. And not the one that killed people. The one I'd erected around my heart to keep it safe.

"Ya know I saw a snow leopard once while I was on the mountain alone. This tattoo is my recollection of the most powerful moment I've ever experienced. It was like she appeared out of thin air when I needed her the most. As if I'd joined her in *her world.* Where she was the apex predator, and I was merely a guest. Her eyes," I dipped my head in remembrance, "I'll never forget their exact shade, they bore a hole into my very soul." I double-tapped my chest with my hand before dropping it to my side, "I swear, she told me even though I was dangerous, everything was going to be okay. Then, like a ghost, she vanished into the fog." I turned my head away and gazed out over the lake watching the ripples in the water catch the light. Holding my breath, I waited for her response.

"Gin, that's the most amazing thing I've ever heard.

It is fitting. You do kind of remind me of a cat."

Relief flooded through me and loosened the tension in my shoulders. She didn't think my story was outlandish. "So, are you a cat person or a dog person?"

She snorted and then covered the lower half of her face with her hand. "Honestly, I like all animals. I'd pet a badger if I didn't think it would try to kill me. But often they're scared of me as if they can sense that I'm bad." She glanced at the ground.

I reached out lifting her chin with my finger forcing her to look up at me. "Regan, you're not bad. But animals are smart, and they pick up on the fact that you're a predator." I removed my finger from her skin, though I didn't want to. I clenched it next to my side forcing it to stay put.

Her mouth shifted to one side as if she were unsatisfied with my appraisal but accepting that I was probably right.

"Do you have to kill people?" She shifted her feet.

"No. I don't have the same kind of urges you do. My fight is when I touch someone. I have to be very careful to contain any emotions I'm having at the moment. The worst is when I'm upset." *Or aroused*, but I had no plans to mention that to her just yet. "To be safe, I avoid touching people just in case I slip."

"I'm so sorry," she repeated.

"That's why I told you. I figured if anyone could understand, it'd be you." Now if I could just tell her about her father, because I feared the longer I kept *that* secret, the angrier she was bound to get. I planned to argue my case with my uncle and Dr. Gloria again.

She stared at me for a long moment as if she wanted to say something else but changed her mind. Instead, she grabbed my arm and turned us both toward the lake. She pressed her bare shoulder into my arm and stayed that way as if to tell me I couldn't hurt her. The gesture tightened my throat.

"Just so you know, when you touch me, I don't feel a thing."

I chuckled, not knowing whether to be pleased or insulted, but I certainly hoped that wasn't the case. Because when I touched her, I felt like I could fly.

Chapter 16: Regan

The vulnerability, not well-veiled behind Gin's eyes, had the blasted butterflies somersaulting inside my stomach. They needed to be captured in a net and drowned in the lake.

I turned away from him to escape the unwelcome feelings.

We stood, shoulder to shoulder, as the breeze blew through the trees and the ravens cawed overhead. His tattoo, the snow leopard perched on a rocky cliff, hovered in and out of my thoughts. I desperately tried to keep it there, but other images—hard pecs, rippled abs, and defined biceps, insisted on taking its place. I knew he was fit but I had no clue what he'd been hiding underneath his trendy clothes. I mentally groaned.

I elbowed him lightly, attempting to lighten the mood or distract myself. "Call me impressed. After studying with the monks, I bet you could kill me without even using your powers."

He brushed my forearm hanging at my side with his fingers. A flash of electricity and tingles scattered.

"Never you. But the others—definitely."

A laugh erupted from my mouth, and I glanced up at him. "You know Gin, I'm starting to get the impression you may not be the sweet southern gentleman I thought you were."

"Looks can be deceiving," he said. A lock of shiny

hair flopped on his forehead, and he tossed it away with a shake of his head.

Something inside of my chest quivered unnervingly. The golem scratched on the glass as if it were trying to break free and reach for Gin. I froze for a second, tongue-tied with nerves and a healthy dose of guilt. I shouldn't have been having those kinds of thoughts.

I took off jogging down the beach. Right before hitting the water, I paused to rip off my tank top and tossed it aside as I slipped off my shoes.

My teeth chattered as my feet hit the water. Ignoring the cold, I pushed through the pain. It was a good distraction from my confusion. Once it was deep enough, I dove in.

"Whooo!" My head popped above the surface and the water slicked my long bangs away from my face. The others were sprawled out on the dock soaking up the sun. "Come in! It's perfect."

"Liar," Mae hollered and flipped me double birds from her prone position.

I splashed water toward them, but I was too far away to pose any danger.

Gin swam out to meet me and turned over on his back to float. The sun gilded the peaks and valleys of his muscled stomach while water beaded on his tan skin. To keep from staring at his glorious form, I flipped over on my back to join him.

Before I drifted too far, he grabbed my hand. Startled, I tried pulling away.

"I'm not holding your hand," he snapped, griping me tighter, "I want to talk and you keep floating away."

I relaxed as much as possible with tiny sparks tickling my arm. It had to be my pet's reaction to what

Gin referred to as his alter ego. They recognized one another. *That was the issue.* Thankful that I'd solved the problem, I felt slightly calmer and a fraction less guilty. I could only control the golem to a point—but I couldn't seem to control its feelings toward Gin. But they weren't *my* feelings.

"What exactly happened during the training exercise earlier?" he asked.

"Tim pretty much covered the bases," I said because it was mostly the truth.

"Knock it off, Regan. Which person on your team shot you?"

"Rory."

His grip tightened. "I thought so. I'll have her removed by the end of the day."

I scoffed. He'd repeated his uncle's words almost verbatim. "Don't be stupid. She's not an issue. Ben, Tim, and Mae will take care of it." Besides, Rory was the ideal test subject.

Gin let go of my hand and started treading water. "Did you just call me stupid?"

"Sort of." I flipped over so I could see him.

"Do you have any idea whom you're talking to?" The afternoon sun sparkled on the blonde hairs of his arms and absorbed into the water creating a hazy green gold around the rest of his submerged body.

A naughty smile grew on my lips.

"Regan," Gin warned. "Don't do it."

I splashed him in the face and swam away.

He caught me by the ankle and pulled me under, holding me there for a few seconds just to prove he could. I came up gasping for air while laughing. The retribution was warranted.

"Is anyone going to help me here?" I howled, waving at the others.

Mae and Tim dove in and surfaced with colorful language, most likely regretting their decision to save me. It *was* cold. Ben flew off the dock with his arms clasped around his legs in a cannonball. The water exploded around him creating a faint rainbow as the mist dissipated.

Rory stood on the edge and nervously adjusted her black bra and matching panties. She was flawless. Soft curves in all the right places, long sexy legs, and a face to match. I couldn't for the life of me figure out why Gin wasn't interested.

"Come on, you sloths!" Mae yelled at Rory and Navi. "Stop being such babies!"

Navi shrugged and jumped in feet first, her long dark hair floating above her before she splashed into the water. Rory sat on the side and stuck her toe in the lake.

"So, much for being one with nature," Mae harassed her.

Rory's eyes flexed before she slipped gracefully into the water. "Brrrr!" she said as she swam over to the rest of us.

We visited and joked around, but it wasn't long before our lips started to turn blue.

To keep anyone from going into hypothermia, we returned to shore, dried off, and headed back to camp.

"So," Mae said, hanging behind with me. "Rory, huh?"

"What?" I asked.

"Rory shot you."

"Did Ben tell you?" It was pointless to deny it.

"Yeah, but give me some credit, I figured it out

before that. I'm ticked. We could've won."

"Maybe."

"But I did manage to get a trophy." Mae pulled a pair of gold hoop earrings out of her pocket.

They were easily recognizable. The last time I'd seen them, the girl from the opposing team had been wearing them. I glanced at Mae.

She rubbed the jewelry with her thumb, waiting for my reaction. "Sometimes I feel compelled to do it. Like if I don't, I'll lose my mind."

My hand shot over my mouth as a strangled sound burst forth. "I completely understand."

"Really?"

"Yeah. I have similar urges—though mine get me into more trouble."

She sighed and her posture softened. "But what if these earrings were important to her? What if they were a gift?"

"Then she shouldn't have been wearing them out here." I looked around at our rugged environment, then at the earrings she was holding in her palm. "And if some cheap loser gave her those," the plating was peeling away leaving a cheaper metal peeking through, "then she deserves better. Besides, they just won one thousand dollars, she can buy new ones." There could've been other possible scenarios for those earrings, but I didn't want Mae to feel worse than she already did.

"And if you're worried about it, give them to Mr. LaCroix or Ron. They'll make sure she gets 'em back."

She chewed on her bottom lip. "They don't know I'm a raging klepto."

"I'm sure it's not that bad." I elbowed her playfully.

"Oh," her tiny lips formed a big O and held it for a

few beats, "it's that bad."

"Fine, give them to me." I held out my hand. "I'll make sure they get home. I'll just say I found 'em on the ground."

"Dang, girl, I've only known you a few days, but I already love you!" she said.

"It's mutual," I answered. The prospect of having real friends, ones who knew all about me and still liked me, was exciting.

"So, now that we're friends, give me the scoop on you and Gin," she whispered and grabbed my hand to hold me back.

Gin was walking in front of us chatting with Tim and seemed to be ignoring Rory as she walked next to them. She was only a couple of inches shy of his six-foot frame. Ben and Navi were way ahead and appeared to be deep in conversation.

Once they were far enough away not to overhear us, Mae prompted, "Is there something going on between you two? Rory's quite convinced and not pleased that he would choose you when he could have *her*." She mimicked Rory by pretending to toss her hair over her shoulder. Though it lacked the punch of Rory's magnificent locks, Mae's dark straight bob shone like an oil spill.

I pursed my lips to the side and shook my head. "No," I said with exasperation. "We're friends." Now that Gin and I knew each other's dirty little secrets, I was comfortable with the label. "And am I really that far down the food chain?" Sure, Rory was tall and gorgeous and looked like she could be a model on the cover of a magazine, but I wasn't ugly.

"No," she spat like the answer was obvious. "But I

think sometimes us short people get a raw deal. Like we're always categorized as cute, never beautiful. People are stupid."

I couldn't argue with her.

"And speaking of stupid." She bumped me lightly with her arm. "Girl, Gin watches you like he's the shark and you're chum in the water."

"Chum? Really?" I glanced at her with a look that said *whatever.*

"Okay, so a nice juicy tuna?" She snapped her jaw a couple of times revealing crooked front teeth and pointed canines.

I could do nothing besides laugh at the innuendo.

"No. Really. The way he stares sometimes gives me chills. I've been around. I survived years by reading people. That delicious specimen wants you something fierce. If somebody put a gun to my head, I'd say that boy's halfway in love with you."

I scoffed at her theory. The mere notion that Gin could have feelings for me was dangerous. If I would have met him before Jude—I shook the thought away. "Don't be ridiculous. Gin and I are friends and nothing more," I said a bit louder than I meant to.

Gin, obviously having heard my outburst, turned his head and winked.

My cheeks grew hot as I focused on the ground ahead.

Mae clasped my elbow with hers and chuckled, though she wisely kept the rest of her thoughts to herself.

Chapter 17: Regan

Dappled light shimmered through the overhead canopy and flickered over Gin's hair. The green colors of his irises flashed like faceted emeralds as his half-closed eyes caressed my face and paused at the swell of my mouth. A deep breath escaped his chest and fluttered over my long bangs tickling my forehead. He reached up and hooked them behind my ear as he traced the curve of my cheek with his fingers. Fire, ice, and electricity ignited from his touch and spread like dancing blue flames over my skin.

Desire clenched in my core, and I inhaled sharply to keep from gasping out loud.

He wove his hand behind the back of my neck and pulled me closer. My pet, not normally interested in anything but anger and occasionally sorrow, purred so loudly inside its prison that the glass walls nearly vibrated.

Gin leaned down and kissed me hesitantly, his lips light as a feather as if he expected me to break. I wound my fingers into his soft hair and forced him to kiss me harder. Our tongues tangled together, and he gripped the back of my head with one hand and low on my waist with the other. My chest rubbed against his and I moaned.

He froze but he didn't pull away. "Are you okay?" he asked with his mouth still against mine.

I could barely hear him over the pounding of my heart. "Better than okay," I answered, curious as to why he stopped.

"Are you sure?"

"Positive." I nodded my head, my lips lightly brushing his.

Relief loosened his shoulder. I could feel him smile before he kissed me again. This time without hesitation.

My fingers snuck under the edge of his shirt searching for the warmth of his skin. He leaned his head back and groaned, then dove toward my neck. His lips scorched, leaving behind colossal flames in their wake as if a trail of gasoline were fueling the fire. I tilted my head, giving him better access. Euphoria traveled along my nerves making me feel lighter than the air. If I didn't hang on, I'd float away. He bit down gently on the sensitive spot between my shoulder and neck. My knees buckled. Before I could fall, he reached down and grabbed me under my thigh. The nearness of his hands to my pulsing core did little to steady me.

As the flames burned out of control, I devoured him. He was the oxygen I needed to breathe. His hands crept upward until his fingers curved around the sides of my ribs and his thumbs rested at the base of my breasts.

My nipples hardened, begging impatiently for his touch. I grabbed his hand and guided it to where I wanted it to be. A barrage of fireworks exploded. I tossed my head back and a gasp of pleasure tore from my throat.

He nuzzled his face into the side of my neck. "God, Regan, you smell so good."

My eyes snapped open, and I shot up in bed.

Sweat drenched my hair. Mortification blazed over

my cheeks as the pleasure from my dream began to fade away leaving behind a dull unsatisfied throbbing between my legs.

"Knock, knock." The door of my tent began to unzip. To my utter horror, Gin stepped inside carrying a steaming cup of coffee. His brows crinkled with concern when he saw me.

"Regan, are you okay?" In two steps he was in front of me with his free hand on my damp forehead.

I shied away. "Yeah. Fine. I had a nightmare," I lied as images of my dream flashed in my brain. Another round of humiliation erupted over my skin.

Gin cocked his head. "No need to be embarrassed, I have them too from time to time."

No. Not like this, you don't.

I pressed my cold hands to my cheeks hoping to calm the blush. "Mm-hmmm," I mumbled but it sounded more like I was questioning his sincerity.

He handed me the coffee.

"Thanks." Refusing to meet his gaze, I stared into the mug focusing on the creamy color of the liquid. If only it had a shot of fairy dust swirling in its depths that would allow me to forget the images burned into my retinas.

"Yeah, okay . . . well, when you're ready, meet me outside."

After he left, I crossed my legs and slowly sipped the hot drink, wishing it were iced.

Of everything holy, what was that all about? I groaned and scrubbed a hand through my hair. An erotic dream with Gin playing the starring role was a good way to make working with him awkward.

I knew *exactly* where the dream originated from. It

was because of Mae and her creative imagination. And Rory because she was convinced Gin and I had something going on.

It wasn't true. Jude was mine and I loved him. Desperately. At times, it probably bordered on an unhealthy obsession. My mom told me not to worry, she said that's the joy of new love. I remember rolling my eyes at her, insinuating that she was ridiculous, though her advice did make me feel better.

While I was having a good time with my newfound friends, I couldn't wait to get back to the cabins and call Jude. The last time I'd talked with him was the day I left Wyoming, almost two weeks ago. We'd texted here and there but the service was crap and most of the time my phone failed, and I received a *not delivered* waring in red.

Our bond gave us a daily connection, more on his end than mine, but occasionally Jude misinterpreted the signals or the reasons behind them. I needed to touch base with him. I needed to hear his voice.

I wanted to tell him about all of the friends I'd made and everything that I was learning. Well, mostly everything. He was my rock—truthfully. He was my compass when my anger, fueled by the golem's desire to create chaos, got the better of me. With just a touch of his hand, he could soothe the monster into submission, no matter how out of control we were.

Here, without Jude around, I'd relied on Gin to be there for me—just in case. So far, so good. I'd yet to kill anyone. But this new development was concerning.

The scent of bacon, eggs, and frying potatoes combined with my growling stomach coaxed me out of bed. I dressed and joined the others for breakfast.

Gin caught my eye and tapped the armrest of the camp chair next to him. I pointed to the spot by Tim and sat down there instead. Gin frowned slightly. In no way was I keen on hurting his feelings, but some time and distance were required to compose myself.

"Crikey," Tim said with a mouthful, "you got Gin's knickers in a twist."

"He'll get over it." I waved. I was more interested in Tim's adventures from the day before. "So, what was it you said to the big guy to make him stand down?"

Tim choked on a piece of bacon. I handed him his OJ and waited for him to stop coughing.

"You saw that?" he asked, his voice hoarse.

"Yeah, they had cameras set up and monitors in the cabin."

"I should've guessed. Anyway, I told him if he didn't back off, I'd make him give me a . . ." he glanced at his lap.

It was my turn to choke on a piece of bacon.

Tim patted my back until I stopped.

"Dude, you make me laugh."

"I aim to please. Speaking of being pleased." Tim jutted his chin toward where Rory had sat down in the camp chair next to Gin.

As she tried starting up a conversation, he got up, threw his paper plate in the fire, and went back inside the cabin.

She glared at me and Tim as if was our fault Gin left.

Mae came over and softly kicked the leg of my chair. "Makin' friends?" She propped her hands on her hips. "I don't get her. She's angry at you because he wants nothing to do with her. It doesn't make sense."

"Welcome to my world,"

A mischievous smile bloomed on her lips. "Oh, do tell."

I gave them a brief summary of my senior year spent in Wyoming—Jude, Layne, and the Three Musketcheers.

At some point, Ben and Navi came over to listen. All of them were laughing holding their stomachs by the time I finished. Mae had tears pooling in her eyes. Navi seemed shocked but was still giggling.

"Isn't Gabby Mr. LaCroix's daughter?" Navi whispered.

"Yup."

"How can he possibly be okay with you?" Her eyes darted nervously to where Mr. LaCroix and Ron stood together talking.

I shrugged.

"I think those boys like your 'don't mess with me' demeanor. Means there's hope for me yet." Mae rubbed her hands together as if she were plotting. She was wearing a collection of jingling bracelets that looked suspiciously like the ones Navi had on yesterday.

"I don't know what they like," I answered surly.

Ben nudged my foot with his. "Oh, girl, please. Look at you. Once you get past your demons, you're quite the snack."

I threw him a dirty look even though I was sure he meant it as a compliment. But he was right, I kind of did have a demon attached to me. I'd never thought of it like that, and it got me worrying. Was I possessed? Were we all? I needed to talk to Gin; he might have some answers.

Ron clapped his hands interrupting my alarm, "Okay, everyone, sorry to disappoint but we're headed back to the lodge a day early. Something's come up and it requires our attention."

My shoulders drooped momentarily, but then my spirits brightened. Once we got back, we'd have an entire day with cell reception. I could ask Jude about this newest theory, and he could run it past his grandpa. He had insights that others didn't. Much of their culture's history had been passed down by word of mouth, not written.

After I disassembled my tent and helped a few of the others with theirs, we took the boats back to the lodge.

Back on the dock, I asked Gin, "Do we have plans after this?"

"No. The rest of the day is yours. I'll be in a meeting," he said brusquely before he turned away to talk to Mr. LaCroix.

I smiled tightly and pulled my phone out of my pocket. Three bars. I hurried back to my cabin and made myself comfortable on the bed. My heart pounded with excitement as I dialed Jude's number.

"Hi!" I said when he answered. My grin was almost too big to contain.

"Hi," he said but his tone lacked enthusiasm.

My smile vanished. "You okay?"

"Fine."

I inhaled sharply. Something was definitely off. "What's wrong?" He could be a bit moody at times.

"Why don't you tell me?" he said snidely.

"What? What are you talking about?"

"Seems as if you've been having fun out there," he accused as if it were an enormous sin.

"Surprisingly, I have. Is that a problem?" I didn't think he would begrudge me for having found some friends.

"It might be. It depends on how much *fun* you've been having." His behavior was disconcerting, and something about the way he said the word fun made the muscles in my neck tense.

He was hinting at something without saying it. Jude and I suspected our conversations were being recorded. Though I worked for GSS, I didn't trust them.

My breath caught in my chest when I realized the problem. Did he really think I was cheating on him? At least that's what I assumed he was suggesting with his attitude.

Oh, God. My cheeks flamed. Because of our connection, Jude and I could feel each other's emotions. It wasn't foolproof as we'd learned this summer. Trying to process another person's feelings was like trying to read a book backward without the vowels. "Well, I did have quite the dream this morning. I woke up, uh . . . flustered. I figured it had something to do with you." I hadn't thought of that until now, but it was a possibility. What if Jude was having an erotic dream at the same time and his emotions bled through to mine? That, plus everyone's insinuations equaled my morning adventure wrapped in Gin's arms instead of Jude's. *Case closed.*

I released a heavy sigh feeling so much better now that I'd solved the mystery and prepared to do some long-distance flirting. Jude, obviously not convinced with my reasonable explanation, had other ideas and our conversation sped downhill. By the time I hung up, I was sure Jude was on the verge of breaking up with me. It felt as if my heart stopped beating.

I gazed out the window taking long slow breaths and exhaling to the count of five. I wasn't mad just yet, I was in shock. Last year, after Gabby LaCroix released the video footage of the day my dad died, I lost my temper and let the golem loose on the entire student body. I ended up in the hospital. Jude thought I was about to die because my aura had faded from swirling black smoke to white cumulus clouds. In order to save me, he permanently tied his essence, his soul, or something similar, to mine. Our connection was stronger and more enduring than wedding vows. Or at least that's what he'd told me. It was our little secret. Though having discussed it with Jude extensively, his ability to read my feelings was much stronger.

Attempting to salvage the situation, I shot Jude a quick text.

—*I need you to know, I love you. You're my one. Before you do anything drastic—we need to have a face-to-face. TRUST ME. I love you.*—

I held my breath as tiny bubbles popped up on the screen and then disappeared. I scowled at my phone, willing him to say something. Anything. Having to control my powers when I was in a stable state of mind was difficult enough. Letting my pet loose when my emotions were volatile, was irresponsible. The little bubbles popped up again.

—*I love you too.*—

A sob of relief trembled inside my chest. My heart, frozen in fear, finally started beating. I sniffed and held back the tears, wishing I could see him in person. Then he'd know I was telling the truth.

Chapter 18: Gin

Walking down the hall toward Dr. Gloria's office in Anchorage, my feet echoed loudly over the gold-flecked tiles. I was stewing over Regan's strange demeanor in her tent this morning and her avoidance of me for the remainder of the day. I had to remind myself that she didn't remember our kiss and that the connection I had to her wasn't necessarily shared. She had a boyfriend. Though she did call me freaking good-looking and she hinted that my powers were alluring, so there was hope.

With a closed fist, I knocked on Dr. Gloria's door.

"Come in, Gin," she said. In the background, she was listening to the playlist I'd given to her for her birthday a few months ago. It was of all my best work and one of the songs I'd recorded especially for her. Dr. Gloria was my biggest fan. Though Regan seemed to be a close second.

I was positive Regan was the girl of my dreams. Our powers nullified one another, allowing me to be close to her without killing her *and* she loved opera. How many eighteen-year-olds had even heard of opera? Sure, I had some young fans—but most of them followed me on social media because in Regan's words—I was freaking hot. Plus, I could sing, and not just opera. Pretty much anything. Originally, I'd chosen the genre because it allowed me to sing without garnering too much attention, leaving me free to work. It's hard to kill people unnoticed when you're easily recognizable.

During my operatic performances, I was usually in a wig, wearing make-up to look older, and often covered in blood. It was a good disguise. Although, in the last couple of years, I'd had to back off from singing professionally to keep my cover a secret. Sometimes I missed it, but most of the time I was content traveling the world and discovering new places while I worked. The idea that Regan and I could someday work together lifted my spirits. It was the first time that I saw a future not spent alone. The mere notion had my insides feeling a bit fluttery—for lack of a better term.

I shut the office door behind me and sat down across from her desk. "Doc, I think in order to maintain Regan's trust, I need to tell her about her dad. Keeping this from her isn't going to end well."

She glanced over the top of her red reading glasses. She had pairs lying all over her office. From my chair I counted three. "Soon, Gin. I promise. Let me have another couple of sessions with her so I can lay down some solid groundwork. We need to give her the best possible foundation first."

I pinched the bridge of my nose. Over the years, I'd learned arguing with Dr. Gloria was pointless. It's not that I thought she was wrong, I was just afraid when Regan learned how long I'd been withholding the truth, she'd never forgive me. Or she'd try to kill me.

"You'll be happy to hear the memory replacements have been helping. Do you think you can manage more?"

"Yes, ma'am."

Her relief, the slight drop of her lips to the softening around her eyes, wouldn't have been obvious to anyone except for those of us who knew her well. I'd been friends with her for a few years now and truthfully, she was family.

"Good. Because Gin, Craig's strength goes beyond measurement and I'm not sure how much longer my shield will hold out against him. If we can give him more to hang onto than just videos and pictures, I think it'll help. And the sooner he's stable, the sooner we can reunite the two."

I glanced at the clock above her head. "Well, let's get it done." My hands gripped my knees, and I pushed up. Because of the inclement weather, the flight here had taken longer than anticipated and my uncle had a meeting scheduled soon, so time was limited.

We hurried from her office to the basement.

Craig, still in the same room he'd been confined to the last time I was here, sat in a chair watching something on a laptop. The handcuffs he'd previously been wearing were missing. I took that as a good sign.

Dr. Gloria inhaled and I could feel her pull the surrounding energy to her like a cloak. "Craig," she said, "do you mind if we come in?"

He glanced up. The expression on his face was as indifferent as ice.

"Suit yourself," he answered.

Dr. Gloria nodded at the camera above our heads and someone in a separate building unlocked the door.

"Do you remember Gin?" she asked after the lock clicked behind us.

"Not really." He didn't bother to acknowledge me.

"He's Regan's mentor."

He lifted his head slowly while his eyes took on an eerie silver hue.

Even standing behind her shield, the hairs on my

arms began to prickle, hinting that Craig's abilities were indeed growing. "Don't."

He chuckled. "It's imperative I know who I'm dealing with."

"Not in this case, it isn't. I'm more than happy to tell you what I'm here for."

He blinked and shut the laptop, the color of his eyes fading to their normal steel blue.

"If you'd like, I have some more memories of your daughter. I think you'd be quite entertained by a few of them."

He rubbed his hand over the scruff on his chin and thought for a moment. "Yes, I think I'd like that."

"Excellent. But I'm warning you now, if I get a hint of your powers, I will not hesitate. I'll shut you down."

His lips dipped into a frown. "Understood."

"Your hand," I said.

Together Dr. Gloria and I stepped forward. With her close, I could stand behind her powers making it easier for me to replace memories without fearing that he was going to take control of my actions. Dr. Gloria didn't have any more problems with him harming the staff, after the last time I'd given him my memories of Regan. But she'd warned me he had the markings of a psychopath. Of course, her diagnosis was far more technical.

With my eyes closed, I reached out with my powers to the base of his brain stem. Pausing to get a lay of the land, I found the desired pathway and began to transfer the data. The brain was the motherboard of all humans, and though each one was slightly different, they were also similar in the way that all cars were. The engine. The transmission. The drive train. All worked together to make the body of a car move. The brain wasn't much different and after many years of using my gift, the minor variances were easy to decipher. As the memory began to weave inside Craig's mind, he stiffened up. Soon he began to laugh and said, "That's my girl."

I'd chosen the day Regan had made my cousin Gabby urinate on her fellow cheerleaders while she was balancing at the top of their human pyramid. My perspective bounced between watching Regan work and the structure as it toppled to the floor.

At that point in my undercover mission, I was already convinced she had powers. Afterward, my uncle agreed. Especially when Gabby wrote a letter to the school newspaper admitting that she'd used an inside man working for GSS to blackmail her fellow classmates. As his daughter, he knew she would never admit to doing those horrible things of her own volition. Gabby was practically a clone of her mother and I never understood why my uncle married a woman like that. But it was none of my business, so I never asked.

Over the years, I'd noticed their relationship had dwindled. I assumed he'd married her for her money, though I hated to think poorly of my uncle. My aunt was the niece of a U.S. senator and was one of the original investors in GSS. Together they'd made a sizable fortune with the business. What most people didn't know was that my uncle donated millions of his own money to fight sex trafficking and other horrific crimes. It was part of the reason he took on government work. They paid handsomely when they needed our help.

Craig swiped the tears of enjoyment from his eyes with the back of his free hand as I finished up.

Then I gave him the most recent memory I had of

Regan's powers. Wisely, I cut it off well before I kissed her. There was no need to make him angry.

"Boy, she's fun," Craig said. It was the first time he'd used any emotion. Hope coiled—maybe this would work.

"Yes. But she's also smart and kind."

He scoffed. "She humiliated a girl in front of an entire audience and made her admit to her crimes in the school newspaper."

"Yes, she did. But she did it to keep the girl from harming anyone else. Regan is a unique individual. She has to use her powers in a way that creates chaos, or she gets punished herself. I don't know why, but she does. So, she opts to take down the bad guys to keep her darkness under control. She's remarkable."

Though, I had my own theory as to why. I believed her pet doled out the punishment. Negative and positive reinforcement were good ways to train any creature. Even humans. The golem punished her with physical ailments if *Regan* thought Regan's actions were good. It rewarded Regan with euphoria if *Regan* thought her actions were bad. I had plans to address it later in her training.

"When do I get to meet her?" Craig asked.

"Soon," Dr. Gloria said. Tiny lines of red lipstick fanned into the dark wrinkles around her mouth and the short curls at her temples were damp with sweat.

The muscles around his eyes tightened. "You said that last week. I want to see my kid," he demanded.

"You'll see her when I can trust that you won't hurt her." I clasped my hands behind my back.

His eyes flashed to mine. "I would never hurt her."

"Then prove it with a month's worth of good

behavior and we'll talk."

I glanced at Dr. Gloria, nodded that I was finished, and together we left the room.

Inside the elevator, I tapped the screen of my phone and internally groaned. "We need to get upstairs, we're late."

Dr. Gloria was looking into the shiny surface, fixing her lipstick in the warped reflection. "We still have ten minutes."

"You know my uncle," I said.

A smile of fond exasperation flashed on her visage, and she shook her head. "Once a military man, always a military man."

As we hurried into the conference room, my uncle glanced at his watch. In his opinion, five minutes early was late.

The three of us and Ron gathered around the table.

"Here's the deal," my uncle said, wasting no time, "we need to know if Regan's as powerful as we think she is. And though I have all of your assessments," he patted the thick red folder near his right hand, "we need to see how she reacts in the field and not just during training exercises. I have a few missions here." He pushed one in front of each of us. "I'm leaning toward this one." He indicated the papers in front of me.

I quickly scanned the documents, shaking my head. "This requires her to control and execute two people at once. I don't think she's ready for this yet." I slid it toward Dr. Gloria.

She put on the glasses that hung from a chain around her neck and took a few minutes to study the file. She handed it to Ron without commenting.

I wasn't comfortable with Regan killing anyone on

her first job. I was hoping for something less damaging to her soul. It required time and a lot of therapy to kill people and not retain the scars. From the beginning, I had Dr. Gloria's help and still, occasionally, I struggled.

Once Ron finished, he tapped the top of it and said, "I think you underestimate her, Gin."

"No, it's not that I underestimate her powers. And I understand both of you have taken lives before." My uncle and Ron served together in the Navy SEALS and had been on plenty of missions where lives were lost. "But this is different. It's far more difficult to take a life when yours is not in danger."

"I agree," Dr. Gloria said. "But with the circumstances the way they are, I think we need to push her to the limits. It's better if we know now. Even though I've only had a couple of therapy sessions with Regan, I believe she can handle it. With the speed her father is strengthening, we may need her powers sooner rather than later. I know this isn't a professional diagnosis, but I have a bad feeling about him."

Dr. Gloria had had an initial therapy session with Regan before she was hired, and like me, Dr. Gloria was instantly intrigued. Though she wouldn't tell me any of the particulars of that meeting, she did say she believed Regan's abilities were similar to mine. It gave me the confidence I needed in order to train her.

My uncle nodded. "So, it's settled?"

"If I'm to agree to this." I rolled my chair back and crossed my arms. "I'll lead her to water, but *I will not* make her drink." I quirked an eyebrow audaciously challenging any of them to argue with me. Not that anyone could force Regan to do something she didn't want to, but I wouldn't push her in either direction. She had to decide on her own. It was the only way she'd continue to trust me. "If she chooses not to do this or backs out at the last second, *I will not* attempt to alter her decision."

I left the room unsettled. This test was supposed to come at the end of Regan's training, not two weeks into the process. I feared that it might lead her down the wrong path. Sometimes when a predator gets their first taste of prey, it's hard to rehabilitate them. I believed with the proper foundation, Regan would be okay—but without it—I was worried.

Chapter 19: Regan

Just as I was about to head to another titillating day spent under Pamela's tutelage, someone pounded on my door.

"Yeah, yeah, hold your horses." I grabbed my raincoat off the bed and yanked it open expecting to see Tim and Mae.

Surprise and something resembling joy leaped inside my heart. Gin was standing with his back to me staring out over the lake. It was a chilly morning, and he was dressed in a fleece vest over his long-sleeve t-shirt. When he turned around, his stony expression softened. "Regan, are you okay?"

He reached toward my face but I backed away, pretending that I was opening the door for him, not avoiding his touch. My puffy red eyes were a dead giveaway that I'd been crying for half of the night. Again.

I'd spent the last few days divvying my worry between Gin and Jude.

After Gin left for Anchorage, I hadn't seen nor heard from him. Not even a text. Had he decided to forgo my training? Had I done something wrong?

I'd been forced to listen to Pamela drone on for three days about where our powers might've come from: Were we descendants of Roman, Greek, or Norse Gods? Perhaps Ancient Egyptian, Mayan, or Aztec deities?

There was speculation about God and Mother Earth in all forms. Or was I possessed? Pamela assured all of us that what we were experiencing was not possession. She showed us a video of true possession, apparently, my theory wasn't new. Afterward, I was fairly certain my pet was not a demon.

We went on to discuss if we were genetic flukes of nature. Or was it all of the above and then some? I had to admit, our conversations got quite creative. The others had concluded—whether right or wrong—I'd gotten my powers from Loki, the Norse God of Mischief since I was a full-blooded Scandinavian.

Before we'd even started dating, Jude was the one who'd introduced me to the idea. I didn't give it much credence in the beginning but after researching the lore, I started to become concerned. Loki had a child named Fenrir; a black wolf that brought around the end of days called Ragnarök. Initially, I'd brushed it off as a silly coincidence that my pet often resembled a wolf in my mind's eye. I was hesitant to mention that to my friends for fear of them running with the idea. They were prone to rabbit holes.

Now, I was starting to worry that Jude might've been on to something. He was intuitive to the point of scary sometimes, even when the subject wasn't about me. And since he'd been refusing to take my calls and ignoring my texts for the last couple days, I couldn't ask him.

Tim, it was obvious he'd been armed with Cupid's arrows and Rory was a strong candidate for Mother Earth. Jude's abilities, though I didn't mention them, had to come from his heritage. The rest of the gifts, we were still researching and debating. And though it was fun, I was more concerned with Gin's avoidance of me and my suspicion that Jude was searching for ways to end our relationship.

For days, Jude's anger had pummeled me in sickening waves. He must've been really angry about something for me to feel his wrath so readily. Even after he fell asleep, I couldn't calm down. Eventually, I started taking one of the medications Dr. Gloria had prescribed at our first meeting. They were supposed to dampen my anxiety, but all they did was knock me out.

Still avoiding Gin's gaze, I opened my cabin door wider. "Come on in," I said politely, foregoing the normal sarcasm I usually lead with.

He stayed put and pushed his hands into the pocket of his vest. With a big sigh, he said, "I need you to come with me. There's been a change in plans. I'm going to grab us a bite to eat, and I'll meet you on the docks."

"Okay," I said concerned by his morose demeanor. With a big gulp, I nodded and spun away before he could witness more tears pooling. His feet pounded down the stairs shaking the deck as he left. Was he going to fire me? Maybe they thought I wasn't a good fit for the company and decided to pass. I dabbed at the corner of my eyes with the cuff of my sweatshirt and shut the door. Why did the thought of being fired worry me? In reality, it might let me off the hook. But the idea of leaving my friends bothered me even though I hadn't known them long.

Nerves battered my stomach as I packed. I dragged my bag and my feet down to the docks. Gin handed me a to-go cup of coffee along with a breakfast sandwich wrapped in paper foil and had me climb into the plane as he tossed my things in the back.

Once in the air, Gin looked over at me. "Do you want to talk about it?"

I swiveled my head toward the side window staring at the marshy area with no trees. A bull moose with a massive rack was belly-deep in the muck. Did I want to tell Gin I'd been fretting that he'd decided against training me? Or that my boyfriend was planning on breaking up with me? Or that I was worried that I was being fired? "Nope."

"Fair enough," he sighed as if I'd disappointed him. "Aren't you curious about where we're going?"

"Nope." I closed my eyes to catch a much-needed nap before we landed. Once in the car, we drove to the medical district.

Inside a small building tucked into a grove of trees, we walked past a secretary who grinned at Gin and waved like an over-excited puppy. Who could blame her? He was quite the catch. We took the elevator to the top floor and entered a conference room where Ron and Mr. LaCroix waited. I sat next to Gin as anxiety stabbed my ribs.

"Here's the issue," Mr. LaCroix said after his greetings.

I traced my fingers over the unique table. It was made of live edge wood with a deep blue epoxy resin running down the center like a lazy river. I knew that Jude had designed and built it, but the thought gave me no comfort. Though today, his anger was more subdued. It swirled with uncertainty and fear.

Noticing that I was mentally adrift, Gin set his hand on my arm forcing me back to the present.

Mr. LaCroix continued once he had my full attention. "Surprisingly, Anchorage has some deep roots in the sex trafficking arena."

The city did have a large community of immigrants, a Native Alaskan population that no one seemed to care about when the women went missing, and a significant number of homeless people. So, no it wasn't that much of a surprise.

He clasped his fingers together and leaned forward resting his elbows on the table. Light from the overhead fixture glared against his glasses. "We've been keeping track of one organization in particular. They tend to run under the radar due to their youth, but we have intel that suggests they're about to join the big leagues. Their first annual gala is called The Big Game Hunt." His lips dipped into a disgusted snarl. "Next week wealthy clients from all over the world will gather in the city under the pretense of attending an auction to raise money for a fake wildlife preserve in Africa. Unless we can stop them. We know where they're keeping the victims, and we have a plan in place to rescue them. But if we don't cut the head off the snake . .."

Ron passed a stack of paperwork across the table so I could take a gander. I glanced at Gin, his jaw muscles knotting, and he nodded tightly.

I scanned them along with some photos, my stomach twisting with horror. There were dozens of pictures of women and men dressed up in all levels of seduction everything from gowns and tuxes to gear designed for darker tastes. But in each photo, despite their smiles, terror hid in the depths of their eyes.

Quickly, I read a ghastly account of a stunning young Russian woman. She'd come here to attend college and worked as a nanny in exchange for room and board. Her second weekend in Anchorage, she'd gone out partying with a couple of new friends and had disappeared. But she was smart—and lucky. She was one of those rare individuals who was an ultrarapid metabolizer. Meaning medication, including narcotics, burned through her system faster than normal. When the yacht she'd been imprisoned on docked, she'd escaped. However, during the three-week-long trip through the inside passage, she'd confronted enough trauma to fill multiple lifetimes. Her account of the long nights with different partners, many of whom had sadistic fantasies, was more than my stomach could tolerate. Before finishing her nightmare, I pushed the stack of papers away. I'd read enough. With my fists clenched, I stared down at the table willing the tears away. I sniffed and looked up.

Empathy etched both Mr. LaCroix's and Ron's faces. "Regan, this mission is level red, which means people die. Bad people. But, as you've seen, by killing these guys you'll be saving many innocent lives. They specialize in young people around your age. You'll want to read the rest of that, but right now just take a look at the last two pages."

No. Really. There was no need for me to delve further. I hesitated but did what he asked. I placed a pair of photos with bios in front of me. One was a chubby dude in a suit. Under his picture was his life summed up—he was the son of a prominent East Coast businessman who attended an Ivy League college. He graduated near the top of his class with honors and instead of choosing to do good with his life, he started a fake company that was a front for his sex trafficking and drug operation.

The other picture showed a dazzling gorgeous guy

with gleaming blonde hair and dimples. His bio was much the same—rich, spoiled, and educated. Though he barely managed to graduate, he did get voted most charismatic by the student body. Together they had brains and beauty.

In theory, killing these villains sounded great, but in reality I wasn't sure.

I placed my sweating hands on my lap and clutched them tightly together. An outline of where they'd been evaporated off the table's smooth surface. The clock above Mr. LaCroix's head ticked loudly in the room.

"If you're not ready, I understand. What we're asking of you is extreme. But I thought you should be made a part of the process sooner rather than later. We have big plans for you in this company, Regan. From the beginning, I want you to know what it is that we," Mr. LaCroix glanced at Ron and Gin, "do here."

I grabbed the glass of water sitting in front of me to sip away my dry throat. "So, you want me to be an assassin?" My worst fear was coming to fruition. It's not like I didn't suspect why I was here. Me, my mom, Barry, and Jude had predicted it. *Why else would someone want me?* Besides—Mr. LaCroix wasn't joking—by killing these guys, I could save lives.

"Sometimes, yes. But not all the time. Your gift has many possibilities." He nodded thoughtfully, the lines on his forehead puckering. "But only if you decide it's the right fit for you in this organization. I need people who are willing and able to do what others can't. It's a tall order, I know."

My eyes met Gin's. "So, I'm not being fired?"

His brows slammed together. "No. Why would you think that?"

I shrugged. "Because you haven't returned my texts." I left out that he'd departed on an awkward note.

He chuckled. "I dropped my phone in the lake and didn't manage to get another one until this morning. I would've texted that I was coming to get you, but it wasn't charged yet. And then I didn't have service most of the flight there."

The relief that spread inside my chest was embarrassing. I was less worried about becoming an assassin and more worried about losing Gin.

Mr. LaCroix interrupted with a small cough. "You'll always have a home here, Regan, even if I have to find you another position. You, by choosing to work for us, knowing who your boss would be," he paused and smiled, "shows me exactly how brave you are. And that's the type of person we welcome into our family."

Gin reached over and squeezed my arm. I chewed on the inside of my bottom lip.

"I can do this one myself," Gin said decisively, grabbing the stack of papers and neatly situating them. He leaned back and crossed his arms.

Mr. LaCroix rubbed his chin. "Of course, you can, but I was thinking this would be good training for Regan. It's not like she doesn't know what we do here."

"Why don't you just have the criminals caught and leave it to the justice system to punish them?" I asked.

"In the beginning, that's exactly what we did. Unfortunately, we overestimated the power of truth and having an overwhelming amount of solid, factual evidence." He pointed to the stack of papers. "Don't kid yourself, a corrupt court system and an expensive attorney are powerful weapons. After so many criminals walked away, despite the fact that the evidence was damning, we revamped the way we worked. When Gin came aboard, it made our jobs easier. But I fear that it's only a matter of time before he gets caught. Unlike you, he has to touch the person in order to kill them."

"So GSS isn't a hired hit man for the government?" During my senior year, that had been the rumor. Curiosity and skepticism drove me to gather more information about the organization I'd agreed to work for. I didn't want to commit to killing someone without good reason. Though the notion that Gin might get caught wielded heavily in their favor.

"At times, we contract for *our* government," Mr. LaCroix emphasized. "Very few people, even amongst the higher echelon, know about our capabilities."

Trying not to be rude, I raised my hand to interrupt. "How do people not know about us and our powers? We just trained with a bunch of normal people. I doubt you could pay them enough money to keep their mouths shut." Not with the way social media was these days.

Mr. LaCroix's eyes darted to Gin before he answered, "That information I consider classified. At least for now. Will that be an issue?" His tone was fairly gentle for a dismissal.

I shook my head. I had my secrets, I supposed they were entitled to theirs.

"Good," he said with a pleased smile. "And the only way I've ever agreed to take on one of the government jobs is if we, as a team, investigate ourselves. I don't trust that they always have the people's best interests at heart. So far, they've been respectful about only hiring us for jobs that we've all agreed are pertinent to the security of our country. These smaller jobs are more for the safety of the individual. Some believe we don't make a big enough impact, but I disagree. To the people we save . . ." He held up a hand, his palm facing the ceiling.

My leg bounced nervously in place, and even though Mr. LaCroix wasn't willing to share everything, I couldn't let Gin continue to be in harm's way when I had the power to fix it. He had to touch people to kill them. In doing so, he was exposed to discovery. Unlike me. I was undetectable.

"I can do it," I said, glancing at Mr. LaCroix and Ron.

Gin noticed my leg and then caught the corner of my eye as if to say *yeah right.*

I tried to force my limb to quit shaking, but adrenaline and fear wouldn't let it stop completely. "No, really," I spun my chair toward Gin, "if you're there with me—I can do it."

An expression like he was pleased with my admission but worried for my safety, etched his handsome face. "I know you can Darlin'. And I would never let you do this alone."

He hesitated as if he wanted to say more but changed his mind and left it at that. He rose from his chair and held out his hand. "Are you coming? We have work to do."

I wanted to take it—and against my better judgment, I did.

Chapter 20: Regan

"They deserve to die," I said to Gin. My breath fogged over the panoramic window, momentarily obscuring the view of the condo complex across the street. I shifted my weight from one foot to the other as we waited for my targets to enter the office.

For the last week, I'd been training with Gin at GSS's Anchorage facility. Mainly it consisted of meditation and strengthening my will. I'd spent hours around town causing mischief and mayhem to tire out my pet, thus making it easier to control.

My insides somersaulted—today we were advancing to murder.

Earlier in the week, I texted Mae, Ben, and Tim to let them know what was going on. I conveniently left out the—*I'm going to kill people* part. Predictably, Mae texted me an eggplant and peach emoji followed by a bottle of alcohol which I assumed referred to Gin. Ben said to have fun and Tim told me to be careful. Though he didn't know about my mission, the nature of his text was one of concern. My band of misfits was steadily growing on me.

My second goal this week had been to avoid Gin as much as possible. Unfortunately, it's hard to do when that person is your instructor.

The erotic dreams about him hadn't stopped. At times, I thought they might be getting worse as my night dreams started to bleed into my daydreams. It didn't help that every time he was near, butterfly wings unfurled inside and began to flitter-flutter around like drunk beasties looking for attention. My awkward attempts not to act like a fool around him were mediocre at best. After our training sessions were finished, I successfully dodged further contact.

Except for the night that he insisted we go to a seedy bar to observe the predator I was about to kill.

"You don't have to do this, Regan," Gin said, interrupting my musings. He was standing behind me staring out the window over my head. His warm breath tickled through my hair and the blasted butterflies almost fainted as he laid his hand on my shoulder.

I shoved those unwelcome feelings aside and concentrated on my task.

My body stiffened momentarily when the targets entered the room directly across from our location. I placed the binoculars to my eyes—an unnecessary gesture since I could see them clearly without them. I needed something to do to keep my focus on them rather than the man standing behind me.

The chubby one flipped on the light and sat behind the ebony desk at the far end of the room. The blonde strode to a bar lined with glittering decanters and crystal glasses. He poured himself a shot of amber liquor before he took a seat across from his buddy.

The golem pushed excitedly at the edge of its prison, virtually leaving wet nose prints on the glass. I returned the binoculars to my jacket pocket, inhaled one deep breath, and exhaled slowly. If I didn't act immediately, I was afraid I'd chicken out.

I wish.

Tingles spread from my chest to the ends of my fingers to the tips of my toes. Black smoke nudged open the prison and tumbled over the edge in curling waves.

Knowing the crimes that they had already committed and the ones they had planned for their *Big Game Hunt* tomorrow evening, I didn't feel bad when I reiterated, "They deserve to die."

The chubby dude hastily slid his laptop in front of him. His double chin tripled as he looked at the screen and opened a new document. He didn't begin to fight against my control until he started typing his suicide note—or really, mine. Sweat dampened my skin and, though I couldn't see it because I was in the condo across the street, chubby was sweating too. Or at least he should be.

"As soon as that's written, don't waste any time. It's going to be difficult, Regan, but you can do this. I'm here with you."

I nodded but didn't let my concentration waver. This wasn't as easy as controlling a cheerleader. This guy was a psychopath. Monster vs. monster. And I didn't plan on losing.

The good-looking blonde rose from his chair and wandered around the room. He pulled a book off the shelf and opened the first page only to return it a second later and repeat the process.

He swiveled from the waist up and said something to his friend with a smile. I was too busy controlling what he wrote to let him respond to what seemed like a joke.

The blonde walked over and snapped his fingers in front of the computer screen trying to capture his buddy's attention.

Chubby quit typing long enough to slap his friend's

hand out of the way and point for him to sit back down. Controlling people wasn't that hard unless they were gifted, but if I let Chubby have his voice, he was bound to start screaming.

Gin and I needed to be in and out as soon as possible.

After he finished, I made him open the desk drawer and pull out a gun. GSS had performed a thorough sweep of Chubby's house last week and it was determined that he kept a loaded pistol in his desk and a shotgun in a secret compartment in one of the cabinets behind his desk. That didn't include all the other weapons spread around his condo.

Bile crept from my stomach and burned the back of my throat. My muscles tensed. I couldn't even swallow the nasty taste out of my mouth.

I can do this. I had to. Because at that point, he was a witness to my powers. Though people couldn't see me inside their heads—they could feel me. And he was the kind of guy who wouldn't let a mystery like *me* go unsolved. He had the resources and the connections to dig into the little phenomenon he'd experienced here. So—he had to die in order to keep my friends safe.

He charged the 9mm and aimed it at his friend. The blonde guy just laughed before he threw back the last of his drink. After he set the glass down, his eyes narrowed. I assumed he noticed the vacancy behind his business partner's eyes as he was no longer in control of his faculties.

Without hesitation, on my part or his, I made Chubby pull the trigger twice.

The blonde guy's head hit the back of the chair violently, his surfer-style hair flipped in slow motion, as one bullet hit him in the shoulder and the other in center mass. He grabbed his chest, pulled his hand away, and stared at the blood, dumbfounded. He looked up, his expression one of shock. Then I imagined the life drained from his eyes while he slumped over in the chair.

Wasting no time, I made Chubby place the barrel of the gun above the top of his ear. His panic flared inside my brain and kicked at the walls of my skull. Apparently, writing a suicide note and killing your friend was acceptable—killing himself wasn't.

The box opened further, and I let my pet off its leash. White spots flared at the corner of my vision and all sound disappeared as if consumed by a silent vacuum. By a thread, I managed to maintain control without shorting my circuit.

I wish.

Blood and brain spattered the expansive window inside his condo and ran down the side of the glass. I flinched before spinning around to bury my face into Gin's chest. He stroked the back of my hair and pressed his lips to the top of my head. My horror only lasted a few seconds before my euphoric drug began to kick in, numbing any of the remorse I might've carried.

A smile and the feeling that I was *more* swept through me. A chuckle began deep in my belly and spilled out of my mouth. I was a step up on the evolutionary chain. *And it was good.* I inhaled divinity and exhaled mortality. I was a God.

Chapter 21: Jude

My eyes drifted closed followed by my head toppling forward. I snapped upright and then glanced over each shoulder self-consciously. I swallowed the rest of my coffee hoping the caffeine would keep me alert.

Normally, I'd be hanging on the carpentry instructor's every word, but after almost two weeks of dealing with Regan's roller coaster of emotions—desire, sadness, anxiety, and guilt— mixed with my anger and fear, I was having a hard time staying awake. It was irritating. I paid good money to be here. If I wanted to succeed in the contracting business, this class was necessary.

I scrubbed my hands over my face and huffed. I suspected Regan was cheating on me and lying about it. If that were the case, then there was no way we could stay together. I couldn't live having my heart ripped out and my pride stomped on like it was nothing.

"It is nothing to a girl like her," the voice inside my head reminded me. I'd been burned before, and I'd be damned if I let it happen again.

Though I'd promised her forever, I'd never considered a scenario in which she'd be unfaithful. It was naïve of me because she'd cheated on her ex-boyfriend Layne—with me. Somehow, I thought what we had was different, something more. Something epic. But as of late, those feelings were being questioned.

Directly after I learned that she might be cheating, I found the address my grandpa had given me of our local medicine man still tucked safely between the pages of my book. Furious, I'd grabbed my keys and driven to the reservation. When I arrived, my anger had abated slightly, but I'd knocked on the elder's door anyway.

He nodded and gestured for me to enter. As if he'd been expecting me, he handed me a bag filled with supplies and sat me down at his table for instructions on how to use them and the repercussions should I attempt to sever the bond with Regan.

When I left his house, I didn't feel any better. I felt worse. Guilty that I would even consider such drastic action.

For now, I was trying to have faith. I loved her and didn't want to end our relationship until I could look her in the eyes to know for sure. The idea of her infidelity had jealousy rising up inside of me overtaking my every thought. The voice had been getting worse. It prodded and poked, antagonizing me when I let my guard down a fraction of an inch. It made me sick to my stomach. Or was that Regan on the other end? It was hard to tell the difference sometimes. I assumed, because I'd initiated the bond, I felt her emotions more clearly. Or the monster living inside of her kept my feelings muted in comparison.

I pulled out my phone, not only to check the time, but to see her latest text. Though I'd been reading them, I hadn't responded to any. I scrolled through the long line of unanswered script. First, she'd begged me to call, second, she'd promised she wasn't cheating. Eventually she gave up and started telling me about her day and asking questions.

—Do you think I could be possessed?—

—Is there a demon living inside of me?—

—Your Norse Mythology theory is starting to scare me.—

—Jude are you even reading my texts?—

—Jude???—

Every time I started to answer her, the voice in my head yelled that I was an idiot if I believed her to be innocent.

I glanced at the latest one sent this morning.

—This afternoon my emotions are going to skyrocket. I just didn't want you to worry. XOXO—

Without answering, I shoved my phone in my pocket and stretched my arms above my head to ward off the sleepiness. As I yawned, another emotion shoved my already overloaded senses into a hard-core fight-or-flight response.

My nerve endings flared with adrenaline, and I stood up knocking over my chair in the process. It clattered to the floor interrupting whatever the instructor was saying.

"Jude," the instructor said cautiously, noting my distressed behavior. He tilted his head down and glanced over the top of his glasses. "Are you okay?"

"No. I gotta go." Something was wrong with Regan. It was as if her monster had slithered up from its hole, granting itself control. The only other time I'd experienced something similar was when she made Gabby humiliate herself in front of the entire school. But this—*this* was different. Back then I could still sense Regan's presence amongst the darkness. Now, all I could sense was utter and complete blackness. Had GSS hurt her? Or had they finally made her do something so morally devoid that she couldn't return? Was her golem forever in control? Not sure what the problem was, I rushed from the classroom, leaving my books behind, and jogged into the parking lot. With an unsteady hand, I yanked my keys out of my pocket and jumped into my truck.

I rolled down the windows to combat the dry stifling heat. My a/c had bitten the dust somewhere in the middle of Wyoming when I was driving to Billings, Montana in order to attend these classes. At the stoplights, I booked a flight to Anchorage, Alaska. Then I called my grandpa and informed him of my plans.

He'd warned me about Regan early on in our relationship. It's not that he didn't like her, he did. But he said dating her was the equivalent of dating yin and yang. Dark and Light. Good and Evil. And though she was a good girl, the darkness living inside of her would always be a problem. I told him, because I loved her, I was willing to deal with the consequences. He had said, "Son, I love you, but she's going to break your heart. She won't even be able to help it, it's who she is by nature. I don't know where her powers come from, whether it's the Norse God Loki or just some cruel chance of fate, but she's similar to our trickster."

He had said even if she didn't break my heart, having a direct line to each other's feelings would never work in a romantic relationship. It would tear us apart at the seams. Everyone was entitled to their private thoughts. No one, especially someone we loved, should *ever* have access to those feelings at all times. According to him, it was a recipe for disaster. I had refused to believe him.

But the last two weeks had me questioning everything.

Because of our unique connection, I could feel the creature that resided inside of Regan celebrating whatever it was she'd just done. I'd never felt its presence, its utter darkness, so clearly before. It was truly terrifying. It even managed to drown out the voice inside my head. I had a barometer on my girlfriend's emotions, but this joy, this elation, this insane euphoria was not hers. Power blazed inside my chest as if I were a God and the people around me were nothing. Zero. Zilch. Nada. The feeling was so overwhelming I had to swallow back vomit.

The wind whipped through my hair as I stepped on the gas and wove in and out of traffic, needing to get to Anchorage in a hurry, not only to help Regan but to save my sanity. By the time I got to the airport, I ran to the bathroom and puked.

Looking in the mirror while I washed my hands, it was apparent that the last couple of weeks had taken their toll. I splashed my face with water and rinsed out my mouth. On my way to security, I could feel the darkness starting to recede and Regan taking its place. Relief loosened inside my chest, but it didn't make me rethink my plans. I'd be damned if I let my insecurities prevent me from being there if she truly needed me.

Chapter 22: Regan

"All right, my little junkie, we have to get out of here." Gin clasped my elbow in his as he escorted me from the condo, down the emergency stairs, and out the back of the building to where our car was parked a few blocks away.

After killing the criminal scumbags, the first hour of my high was glorious. The longest and the best I'd ever experienced. Once we'd arrived at the hotel, the guilt edged alongside the pleasure, then began to outpace it, erasing the earlier decadence and leaving me in misery.

I sat on the corner of the bed trembling.

Even though Gin had spent most of the week training me, guiding me physically, spiritually, and intellectually, I couldn't control my body's biological reaction. After the high wore off, my fight vs. flight mechanism kicked in. My breathing turned shallow and ragged. A clammy sweat dampened my entire body. Gin sat next to me with his arm tightly gripped around my shoulder to keep me from shattering.

Tears streamed down my cheeks.

He'd told me repeatedly it wasn't going to be easy. He said after the high wore off, the shock would set in. And after the shock wore off—I was going to be an emotional basket case.

Miss cocky predicted a different outcome. There was no way killing two repulsive, horrific, sub-humans was going to make me feel an ounce of remorse.

I.

Was.

Wrong.

My mouth began to water, and I started to gag.

Gin hopped up to grab the trash can next to the mini-fridge barely in time. I wrapped my arm around the cold metal and vomited. Gin tucked my hair behind my ears and rubbed my back in a soothing circular motion. My spine curled, heaving until there was nothing left.

"I'm so sorry, Regan." He leaned down and kissed the top of my head. I was too shaken up by what I'd just done to read too much into his gesture. But despite my love for Jude, Gin was the only person I wanted with me during the aftermath. He was the only one who knew the confusing depths of my raw emotions; how I was proud of the fact that I'd saved lives. And how I hated myself because of the way I'd accomplished it. How I enjoyed the high and how I hated the despair even though I deserved it. This was me, and Gin was the only one who understood.

Not surprisingly, the golem was snuggled happily in its cage. It was comatose with satisfaction, leaving me to deal with the fallout. *Traitor.*

It was a strange feeling having another side to my personality or what often felt like a completely separate entity living inside my head. It was comparable to keeping a dragon locked in a cage and only letting it out to eat on occasion. It was a dangerous balance. But with Gin's help, I was learning how to co-exist with my pet. He'd told me his powers were much the same, though he'd learned to live without locking his alter ego in a prison. The idea of letting my darkness permanently loose was terrifying. I knew, without a doubt, becoming a psychopath would only be the beginning. I didn't want to imagine the monster that would follow.

After I finished puking, he tipped my chin up with a finger and said, "Let's get you cleaned up and into bed, shall we?"

I nodded.

He took the gross trash can out of my grasp and set it down before wrapping his arm underneath mine to lift me up. We walked to the bathroom and he stood beside me holding me steady as I brushed my teeth. My skin matched the white countertops except for the dusky purple smudges below my haunted blue eyes.

"Better?" he asked when I set my toothbrush down.

I smiled weakly. "Gin, do you ever feel guilty?"

"Yes. Every time. Even though they were garbage. If I'd let them live, they would've hurt more people. That very thought lets me sleep at night. I don't like killing them, even if they do deserve it. You don't either." The look in his eyes said *I told you so.* But being a gentleman, he didn't add salt to my wound.

I shook my head. The golem enjoyed it. I didn't.

"Come on." He held out his hand. I hesitated before taking it.

His touch, his very presence comforted me far more than it should have. He led me back to the room and sat me down on the side of the bed. He dug through my bag and pulled out a pair of plaid pajama bottoms and a T-shirt.

He knelt on the floor, untied my shoes, and pulled them off. "Do you need help with the rest?"

I sniffed and shook my head.

"Okay, I'll step out to order us some food."

My eyes widened. "No."

"Ya don't have to eat it Darlin', but I'm ordering it anyway. We're going to sit here, eat—or not—and watch TV until you fall asleep."

The soft glow of the table lamps reflected in his eyes. I wondered who'd been there for him after he'd made his first kill. Probably Mr. LaCroix. The notion increased my respect for the man. I was struggling to find any faults in his actions.

Gin left then came back twenty minutes later wearing sweats and a fitted tank top, his biceps flexing as he carried in a bag of food and set it on the table. Even though my stomach was queasy, it smelled good. Due to my nervousness, I hadn't eaten much all day.

"I got you some fresh rolls and Thai soup with rice." He rifled through the bag. He placed my food and utensils on the nightstand. "Do you want me to stay? Or do you need some time alone?"

"Please stay." My voice was desperate. It was easier to keep the bad thoughts at bay with him near.

A tiny smile bowed the corners of his lips. He reached toward me as if to touch my cheek, but veered away at the last second deciding, instead, to grab the remote control sitting on the nightstand next to me.

"Anything in particular you want to watch?" He flipped through channels.

"A romance," I said, knowing he wouldn't deny me in this state of mind. It was the only thing I could think of that wasn't full of violence and killing.

He climbed into the other queen-sized bed, found a romantic comedy, and said under his breath, "As you wish."

Chapter 23: Jude

As I sat down at the back of the plane and stuffed my carry-on bag under the seat, my nausea turned to guilt accompanied by intense sorrow. The pretty woman seated next to me smiled and looked as if she were about to start up a conversation. To keep that from happening, I leveled her with a stare that said *don't*. I'd been told my dirty looks were enough to kill. So, I wasn't shocked when her eyes widened in surprise followed by a small measure of irritation as she turned back toward the window.

The entire flight, I had to concentrate to keep from crying, though the tears wouldn't have been mine. Regan's guilt and self-loathing was all-consuming and soul-crushing. I wasn't sure she was going to survive it and my heart ached for her.

Thankfully, the voice in my head was on radio silence, leaving me a moment to breathe, regroup, and remember all the reasons why I loved her in the first place. It wasn't just the way she looked, though I enjoyed her exterior to the fullest. It was her sarcastic sense of humor, her ability to laugh at herself, and the way she thought she was a horrible person, when she really wasn't. I'd been there while she defended people who couldn't defend themselves. I'd been one of them. She was a knight in shining armor, carrying a very dangerous sword. One that would slice her apart and watch her bleed.

I propped my elbows on the tray table and rested my head in my hands. I should've never let her go alone. My earlier anger faded to worry. Her roiling emotions were mind-boggling. How did she do it and stay sane?

My only hope in saving her was to get her to quit and come home with me. I'd finish trade school and she could go to college like she wanted to. Eventually, we'd get married and start a family. I knew if given enough time, she'd come around to the idea of children. And if she didn't, there was always adoption. With the way things were going, I wasn't sure that the future I'd so carefully planned would materialize.

After the plane landed early the next morning, I ran past the gates, down the escalator without stopping, and out the doors. The smell of the ocean and jet fuel tinged the air. Pushing in front of a crowd of people, I grabbed the nearest cab despite the complaints coming from behind me. I climbed in the back seat and said, "I don't know the address, I'll tell you where to go."

He put on his blinker light and pulled away from the curb. I closed my eyes and focused on Regan's smoky black aura. The tug in the spot below my heart and above my stomach guided me onward. "Just go straight for now."

Once we neared the highway, it veered away. I directed, "Go left."

A short time later, I had him pull over in front of a hotel overlooking downtown and the ocean. I threw him some cash and jumped out of the cab. There was no need for me to stop at the front desk and get a room number. I ran up the stairs, taking them two at a time until I hit the fifteenth floor.

Without a moment's hesitation, knowing she was inside, I banged on the door. "Regan," I yelled through the wood.

I almost fell over when Gin, wearing sweatpants, a tank top, and with messy hair, answered. I pushed down my instinct to knock him out and shoved past him.

"Jude," Regan yelled and flew into my arms. I held her as tiny cracks in my heart fractured. My eyes roved the room, taking in the half-eaten cartons of food to the unmade beds that had obviously been slept in.

The voice inside my head came back with a vengeance. *"One bed to sleep in and the other for play. You know what they say about the mouse when the cat is away."*

My trust in her, already on shaky ground, vanished. I pushed her away and stepped back out of reach.

"It's not what it looks like." She yanked the sleeves of her sweatshirt over her hands.

My nostrils flared, my teeth clenched, and my fists curled.

"Liar, liar, pants on fire," the voice said.

"If ya just chill for a second, I can explain."

I ran my tongue under my closed lips over my front teeth. Not able to speak, I gave a curt nod.

"Regan," Gin said from behind me. "Everything okay?"

With my arms crossed, I turned and leveled Gin with a nasty look. He seemed completely unconcerned by my presence, which made me even angrier. A shiver of fury ran down my spine as the voice cackled, *"And what are you going to do about it? Kill him?"*

"It's fine, Gin. Can you give us a few minutes?" Regan said.

"Absolutely, but I'm right next door if ya need me."

I barked out a harsh laugh at the same time the voice said, *"If he had a room next door, why did he stay here for the night?"*

"Do you want to sit?" Regan asked.

"No," I snapped. I'd been so mad at her for the last two weeks imagining her wrapped in Gin's arms and now having found her in a room together with him, that the inferno burning inside of me was almost past the point of control. Because of those images playing on repeat, my lack of sleep, and that damn voice, I was struggling to say the least.

"Have it your way," she mumbled. She grabbed a throw pillow off the hotel chair and tossed it on the floor. "Last night I killed two people."

Another surge of anger jolted, though this time it wasn't aimed at her. Those bastards were going to pay.

She licked her bottom lip. "I thought it wouldn't bother me. They were bad guys. The worst kind of people. But I was wrong. It was awful." She walked over to the window and pulled open the curtains. Outside the clouds hung low over the mountains. "It wasn't the same as killing my dad." A sob caught in her throat, and she hiccupped it away. "But it was bad."

I swallowed. It was like I had people warring inside of me. One that wanted to hold her in my arms and take away her pain, and the other one who wanted to walk out the door and never look back. And a third one that was urging me toward murder. I just wasn't sure whose. GSS for making Regan kill? Gin for taking advantage of my woman in a vulnerable state? Or Regan herself for allowing any of it to happen?

"I asked Gin to stay until I fell asleep. The thoughts

going through my mind . . ." She squeezed her eyes shut looking as if she were trying to keep the memories at bay. "I didn't think it was wise to be left alone." She glanced at Gin's unmade bed and shrugged. "It looks like he just fell asleep too."

Though her reasoning made perfect sense, she had spent the night struggling with guilt and sorrow, it didn't explain away her other emotions for the past two weeks. My first taste of her dishonesty was while having lunch with my Grandparents. Luckily, I'd excused myself and was in my bedroom when her desire hit me like a freight train. For approximately five minutes my body pulsed and throbbed with need that was not mine. It was humiliating. Then without warning all the sensations disappeared as if they'd never existed. I might've believed it was a figment of my imagination if it weren't for the following mornings. Like clockwork, something aroused her—therefore arousing me. When she'd finally called me, she blamed her erotic dreams. But if they were about me, why did guilt and shame follow? She was cheating on me. I was almost sure of it. So was the voice inside my head.

Chapter 24: Regan

"Jude, I'm telling the truth," I said for the umpteenth time. I rested my head against the headboard with my legs curled beneath me. "Please, sit down," I begged as he paced over the hotel carpet.

He ran his hand over his black hair and crashed down into the chair with such an attitude one would've thought I'd asked him for a kidney. His bronzed skin was pulled and drawn, and his eyes held a harshness not usually there. I'd never seen him look so exhausted. He wasn't less handsome than usual. His angles and edges just seemed sharper making him look older than his nineteen years.

My fingers fiddled with the edges of the comforter. "Why don't you believe me? I've never lied to you. Seriously, you're the *only one* I've never lied to."

It's not like I went around lying because I wanted to, but how many people were going to believe me if I told them I had the power to control them with my mind? I'd sound crazy.

He huffed angrily and shook his head. "I have a window inside your brain, remember? And something's going on. I'm assuming between you and Gin. Or maybe it's more than one person," he said flippantly.

My mouth fell open at the accusation and the air rushed from my chest like I'd been punched. "How can you say something like that?" My pet, usually keen on

Jude's company, darkened from a smoky gray to pitch black.

He pounded his chest. "Because I can feel you. And more than once, something—" he held a finger in the air, "no scratch that—someone *else*, turned you on."

"First," I held my finger in the air matching his, "being turned on doesn't constitute cheating. You know what happens to me when I let my pet out of the bag. I can't help it." It was disturbing enough without him pointing it out. I couldn't fathom why he was condemning me for something beyond my control. My cheeks started to warm knowing I was about to embarrass myself further. "Second, I told you I've missed you and I've been having . . . colorful dreams," I choked out. I didn't lie and tell Jude they weren't about him.

No, omission is not lying.

"Plus, I don't know!" I shrugged, my hands splaying with the motion. "Tim has the power to make people fall in love with him. Maybe his voodoo hoodoo is messing with me." *Again, not necessarily a lie.* I knew of three people whose powers worked on those of us with gifts. It was possible, if not probable. I couldn't figure out why Jude was getting these emotions from me. Sure, I'd had erotic dreams of Gin, and I kind of had a tiny moment with him on the mountain. But thankfully I passed out before I did anything stupid, and then again last night. That high was intense, but Gin was too concerned about my well-being, or too much of a gentleman, to notice the pheromones I was tossing around like confetti.

"Well, you've done it before," Jude growled.

It seemed the more I explained the more irate he got—as if he wanted to be mad at me.

My nostrils flared and I cast him a dirty look. "I have *not* lied to you."

"Maybe not, but you've cheated." He crossed his ankles out in front of him looking relaxed and comfortable. He wasn't. His anger and hurt were swirling inside, fueling the fire.

"No! I have not!" I slapped the pillow on my lap.

"Not *on* me. But with me, when you were dating Layne." His tenor was snide.

I sniffed sharply at the low blow. I'd seen Jude mad before but never like this. Being angry with someone and being purposely mean were two different things.

My first instinct was to pick up my water glass and throw it at his head. Instead, I glanced away counting to five as I breathed. Thankfully, my powers didn't work on Jude, so there was no worry that I could hurt him. "You're right, in a moment of weakness, during a low point of my life, I kissed you while still dating Layne. But I stopped and didn't do anything further until I'd broken up with him. I'm not proud of what I did." I looked back at him and waited until he made eye contact. "Funny, I thought you'd be the last person to throw that in my face."

He shrugged. "Well, it's true."

I gulped and nodded. It was.

"And then—what you did last night? You *killed* people. And don't tell me you didn't like it. I know you did," he said. The venom and judgment in his voice unraveled me.

It was like talking to a stranger. The blood drained from my face. "Yeah, but then I spent the next few hours in shock, an hour puking, and intermittent hours of crying until finally I could eat something and get some sleep. When did you become such an asshole?"

He laughed jadedly. "I'm the asshole, that's rich."

"Jude, I don't know what else to say. I'm not cheating on you. I love you. Sometimes so much it hurts. But you've read my emotions wrong before. Can you just consider that?"

For a few seconds, he stared out the window. The gray, overcast light softly accentuated his high cheekbones and perfect lips. "So, where do we go from here?"

"I don't want to lose you," I whispered.

"Then quit and come home with me." He leaned forward and rested his forearms on his thighs. The sleeves of his plaid shirt were rolled up exposing his smooth bronze skin.

"But I like it here. I've found a group of people that I fit in with. You'd like them too. I don't think an opportunity like this will ever come around again."

He clasped his hands together. They were calloused from working with wood and discolored from using paints and stains. "You mean the opportunity to kill people with impunity?"

His barb hit like a knife to the heart. Not wanting things to escalate, I said, "No. Jude. To bond with people like myself."

"I'm like you." He sat back and scratched his fingers over his hair.

"Then stay. Tell them what you can do and stay with me."

The muscles in his jaw flexed as he stared at the floor. He stood up and pushed his hands into his pockets. "I'm mad at you. I get it—all your excuses add up, but I just can't shake the feeling that you're lying to me."

He cocked his head as if he were listening to something I couldn't hear. His fists curled and again his anger rose like lava just under the surface of an active volcano. "Don't worry, I've found a way to break our bond if I need to."

I inhaled the words on the tip of my tongue, forgetting what I was about to say. A cloud of panic gripped my chest and knotted up my throat sealing off my ability to speak.

"I'm going to take a walk. I'll be back in a couple of hours."

Chapter 25: Jude

Having settled on my decision to become GSS's latest recruit, I stood outside the log building, enjoying the crisp morning air and admiring the views. This part of Alaska displayed a rugged beauty similar to where I lived in Wyoming but it smelled different. Moss, spruce trees, and wet earth instead of arid, pine trees, and grasses.

Once composed, I opened the door into an entryway before I hung up my sweatshirt and entered the room.

All eyes turned on me as I strolled across the floor and sat down as far away from my girlfriend as I could get. I wasn't ready to be all kumbaya with her just yet. The guy next to me, with red hair pulled back in a short ponytail, lifted his chin in greeting. If he thought it was strange that I chose a seat next to him, it didn't show. He was wearing a pair of cowboy boots, ripped-up jeans, and turquoise jewelry. Ben, if I was correct.

On the short plane flight over, Regan had filled me in on all of our classmates: what they looked like and what abilities they possessed. She was so excited to have me with her that I almost forgot that I was angry.

After I'd confronted Regan in the hotel, I'd taken a long walk. I concluded the only way to keep her safe and convince her to come home with me was to stay. Though I hated Mr. LaCroix—his daughter had falsely accused me of sexual assault—I'd called him and told him what

I was capable of. He sent a car to the hotel to pick me up. During our meeting, I conveniently left out that Regan and I were bonded. That was nobody's business but ours.

After hearing about my abilities, Mr. LaCroix offered me a position with GSS and filled me in on what to expect. They usually spent three months training new recruits and, in the end, if they were a good fit with his organization, they were offered a permanent position. He chuckled that Regan had guarded my secret and hadn't told him of my gift. I was surprised by his reaction. My expectations of his response would've been that of anger, but he seemed pleased by her loyalty.

This morning Regan had asked if I wanted to go to breakfast with her to meet everyone before class.

I declined, informing her I needed some space. Our relationship was already rocky and when angry I tended to say things I'd regret. I wasn't one to get over *things* easily. My mother said I was just like my father in that respect and held onto grudges like a dragon guarding its gold.

The voice inside my head hadn't shut up, but it was easier to ignore when I could keep an eye on Regan.

Pamela rose from behind her desk and straightened out her hippie skirt. Its length swished as she walked to the center of the room. "Today we're going to be separating into two groups. Those that have powers over the mind, body, or spirit." She touched her hand to her head, heart, and then swept it lengthwise in front of her. "And those that have more of a connection with the outside world. We categorize them as internal or external manifestations."

"The innies and the outies," Tim said. He elbowed my girlfriend who was sitting next to him.

Pamela squinted. Clearly, Regan was correct and Pamela lacked humor.

She glanced at her watch phone and tapped it with a finger. "While we wait for Mr. Templeton to arrive, let me introduce Jude."

"We know who he is," Tim said. "He's Regan's boyfriend." He waggled his eyebrows making his oversized glasses twitch.

Pamela's forehead wrinkled, her eyes taking in mine and Regan's distant seating arrangement.

She harrumphed. "Well, Jude, what are your powers? And no demonstrating on me." Her lips thinned with disapproval. Regan had outlined their history on the flight over. She made enemies like I held grudges.

"I can see people's auras and differentiate between those who have powers and those that don't."

Pamela swallowed hard and choked on her own spit. She held up her hand and took a sip of coffee. Once she stopped coughing, she said, "How fascinating."

By her reaction, Mr. LaCroix had not informed her of my capabilities. With me on staff, they would no longer need her abilities to recruit candidates. She had to interview family members and determine if they were lying in order to see if people had gifts. I could do what she did for the company far more efficiently. Though I didn't feel bad, her skill was still one of great power and I had no doubt GSS would find a different way to utilize her gift.

"Can you tell us what everyone's auras are?" Pamela asked.

I sat forward and propped my forearms on my thighs. I rubbed the polished arrowhead dangling from my leather necklace between my finger and thumb.

The dark-haired girl, Navi, blushed as she looked at me. The redhead smiled, fluttered her long lashes, demurely looked away, and bit down on her bottom lip.

Regan's anger flared. And to be honest, I enjoyed it.

"Absolutely. But you guys need to realize it's not an exact science. Most auras change with time and life experience. And there's a lot of conflicting information out there about what certain colors mean. May I read you?" I asked Pamela.

Curiosity won and she smiled while nodding permission. So much for not demonstrating on her.

"Yours is orange and has a slight shimmer." I teetered my hand back and forth. "It's opalescent. I've seen a few like this, but at the time, I didn't realize they were special."

She placed her palm over her heart. "Thank you, Jude. It's nice to hear."

I nodded then shot my girlfriend a scowl. "Regan's is black smoke." Even I winced at my tone.

"Tell them. Tell them what a horrible person she is. Tell them how she killed those men," the voice urged. And though I wanted to, I refrained. Both Regan and Mr. LaCroix asked that I not say anything to the other recruits.

"Of course, it is," Pamela scoffed under her breath.

A smirk lit up Rory's face and with a flick of her hand, she flipped her long hair over her shoulders.

Their dismissal triggered my temper but this time it was aimed toward them. It also negated the voice allowing me to come back to my senses.

Mae tossed Regan a peace sign and stuck out her tongue. The piercings above the corner of her lips caught the light.

"Bruh, wicked," Tim said, pushing against the side of Regan's face. With false irritation, she slapped his hand away and caught my eye.

The trepidation hovering around her made my guts clench. I was the one who was supposed to be defending her, not destroying her. "But," I continued having regained control of myself, "inside the smoke, tiny diamonds glitter like the midnight moon shining on freshly fallen snow." My goal was not to demonize her in front of the other new recruits. I was mad at her, but my issues weren't theirs. My reaction seemed unreasonable, even to me.

She smiled softly at me, and my heart skipped a beat. One side of my lip curled into a crooked grin. I loved her. And I hated her. One minute I wanted to throw her against the wall and make her scream my name. Destroy the memory of whoever was taking my place. The next minute I wanted to throw in the towel and leave. It was exhausting. I was exhausted.

Before I let my gaze linger too long, I moved on. "Tim, yours is magenta—a little pink, and a little red but it also has a slight sparkle. More than Pamela's not as much as Regan's." The slight acne on Tim's cheeks blazed and the tip of his nose and ears flared bright red.

"Navi, yours is silver and it intermittently quakes. It's quite pleasing." Her face flushed deeper, almost matching Tim's. Regan's ire sparked like a hot poker to my sternum.

"Ben," I said, glancing at my couch mate, "yours is purple and slowly fades in and out like it's breathing."

"Rory," I said. She sat straighter and licked her lips. "Yours is greenish. It swirls with some blues, browns, and whitcs crcating all different shades of green."

"Mae, yours is bright yellow but the perimeter is finite." I lifted my hand in a fist. "Most auras have a soft edge that fades into nothing."

Having never been in a situation where there were so many of us with gifts in one room, I was starting to see a correlation. Those of us that were innies shimmered or sparkled, and those that were outies had edges that were unusual.

"And mine," Gin said as he popped his head inside the door. His southern drawl had the sharp edge of humor knowing his presence would irritate me.

Gin held open the door and in walked Andrew Templeton, one of the guys GSS sent to Wyoming last year to spy on Regan. Eventually, he offered her this job. I sat up, leaning back. I propped my hands behind my head and glared Gin's way. As my T-shirt stretched over my abs and chest, Navi sighed loudly and quickly covered her mouth. Her cheeks again blushed.

"Green. With glitter."

Regan cocked her head. I stuttered on the inhale and her eyes narrowed at my reaction. I'd made a mistake. I'd told her a few months ago, that his aura was green but shook like an earthquake. When in reality, it looked much like hers except for the color. The specks of glitter weren't as obvious because the shade was lighter. But it moved much the same. Like they had a living breathing creature made of smoke cloaking their bodies in armor.

I blew past my gaffe and continued as if I hadn't been caught in a lie. "Andrew's is steel blue and the edges slither."

"And yours is?" Rory asked while twirling a lock of curly hair in her fingers. If she had any idea of what her flirting with me was doing to Regan, she'd quit.

The voice inside my head laughed at the chaos it was creating.

Regan's aura darkened from a deep gray to pitch black as it swirled and coiled over her shoulders. It curled into her hair and around her neck like a noose.

Gin looked at her. "You okay," he mouthed as he took a step closer. His aura reached out for hers and they started to mingle spiraling around one another like lovers.

My fury flared at the sight.

"Told you so," the voice said.

Regan's eyes widened at my response and she nodded quickly to Gin.

While she might be okay, I was beginning to question whether Gin was going to survive.

But if I touched him, he could kill me, so I adjusted my tactics and threw Rory my best flirty smile. Two could play this game. "My grandfather says mine is gold on gold. Which now, after seeing everyone else's aura, I'm assuming it's gold with a shimmer."

"Fantastic." Pam clapped her hands in front of her, seemingly unaware of the tension choking the air. "It means we're on the right track with our groupings. Jude, Tim, and Regan, you'll be with Gin."

I closed my eyes and shook my head, not even attempting to hide my annoyance. I pushed my hands against my knees and rose.

Regan yanked Tim up by the hand.

"Rory, Navi, Mae, and Ben will be with Andrew Templeton. He has the ability to slow time. So, I think you'll learn a lot from him."

Andrew gave a small wave, then caught Regan's gaze and tipped his chin. She smiled and waved back with fluttering fingers. She'd spent hours as his waitress when he and his partner, Paul Metz, were stationed in Wyoming trying to figure out if she had powers. She said he had quite a sense of humor. But I'd never gotten any vibes from her other than a feeling of fondness for him. What she felt for Tim seemed like that of a sibling, rivaling what she felt for her twin brothers. But what she felt for Gin was astronomically different.

Andrew smiled back revealing his dimples.

Mae bounced her eyes between Regan and Andrew and fanned her face, basically swooning.

Determined to keep Gin away from Regan, I sidled up next to her and stood close enough that my arm was touching her. Tiny sparks of static electricity sparked between the two of us. It had been so long since I'd held her, kissed her, and done other things with her. I missed her and all the benefits. I pressed closer and placed my arm over her shoulder with my hand draping loosely which irritated her. Earlier I told her I wanted space and now she thought I was marking my territory. Maybe I was.

Chapter 26: Regan

Pam sat across from me in the dining hall staring into my eyes. "I like your skirt," I said. Her lips flattened into a non-existent line and the muscles in her face contracted in concentration. Her job was to see if I was lying or telling the truth.

Gin had stuck a note on the door warning no one to enter for the next two hours. Today, GSS was trying out a new curriculum, one that allowed us to experiment on each other. Given that Gin's and my abilities worked on the others, Mr. LaCroix and Ron decided to test a theory. They thought that perhaps because there were so many of us, our powers might amplify one another. The largest class they had up until now was three students and we had a whopping seven with Jude. I didn't question their reasoning. After all, my brothers Kennedy and Lincoln's abilities only worked if they were together, though I didn't tell anyone that information. I kept my promises.

Gin laid out the ground rules—we could practice on each other but nothing dangerous or too humiliating. The last tidbit was aimed at me. Go figure.

Pam, being a surprisingly good sport, volunteered to join our session.

"That's a lie," Pam said. She shook her head making her beaded earrings swing.

"Nope." Though I wouldn't choose the skirt for myself, I did like it. The bright, cheery colors reminded me of a carnival.

Her eyebrows creased. "You like it?" she questioned as if she didn't believe me.

"Yeah, I do."

"Hmmm. Let's try again." She seemed determined, but I was confident she wasn't going to get through my pet's defenses, since I couldn't even feel her presence in my brain. She should've practiced on someone easier like Tim or Jude but she insisted she started with me. I wasn't sure if she wanted the challenge or revenge.

"I made a classmate choke on a hot dog after she flirted with my boyfriend." I sat forward and folded my hands together on the table smiling politely while wishing Navi and Rory were here so they could heed my warning. If they kept flirting with Jude, I was bound to lose my temper.

Pamela stared at Jude and blinked a few times. "Truth," she said.

"Nope." I leaned back and crossed my arms. "And you can ask him because he's right here to verify that I'm not lying."

"She's not. Regan doesn't often use her gift to help herself. Mostly she defends those of us who don't have the means to defend ourselves. Like me." His answer made me feel slightly better about our situation.

Pam's forehead gathered in surprise.

"Pamela," Gin said, coming to stand behind her. "I think your first impression of Regan is clouding your judgment. Jude, why don't you sit down."

Before I got up, I said, "Ya know Pamela, I'm sorry I demonstrated on you the first day of class." Mr. LaCroix had asked if I would consider apologizing to Pam for his sake. He said even though I wasn't aware of the rules, I had made a fool out of her and I knew better. It was such a parent move on his part. But he was right, so I swallowed my pride. "In my defense, nobody told me we couldn't use each other. Plus, I didn't know our powers *weren't* supposed to work on us. After Tim had practiced on Cammy," I glanced at Tim and he shrugged, "I thought I'd save her more humiliation and use you. For that, I'm sorry."

Her eyes fell to the table before she took a deep breath and looked at me. "I apologize too. The miscommunication was my fault. And truthfully, I was having a rough morning."

"I'm sorry for that." I scooted off the bench making room for Jude.

Jude grabbed his arrowhead and said, "My father made this for me for my fifteenth birthday."

Lie. On Jude's fifteenth birthday, he'd been sent out by his grandfather on his vision quest. During his adventure, he'd found that arrowhead. Upon his return, his grandpa fashioned it into a necklace. To this day, I'd never seen him without it. He even wore it in the shower. A vision of him standing naked with water running down his glorious muscled body had my insides warming under the memory.

Pamela cocked her head to one side and then to the other. A sheen of sweat broke out on her upper lip. "I— I feel like that's a lie."

Jude's surprise jolted behind my ribs. Because my powers didn't work on him, he was cocky and thought nobody else's gift would either. But a broken clock gets the time right twice a day.

"You're right," he said. "How about another one? Coffee's my favorite."

Lie. Hot cocoa was his favorite.

Pamela shook her head. "You're lying."

Jude frowned and nodded. "Okay, one more. Though I plan on being a general contractor one day, my passion is building furniture."

Truth. The table in GSS's conference room was built by Jude, though I wasn't sure if he knew Mr. LaCroix was the one who'd purchased it.

A huge grin lit up Pamela's face. Her teeth were straight and white but too large for her tiny mouth. "Yes. You're telling the truth!"

"I am," Jude said. He sounded casual, but he was annoyed.

"Amazing Pamela," Gin said. "This is the first time you've been able to use your gift proficiently on one of us. How did you do it?"

"Honestly, trying to get through Regan's defenses made it easier to get through Jude's. Hers is like a black sticky web. I couldn't even get in. Jude's was more like climbing a cliff—difficult but with careful planning, I was able to find hand and foot holds."

"Awesome," I congratulated her.

"Thank you," she sighed, "but it's someone else's turn because I feel as if I've actually climbed a rock wall and now I need a rest. "Do you mind if I go take a nap?" she asked Gin.

"You don't have to ask my permission, I'm not the boss," Gin said. "Tim, have a seat." Gin gestured to Pamela's vacated spot. "Let's see if you can break Jude." The timber of his voice didn't give away his humor, but his eyes sparkled with mischief.

Jude leaned back and crossed his hands behind his head pretending to be unconcerned. He was nervous.

Adrenaline pounded through his heart. I pressed my palm against my chest and willed Jude's emotions away.

Though Jude never let on that Tim's powers were working on him, I could tell by the tingling in my groin they were working. I had to bite back my laughter. After a few minutes, Jude stood up with his hands raised and his face hot with embarrassment. "That's enough. Your powers work on me." He pointed at Tim. "Don't ever do it again."

I patted Tim's back and scooted him over. "You and I have the same effect on people. We make them mad." I raised my eyes to Jude and blinked innocently. My pet paced around its cage. "My turn."

"Why bother, your powers don't work on me." He shoved his hands into the pocket of his hoodie.

"They don't?" Gin glanced between us.

I tapped the surface of the table with my finger for him to sit back down. "I think they might, now that my pet is mad at you."

Jude's emotions flared from irritation to fear to resignation and then morphed into what felt like a battle of wills. Good vs. Evil. I knew where I stood in his line-up. He sat down and leaned closer with his arms resting on the table. His eyes were black and hard like polished onyx. I licked my lips. "Are you planning on breaking up with me?" I needed *him* to make *me* mad and this was the quickest route.

He huffed. "I don't know. Besides, that's private." He glanced at Tim and Gin standing behind me.

I cocked my head and ignored him. "You promised me forever. You told me that if we slept together our bond would become more permanent than marriage. And at the first sign of a problem, you're already thinking of bailing?" I didn't hide the hurt in my voice.

"That's before you cheated on me!" He stood up abruptly.

My pet didn't like his false accusation any more than I did. It lifted its head and showed its blackened fangs.

I wish.

"Sit down," I ordered. Tingles rushed from my chest to the tips of my fingers and the tips of my toes.

His eyes widened in distress. He started to tremble and sweat sheened his forehead. He was putting up a good fight. Before today, my powers hadn't even made a dent in his free will.

I opened the box further and smoke rolled over the side of the glass.

"Now!" I hissed.

He dropped into the seat snarling at me. His anger seared through our connection. I probably hadn't made our situation better by confronting him with witnesses. *But we know, I don't always make smart decisions.*

"Remember when you accused me of being scared of you?" I was referring to the time before we took our relationship to the next level. He thought I was physically scared of him because of Gabby's accusations. When in reality, I was scared to go further with him because he'd yet to admit that he loved me. I'd already said the words out loud. "I was scared, but not for the reason you thought. You read my emotions wrong. And you're doing it again." I stood up, only a little wobbly from the high. It took more than a few seconds of controlling someone for me to catch the dragon these days. "I've never cheated on you, Jude. Why can't you just trust me?"

He scrambled out of his seat. "Trust you?! It's not

as easy as you think. I helped you through every difficult situation, believed in you when others couldn't, I saved your friggin' life, and still, you chose another."

My feet shuffled backward. He was talking about Layne. I hadn't realized he was holding on to that grudge too. I'd only chosen Layne because I was scared to pick Jude. He was dangerous. At the time, I couldn't control him, and he seemed overly fond of my powers. I wasn't sure if he liked me or if it was the golem that had captured his interest.

I swallowed trying to relieve my dry throat. "You once told me you loved all of me—even the darkness inside. I guess you were just fooling yourself." I threw my arms in the air. "Because *this* is the reality. I can't change who I am. And not because I don't want to. Because if I do, I'll go crazy and end up back in the psych ward or dead."

I turned abruptly and yanked my rain jacket off the coat rack before I stormed out the door.

Chapter 27: Regan

When I arrived at my cabin, I had good intentions of calling my mom. I really needed the comfort of her voice, but instead I accidentally fell asleep on my bed until a soft knock woke me from a pleasant dream. One without Gin or Jude.

Tim was standing on the small deck waiting for me wearing a silk shirt that reminded me of an orange and green retro kitchen. I opened the door for him to enter.

For some reason, I expected it to be Gin coming to soothe my temper. I knew better than to think it was Jude. After my little stunt, I'd be surprised if he ever spoke to me again. The boy could hold a grudge. He'd weaponized his silent treatment against me before. The last time he was mad at me, we'd gone almost four months without having a real conversation. Not for lack of trying on my part. But if he was going to break my heart, he needed to get it over with. I felt as if I were balancing on the edge of a razor blade and no matter which path I took, I was bound to get hurt.

Tim glanced around and then stepped inside. "Here, I want to show you something."

He pressed play before handing me his phone.

On the screen, Gin and Jude stood across from one another with the dining table between them. Though I wasn't there, the tension radiating was charged even on the video.

Gin swiped a hand through his hair and said in a calm tone, "Aren't you going to go after her?"

Jude pointed a finger at him. "You stay out of this!"

Gin's lips dipped into an irritated frown. "Normally, I would. But this instant, I'm afraid I can't bite my tongue. If you don't go after her you're an idiot."

"What would you know?" Jude snapped.

"I'm here to tell you Regan is not cheating on you. At least not with me. Tim?" Gin looked at Tim.

I couldn't see Tim since he was filming. From the strange upside-down angle, it seemed as if he'd hidden the phone in his hand with his shirt sleeve covering everything but the lens.

"Not me," Tim said. "And it's not like I haven't thought about it."

Jude's eyes slivered and Gin blinked a few times as if surprised.

The camera lens jumped when Tim shrugged his shoulders. "What? She's really pretty and nice to me. I'm fourteen. It would be weirder if I didn't. And not once has she shown any interest in me."

Jude glared with his arms crossed and legs spread shoulder-width apart.

"And you," Jude jutted his chin toward Gin. "You claim the two of you haven't . . ."

"We haven't. But I'd like to," Gin said, shocking the hell out of me. I held my breath listening to the rest. "Regan and I are the perfect match. And it seems to me, I care for her far more than you do."

"That isn't true! I love her!" Jude stepped forward as if he were about to spring over the table. This was like watching reality TV.

Gin, looking completely unconcerned, cocked an

eyebrow. "You have a strange way of showing it. By falsely accusing her of cheating on you? Correct me if I'm wrong, but didn't my cousin Gabby do something similar to you?"

Ouch.

I handed Tim back his phone.

"I just thought you should know," Tim said.

"Thanks," I said. I glanced at the time. "Oh, crap, I gotta go or I'm going to be late for therapy."

"No worries. Probably not something *you* should miss," he teased as I rushed past him out the door.

I ran through the pouring rain, my feet splashing on the wooden walkways, and entered Dr. Gloria's office out of breath and sopping wet.

Upon our initial meeting a few weeks ago, I had been determined to keep everything close to my chest even though she'd promised me doctor-patient confidentiality. She'd said her job with GSS was to make sure its employees were mentally stable enough to perform their duties.

Thinking I might not be the ideal candidate, I had risen from the chair she had me sitting in and pointed at the door behind me with my thumb over my shoulder. With a straight face, I'd asked, "So, should I head to HR and resign now?" *Mentally stable* wasn't really in my wheelhouse.

Her perfectly painted lips dropped open, then closed, then opened again like a fish out of water. Then she surprised me and broke out laughing. The lovely sound echoed in the room. "Gin warned me that you were funny." She'd pulled a tissue off her desk and dabbed the corners of her eyes.

Even back then, the idea of Gin thinking I was funny

warmed my heart.

"He also told me that you think you're a bad person, but he said you're not. He said you're the most morally committed person he's ever met. Coming from Gin, I can't imagine a higher compliment. So, are you comfortable telling me why you think you're a bad person?"

My plan to keep everything close to my chest had flown out the window. I told her almost everything. I hadn't realized how desperately I needed to talk with someone. How desperately I needed a helping hand. And not one that was six-foot-tall with wide shoulders, sculpted muscles, and a handsome face.

Thankfully, Dr. Gloria was the polar opposite—well into her sixties, short and curvy with a cap of curly white hair. Plus, she had a license to analyze me. It wasn't the first time someone with a degree had a crack at me, but Dr. Gloria was armed with more knowledge than the rest. Therapy seemed to be helping.

I was actually excited to see her today.

"Goodness," she said as I walked into her office and stood in her doorway with water dripping from my hair. She grabbed a towel out of a cupboard and handed it to me. "Dry off and have a seat."

I scrubbed it over my hair and face before giving it back. I sat down on the cute velvet settee with my hands crossed over my lap. Her office at the lodge was decorated much the same as her Anchorage office, in a soft shade of gray with white and baby blue accents.

"So, how's it going?" Dr. Gloria asked. She came around her desk and sat in the barrel chair across from me. She grabbed her glasses hanging around her neck and slipped them on her face. Her dark eyes grew twice their normal size.

"Uh, good and bad?"

She crossed her legs giving me a peak of her socks printed with musical notes, under the hem of her trousers. In the background, classical music played softly. We'd bonded over our love of opera. She'd gushed over Gin's talent and showed me some of his work. It's not like I hadn't cyber-stalked him once I found out his stage name, Christian Lansing, but Dr. Gloria had the stuff the internet didn't. He was one talented young man. Hearing his voice gave me full-on goosebumps that tickled my spine in a most delicious, dangerous way.

"How about we start with the good first?" she said.

I told her how I managed to control my temper after Rory shot me last week with her paintball gun.

"Regan, that's fantastic. What an accomplishment. Does that make you feel more confident using your powers out in the real world?" She leaned forward in the chair clasping her hands together. Her shiny red nail polish matched her lips.

"Yeah, but I still need to work on it. It was touch and go for a few minutes."

"It will always be a work in progress, but it'll get easier the more you do it. Just like anything else."

"I know, but I wish there was an easy way." I picked at the cuticle of my thumbnail with my index finger. It was a habit that I'd inherited from my dad. I usually did it when I was uncomfortable. He did it when he was lying.

"We all do. But I hear you have other things to deal with at the moment. I've been informed your boyfriend's here. Jude is it? I haven't had the chance to meet him."

I scraped my teeth over my bottom lip.

"Don't worry," Dr. Gloria chuckled, reading my hesitation. "He's been placed with Mr. Ling. I think they'll be a good fit."

"I wasn't worried about that," I said.

She pulled off her glasses. "What then?"

I told her that Jude thought I was cheating on him even though I wasn't. Then I came clean about the fact that we could sense each other's emotions and how all of that came about.

"Well, that's a lot to process. So, he doesn't believe you even though you've explained why he's having those feelings?"

I shook my head.

"And how does that make you feel?"

"Unworthy." My dad once told me that I was never to care what strangers thought of me—to only take criticism from people who respected me and were trustworthy. But Jude *had* proven he was trustworthy. And I loved him.

"How so?" Dr. Gloria urged.

"When he looks at me with mistrust in his eyes, it breaks my heart and makes me feel bad. Emotionally bad and bad like he thinks I'm evil personified."

She tapped her pencil on her lips. "Does this make it harder to control your temper?"

I sighed. "I don't know, but feeling like this makes me unhappy. And when I'm sad, my emotions are hard to control. So, yeah, I guess it does. But I don't want him to leave. I just want him to believe me. Mostly, I don't want him to think that I'm evil."

"I understand. But as we talked about last time, the only person you can control is yourself. Jude's actions and thoughts are his alone. No matter how badly you want him to believe you and believe in you, all you can do is stay true to yourself. Having said that, I can see how it would make this," she motioned in front of me, "more difficult. I have no doubt you're up to the task."

I nodded, wanting to think she was right.

"How are you dealing with the fallout after your first mission?" She addressed the real elephant in the room.

"You know, better than I thought. Gin was really there for me." I was glad that I hadn't known at the time that he might have feelings for me. I wasn't sure if he was being truthful in the video Tim filmed or if he was trying to make Jude jealous so he would run after me. "And with Jude showing up right afterward and now with him on the team, I really haven't had time to deal with those feelings." Issues were adding up faster than they could be filed away.

"Well, you seem okay. I'm comfortable waiting until our next session to go over those if you'd like. Sometimes it's easier to talk about it once you've had some time to process them yourself. But, as always, I'm here if you need an emergency session."

It was comforting knowing there were multiple people in my corner. "Thanks." I let my head lull backward. For me, solving one problem at a time was always easier than tackling multiple ones.

"Before you go, let's work more on your meditation and breathing techniques." She turned down the lights leaving only the glow of candlelight in the room.

By the time I left Dr. Gloria's office and headed to the dining hall, I felt better than I had in days. Not wanting anyone to spoil it, I snuck in, grabbed some food, and took it back to my cabin. I ate while I called my mom, then Miss Molly. Though she was my ex-boyfriend's mom, she was still my friend and I'd promised her I would keep in touch. It was good to hear their voices, even if I had to pretend nothing was wrong.

Chapter 28: Gin

I opened the door to Pamela's classroom and leaned against the frame. "I need to steal Regan."

Jude glared as if he wanted to flay the flesh from my body. I smiled at him pleasantly, enjoying that my presence irked him.

Seeing that Regan was seated next to Tim, not Jude, made a weird sensation balloon in my throat. I'd been attending meetings for the last few days and hadn't seen her. Many of those hours I'd spent fretting that she and Jude would repair their relationship. It's not that I didn't want Regan to be happy, I just wanted her to realize there were other options available.

She patted Tim on the leg and winked. "Later, sucka." She got up and headed my way without bothering to say goodbye to her boyfriend.

"Save some for me," Mae hollered.

I chuckled. Mae was quite the character. Bold and brash. It amazed me the things that could crush one person's spirit often made another strong as steel. Mae was a perfect example. Once she escaped the cult and found safety in Montana, though often homeless, she got a library card and educated herself. During the summer she played guitar on the street corners for tourists and in her free time she studied. She was a force of nature, and I was pleased she and Regan had become fast friends.

Regan brushed by me without a glance as I held the

door. On her way past the coat rack, she snatched her jacket off the dowel and fled outside.

"Trouble in paradise?" I jogged to catch up to her.

"You're the last person I should be talking to." She pulled the hood of her rain jacket over her head.

"And why's that?" I yanked it back down so I could see her face. She had no excuse, it wasn't raining.

She tossed me a scathing look. "Because he hates you."

"Well, I'm not a fan either." During my brief stint in Wyoming, I liked the guy. It seemed as if he was good for her, but after his stunt earlier this week, showing up uninvited with accusations of cheating—granted he may have known about my indiscretion even if Regan didn't remember—and the way he'd been treating her since, I'd reformulated my opinion. "But that's a silly reason not to talk to me. I know it's much easier to contain the beast when emotions are stable. At least, it always has been for me."

Apparently, having won the argument, she sighed and said, "He's hardly spoken to me, and he barely looks at me. The only time he pays any attention is when we're around other people. You and Tim especially. I understand he needs time, but it hurts. It doesn't help that Rory and Navi can't keep their tongues in their mouths when he's near."

Rory was a snake. Once you got past her looks, it was a rational conclusion. In her family, she was the center of the universe, their gorgeous princess, and it bled over into her ego making her into a shallow, ugly human being despite her lovely face. Navi was a sweet kid but naïve. Her parents had sheltered her terribly and controlled every aspect of her life. I found her awkwardness around the opposite sex endearing. At the moment, I dared not share my opinion with Regan.

"I'm sorry to hear that."

She quirked an eyebrow and said sardonically, "Are you?"

I blinked lazily. "No. Not really. I mean, I'm sorry you're in pain, but I think you can do better."

I was hoping she would ask who because I was prepared to tell her. But she didn't. Instead, she pulled her hood back up to hide her face. I assumed Tim had told her that I'd openly admitted my feelings for her, but I wasn't positive.

"Would you rather go for a walk or head over to my office?" I said after a minute of tense silence. I needed to tell her about the kiss I'd erased from her memory. It wasn't a secret I could keep any longer. If I did, I'd lose Regan's trust. Right now, that was even more important than capturing her heart. Because I was keeping an even larger secret from her, her dad. And once she learned about that, I was going to need all the help I could get.

She shrugged.

"Well, if you're not cold, let's go to the gazebo. My office is small and doesn't have the same view."

We followed the boardwalk, our feet squeaking on the damp wood, past the dining hall into a small meadow flanked by mountains on one side and the lake on the other. Tall stalks of fireweed grew around the large circular structure almost touching the green overhang of the metal roof. The delicate blooms shifted slightly in the breeze perfuming the air in its bouquet.

Once we stepped inside the structure, I turned on the overhead heating unit. As it warmed up, I held my hands near to take the edge off the chilly day.

"That's cheating," Regan teased. "Today's the first day of summer."

It was the summer solstice; the longest day of the year and the sun wouldn't actually set. For a few hours, a dusky haze would paint the horizon until it rose again. Though I often enjoyed the long hours, I missed the warm Southern evenings watching the stars cascade across the midnight sky while the fireflies darted in the darkness. "I'm used to real summers." I picked a bench along the outside edge of the gazebo. I sat down before patting the space next to me.

"Do you mind if I just stand here for a minute?" She stared out over the lake. I believed she was using the view as an excuse to avoid me.

Not taking the hint, I got up and stood beside her.

She fiddled with the hem of her sleeve. "Gin, how do you do it?"

"Do what exactly?" I stepped closer to her, our arms brushing.

Her eyes narrowed in contemplation. "You're always so calm. It's as if nothing or no one affects you."

Not true. The energy traveling up my arm to my heart was proof that *someone* had broken through my defenses.

"That wasn't always the case. While living with the monks—I figured out something. Much of their training was letting me learn the hard way. Lessons sink in better that way." I nudged her slightly. "But since you don't have the opportunity to study with them, just me, I'll let you in on a secret. The monks are exceptionally tough. They can withstand immense force without succumbing to the pressure, whether it be mental or physical. I learned they don't react simply because they don't have to."

She cocked her head toward me.

I let my gaze slide over her face. It had a habit of stopping on her full lower lip. "When you know that you are the most powerful creature in the room it makes it easy to ignore outside forces. Call it arrogance. Call it confidence." I shrugged. "I know—like the monks—the chances of anyone being able to hurt me are slim. There is peace within that knowledge. Do you understand?"

She looked toward the lake. "Yeah, I think I do. I can't imagine anyone, unless they're a sniper, being able to hurt you."

"That's not entirely true," I said softly. "Not all wounds are tangible."

Her jaw tightened as if she understood my veiled message. *She* had the ability to hurt me.

My heart knocked against my ribs, though I kept my shoulders neutral, as well as my facial expression. When she didn't say anything in return, I moved the conversation forward in an attempt to hide my apprehension. "So, I've been thinking, our powers have never worked well on one another until now. I have a couple of theories I'd like to test," I said.

"Okay, what are they?" She smiled but it was strained.

"In order for this experiment to have little bias, you need to be in the dark. At least for now. Okay?"

She climbed up on the bottom rung of the gazebo railing so she could brush her hand over the soft petals of the fireweed plant. When she stepped down our bodies no longer touched. She looked up at me with her gray-blue eyes partially obscured by her long bangs and said, "Sure. Just tell me what you want from me."

Your loyalty, your heart, your soul, your body. Is that asking too much?

I opened my mouth to tell her about the memory I'd erased. But honestly, the thought soured inside my stomach and my confession caught in the back of my throat. Was I a coward? Apparently so. Did I want to know about Regan and Jude's bond? Not really. Consulting Dr. Gloria on how I should approach the situation seemed like a reasonable excuse not to tell Regan just yet. Dr. Gloria was my sounding board and though she wouldn't outright tell me anything that Regan had said in confidence, she had difficulty masking her opinions around me. During my years spent with the Monks, I'd learned how to interpret body language efficiently. Their philosophy was that, like animals, a large part of human communication was done silently. Once I had Dr. Gloria's views—verbal or nonverbal, I would confess.

Regan shifted closer to me with her arm almost brushing against mine. It often felt as if we were magnets drawn together by an unseen force. The energy that ricocheted between the two of us, at least on my part, made it hard to concentrate when all I wanted to do was kiss her again and not erase it this time. "What I need is a list of who's the easiest for you to control to the most difficult. Can you do that without anyone knowing?"

"Sort of. It's obvious to anyone when I'm inside their minds. But I can erase their memory of having been there."

I stiffened. "You can?" She'd never mentioned that ability before.

"Yeah, but only tiny pockets. I call them mystery minutes. I can't seem to erase the big things. But, to be honest, the idea of even doing it on a small scale to my friends makes me uncomfortable. It's a line I'm not willing to cross."

It amazed me that she always thought she was such a bad person. "But you're willing to use it on strangers?" I clarified.

"Yes," she snapped. "But just to keep my pet under control."

She'd been uptight and defensive since Jude had arrived *uninvited*. "I think you misunderstand me. I find your loyalty to your friends admirable."

Her shoulders slouched. "Sorry. I'm being overly sensitive. Having Jude question my moral compass is making me crazy."

The idea that he was not only questioning her loyalty, but her heart, made the muscles in my neck seize. Despite wanting to talk with Dr. Gloria first, I couldn't let Regan suffer when I had the ability to fix the problem. Besides, she couldn't get that mad at me, she'd begged me to erase the memory. "Regan, your moral compass is far better than most people that I know. And they don't carry your baggage, so to speak."

"Thanks." She inhaled a slightly trembling breath. "I needed to hear that."

"You said something the other day, and I've been wondering . . ."

"Yes?"

"You said that when you and Jude slept together, your bond became more permanent than marriage."

Her eye began to twitch and her skin paled.

"I see I've struck a nerve. I'm going to need you to elaborate." If Jude knew about my transgression, which I suspected he did from his behavior, I needed to share no matter the outcome.

Her eyes darted away. "It's nothing," she choked out and flicked her wrist as if it were *just nothing*.

I cocked a brow. "Well, forgive me for prying, but I think you might be wrong. I'm the one training you, and to do it properly, I believe I need to know what you meant."

Her jaw flexed as if she were trying to trap the words on the tip of her tongue. "Remember the day when I destroyed the gymnasium after Gabby showed a video of my dad walking in front of the bus, then all my medical records played for everyone to see?" she said in one big breath.

"I'm aware." At the time of the incident, I hadn't been attending her high school. It was *that* very mistake on her part that landed me there. After the debacle, my uncle had me pretend to be a student in order to spy on her.

"When I was in the hospital, I almost died. Jude saved me. He somehow tied his soul, his essence, *his whatever*, to mine so I didn't die. It created a bond and now we can tap into each other's emotions." She blushed.

I clenched my fists inside my jacket pocket and swallowed waiting for her to continue. When she didn't, I removed my hand and raked my fingers through my hair away from my eyes. "I see. And this bond is permanent?" My voice was barely above a whisper.

She stared at the ground and shook her head. "I thought so, but apparently, Jude's found a way to sever our tie."

"I'm so sorry."

She raised a hand to stop me. "Don't be. It might be

a good thing."

"No, I'm so sorry because—" I said, wiping my sweaty palms on my pants. "Do you remember that first time we practiced together on the mountain?"

She nodded.

"I kissed you that day."

Her laughter started silently in her chest and gained sound as it rolled off her tongue "No. No, you didn't. I think I would remember."

I sighed, knowing I was about to blow any shot I'd ever had with her. "I did. You were glorious standing there with silver flashing in your eyes and a dare on your face I couldn't resist." I shrugged playfully as if that would conceal my racing pulse and the dread in my stomach. "And the whole time you were wishing for me to kiss that tree, I was wishing it was you."

She sucked in a surprised breath and the color on her cheeks deepened.

I clasped my hands behind my neck and tilted my head back as I exhaled. "My uncle would strangle me if he knew what I was about to confess. Very few people know." I caught her eye and held her stare. "But along with being able to kill people with my touch, I can also erase memories."

She froze.

Her reaction spoke volumes—she knew that I could kill a person with my touch but now she knew that I could navigate someone's private moments and erase them or change them at will.

With nothing else to lose, I continued. "That day, I kissed you. Then I said something that seemed to upset you. When you realized what was going on, you broke down and started sobbing. You were horrified by what

I'd done and what it would mean for your relationship with Jude. So, I did the only thing I could think of to ease your pain. The pain that I caused. I asked you if you wanted me to erase the memory. You begged me to do it. I didn't know at the time that he'd already be aware of my indiscretion."

She stood there staring at me seeming too shocked to even blink.

Trying to clarify further, I soldiered onward. "And you weren't thinking clearly. You were in a panic. So, I erased the memory. I thought you should know. I don't like keeping things from you. I'm so sorry."

I didn't want to harbor secrets, but my uncle, Ron, and Dr. Gloria had again vetoed my request to tell Regan about her dad. I hoped by the time we shared the news, she would understand the reasoning behind the decision.

She shuffled her feet and pulled her hands deep inside her sweatshirt. "Well, that explains a lot. You didn't erase my memory."

"No, I did," I said firmly.

"No," she copied my tone, "you didn't. Not really. You told me I smelled good."

My brows slammed together. "How do you know that?"

She licked her lips and glanced away. Her long lashes cast shadows on her cheekbones. "Because I dream of it every night. I wake up right after you tell me I smell good. I was wearing the perfume Jude gave me last Christmas. That must've triggered my meltdown."

My mouth dropped open. My power had never failed before. "So . . . you sort of remember?"

"No. I remember. But not until my subconscious brought it back. After that, I assumed it was a reoccurring dream. A *very persistent* one that baffled me—until now."

"I feel like I have to ask this again, can you forgive me?"

She huffed out a laugh like I was being ridiculous. "There's nothing to forgive. Besides, how can I be mad? I know what I'm like when my pet gets too much leash."

"No, Regan," I said sharply. "None of this is your fault. I kissed you."

"Part of the blame is mine—I didn't stop you. I . . ."

"Darlin'," I pleaded, "you did. Believe me, you did."

Chapter 29: Regan

Gin stepped close enough that I could see his sneakers in my peripheral vision.

Don't come closer. Please come closer. The war inside of me was almost as exhausting as the one with Jude. Now that I knew that Gin might have feelings for me—plus every morning I woke up with his phantom kisses burning my lips—it left me confused and directionless like a kayak without a paddle. His green eyes darkened as his voice took on a sliver of desperation. I'd never seen him look anything other than composed or moderately bored. The slight heaving of his breath and the pain pulling at his face led me to believe I was getting a peek under the surface.

My pet coiled around the perimeter of its cage, nudging up against the side as if encouraging me to grab Gin's hand, pull him closer, and repeat the kiss. I took a step back afraid that if I didn't, I would capitulate to its desires. Anything to ease the emotions running across Gin's face.

I didn't know it was possible for joy and regret to live inside the same breath. But the most confusing part was I didn't know which reaction to attach to which man. Was the joy because Gin kissed me or was it because I could finally fix things with Jude? And where did the regret belong? How could I regret losing someone that wasn't mine to begin with? Because as much as I hated to admit it—I certainly didn't regret that kiss. God, I was going to hell. I was pretty sure I was destined to fall from the beginning—now I was positive.

Gin reached out and placed his fingers under my chin, tilting it back so I had to look at him. My pet whimpered and scratched at the glass. My heart beat faster—then stopped—then started again at a nonsensical pace. Both it and my pet were acting ridiculous, but I couldn't seem to control either of them.

"I—I gotta go." I panicked, backing up.

Gin swallowed and nodded once as he looked away.

My feet pounded over the wet boardwalk while I rushed back to the classroom desperate to speak with Jude even though my thoughts were scattered.

The others were just walking out for lunch while Jude held the door for them to exit.

"Jude," I yelled and waved.

He said something to the others that I couldn't hear before they left him behind.

"What?" he said when I got close enough.

"We need to talk."

He held his hand out. "Lead the way."

My eyes narrowed at his brusqueness. I wondered what conclusions he'd come to with my latest emotional outbreak.

Once we made it back to my cabin, I motioned for him to sit down. He declined. I insisted.

Not having a plan, I opened my mouth and blurted out the news. Good news? Bad news? I wasn't sure how he was going to take it. His mood was sour lately. "Gin kissed me."

Jude slapped the table as he stood up. The vase of flowers toppled over and water spilled to the floor.

"Wait!" I yelled, pushing myself away from the table and getting to my feet. "It's not what you think." Okay. Maybe it was. "It was during our first round of really intense training. You know how I get. I'm so sorry."

I didn't plan on telling Jude that Gin had erased my memory of the events. He'd mentioned that his uncle was going to be furious for telling me. And though it would help me explain why I didn't confess the mistake earlier, throwing Gin under the bus didn't feel right.

"And you thought I wasn't going to know about it?" Jude growled, crossing his arms.

"Um . . ." I stuttered. I hadn't thought out my lies well. "It didn't mean anything." I lied again. Or at least I think I did. I probably should've waited to tell Jude about the indiscretion until I'd established a solid plan.

Jude cocked an eyebrow as if he could read my mind. More and more I was beginning to hate our connection. It was a strange violation—one that wasn't easy to explain. Having someone present for every emotional upheaval and not having time to process those feelings for myself first was exhausting.

"It didn't," I insisted. "I lied about it because I knew exactly how you would react." I slapped my hands on my hips.

"And how am I doing?" he mocked. "Am I living up to your standards?"

"You're the one with unobtainable standards," I shouted. He was the one who wanted a perfect job, a perfect house, a perfect wife, and a dozen kids. The American Dream. Right? Wrong!

"Me?" He pointed to his chest before pointing back at me. "You're the one who kills people without a second thought!"

I inhaled sharply. This was not going *at all* how I wanted it to. Black smoke crept up the corner of the box and pushed on the lid. I clamped my teeth together holding the prison secure. "We should probably wait until later to finish this conversation."

"There's nothing left to finish." He spun around and slammed the door behind him.

Chapter 30: Jude

Regan's cabin door shook on its hinges as it crashed shut. I stomped down the steps toward my accommodations with the voice in my head whispering, *"you were right all along."*

I *was* right all along. How did she think I wouldn't know?

"Because she's a lying, cheating, whore just like your last girlfriend."

I grabbed my skull attempting to silence the voice. It had always been there, especially with what I'd gone through after Gabby LaCroix had falsely accused me of sexual assault. My subconscious battered me with my insecurities—that I wasn't good enough, that nobody liked me, that's why all my friends disappeared, and that my dad hated me and that's why he didn't show up to help. Those self-doubts had only gotten stronger after I'd bonded to Regan. The worst of it was when I physically touched her while she was out of control. It was like I could siphon some of her darkness before it erupted and killed her. Or someone else. It was manageable, but after I had learned that she was cheating, the voice became a physical manifestation. For the most part it had laid off my insecurities and started telling me why Regan was a horrible person and that I should get rid of her.

Lately the anger had grown so heavy, I didn't even need its help to come up with reason why *she* was no longer good enough for *me*.

First—she killed people. And having a direct connection to her emotions—she enjoyed it. They had a name for people like her.

Second—as if reason number one wasn't enough—she was a liar. And now I had proof. If she would've just admitted to kissing Gin from the beginning we could've put it past us. I knew better than anyone what happened when she let the golem lose. Her hormones raged out of control, but I used to be the one who benefited.

"You don't want to be with someone you can't trust," the voice reasoned.

Exactly.

"Fuck!" I yelled and kicked the chair. It toppled over and scooted across the room stopping when it hit the wall. The above painting wobbled and ended up hanging crooked.

With every intention of calming down, I inhaled through my nose and exhaled out my mouth several times. I'd always struggled with anger but it was becoming unbearable. And dangerous. The thoughts mulling inside my brain were borderline homicidal.

The therapist GSS had assigned me said that I was welcome to stop by anytime. I couldn't think of a better time even though I'd seen him three days ago.

Desperate for help, and perhaps answers, I threw on my sweatshirt and ran out of the cabin.

I stopped in front of Mr. Ling's office and hesitated before I knocked.

"This is stupid. You don't need this quack. Do you really want to tell him all your secrets?"

No. But if I didn't talk to someone . . .

"Come in," Mr. Ling said, as he opened the door.

"Ah, Jude. How nice to see you? Why don't you sit down?"

"You don't have anyone else here?" I stuck my head in and looked around. The black and white room was empty.

"No. You have good timing."

I puffed a long breath of resignation between my cheeks. I really didn't think he would have time to see me on such short notice. With my internal war raging— me insisting I needed help, and the voice disagreeing—I would've been partially relieved if he didn't have an opening.

Having no way to back out, I slouched into one the curved chairs and gripped the armrests with my fingers. I stared at the colorful fish swimming in the tank behind his desk.

His eyes darted to my hands as he sat down. "Let's just get straight to it, Jude. What's bothering you?"

Though I'd only seen him once, I liked how he didn't beat around the bush. He was upfront and straightforward our entire session. Knowing that he'd probably heard worse than what I was about to spill, I dove in.

"The anger's getting worse. I thought once I got here, it would get easier."

"Do you think it's residual from your past experiences or is this something new?"

During our last session, we'd visited my past. How Gabby threatened that if I broke up with her I would regret it. Though after everything she put me through, I still didn't regret it. She was a monster of her own making. Not like Regan who didn't have a choice in the matter.

Then I told him about my friends abandoning me to save their own skin despite that Gabby had no evidence. How my parents divorced shortly afterward and all the guilt that came with it. And that I often believed everything really was my fault, leaving me to question my worth.

Thankfully, Mr. Ling assured me that none of those problems rested on my shoulders.

He said Gabby was wrong and what she did to me was horrific and my parents' issues were their own—not mine. As for my former friends, they would have to live with their decisions which would have consequences.

After having left his office that day, my load seemed lighter.

"I think this anger is new. Regan just admitted that she kissed Gin—or he kissed her." I shrugged as if the order didn't make a difference. It did. I was being stubborn.

I hadn't told Mr. Ling that Regan and I had a bond. It was nobody's business, but since Regan had announced it to everyone, he would know soon enough. Instead of letting him hear it second hand, I said, "Regan and I have a bond that allows me to read her emotions. I knew the exact moment they kissed and I questioned her as soon as I had the opportunity. She denied it. What I can't understand is, why she lied."

The expression on Mr. Ling's face didn't change despite the bomb I dropped. He simply nodded his head as if things of this nature were an everyday occurrence. Maybe they were. "Let's go back to this bond? I think I need to hear more about it." He tapped his pencil on his note pad.

So, I started at the beginning of mine and Regan's

story. By the time I finished, he pushed his notes away and folded his hands over his desk.

"Jude, I can't say for sure, seeing as this is an unusual situation, but hear me out before you make any judgments. Do you think it's possible that whatever resides inside of Regan is capable of feeding off your emotions through this bond you've created?"

The clock on the wall stopped ticking, my heartbeat froze, and I quit breathing. Everything resumed as I realized that my insatiable anger might not actually be mine.

A hesitant smile lifted the corner of my lip. "Thanks Mr. Ling!" I bolted up from my chair and rushed from his office leaving his protests behind.

I couldn't tell Regan what my problem was because if I did, she would insist we break the bond. But now that I knew the monster—I could slay the beast. I just needed a few days to figure it out on my own.

Chapter 31: Gin

The next afternoon, we reconvened in the classroom with me, Pamela, and Andrew supervising.

"We're here to see if the innies," I said, adopting Tim's term, "have the ability to control the outies." Yesterday in the dining hall we let those of them with similar powers practice on one another and for the most part everyone was successful. "If anyone has objections, let me hear them now."

"I don't want her inside my head," Rory said, angrily flipping her hair over her shoulder.

Everyone knew she was talking about Regan.

"Anyone else?" I asked, ignoring her for a moment.

"Bring it on." Mae held out her hands and wiggled her fingers. She loved a challenge. It was admirable. I could see why she and Regan gravitated toward one another.

The rest shook their heads.

I returned my attention to Rory. "If that's what you wish. But this will be the end of your journey here."

"So, if I don't let her in my head, then I'm fired?" She slapped her hands on her hips. A stream of red crawled up her neck to her cheeks.

"If that's how you want to look at it. We're here to learn from one another. The only way we can discover what we're all capable of is if we push the limits. If you're not willing to do that, then you're welcome to go home." I was hoping she would comply.

She had the nerve to look over at Jude. He shook his

head like he didn't want her to leave.

Regan's eyes flashed silver. From our conversation earlier, she said she was having a hard time with Jude flirting with Rory and Navi.

I knew that Regan had talked with Jude. And from their demeanor, the conversation hadn't gone well. Part of me was relieved because my feelings for her were growing deep, but it upset me to see her in pain. Especially knowing I was the one who caused it. I reached over and squeezed her arm. The stiffness in her body loosened under my touch as she shot me a wisp of a smile.

"Fine!" Rory huffed, flipping her hair over her shoulder again.

With that settled I said, "What we're going to do is like speed dating in a sense. Andrew, if you don't mind, I'm going to pair you with Regan to start."

He nodded before he slapped his hands together and rubbed them creating friction. "Oh, this should be fun! I've yet to have the honor." He curtsied in front of her like he was wearing a skirt. She bowed back nearly touching her nose to her knees.

"My powers are too dangerous to use on anyone," I wanted to glance at Jude, but I refrained, "and Jude has already demonstrated his, so the two of us will sit this one out. Pamela, if you'd please stand in front of Rory and Tim, let's see what Ben thinks of your talents."

"No hard feeling, right mate?" Tim said to Ben.

Ben swept his hair into a ponytail. "Bruh, you never know, I might like it."

Tim's face flushed the color of his burgundy bell bottoms.

Regan stepped in front of Andrew and pressed her

hands together in a prayer position.

He blew her a kiss.

With a glint in her eyes, seconds later, she wiped those dimples from his face. Concern rippled over his features before he slid the heels of his feet together, bent his knees, and held his arms in a delicate circle out in front of him.

A devious smirk lifted her lips showing her straight white teeth with slightly pointed canines. That look, so similar to the one she gave me right before she demanded that I make out with a tree, was enough to ignite my feelings. I averted my gaze before I revealed my intentions to everyone.

With Regan's encouragement, Andrew straightened and followed with en pointe almost getting up on his tiptoes though he was wearing sneakers and not ballet slippers. She had him finish with a grand jete jump with splits in the air. If he hadn't been wearing jeans, he might have pulled it off. He landed surprisingly well.

The others, too distracted by Andrew's talent to practice theirs, applauded.

When Regan released control, his shoulders heaved downward and he inhaled deeply as if finding his feet again, so to speak. Once composed, he bowed before meeting her gaze. "Did you know I studied ballet as a kid?"

Mae's head snapped toward Regan and said in a false whisper loud enough for everyone to hear. "Oh, he's quite flexible then."

"I am," Andrew said confidently but his cheeks took on a small blush.

Mae was anything but subtle.

Next, Regan picked Mae.

She kept it simple and forced Mae to serve Rory a cup of coffee as if she were the Queen of England. Though Regan could make her serve the tea, she couldn't wipe the snarl off Mae's face nor the tremor in her hand as she passed the cup to Rory almost spilling it on her lap.

When Mae sat down in a huff, Regan winked at Tim. His normally tan face paled, highlighting the acne peppering his cheeks. He stiffly walked toward where I sat on one of the couches in the room. His eyes darted at Regan before he kissed the top of my head. Afterward, he stuttered an awkward apology as he scurried to the couch across the room. I waved it away with my hand.

Once it was Ben's turn, Regan had him write on the dry-erase board—*I cry when I watch sad movies.* He laughed and said that it was true, especially if the dog died. Then he plopped down next to Tim.

She then made Navi loudly declare that her dad was a proctologist. When Regan let go of control, Navi turned with her hands on her hips and said, "How did you know?"

Everyone looked at Regan with suspicion. "I didn't." Her eyes found me. "I didn't," she insisted.

"Just kidding." Navi giggled. "He's an internist. It's pretty much the same thing."

Navi was beginning to come out of her shell and connect with the entire group. At first, I had thought she was going to stay glued to Rory's side. I was glad to see she had a backbone even if she was a people pleaser. We just needed to redirect her loyalties.

Apprehension built behind my ribs as Regan stepped in front of Rory. The others leaned forward as if they also sensed the tension building in the small space. The history between the two was precarious.

Rory huffed and crossed her arms, her eyes flashing with hate. She licked her lips nervously. Though I didn't care for her, I couldn't blame her.

It took Regan a split second to have Rory under her control. I wasn't surprised by her weak constitution. In Pamela's report, Rory didn't take constructive criticism or direction well. Her training was lagging behind the others. It was disappointing because the ability to control the elements was an interesting gift. One that we hadn't seen at GSS.

Rory went to Pamela's desk and began to shuffle through the drawers. Once she found what she was looking for she held the looped handle by one finger and displayed a pair of scissors.

Everyone inhaled sharply. Silence rolled into the room like fog. She gathered her hair in her fist and pulled the bulk of it over her shoulder.

"Regan," I warned.

"She won't do it," Jude said, leaning back on the couch with one arm resting on the top of the cushions. "No matter how much she dislikes Rory. Regan never weaponizes her power for herself."

I didn't like being corrected by Jude and I liked it even less when Regan smiled at him.

"What about my cousin?" I reminded him.

"What about your cousin?" Jude snapped. "Regan didn't do that for herself. I had to beg her to do it. And she only agreed in order to save the rest of us. Gabby spent three years holding us hostage. *My* girlfriend used her powers to free us. She would've *never* done it to help herself. She doesn't think she's worth the effort."

From the corner of my eye, I caught Regan again

smiling at Jude for defending her, but he was too busy glaring at me to notice her. He was a fool.

When Regan released her, Rory dropped the scissors and they clattered loudly on the floor. Hate burned on Rory's entire face and her hair billowed around her head like flames. "You bloody witch," she hissed and pointed.

Having no fear of Rory, Regan bent over with laughter. Between breaths, she said, "You really aren't very smart, are you? Nobody else got mad."

Rory stormed out of the room and tried slamming the door, but Jude caught it as he followed behind her. The muscles in Regan's jaw flexed and a wave of pain washed over her delicate features.

"All right. Fun's over." I shooed everyone from the room. "We'll pick up tomorrow where we left off. I still want to see how Tim and Pamela's powers work on the rest of you." As Regan strode past me, I touched her arm making her pause.

"Do you mind making me that list?"

She turned back toward Pamela's desk and snatched a sheet of paper and a pencil. She began jotting down her observations with quick short motions.

While I was curious how Regan would rank their strength—this experiment was about much more. During their stay, this particular group had gained power far faster than any other group we'd ever trained. At first, we thought it was because of the sheer numbers. But I had a different theory—Regan's powers acted as a catalyst. To me, it was the only thing that added up. She hung around with everyone but Rory. And everyone but Rory had gained power quickly. After yesterday's performances in the dining hall—I was almost positive I was right. The knowledge left an oppressive weight behind, because if I was, and her dad ever got ahold of her, he'd be unstoppable.

Halfway through ranking their strength, she stopped and looked up at me. "You know I wouldn't have done it. For the most part, what Jude said was true. Sometimes I slip but not when it comes to the big things. I would never make Rory cut her hair off no matter how much I disliked her. Unless she was hurting someone I cared about. And the only person she seems intent on ticking off is me. So," she shrugged, "she's safe."

I nodded, mortified that I even considered she would do something that egregious. "What's it like?" I asked. "Controlling people with different abilities?" My powers worked the same on everyone. Personality and constitution played no part in my ability to circumvent the brain. Regan was the only person I'd ever met who could truly resist my touch.

"Her energy's weak and snapped easily. Everyone else here is strong but flexible. It isn't just the strength of their energy that makes them formidable. It's more like their ability to bend without breaking that makes them stronger. Once they're broken, I'm inside and free to do as I please. Most of you are like trying to walk through water against the current. Some are raging rivers, others are merely creeks. Rory's a dry riverbed."

"And I am…?"

She bit down on her bottom lip and slid it through her teeth but didn't answer. Instead, she handed me the sheet of paper.

Levels 1-10 Weak to Wicked

1: Rory and all the other humans with no grit. I pushed her hard to make my point—very uncool that you thought I'd actually make her do it.

I swallowed, shame binding in my throat.

2: Navi—I didn't push her because I didn't want to embarrass her. If she can come out of her shell and stop worrying about what everyone thinks of her—she'll progress.

3: Humans with grit like my mom's boyfriend or my grandpa.

4: Ben and Pamela—both will get stronger with practice.

5: Tim—easy to get in but he also trusts me. He gave me pushback once inside—guess he didn't want to kiss you. Can you blame him? ;)

I chuckled and looked up at her with a raised brow. She smiled sweetly, though the curl of her lips held an edge of teasing, before strolling over to look outside the window. With her back to me, I kept reading.

6: Mae—harder to get past her defenses but once inside she was easier to control than Tim.

7: Andrew—it might have been worse if I'd picked modern dance or a strip tease (Mae would've enjoyed that)—there's always next time.

8: Jude—going against him I have to be angry or it doesn't work.

9: Gin—I'll hit you with some wild wishes. And with a bit more practice, I'll succeed.

My heart practically stopped, and then it fled into overtime. My mouth went dry. She wasn't going to need her powers to make me bend to her wishes. I'd capitulate willingly if they resembled my imagination. I reached out and grabbed my water bottle sitting on the desk, the plastic crinkled under my fierce grip. I took a sip while continuing to read.

10: Hopefully, I never meet this person in a dark

alley . . .

With my heartbeat semi-under control, I laughed. I often did with her around. It wasn't something I was accustomed to, but I enjoyed the way she made me feel. That might've been an understatement. With my head hung sheepishly, I said, "I'm sorry about that. I should've trusted you."

"It's okay. You haven't known me long."

I stared her in the eyes. "What did Jude mean when he said you don't think you're worth it?"

She itched her nose and heaved a long breath between her cheeks. "I try not to defend myself when others are mean to me. It's my penance for killing my father."

"You allow other people to treat you poorly because you think you deserve it? It was an accident."

She shrugged a shoulder as if she were trying to dismiss the importance of our conversation. "Pretty much. It was nice to hear Jude defend me for a change. It was like the old days when he thought I was the hero and not the villain." She glanced at the floor.

I stepped in front of her and lifted her chin with my fingers. Once she was looking at me, I said, "You listen to me Regan Braaten, you are worth defending. And if you won't do it, there are plenty of us that will. But most importantly, you are not a villain. As far as I'm concerned, you are," I took a breath, "perfection." My gaze traced the lovely contours of her face.

She tried pulling her chin away but I didn't allow it. A tiny smile quavered on her lips. "Thanks."

My arms closed around her and she pressed her face tight to my chest. I rested my chin on the top of her head and inhaled her sweet scent into my lungs. The yearning to have her, to possess her, to make her mine, and give her my heart in return was overwhelming. I needed to let her go, but my alter ego refused. And despite my better judgement, I didn't want to let her go either.

Chapter 32: Regan

In the far distance, the jagged peaks of the mountains were blanketed with everlasting snow. The cool morning breeze fluttered through my hair while I stood on the main deck of the lodge overlooking the lake.

I stuffed my hands into the pouch of my hoodie as the other students gathered around all in varying degrees of outerwear even though it was June. It was comfortable by my standards. Jude, accustomed to the brutal winter temperatures in Wyoming, was dressed much like me in jeans, sneakers, and a sweatshirt.

"Hey, everyone," Pamela said, coming out of the lodge. She was wearing an insulated skirt over leggings and a puffy winter jacket while gripping a steaming cup of coffee.

These people were crazy if they thought this was cold. I shook my head and shot a knowing smile at Jude. Shockingly he returned it. My heart fluttered which made him scowl.

Not wanting anyone to witness my disappointment, I walked over to the deck railing to watch Mr. LaCroix, Ron, Gin, Andrew, Cammy, and Casey pack our camping gear into multiple boats. It seemed as if whatever they had planned for us was a big deal.

It had been almost a week since I'd told Jude about the kiss Gin and I shared. It probably didn't help that I could control him now. His ability to resist my power was a point of pride for him, though he'd never admit it.

I'd tried getting him alone to see if we could mend the chasm we'd created, but he'd managed to avoid me for the most part. He'd told me he needed some time and most of that time he spent hanging out with Rory and Navi. I thought about showing up on his doorstep, and demanding we fix this, but decided against it. He'd requested space and I thought it best to honor his wishes.

But that also gave me time to reflect. Our differences were becoming glaringly obvious. Not only what we wanted out of life, but how we handled disagreements. I didn't like the silent treatment—and that was Jude's M. O. It's not like I didn't know, he'd weaponized it against me before.

Tim had deleted the video of Gin and Jude's argument and promised to keep Gin's declaration our little secret. I didn't know what to do with Gin's confession. Or that he told me I was *perfection.* The last few days—or nights—hadn't made it easier. Every time I fell asleep, I dreamt of Gin and the kiss that never happened. But it had. Surprisingly, I continued to act normal around him.

"Let's head down, it looks like they're almost ready for us," Pamela directed.

"What are we doing this time?" Ben asked. We'd only been here a month, but already he was getting much better with his illusions. He'd moved on from creating images of dead people to the scenery. It was weird to see the mountains vanish and a tropical beach magically appear in its place. Though he could fool the eye, he couldn't change the air temperature or the sounds to accompany the scene change. He promised that was next on his list.

"It's a surprise," Pamela said. She led us down the trail bordered by devil's club, ferns, and long wisps of fireweed. Half of the tiny flowers had bloomed, coloring the path in magenta and deep green. Soon they would be covered in wisps of cotton-like seeds that would eventually float adrift until they piled on the ground like colossal dust bunnies.

We separated into four different boats. I chose one without Jude or Gin. There wasn't enough coffee in the world for me to deal with them this morning. Plus, I had no intention of fueling Jude's anger by spending extra time with Gin.

I hopped in alongside Ben, Mae, Andrew, and Casey and strapped myself into an orange life vest.

Gin threw me a look of *seriously, what the hell*— since he'd been stuck in a boat with Rory and Pamela.

I didn't hide my amusement. "Sorry," I mouthed to him. *Better him than me.*

Casey started the engine, the noise vibrating my teeth, and slowly pulled away from the dock.

"Hey, Regan, how's your mom?" Andrew asked.

"Good. I talked to her yesterday." The remodel of the house was coming along nicely and she excitedly texted me pictures of light fixtures, faucets, area rugs, and new furniture. When she asked how Jude was doing, I lied and said he was great. And then I lied about what made him freak out and jump on a plane. I claimed that he overreacted to a particularly tough training session that I'd complained about over the phone. So, it wasn't completely a lie, more like an omission of truth. I was getting good at those.

"She still got that boyfriend?" Andrew asked.

I blinked slowly with my lips pursed in mock

disapproval. "Yup. And I like this one too. So, don't think about it." I aimed a finger at him.

"Okay, I have to ask," Ben said. "Is your mom really all that?

I got out my phone and showed him a picture.

"Oh, wow. No offense Regan, you're hot but she's smokin'," Ben said.

It's not like I wasn't aware. My mom was stunning, outside and on the inside. And I appreciated Ben still thinking I was hot though I had an inkling that he didn't bat for my team, which made the compliment even better.

"It's not just that." Andrew scratched his head. "It's like she has something extra. If she had been alive during the Renaissance era, she would've been someone's muse and not just because of her looks." Andrew glanced my way. "I know everyone says you got your powers from your dad, but I think you got something from your mom too."

I'd never really given it much thought, but she had that effect on all people, not only men. She was the flame. "It doesn't matter. Besides, you're like what, fifteen years younger than her?"

Andrew clasped his heart. "Age is just a number, Regan," he said, taking false offense.

"Yeah, that's what our cult leader said when he publicly announced I was to be his bride," Mae said with little inflection. If you didn't know her, you'd think she was indifferent to the horrific situation. She wasn't, she was simply past it. Her resilience was steadfast, and I aimed to be more like her.

Andrew's eyes shifted uncomfortably. Mae started laughing and he tilted his head in confusion like he couldn't tell if she was lying or not. She wasn't, but she was messing with him.

"I don't know," Ben said. "My mom likes 'em young. Legal but young."

"Seriously, do any of you have normal lives?" I questioned.

They all shook their heads. Casey said, "My dad talks to animals. When my mom found out she ditched us."

"Ouch." I swiveled around to see him.

"Honestly, things got better after that," Casey said. "I keep threatening to hook him up with Pamela. At least she knows what he is."

Now that Pamela and I were getting along, I could see it. "You might be onto something." I tapped the side of my head.

"I said I'd ask Tim to give her a push." Casey lifted the brim of his hat with a tilt of his chin so we could see the mischief sparkling in his eyes. "Dad *did not* think I was funny."

We all laughed. It wasn't hard to imagine Ron's reaction.

"Get this," Ben said. "When my mom turned twenty-one, she went to Mexico to celebrate and came home knocked up with me." Ben winked. "My grandparents were so upset I was half-Mexican, they threatened to disown her. So, she went and did it again."

Everyone's expressions varied from disbelief to horror.

"I have four siblings, each one of us from different cultures. The joke in our family is that my mom's collecting ethnicities," Ben said.

"Oh. My. God," Mae said with tears streaming down

her face. "Your story is as warped as mine and Tim's." She clenched her fists and shook them like she was cheering on her favorite sports team. "I love it so much. We really are a bunch of misfits, aren't we?"

"More like the miscreants," I muttered.

"Oh, I like that! I'm telling the others. That can officially be our title," Mae said.

"Just tell them you came up with it and not me."

"Good idea." Mae nodded. "It's not like I'm opposed to stealing things." She raised her palms upward next to her face, her newly acquired bracelets clinking together. She glanced at them and shrugged. "I told Navi I stole them. She said not to worry, I could keep them."

Mae had finally come clean with her kleptomaniacal proclivities so that she could return our possessions instead of throwing them away when she felt too guilty to keep them. It was a win-win plan. And now we teased every time we lost something as *pulling a Mae.*

Too soon, Casey maneuvered the flat-bottomed boat on the sandy shore. We hauled our gear up the slight hill to the clearing.

Standing on the porch of the cabin, Ron hollered, "Two tents for the girls—two tents for the guys. Figure it out."

My head snapped toward Mae and her head snapped toward me. We nodded in unison.

"Cammy," Mae said, "you can bunk with us if ya want to."

Cammy's shoulders dipped. She was the odd person out considering she didn't have powers.

"I'm going to bunk with those two," Pamela said, motioning toward Rory and Navi.

"Ahh, yeah, whatever you want," Ron dismissed but

I swear he looked disappointed. "You have thirty minutes to get your tents set up and your things situated inside. Then meet us around the campfire."

Finished in record time, the three of us girls congregated around the firepit as we waited. When the others joined us, Ron walked over rubbing his hands together with excitement. "Ladies and gentlemen, in the next few days we will not be messing around. You'll be going up against some of the finest ex-military and security people in the business. Your first mission will be to guard a high-profile target against our elite team. Your next mission—to capture said target from enemy forces."

My pet sat up straight and perked a proverbial ear. I glanced over at Jude and he met my gaze and held it. He nodded once as if calling a truce.

"The rest of today you'll be given time to plan your operations. But," he raised a finger, "in order to accomplish this with any amount of success, you must elect a leader."

"That's not fair." Rory slapped her hands on her hips. With an overexaggerated swing of her neck, she tossed her hair over her shoulders. Her blazing red spirals had almost as many personalities as my pet.

Ron pinned her with a hard stare. "Life's not fair. So, instead of whining, perhaps you should work on your skills," he admonished.

"This is just a popularity contest," Rory snapped. Pamela set a hand on her arm as if to caution her to keep her mouth shut.

If Rory spent half as much time practicing as she did complaining, she'd be high on that list. She could control the elements. But after a month, she wasn't much better than when she started. Sure, flowers and veggies were bigger and brighter after she'd spent some time with them, but what could she do with that? Bludgeon someone with a zucchini? Stab them with a carrot? And it's not like she could hurt anyone with the slight breeze she could create. The only advantage of that was she could keep us upwind. As for fire and water, her skills were non-existent. The other students had come much farther in their training.

Ron shook his head in exasperation. "No, Rory it's not. Often in our line of work, it's called survival."

"Not everyone has to go around *killing people*," she snarled and looked directly at me. An arrogant, knowing sneer ghosted the edges of her lips.

Jude's eyes widened and guilt exploded in his chest along with a measure of anger as if it were my own. No one was supposed to know about that. He'd been asked by me and Mr. LaCroix not to say anything.

His betrayal burned hot over my skin but despite the heat, a cold clammy sweat sheened my forehead. He'd been being a dick lately, but this was a low point even for his new, less improved, attitude.

Mr. LaCroix, Gin, and Ron glared at Jude. Their expressions ranged from disappointment to irritation. The rest of my friends gawked at me. Pamela pursed her thin lips while shaking her head, refusing to look Rory's way.

Ron passed us each a sliver of paper and a pencil. "Write down who you'd like to choose as your leader."

Without hesitation, I wrote Jude's name. Though I was hurt, I wanted to win. He'd spent hours in the wilderness tracking and hunting with his grandpa. I folded the paper and passed it to Ron.

Once he'd received everyone's choices, he scanned them before stuffing them in his pocket. "Regan and Jude. Looks like each one of you will be heading up a mission. You have the rest of the day to strategize. Everything you need will be in there." He indicated the canvas tent next to the cabin. "Get some food, then get started. Tomorrow morning it begins."

Tim slid up next to me with Mae and Ben right behind. "What was Rory talking about?" Tim asked.

"That week I was missing, I wasn't just at the airport meeting Jude or training with Gin." I blew a long breath hoping my friends wouldn't be as judgmental as my asshole boyfriend.

After I relayed my harrowing tale, they all stopped walking.

"Are you okay?" Mae grabbed my hand, pulling me to pause.

Ben gripped my shoulder and gave it a firm squeeze. "Dang, girl that's heavy. But I'd have done it too."

"Me too," Tim squeaked. "My parents see sex trafficking often in their business and have helped many people get free. They may make sleazy films, but their actors are always doing it by choice. Lots of people do it to pay for their way through college." He pushed up his glasses.

"Don't leave me out!" Mae said. "I probably would've spent some time torturing them first. They got off too easy if you ask me." She'd lived on the streets for years, so I was betting she had first-hand accounts of life in the shadows.

I swallowed the knot in my throat. "Thank you, guys. I can't tell you how relieved I am that you don't hate me too."

"Is that why he's being such a douche canoe?" Mae placed a hand on her cocked hip.

I half chuckled, half snorted at the term. "Mostly that."

"Those. Little. Beyotches. I'm going to kick their asses. Then I'm going to kick his." Mae spun abruptly but I snatched the sleeve of her coat. Tim was aware of the connection Jude and I had, so I confessed to the other two, explaining why he thought I was cheating.

"Damn." Ben laughed, rolling his finger in the air. "Drama."

"Score!" Mae said, slapping my butt. She was ridiculous and lacked boundaries, but I found it endearing. She danced around with her hands in the air as if we had something to celebrate. "I knew Gin had a thing for you!" she sang.

I wanted to tell them that I didn't know the initial kiss, but then I would have to reveal Gin's secret. And I wasn't like Jude, I didn't throw friends under the bus. *Friends?* Was that what Gin and I were?

"I don't get it," Tim said. He removed his glasses to clean them on the hem of his button-up shirt.

"What?" I watched as Jude and Navi grabbed lunch together and sat down next to the campfire. Pamela had Rory in the tent—hopefully giving her an earful.

"I don't get why you're bothering with that bloke, when you could have Gin. I mean, sure, Jude's handsome enough but the whole 'I'm better than you' attitude is ugly. Then he betrayed your trust and told Rory and Navi something he was asked to keep secret. It seems to me that you deserve to be treated better, is all," Tim said.

"Yeah, but—" I started to say.

"Gin kissed you correct?" Tim asked.

I nodded.

"Were you the one who stopped it?"

"Yes, but—"

Tim waved away my impending excuse. "I get it. I know what it's like using our powers, we're both innies, we get a bit freaky. And you didn't initiate anything. You ended it."

"Thanks, guys." It wasn't that Tim was wrong. The way Jude was behaving toward me seemed extreme and I wasn't sure if I wanted our relationship to continue.

Chapter 33: Regan

I stood inside the canvas tent staring down at the open binder that contained all of the information we needed for this first mission. Jude and I had decided to convene without the rest of our team so we could plan the attack without hurting anyone's feelings.

"What do you think?" I asked him. "About the mission," I clarified, avoiding the elephant in the room, why he told Navi and Rory my secret. Our orders were to rescue Casey from enemy forces. Though we were still in training, we were going up against GSS's global elite team. Some of the members had powers. Some didn't. The docket didn't elaborate on what kind of abilities they possessed but we assumed Andrew was one of them. However, it did inform us that they had six team members as opposed to our seven.

A separate binder contained our second mission; protect Cammy and keep GSS's elite team from kidnapping her. Again, six against seven.

The canvas tent was stocked with everything else: camo clothing, communication devices, zip ties, and more. Except for weapons. According to the information, *we* were the weapons and only the opposing team would be armed with paintball guns.

Jude pulled off his stocking cap and scratched through his short messy hair, ruffling it further. "I think I should head up the rescue mission and you should be in charge of the protection detail." He grabbed the other binder, opened it, and passed it to me.

"Agreed." His tracking skills would be put to better use that way. "And what about Rory and Navi?" I flipped through some of the pages not actually reading them—I was busy *looking* busy and keeping the jealousy out of my voice. My pet was awake and prowling. But after having been properly fed, it had been easier to contain. Though the desire to create chaos and mischief was like a constant itch I couldn't scratch. It vibrated above my muscles and under my skin as if tiny creatures were trying to break free.

"What about them?" he said cautiously.

I halted what I was doing and looked up. "I don't want them on my team."

He quirked a dark brow. "Noted," he said.

I scoffed and flattened my palms on the table. "No. Not noted. I'm in charge of the protection detail. The last time Rory was on my team she shot me with a paintball gun just to make me look bad. I don't trust her, and you shouldn't either." Especially, since an hour ago, she'd thrown him under the bus to make me look bad *again*. "I won't rely on someone I can't trust. As for Navi, she's Rory's lap dog."

Jude rubbed the back of his neck. "Yeah, you're right about Rory, but that whole 'I can teleport' thing might come in handy."

He was right. With practice, Navi had gotten much better. She could teleport three times without losing her strength. Plus, she could get through drywall now.

The corner of his lip rose in a cocky grin, his straight teeth showing bright against his skin. "Besides, she'll behave if I tell her to."

My jaw clenched and my pet hissed. "I'm sure she will," I muttered under my breath. Then I broke, "Are you even going to say sorry for telling them?" I wasn't letting him get off the hook that easily, even though it killed me to beg for an apology.

He glanced sheepishly at the ground and shifted feet. Remorse tightened in his throat. "I'm sorry. I shouldn't have said anything. It was wrong. I told them before I realized what the problem was—"

I was so fed up with his attitude, I couldn't even let him finish. "I said I'm sorry about what happened. I wasn't the one who initiated the kiss, I was the one who ended it. But I'm not sorry for killing those scumbags. They deserved it. And what did you think GSS hired someone like *me* for?" I said the word me like I was talking about a rotting animal carcass crawling with maggots. Because that's how he made me feel. Like I was garbage.

A millisecond of alarm flashed in his eyes before he erected his emotional wall. He picked up the binder and started examining it for the umpteenth time. "Look, I only said something to Rory and Navi because I'm worried about you."

My hackles rose but before I could yell, Jude held up his hand. "I wanted to see if GSS required the same amount of commitment from them as they do you. But you already know the answer. The others haven't harmed a fly with their powers, and you've already killed." He stared hard, daring me to argue. "GSS—Gin—all of them, I don't know. They're manipulating you, Regan," Jude said brusquely.

"But are they?" I almost burst out laughing. It's not like I hadn't thought the same thing in the beginning. But no matter how hard I searched for signs of insincerity in both Mr. LaCroix and Gin, I'd yet to find much. The only thing that bothered me was Mr. LaCroix's constant presence here in Alaska when his wife and daughter were in Wyoming. My parents were miserable to be around when they were separated. Deployments were hard on our entire family. I couldn't understand why Mr. LaCroix seemed so blasé without them around. But a strained relationship was a flimsy reason to suspect him of greater sins. I'd continue to dig, but so far, I'd come up mostly empty-handed. "They haven't lied to me. At least to my knowledge. Mr. LaCroix gave me the option of doing the job—or not." I shrugged. "I read those files, and if you'd read them, I'd like to think you would've done the same thing."

He slapped the book shut and dropped it on the table with a loud thunk. "Regan, it's a slippery slope. Especially, for someone like you."

My mouth hung open as a stab of pain knotted behind my ribs. "What's that supposed to mean? I've kept my pet on a leash. I haven't hurt anyone that I didn't choose to. And believe me, I've disappointed it a number of times. As I'm sure you know." I patted my chest referring to the fact that he could feel my emotions. "Instead of condemning me, maybe you should try and put yourself in my shoes. You've done it before, why can't you do it now?"

He shoved his hat back on his head. "That wasn't the same. You weren't playing God."

"But wasn't I? Besides, if God was the one who made me like this, then maybe he needs some help. So long as I'm able to balance the angel on one shoulder and the devil on the other, perhaps I can make this world a better place by killing one bad guy at a time." *A serial killer with a conscience.*

He leveled me with a stare. "*Thou. Shall. Not. Kill,*" he quoted one of the Ten Commandments. "It seems pretty clear. Besides, killing people leaves an irrevocable stain on your soul, Regan."

The need to defend myself from the one person who promised to love me—all of me, the dark and the light, was taxing. He wasn't wrong, killing did leave a stain on my soul. But being treated like this felt worse. Jude, of all people, should know.

Gin promised me that killing people, even though they were evil, *didn't* get any easier. And knowing that made me feel better. I didn't want to become indifferent to something so heinous. "I guess you're going to have to trust that I'm strong enough to carry the weight." Not that trust was high on his list. "Jude, what's going on with you? It's like I don't even know you. If you're going to break up with me, just do it already." The relationship limbo was wearing me down, making it harder to keep control of my pet.

He took a step toward me, then another until he stood directly in front of me.

I stared up at his face. His eyes were so dark they appeared black, his skin nicely bronzed from the sun, and his lips were so exquisitely sculpted, that I wanted nothing more than to reach out and trace them with my finger.

He swallowed. "Regan, we have to talk." He rubbed his sternum as if it caused him physical discomfort.

"Yeah. I know. But I'm not the one avoiding you."

"You're right. I have been avoiding you." He looked up at the top of the tent and cussed. "I saw Mr. Ling the other day and he said something that made a lot of sense. And for the last week, I've been in denial. I thought I could figure this out on my own. If I tried hard enough, I could control it like you do. But I can't. I can't seem to make it go away. I've tried."

"Jude, what are you talking about?" The war raging inside of him was like a fierce thunderstorm striking aimlessly starting fires. Only there was no rain to extinguish the flames.

I reached up and placed my hand over his, begging him to talk to me.

"When I forged our bond, I believe it created a pathway between our souls. Unfortunately, I don't think we're the only ones who can use it."

I cocked my head trying to think of anyone else able to navigate our connection. It hit me like a ton of bricks burying me in what should've been obvious. The blood drained from my face. "The golem. It affects you too?"

Tears welled up glossing his dark eyes and he nodded.

"Oh, God! It explains everything." I pressed my palms to my forehead.

The muscles in his jaw flexed, sharpening his already sculpted cheekbones. He grabbed my shoulder and held me in place. "Regan, what are we going to do? I don't want to lose you but I'm afraid if we don't break the bond, I'm going to hurt someone. Is this how you feel all the time?" The desperation clinging to his voice shattered me.

I hadn't felt that way since Jude had saved me. "With training, I'm getting a handle on it." There was no way I would admit the level of pressure Jude took from me that day. I couldn't—wouldn't—let him suffer because of my affliction. A sob caught in my chest but with a deep breath, I covered it. Between his breaking heart and the panic gnawing a hole in my stomach, my mouth watered as if I were about to vomit. He was my first love, and always would be. And now that I knew his awful behavior wasn't really his, I wondered for a second if there wasn't a way to fix us. But I couldn't let my selfish desires keep him from his dreams. "We have to break our bond."

He shook his head rapidly.

"Jude. It's not just that. We don't want the same things out of life and we both know it. I'm never going to be able to give you what you want. A normal life."

He started to protest.

I reached out and held his bicep. "No. You know I'm right. In order to stay sane, I'm going to do things that you will never approve of." And once we broke the bond, I had a feeling it was going to get much worse.

He licked his lips and inhaled slowly. "I can break our bond. It'll hurt, but as strong as we both are—we'll survive." He scrubbed his trembling hand over his mouth.

My heart already fractured, buckled under the weight until it shattered into a million pieces. We were really going to do this.

Chapter 34: Regan

After our agreement to separate, I was on the verge of tears. Not a fan of public displays of emotions, I grabbed some dinner off the picnic table and brought it back to my tent.

With a sniff, I held back the impending waterworks. Inhale. *One. Two. Three.* On the exhale, I meticulously separated my feelings and stuffed them into the appropriate boxes inside my head.

Later I'd take the time to process them, but I was afraid that if did it now, I wouldn't be able to stitch the pieces back together. Tonight, because of my mangled heart, my pet was fidgety. It liked to take advantage of my weakness. Tomorrow morning's shenanigans couldn't come soon enough.

Jude and I had officially broken up but we agreed to sever the bond after our missions were complete. He didn't know how the ceremony was going to affect us, physically or mentally, and thought it was best to wait. Until then, he asked if we could be civil. Though I wasn't the one having a problem with civility, I agreed. If that's what made his day easier, I would happily comply. I was the reason he was struggling to begin with.

Satisfied that my emotions were sufficiently contained, I stuffed a bite of bratwurst in my mouth. Mustard and sauerkraut squeezed out and dripped down my chin. I fumbled to find my napkin, when Gin said,

"Knock, Knock, I'm coming in."

The zipper of the tent opened, and he stepped inside only to close it behind him. He smiled while I wiped away the mess on my face. "Pardon me, am I interrupting?"

I swallowed quickly, nearly choking. "Yes." Though I was irritated, my pet pawed at the side of the glass like a dog begging for attention.

"My apologies. I'll make it quick." He pushed his hands into his coat pocket. "I needed to clear the air."

I cocked an eyebrow. There was more?

"Do you remember the day you were questioned by John Smith and Willa Zehn?"

How could I forget. They'd taken me and my mom into a private room on the military base without telling us who they were or why they were there. After my mom excused herself to use the restroom, they questioned me about my dad's death My mom's memory of the events and mine were surprisingly different. Or not so surprising.

I chuckled. "Oh, yeah, I figured that was you after you know—when you told me—,"

"I just wanted to be clear."

"Thank you." I bit down on the impulse to tell him Jude and I were no longer an item. Keeping Gin at a distance would definitely be considerate.

He unzipped the tent and stepped out.

"Stay away from her," Jude said loud enough that anyone in the near vicinity could hear.

Are you kidding me? I wanted to scream. We'd broken up. But my darkness was still tethered to him, so I cut him some slack.

I was about to slip on my shoes and put a kibosh on

the situation when Gin said, "That's not going to happen, Romeo." His tone, as always, was the pinnacle of politeness.

Both Cammy and Mae, standing right outside the tent door, giggled.

"I'm her mentor. And if you care for her at all, you're going to simmer down a notch. You are both going to have to be at your best if you have any shot in hell at winning tomorrow's mission."

"I don't care about tomorrow," Jude spat. I could feel his worry, jealousy and rage swirling in the pit of my stomach, making me nauseous. It was as if my affliction was purposely egging him on. I couldn't fathom why.

"Obviously, but Regan does. If you could control your temper, you might notice," Gin admonished him. "Now, if you'll excuse me, I have a meeting to attend."

I tossed my paper plate with half eaten brat to the floor and flopped back onto my cot before I placed my pillow over my face to muffle my frustrated bellow. *Could this situation get any worse?*

Mae stepped inside with Cammy behind her. "Whew!" Mae said with a round hand motion in the air. "That's a whole lot of testosterone flying in the air. So, who's it going to be?" She tapped a finger painted with black polish over her lips.

My brows furrowed. "What do you mean?"

"She means who are you going to pick?" Cammy's expression bordered on excitement. She tied up the garbage, threw it outside the door, and zipped the tent shut. It was Ben's night to make the trash sweep.

"Gin's my instructor," I dismissed like they were being silly.

"Don't be naïve, Regan. I already told you, *you're*

chum in the water darlin'," Mae mimicked Gin's accent.

Cammy nodded as she crawled inside her sleeping bag. "Yeah, I agree. Gin hardly talks to anyone, but he goes out of his way to be near you *and* talk to you."

"He has to."

She wrinkled her nose. "Nah, it's different. And I've known him longer. Plus, I heard Ron and his uncle talking the other day about how it was nice to see Gin comfortable touching another person. Apparently, Gin doesn't touch anyone. Even family. Something to do with his powers draining people's life force. I mean, we all know what he can do, but before he went to study with the monks, he didn't have much control and often wasn't aware he was even doing anything. Or at least that's what Mr. LaCroix said. Then he said it's as if your golem gives you a defense that other people don't have. Is that what you call it?"

"Yeah."

"What's it like?" Mae asked.

"It's like a golem made from smoke instead of clay living inside of my head. It doesn't talk to me or anything. It reacts based on my emotions and my commands—kind of like a dog I guess." *After all I did call it my pet.* "It lives in a glass cage so I can keep an eye on it."

"Fascinating," Mae said. "Mine's so boring. Yours is like having a pocket puppy only instead of carrying it in your purse, it's in your brain."

A snort of laughter shot out my nose at her comparison. A pocket puppy? More like a dragon biding its time in order to escape.

"But Cammy's right," Mae rambled, slipping off her shoes, "Gin definitely goes out of his way to touch you.

Sometimes when he looks at you, it's almost as if you can see the longing in those spectacular eyes. He's smokin' hot, girl. So, who's it going to be?"

"Neither." I threw them a dirty look and fluffed my pillow.

She scoffed at my dismissal while undressing to put on pajamas. She folded her black jeans and graphic t-shirt neatly and tucked them into her bag. "Jude's hot too. But don't take offense, he's a real prick. I guess if you're a sucker for the bad boys."

I wanted to tell them why Jude was acting so poorly, but he asked that I not say anything. I think he saw it as a sign of weakness not being able to control my darkness.

"And then there's Gin." Her voice took on a dreamy quality. "He's hot and *soooo* cold at the same time. Ohhh," she faked a shiver, "I'd like to crack open that glacier and have a peek inside. I'd choose him."

Cammy shimmied inside of her sleeping bag and pulled it up to her chin. "Me too," she whispered.

The golem settled into the corner and purred in agreement as if it were saying *me three*.

"Can you imagine what that boy is like in bed? Mmmm, mm." Mae basically moaned. "All that control. It's making me warm just thinking about it."

I picked up my shoe and threw it at her.

She raised her hand and the shoe slammed to a halt in the air. It hung there for a few seconds before she flung it my way. Her aim was good and I had to duck.

"What? I'm just saying out loud what we're all thinking." She chuckled darkly.

I'd spent plenty of time trying *not* to think of that. I didn't need their help.

After a few hours of tossing and turning in a fitful

sleep, I awoke in the predawn. Remnants of Gin's kisses ghosted over my skin and the distant howl of a wolf reverberated in the distance.

To quiet my racing mind, I slipped into my shoes and pulled my sweatshirt over my head so I could take a walk down the beach. Even though Ron, who had the power to control animals, cleared the nearby area of any dangerous predators, I grabbed a can of bear spray.

My feet crunched over the rocks as I picked my path along the lake shore. A thick fog hung over the water and mist coated my face. A woodpecker tapped a nearby tree like a keyboard and fish jumped out of the water landing with a splash.

The smell of decaying leaves and wet evergreen branches made my insides flow with delight and ebb into a small measure of sadness. My dad's memory was never far. I couldn't count how many times we'd walked together on beaches similar to this one. During the summers we fished, during the fall and early winter, we hunted. Moose meat and caribou were staples in our household.

My bottom lip began to tremble and tears clouded my vision. Misery burdened with guilt weighed on my conscience. I missed my dad. Desperately. I wondered if the pain would ever diminish.

I skipped a rock over the smooth surface of the lake. With every bounce, ripples fanned in a circular pattern all the way to the shore. Rays of light fractured through the pockets of fog creating an orange-yellow haze. On the other side of the water, a dark figure crept silently out of the mist. Goosebumps that had nothing to do with the temperature scattered over my skin.

I held my breath and my pet perked at my interest. I

squinted, thinking my eyes were playing tricks on me. Ron had cleared this area. Despite that, the largest wolf I'd ever seen stepped into a beam of light. Its black coat glowed indigo. It wasn't my first encounter with a black wolf. The last time, I'd been in Wyoming with Jude.

Though I kept perfectly still, he turned his massive head and stared directly at me, his golden eyes bore into mine as if he recognized me. Whether it was as another predator, or something more, I couldn't tell. He lifted his head and howled, the song hung long and lonely in the misty air. A shiver snaked its way down my spine and shot energy into my very soul. It was as if this terrifying, beautiful creature was my spirit animal. He walked over to the edge of the lake, his shoulders rolling with each step. He lapped up some water, took one last look at me—it seemed as if he nodded once—then disappeared into the forest. It was then that I knew what Gin meant when he said seeing his snow leopard was the most powerful moment of his life.

Chapter 35: Jude

I couldn't even look Regan in the eyes as we stood across from each other inside the canvas tent, solidifying our plans to rescue Casey from GSS's elite forces. Everyone else was outside waiting on my orders.

"Liar. Cheater. Whore. KILLER!"

I'd hoped the voice in my head would simmer down, once Regan knew what the problem was. Maybe she could get her pet to behave and stop harassing me. It wasn't working. I suspected it was now feeding off my sorrow. We'd broken up but that didn't stop me from loving her. What we had couldn't be erased in a day. And I wasn't stupid, the minute we broke our bond, she'd be a true free agent and Gin was biding his time, adding another level to my misery.

I couldn't take it much longer, but the thought of leaving her, severing our final tie, was too much to bear. That's really why I'd asked if we could wait until our missions were over. Not because I didn't know how the ceremony would affect us—though that was also true. It was my last-ditch effort to get ahold of the darkness. I was losing. And I hated myself for it. It made me feel weak and pathetic, like less of a man.

"Because you are," the voice whispered.

"You know," Regan said, interrupting my horrific thoughts, "allowing Rory and Navi on your team is a mistake."

"Well, it's my mistake to make, isn't it?" I snapped, dismissing her concerns, though she was probably right. I'd asked Rory and Navi not to say anything about Regan killing those two guys, but yesterday, Rory had proven she was only in it for herself. She found me later and profusely apologized. Though she said it was only right that everyone knew what kind of person they were dealing with. A part of me couldn't fault her, Regan could be dangerous.

Today, I'd decided to give Rory the benefit of the doubt. Her and Navi's opinions on the *'Gin and Regan'* situation had been invaluable. Rory claimed to see Regan and Gin holding hands while they were out on the lake before I got here. When Navi backed up her story, I knew it to be true.

Both agreed there was something going on between the two. Even though Regan still vehemently denied anything other than their kiss. I wasn't sure why I even cared, but I did. I hated the way Gin kept his eyes on Regan like a predator tracking its prey. Though we all knew Regan wasn't prey. And though I was jealous, I was also apprehensive about his influence over her. It was obvious she craved his approval, and it made me furious. How could she be so naïve?

"Your choice," Regan said politely. She gathered some communication devices in her hands before she exited the tent.

"Is it your choice? Or has she been controlling you this entire time? She can do that you know," the voice whispered. "You must sever your ties, it's the only way for you to be free."

It was bad enough her darkness was spiraling inside me, making me question my sanity, now I was questioning every aspect of our lives. Could she control me from the beginning?

I snatched the three earpieces she'd left behind and stormed outside. I handed Navi one. She reached out with a shaking hand. Her skin was pale, giving her a greenish-yellow cast and dark circles marred the skin under her eyes. I pulled her aside. "You don't have to participate if you're not comfortable," I said.

She looked at the ground and hiccupped a few breaths. "I know. I don't want to disappoint . . . anyone."

What she really meant was she didn't want to disappoint me. I wasn't stupid. I noticed the way she blushed every time our eyes met. Rory was much more direct in her attentions, though I believed she was more concerned with getting Gin to notice her. It made me question why she was so keen on Regan and I breaking up. I had no intention of telling her that had already happened. Maybe it was as simple as Regan said—she was stupid. Honestly, she didn't seem sharp. Having spent the last week around her, she was obsessed with herself. She reminded me of my ex-girlfriend Gabby.

"Everyone ready?" I called. They all nodded.

I handed Rory her com device. She wrapped her hair into a puffy ponytail, exposing her neck. "Can you help me?"

I almost rolled my eyes. Instead, I swiped a curl aside and positioned the piece inside her ear canal. Regan's emotions stayed surprisingly empty as I touched Rory. It hurt knowing that she was going to get over me far quicker than I was going to get over her.

"Follow my lead." They all fanned out behind me. Yesterday, I'd given them lessons on how to be silent in the forest and from the lack of sound, they'd learned something.

As we hiked, birds, squirrels, and insects created a cacophony of music all around us. So long as we didn't do anything to frighten them, they would continue to provide cover. About a half of a mile in, I held up a fist in the air for everyone to stop. A disturbance in the energy around me, and the slight hush from the forest creatures, warned that we were close to the enemy camp. I gestured one way with two fingers and then the other way signaling to split forces.

Rory stayed behind. Though I was mad at Regan, I trusted her instincts and after Rory's performance yesterday, it would be stupid to trust her.

I stopped at the base of a large tree with low branches, positioned my hands, and started to climb. The vantage point from above would be much better to locate everyone's auras. I instructed Rory to guard me. Once high enough, I grabbed the binoculars from my pocket and situated them against my eyes to scan the area.

Regan was to my left. I didn't need to see her to know exactly where she was. Our bond was like a tether, it pulled in her direction no matter where she was.

I spotted the four auras of the opposition and assumed the other two were inside the camo tent. Curiously enough only one had an abnormal glow and it wasn't Andrew.

"Sniper," I whispered over the com. "Two o'clock, fifty feet up in the tree. Aura—normal." It was purple with nothing to mark it as special.

"Copy," Regan said thirty seconds later. It took her longer to find the sniper without his aura giving away his location.

"Of the three others guarding the tent, the one on the left has powers. She's an innie," I said adopting Tim's terminology. Her aura was minty green and shimmered but didn't sparkle.

"She's all mine," Tim said. He needed direct eye

contact in order to make someone fall in love with him.

I had to trust that he could manage on his own. He'd been putting in long hours of practice and his powers had become quite formidable. When he'd used them on me, the longing in my groin and more disturbingly in my heart, was difficult to fight. But I had another theory on why he was so strong. One I took from my own experience. People wanted to fall in love—there was no better feeling in the world.

Though the guard Tim was currently enthralling didn't look happy about it. Her face was mottled burgundy and her lips were pulled back from her teeth in a snarl.

The sniper in the tree caught my attention when he tossed his weapon to the ground. "What are you doing?" I hissed over the com. Regan was supposed to make the sniper shoot the three guards.

"He's too strong," Regan said. "He won't do it. It was the best I could do."

"Navi, retrieve the gun," I ordered.

Navi suddenly appeared next to the tree and snatched the gun. She disappeared just as the two unoccupied guards lifted their weapons to shoot her. I was impressed, she was getting quick on the draw.

A millisecond later those guards threw their weapons aside, dropped to the ground, did three push-ups, two leg lifts, and jumped back up. Then they repeated the action.

I assumed Regan was behind their odd behavior. So long as it kept them busy, it would have to suffice. I would've been more comfortable with the situation if she would've complied with my original orders. But sometimes you have to adapt.

Soon, a thick fog rolled slowly like smoke through the trees toward the tent. Ben was good with illusions, but the bigger ones took longer to develop than creating ghosts.

I scurried down the tree and we followed behind Ben and Navi using the curtain of fog to hide our approach. Once we were close enough to the tent, Navi skirted around the back.

Regan was supposed to join us, but she was immobile in the same spot. She had the two guards doing burpees faster than I'd ever seen and the sniper was still in the tree.

Believing she had everything out here under her control, I motioned for us to step inside. Rory and Ben went first. As my foot landed across the threshold, it slowed as if it were swimming through gelatin. I'd expected it. Andrew, who could slow time, was sitting across from Casey waiting for us. Each had playing cards in their hands. They were the only two in the tent. My pulse accelerated as I realized there was an enemy unaccounted for.

I fought my way through the lag in time, but it was like trying to run fast in your dreams. No matter how quickly you needed to move, you couldn't.

Finally, Regan joined us and threw open the flap of the tent. The muted light from outside shined on two paintballs floating through the air as if they were on a Sunday drive. Strangely enough, I couldn't spot where they were coming from. Andrew's weapon was sitting on the table next to him.

I yelled. The single word was slow and distorted, "Duuuuuccccckkkkkk!!!"

Because of the lag in time, neither Ben nor Mae

were able to dodge the bullets. Red paint slammed into their chests with a long thump. Ben, able to maintain his balance, caught Mae before she hit the floor.

As Regan stepped through the tent, Andrew pulled back his power and time resumed. She fell forward and caught the ground with her hands instead of her face. Andrew howled.

She jumped up, wiping the grit from her palms then gave Andrew a thumbs up as if she approved of his tactics. In retaliation, she forced him to hold out his hands as she pulled a zip tie from her pocket and dangled it in front of her.

"Rory, Casey, get out!" I ordered. Once Regan had Andrew secured, he started playing a game of solitaire. "Regan, is he . . .?"

"Yeah, he'll be busy for the next few minutes anyway—I can't hold him for long with the others demanding my time." She tapped the side of her head.

She ran to the exit, thrust her hand through, and held open the flap as Rory busted out with Casey in tow.

The outside guards under Regan's control, their uniforms and faces dripping wet with sweat looked as if they were about to faint. She must have noticed because she let them stop. Both fell onto their knees.

The female guard was still in a mental battle with Tim. The expression on her face said she hated him, but the fact that she hadn't drawn her perfectly good weapon on any of us was proof that hate and love were birds of a feather.

Ahead, two *thump, thump* sounds whooshed from the tree line a split second before Rory was struck in the chest by a paintball. She flailed backward into Casey and they tumbled to the ground.

I ducked and rolled, trying to figure out where those shots originated from. I sprung up into a crouch and scanned the branches. The same guy was still in the tree, but somehow, he'd secured another weapon. I guess Regan wasn't as strong as she thought she was.

At the same time, the female guard collapsed to the ground. "That little mother—" she was interrupted by two more shots coming out of the trees. One hit me in the chest, stinging like a son of a gun, then nailed Regan in the shin, knocking her legs out from underneath her. She toppled over only to be shot in her butt crack.

"Ouch," she hollered. "Okay! You win." She was laughing but I could only imagine that hurt like a bugger. She rolled to her knees and lifted her hands in the air. Tim walked out of the woods swaying as if he were having trouble staying upright.

I gave Regan a dirty look and I hated myself before the words rolled off my tongue. "If you'd have just taken that sniper out like I told you to."

Earlier, we agreed that she would have the sniper shoot the guards, then turn the weapon on himself.

"It's not like she hasn't done it before." I covered my ears as the voice screamed in my head. *"She's a lying, cheating, whore, and a killer! And she can make you one too, if she desires."*

"Jude," Navi came up next to me and set her hand on my arm. She looked up at me with true concern in her dark eyes. "Are you okay?"

I patted her hand, grateful that someone cared. "I don't know."

If I didn't get rid of this thing, I was going to self-immolate and take everyone down with me. And that's when I knew for certain, in my wildest wishes, I couldn't beat this darkness no matter how hard I tried.

Chapter 36: Regan

After the competition was over, Mae sat down in the camp chair next to me. I did my best to ignore Gin sitting across the fire with his legs crossed. Was I avoiding him because we'd lost the mission? Sure. That's what I told myself.

"Does Jude expect you to do everything?" Mae curled her feet underneath her and placed a fleece blanket over her lap.

"No," I said. "You know that bond that we share?"

"Yeah."

"Well, it's been affecting him too. I just didn't know until recently."

"Oh God." Her mouth dropped open.

"He didn't want me to say anything, but I can't sit here and have you think he's a bad person when he's actually not. We plan to sever our connection soon."

"Why wouldn't he want you to tell anyone?"

I shrugged. "Because he's a dude. I suspect he thinks it makes him weak not being able to control the darkness."

As the rest of my friends sat around the campfire, I stared at Jude's beautiful face. The flames licked over the contours of his cheeks, his forehead, and reflected in his ebony eyes. I remembered a time that my staring at him was enough to warrant a desperate search for somewhere private. Though technically, we'd only been together for four months, the promise we'd made to each other was forever. But it was my turn to save Jude, and forever with me would destroy him. The thought tore at my soul leaving a huge, seeping wound. It was for the best, but it didn't make it hurt less.

Instead of dwelling on the ache inside my chest, I got up carefully from my chair—my butt felt as if I'd been crack attacked—grabbed a marshmallow out of the bag and shoved it over the point of the stick. I held it close to the bed of embers, determined to roast it to the perfect golden brown. Resting on each of Mae's knees were graham crackers with chunks of dark chocolate waiting for the pièce de résistance.

"Tim!" Mae said. "You're a rock star!" His face burned red, but he looked proud as a peacock showing off his exceptional feathers.

"No, doubt!" I agreed.

Then I told everyone that I'd met his nemesis once before. Her name was Willa Zehn. But I didn't know what her powers were. She and her partner questioned me after the death of my dad. They were the catalyst as to why my mom made us relocate to Wyoming.

"Tim," Rory asked. "Did you find out what kind of powers Willa has?"

"Nope, once I took hold, I didn't let go." He pushed up his glasses with his middle finger to make his point.

"Like a dog with a bone, bruh." Ben chuckled. "I'm just going to call you Dog, from now on. It fits on so many levels."

We all joined in the laughter. He was right.

"You were in a fight to the death and you hung on until the end. I want you on my team now and forever." I leaned closer to fist-bump Tim.

"Regan, I'll be your team from now on until the day I die," he vowed, crossing his heart.

I looked at him—really looked at him—and said, "Deal." Who would've thought one of my best friends would be a fourteen-year-old boy with glasses and braces who dressed like a 70s porn star?

He reached out with his pinky and we shook on it.

"You guys all did great," Jude said but the emotion behind it was dead.

Cue the guilt always within reach. Because his pain was my doing. "Jude's right. You guys were amazing! Navi, you snatched that rifle so quickly they didn't even have a chance to shoot you. And Ben, wow, man! That fog was serious. I couldn't see a thing!"

"I'm disappointed in my performance," Mae said. "I'm excited to try it again tomorrow."

I rotated the marshmallows slowly so they didn't burn. "Don't worry, I have plans for you. Tomorrow, you're mine. I'm going to have you steal anything you can get your hands on. Preferably their weapons, but should other things go missing?" I shrugged innocently.

"Awesome." She rocked her head.

"But I could've sworn that sniper today didn't get down from that tree. I made him toss the gun, then ordered him to stay. Getting him to shoot his teammates was taking too much time. Willa and the other two guards spotted us just as I took control of the sniper. Tim had her under the influence of Cupid, but the other two were going to shoot him. Sorry, Jude, I had to make an executive decision and I guess I made the wrong one. Are you sure it was the same sniper that ended our game? I swear I had him."

"He was the only one up there," Jude sighed as if he

were tired of explaining it.

His soul was weary, and I probably should've dropped it and taken the blame. But my gut told me we were missing something and if we didn't figure it out by tomorrow, we might lose again. "Yeah, but I thought there were supposed to be six of them. That's what our information said. And so far, I can only account for five: Andrew, Willa, the sniper, and the two other guards."

"Well, maybe they lied to throw us off," Jude said.

"I guess." I pulled the marshmallow out of the fire and scraped it off on the graham cracker. I picked it up, offering it in front of me. "Anyone else?" I'd already fed most of them dessert.

"Or maybe, Jude missed someone," Tim said.

"I didn't," Jude grumbled.

A smile crept up on Gin's face and he turned away trying to hide it. "I'll take one," Gin said.

I walked around the fire and handed it to him. He grabbed my hand before I had a chance to leave. "You did good Regan." Something pleasant quivered in my stomach at his praise. I didn't know how to make it go away. Without letting go of my hand, he looked at everyone else. "Y'all did. I was impressed and I'm curious about how tomorrow's going to go."

Jude's attitude blazed behind my ribs, so I pulled my hand away from Gin and rubbed the spot over my chest as if it were heartburn.

"Well, it's been real," I said, "but my feet are killing me. I'm going to bed."

"Yeah, right, your feet! You mean your butt?" Ben exaggeratedly rolled his eyes.

I snarled a teasing lip at him, "Douche!"

"Me too," Mae said.

"Me three," Cammy chirped.

They sidled up next to me and each threw an arm around my shoulder. Cammy was a head taller.

Mae said over her shoulder, "We're out," and threw a peace sign behind her.

* * * *

Over breakfast the next morning, I asked my core group, "Hey, can I talk to you guys?"

I tossed my paper plate into the fire as we snuck past the tree line so the others couldn't hear us. Rory and Jude took a moment to glare at us, Gin cocked a curious eyebrow my way, and Navi was too deep in conversation with Casey to notice us.

"So, this mission is mine to conduct, and I've been wrestling with this decision all night. Do I leave Rory behind or do I trust that she won't sabotage us?"

"Personally, I'd leave her behind." Ben scuffed the dirt with his cowboy boots. Though the rest of us settled on sneakers, he insisted the leather soles grounded him giving him better access to his powers. "I thought I overheard Navi saying something to Casey about Rory enjoying that yesterday's loss was your fault. I could be mistaken. We should ask her."

I waved Navi over. Jude and Rory started coming our way.

I shook my head and mouthed, "No."

Jude grabbed Rory's arm and stopped, his eyes flashing with ire. She glanced up at him and it looked like she said, "What are they doing?"

Jude shrugged, tucked her arm into the crook of his elbow and led her back to the campfire as if she couldn't find it on her own.

I turned away as Navi pushed into our circle.

"What's up?" she asked. "And why aren't they invited?" She motioned to where Jude and Rory stood.

"I'm conflicted on whether to include Rory in this mission."

Navi's usually buoyant expression faltered. "Uh," she stalled, "why are you asking me?"

"Because you spent all night with her," Mae said.

"Yeah," Ben said, "Plus, I overheard you talking with Casey."

"Oh, well," Navi's shoulders rounded, "if I were you, I'd leave her behind."

"Problem solved. This should be fun," I muttered, heading straight for confrontation.

"You're not alone Regan." Tim rested a hand on my shoulder. "You never will be."

"Nope." Ben grabbed my other shoulder and gave it a squeeze.

"Can't get rid of me that easy!" Mae pushed Tim and Ben out of the way. She jingled my gloves in front of my face. I snatched them out of her hands. "How do you do that? I didn't even notice!"

"I'm magic," Mae said. She clasped Cammy by the arm and skipped ahead.

They stopped in front of Jude and looked back waiting for the rest of us to catch up.

Once we did, I stared at the ground for a long pause before meeting Jude's gaze. He was still holding onto Rory's arm.

"It's unanimous. Rory, you're out."

Her lips parted.

"No, it's not," Jude said. "I didn't agree to this."

"Yeah, you did. When we decided this mission was mine to command. Against my better judgment, I went along with your wishes yesterday."

"Yeah," Rory spat, "and look how that turned out. You're the reason we lost."

The desire to lash out was strong but then Gin's advice about the Monks never reacting simply because they didn't have to, kept me still. As *the* apex predator, Rory was no threat to me. So, I overlooked her jab, even if I didn't like her.

But she was wrong, I had that sniper under my control. We were missing something. I addressed Jude. "Regardless, this is my mission and I get to decide who's with me."

Jude finally let go of Rory and crossed his arms over his chest. He took a step closer forcing me to look up even further. "Fine, then you can do this without me too."

I stepped back, not expecting his venomous answer. The anger roiling inside of him was consuming his every decision. We should've severed our connection earlier, but there was nothing to be done about it now. I vowed as soon as we finished today, the deed would be done.

My pet growled though it almost sounded like laughter, as if it enjoyed pushing Jude's buttons. "If that's what you wish," I said quietly.

"Bruh," Ben said, horrified. "I thought you're supposed to love her—funny way of showing it. Don't worry Regan, we'll figure it out on our own."

"No." Mae shoved her way into Jude's personal space. "We need you and you know it, Jude. Man up, I know you can do it." She smacked him hard in the chest. He took a step back. "Seriously dude, are you hoping we fail? Is that what you want? If it is, get the *flock* out of here. If not, swallow your damn pride, fix whatever is going on, and help us."

His jaw muscles twitched and rolled.

"Screw them," Rory said. "Not only is she a killer, she's a cheatin', lying, whore."

"Are you kidding me?" Jude recoiled as is she'd slapped him. "Don't you dare call Regan that! Wait," he yelled. "Mae, you're right. Regan, please wait! I'm sorry." He jogged up next to me. "I'm sorry," he repeated. "You know that I am." His eyes twisted with regret as did the emotions swirling inside.

The darkness he was experiencing was something I was well acquainted with.

I reached out and grabbed his hand and gave it a hard squeeze. "I know. Now get your ass out there and help me win."

Chapter 37: Regan

The drizzling rain collected in the forest canopy and pelted my black waterproof jacket. Mae gripped my hand reassuringly before we separated into our hiding spots amongst the thick underbrush.

We crouched in silence while Ben, who was standing outside the camouflaged tent, created a heavier, thicker fog. It didn't take him long because it was misty already. I wanted our enemy to think we were using the same tricks as yesterday. Once his illusion was well established, Ben ducked under the flap and disappeared inside.

About ten minutes passed before Jude announced over our communication devices, "Incoming. Again, there are only five. Two on the right flank—three on the left. They're headed straight for the target."

I nodded at Mae.

Willa was easy to spot even though her long hair was pushed up under her black ball cap. She was tall but much narrower than her comrades. Next to her was Andrew, his normally happy face was serious and focused as he scanned the area.

The golem whirled inside the glass box in anticipation. I slid the lid open and a coil of black smoke zoomed over the side.

I wish.

Tingles shot from my chest to the tips of my fingers

and the tips of my toes. *Dance, boys,* I ordered.

The three guys to the left stopped and froze. One of them shook his bald head as if he couldn't believe it was happening again. All of them fought against me, but today it was easier as if yesterday's shenanigans made me more formidable.

Mae took advantage of their brief distraction and ripped the paintball guns from their hands. The weapons flew in the air, one after the other like a wave at a sporting event, and crashed to the ground approximately twenty feet away.

From inside the tent, a kickin' country song with a rap beat started to play. I found it was easier to get people to comply with my wishes when they were fun and accompanied by familiar tunes. It was as if the music relaxed them and helped me get inside their heads.

Having grown up around military bases, I knew that G.I.'s loved to go to the bar and dance. *Let's go gentlemen.*

All three of them placed their hands on their fictitious belt buckles and took two steps forward and two steps back. Hand clap, twirl to the right, hand clap, twirl to the left—all in time with the country hip-hop song blaring on the stereo. I'd worked at a restaurant/bar in Wyoming for an entire year. I had more than enough moves to keep them occupied for hours.

Andrew couldn't help himself and he started wailing with laughter. Mae, always good with her timing, took that opportunity and ripped Andrew's paintball gun from his hands. His smile disappeared and he cussed as the weapon dropped to the ground. Willa jabbed him in the ribs with her elbow. He cussed again, though he didn't look seriously mad. How could he with his comrades burning up the dance floor?

Andrew took a step toward the gun. As he leaned over to grab it, Mae scooted it out of his way.

I had to suppress a giggle at the indignation that crossed his face. He lunged for the weapon, but Mae was quicker. She forced it sideways as Andrew stumbled.

I looked over at her and the smile on her face was a combination of diabolicalness and pure joy.

Willa, having given up on her partner, pushed the flap of the tent open with the barrel of her paintball gun. She cautiously stepped inside.

Though I couldn't see what was going on, we had it all planned.

Ben was hidden inside a wooden crate with enough room between the cracks for him to see out. It was latched with a combination lock so no one would think to look there. His job was to use his illusions to disguise Navi as Cammy. And vice versa. The girls were sitting at the table with Tim. Once an enemy stepped inside, they were to rise with their hands in the air. Whoever the lucky—or unlucky recipient was—they would be subject to Tim: The Dog.

"Oh, my God!" Tim shrieked over the headset.

My eye twitched as I shied away trying to escape the screech. Since the com was attached to my ear, I failed. I rose from my position prepared to save him, but Mae snapped her fingers and shook her head. She was right, Tim had proven himself.

"Oh, my God!" he cried again. "I need the dunny!"

Mae and I both looked at each other with our brows furrowed and mouthed, "What?"

"I'm going to pee my pants," Tim whined.

And then it dawned on me. The day Willa and her

partner questioned me after I killed my dad, my mom excused herself from the room because she had to use the ladies' room. *No way. No freaking way.*

"Tim," I said calmly. "You don't have to pee. That's Willa's power. Willa has pee power."

Laughter accompanied by a few creative comments echoed over the headset. My mom's recollection of that day Willa and her partner questioned me was very different from mine thanks to Gin.

"Uh," Tim groaned again.

"Hang in there, buddy," Mae whispered. "I'm coming."

Andrew, having given up on his paintball gun, went inside.

Mae hurried from her hiding spot and rushed into the tent. My job was to sit and wait. I needed the enemy to think my hands were full controlling the line dancers. When the song switched so did their moves.

Jude, having crawled down from the tree he was hiding in, came and waited beside me. His foot tapped to the beat of the music, even he seemed to be enjoying himself.

"I can't hold it any longer! I need the dunny!" Tim's voice was an entire octave higher than normal, making him sound like a cartoon chipmunk.

At the same time, Andrew came out of the tent holding onto Navi who was masquerading as Cammy thanks to Ben's illusion.

The hiss of a paintball gun being fired and a thunk, echoed over the headset followed by a string of Australian slang words from Tim—which I assumed were not complimentary— but they were comical nonetheless. Willa ran out of the shelter and caught up with Andrew. She grabbed Navi's other arm and they quickly escorted the wrong girl away.

Even though my pet was busy choreographing another line dance, it took a moment to pirouette in joy. We weren't finished.

Jude and I snuck to the backside of the tent where he pulled a knife from his pocket and cut a hole so we could get inside without being seen.

I hurried over to the crate Ben was hiding in and rolled the lock to the correct combination. I snapped it open and helped him out.

"Go," I said.

His job was to follow Navi without being caught. A closer location aided his abilities.

Jude grabbed the real Cammy by the hand and met my eyes. "You got this?"

At odd times, it struck me how handsome he was; his ebony eyes, looking at me for confirmation, those sharp cheekbones I'd traced with my fingers a million times, and his full lips I'd kissed until they were swollen. He took my breath away. But in order for him to survive and live the normal life he craved, we needed to part ways. Hopefully, we could still be friends. Because the idea of not having him in my life was depressing.

"Under control." I signaled for them to go. Mae, Cammy, and Jude slipped out through the back.

"What happened?" I reached down to help Tim off the floor.

"That bloody fruit loop got the drop on me, man." He didn't seem to want to get up.

"Looks like we did it." My lips dipped downward as if I didn't quite believe it.

"Yeah, let's just hope Ben's illusion lasts long

enough for Jude to get Cammy to safety."

"Well, that's what we're staying back for. Glad ya didn't get shot." I was relieved to see that Willa had missed her target. At least with her paintball gun. Red color was dripping down the side of the canvas like spilled blood.

Tim shook his head. "Naw—"

"You got the wrong girl!" A deep, disembodied voice shouted from inside the tent.

My head whirled toward Tim. Our eyes met. We were the only two people in here.

"Stop!" The voice hollered again and our stereo turned off all by itself leaving us in silence. "Stop!"

Instinctually, I grabbed a bottle of soda off the table and whipped it toward the stereo.

It stopped in midair and fell to the floor like it had hit a wall. That wall grunted.

Tim stood up, grabbed a coffee cup, and tossed the liquid toward the same spot. Coffee ran down the side of someone—who was apparently invisible.

"Shit, that's hot!" he yelled.

I could sort of make out a hand trying to remove the liquid.

Tim and I locked glances and nodded once. I opened the box and let a twine of smoke loose.

I wish.

I made the guy press play on the stereo.

Tim made him fall in love.

With both of our powers being used together, it seemed as if our subject was thoroughly disoriented, making him quite easy to control. I reined my pet in before it did something stupid.

All three of us yelled and jumped back in surprise

when Navi popped up in front of us.

"What's going on?" She tilted her head and stared at the strange apparition covered in coffee. Slowly the guy's true form started to materialize.

Her eyes grew round as a naked man took shape. Shock painted her features while pink spread up her neck to her cheeks. "Anyway," she said, drawing it out, blinking a few times. Then she rattled quickly, "With all the yelling the enemy is on their way back. Ben's doing his best to keep them busy. I'll go help him." She ran out of the tent.

I tossed the guy my rain jacket and ordered him to tie it around his waist covering his junk that was saluting the flag.

Seeing the sweat running in rivulets over Tim's face, I made the guy sit down in the chair and grabbed some rope off the table to tie him up.

"Okay, Tim. He's secured." Tim released a huge sigh and his whole body slumped.

The profanities that escaped the guy's lips were impressive. But he didn't sound mad, quite the opposite, he sounded amazed. "I don't even want to tell you what that felt like," he chuckled.

"BDSM?" Tim guessed as he turned away and tied his rain jacket around his waist. I had noticed the wet spot on the front of his pants.

The guy hooted loudly, nearly falling over in the chair. "Yeah, something like that. You can untie me now, Andrew's called it. You guys win."

"Ha, ha. Smooth. I'm not untying you until Mr. LaCroix calls it. We aren't taking any chances."

Over the headset, I heard Mr. LaCroix chuckle. "Congratulations, Regan, your team wins."

Chapter 38: Regan

Upon being declared the winner, I ripped out my earpiece and I threw my fist in the air. "Yeah!" I could hear the rest of my team yelling over the com device even though it dangled by a curly cord over my shoulder.

I reached out to hug Tim, but he put his hand up. "You don't want to hug me," he said.

"The heck I don't! I worked on a ranch—you'd have to do better than that to gross me out." My eyes darted to the front of his wet pants and I rushed in to hug him anyway. I whispered in his ear, "I'd never say anything, but if I were you, I'd wear it as a badge of honor. You held your ground making sure Willa couldn't use her weapon on the rest of us."

Even though I was sure the naked guy couldn't hear us, he said, "Willa's made all of us pee our pants at one point or another. That girl's a few cards short of a full deck. Now can one of you please untie me?" He held out his arms.

"See?" I quirked an eyebrow at Tim and began to work the knots loose. Once finished, I jerked the rope away and tossed it on the table.

"Whoa." The naked guy shook out his hands and rubbed his wrists. "Nice knot work."

"Thanks, my dad taught me." My dad had grown up in Washington state on Whidbey Island. His grandparents, who raised him, owned a sailboat.

Unfortunately, they both died in a house fire right before he graduated high school, leaving him with no family. He didn't talk much about it, but when he did, I could see how much losing them at such a young age affected him.

"Yeah, I wasn't getting free of that and I'm quite adept at slipping out of traps." He stepped closer to me. My first instinct was to back away. It probably had something to do with the fact he was only wearing a coat tied backward and nothing else. "They call me Casper."

Both Tim and I snorted but I shook Casper's hand. He was only a few inches taller than me.

"You're Regan and you must be Tim." He reached over and shook Tim's hand. "Honestly, we've all been excited to meet you kids." His dark brows knitted together in a frown. "I probably shouldn't call you kids seeing how you just beat us."

I said, "It's fine. Technically, we are teenagers."

"Hey, can we head back to camp?" He gestured over his shoulder with his thumb. "It's freezing out here."

As we exited the tent, I handed Casper my gloves and my stocking cap. "I think the weather's particularly beautiful today."

"I'm certain fire and brimstone could be falling from the sky and you'd think today was beautiful," Casper said.

"You're probably right." I was walking on air. The normal feelings of guilt I carried for being *me* had temporarily vanished. Part of it was the high I was experiencing from letting my pet loose and part of it was—we won.

Ben, who'd been waiting for us at the edge of the clearing, fell into step next to us. He didn't say anything, he just pointed at Casper like *WTF*. Tim took it upon himself to clarify the situation.

When we were almost back to camp, I heard footsteps from behind. I swiveled to see Jude jogging toward me with Cammy on his heels, her blonde braid bouncing over her shoulder.

Jude did a slight double-take at our mostly naked companion before he picked me up and swung me around. Now that we were all together everyone started whooping and hollering. I threw my head back and laughed into the wind. We. Won.

My feet slowly descended to the ground. Once planted, I placed my hand on Jude's hard chest to keep from falling over. His warmth radiated into my cold palm and a tingle snaked its way to my heart.

A grin of victory and happiness lit his handsome face and softened the normally hard edges. It had been a long time since I'd seen a sincere one. I matched his grin and bit down on my bottom lip. With lightning speed, he reached behind my head and brought his lips to mine.

Confusion erupted through my system like pyrotechnics on the fourth of July. We'd broken up.

"One last kiss before I have to let you go," he said, breathlessly.

Our emotions tangled together, and I couldn't differentiate mine from his. Love, hate, desire, betrayal. Pain. So much pain.

He buried one hand into the back of my hair and pulled me closer with the other, gripping my lower back almost painfully. His lips were hot and warm and he tasted like peppermint gum.

"Get a room," Tim yelled.

Jude stopped kissing me and pushed me away. His

eyes were wide with surprise, then they slivered into resentment. I stumbled back

He huffed and shook his head like what happened was all my fault. "We broke up," he hissed. "You did this! You've been controlling me this entire time, haven't you?" He stomped away.

I stood there frozen in shock with the breeze chilly on my wet lips. He was the one who kissed me.

"Go," I heard Gin say to the others.

As they passed me by, Tim messed up my hair and Mae squeezed my shoulder. "I still think he's a dick," she said.

Gin stepped in front of me and placed his hand on my cheek. With his thumb, he wiped away a tear I didn't know was there. I blinked slowly trying to clear the fog in my brain. *What just happened?*

I looked up into Gin's green eyes. There was anger, pity, and something else I didn't want to acknowledge, hiding in their emerald depths. It made my breath hitch. Normally, he was very good at hiding his emotions. Or maybe this time he wasn't trying to disguise them.

Having him here to comfort me wasn't going to help with the Jude situation. "You should go," I insisted, backing away. The cold air quickly replaced the warmth of his hands.

He tucked them into his pockets. "What kind of man would I be if I left you here like this?" *Ouch.* That was a not-so-subtle dig at Jude. "Besides, I tried to give the boy the benefit of the doubt." *Double ouch.* "After the fiasco with my cousin, he seemed as if he was good for you. But if I'm being honest, I don't like him anymore. And I don't know why you do either."

"We broke up," tumbled out of my mouth without

permission. I'd planned to keep it under wraps until all of our ties were gone.

His eyebrows rose, questioning the scene he'd walked into but instead he simply asked, "Why?"

"Because my pet has found a way to navigate our connection."

He inhaled sharply. "I see. That explains a lot."

"That's what I said."

"And what are you doing about it?"

I told him that Jude and I had plans to break the bond tonight after everyone else went to bed.

"I'm so sorry. That must be difficult. But I'm not going to stand here and pretend I'm not pleased." He hesitated then shook his head as if he shouldn't say whatever it was he was thinking.

I crossed my arms over my chest and gripped the opposite shoulders with my hands, giving myself a hug of sorts.

"You must realize I have feelings for you. I don't believe I've been that subtle and surely, Tim must have said something?"

I nodded into the crook of my elbow. "But I didn't know whether you were just trying to irritate Jude or make him jealous enough to go running after me like he should've." I slid my arms down and shoved my hands into my pockets. The nerves buzzing in my stomach were making me fidgety.

"Can't it be both? But mostly I wanted him to know my intentions weren't completely honorable. I've never looked at you as my student. Always my equal. Even before you arrived here, I had a crush on you."

My nose wrinkled in disbelief. "You did?"

He tapped the end of it with a finger. "Don't look so

surprised. You're gorgeous. And you're not, by any means, boring." He shifted his weight. "And there's nothing that can be done to save your relationship?" he asked even though he'd just confessed that he had feelings for me.

I shrugged. "I don't know. But honestly, even if there was, Jude and I wouldn't last. It took me a while to figure it out, but we want different things. The way I'm going to have to live my life—he wouldn't be able to live with that monster."

Gin ignored my plea to keep his distance and stepped closer. He slid his hands on both sides of my face and tilted it forcing me to look at him. "You listen to me. You are not a monster. You are NOT a monster. The monks taught me, no matter what preconceived notions people have of you, *you* are the one in control of who you are and who you'll become." He caressed his thumb over my cheek before he released me. "Ultimately life is simple, when we disappoint ourselves, we have two choices—do better or do worse. These choices lead you down every road in life. And you, Regan Braaten, are the type of person to choose better."

I wasn't sure I agreed with him. Often my choices were—do bad or do worse. But I was talking to the one person who actually understood my predicament.

"Nod, if you understand me." He nodded, a crooked grin creeping up as if I were a child and I should mimic his actions.

I copied him, stashing his advice away for a rainy day.

He clasped his elbow through mine—I tried pulling away—but he set his free hand on my arm and refused to let go. As we walked to camp, a feeling of comfort and safety edged with something far more dangerous swelled behind my ribs and pressed against the bone like it was about to break free.

Before we cleared the tree line, I pulled Gin to an abrupt halt, not quite ready to face my friends or Jude. I desperately hoped once we were separated, he would revert to the person I'd known.

Gin gave me a minute of silence before he sighed and tucked my hair behind my ears. "Now, no more tears Darlin', you have a victory to celebrate."

Chapter 39: Regan

Ahead in the clearing, our two teams had gathered around the fire pit and appeared to be happily mingling. Some of them were warming their hands over the leaping and cracking flames. Others were relaxed comfortably in chairs holding drinks. Laughter resonated through the forest. The only person missing was Rory.

One of the guys without powers saw us and threw his hands up in the air as he jogged our way. "There she is!" He stopped in front of us with his hands on his hips in an exaggerated fashion like he couldn't believe what he was seeing. "Regan Braaten. Craig's little girl, all grown up. Time sure does fly."

My jaw dropped. "You knew my dad?" Gin continued walking and though he didn't touch me as he passed by, tingles concocted from inappropriate dreams and desires slid down my spine.

"Absofloggin-loutly! I'm Doug Mack. We went to West Point together. I'm so sorry I didn't make it to the funeral, I was overseas on a mission."

I inhaled in recognition. "Little Dougie Mack?" I questioned because *little* was quite the opposite of reality. He wasn't overly tall but his biceps had to be the circumference of my waist. My dad said he was the best sharpshooter he'd ever seen. According to him, Little Dougie Mack never missed a shot.

Doug's blue eyes crinkled to nonexistent as he

tossed his bald head back and hooted. "I haven't been called that for years. Oh, it's good to see you again. You look just like your dad."

I was so used to that comment, it didn't bother me anymore. "That's what everyone says."

"Come on, let me introduce you to the rest of the crew," he said. He stopped next to the cabin and grabbed a beer from Pamela who was re-stocking the cooler. She handed me my favorite soda and shooed us on our way.

"You were the one in the tree on the first day, weren't you?"

"Yes, ma'am, that was me."

"Can I ask you a question?" I popped open the tab on the aluminum can. It hissed.

"Shoot," he said.

"Why was it easier to throw your weapon than shoot your teammates?"

He stopped walking and crinkled his forehead. "You mean the answer isn't obvious?"

"Well, yes, of course. But I never get to ask normal people what it's like. I could tell getting you to turn on your friends was going to take too long but ditching your weapon seemed easier."

"It was crazy. I felt you in my head take control." He gripped his skull with his free hand. "I was supposed to be prepared for it, we all were. But I wasn't. Your gift is a different beast. That first thirty seconds was like wrestling a giant anaconda wrapped around my brain. Honestly, it was paralyzing. When you gave up and made me toss my weapon, it was all too easy. But I'm here to tell you, another ten seconds and you would've had me."

My lower lip dipped in surprise. The way he was

fighting me, I didn't think he was about to give up. "Good to know. But FYI, you were *a lot* harder to control than the other two."

"You've no idea how happy I am to hear you say that." Everything about him wilted in relief.

"Don't tell them, okay?" I didn't want to hurt anyone's feelings if I could avoid it.

He pretended to zip his lips shut.

"Can I ask you another question?"

He nodded.

"When did you find out about my dad having powers?"

"Well, I suspected he was special early on. The way he could get people to cooperate, even when his suggestions were outlandish, was unusual. But I didn't know for sure what it was until GSS started recruiting him a few years ago. Then all the crazy stuff we did throughout the years began to make sense."

"They've been after him that long?"

"Yeah. Craig wanted out of the military and he could retire with his twenty years at any time. Joining a security company like ours is often a natural progression. But it was a big decision. I mean, the things we do aren't always above board. His biggest concern was protecting you guys. I didn't understand his hesitation at the time." He pointedly glanced down at me. "I do now."

"Huh," I said. Knowing my dad as well as I did, his working for GSS was probably a stretch. He was a good person and never did anything violent or illegal as far as I knew. My mom was more likely to push those boundaries. Maybe I got that part of my personality from her.

"Did you know I was there the day your parents

met?"

I shrugged. I knew that my dad and some West Point buddies had taken a ski trip to Wyoming over the holidays. My mom worked at the lodge. They met there.

"Every single one of us had a crush on Sara. She was so beautiful and it turned out that she was nice too. But after those two laid eyes on one another, the rest of us were as invisible as Casper. I'm still a little disappointed." He rubbed his chin between his thumb and fingers.

I laughed, men often were when it came to my mom.

"Come on, they're dying to meet you." He dragged me toward the campfire.

Mr. LaCroix and Ron stood on the deck barbequing dinner while Casey and Cammy laid a red and white tablecloth over the picnic table. My stomach growled as the scent of fresh grilled salmon wafted through the air.

Tim had changed his clothes, but he took my advice and wore his pee pant story with pride. He was sitting between two of our champion line dancers getting an earful on all their pee pant stories.

"Yeah, the first time she got me," one of the guys said, alluding to the fact she'd done it more than once, "we were five miles in on a ten-mile run. She hit me so hard I didn't even have time to whip it out. It ran down the leg of my BDU right into my boot and by the time I got back, I had blisters."

"Nice of you to explain why I retaliated. You put toothpaste in my shampoo bottle, ya dick," Willa defended herself from across the fire.

"I probably deserved it." The guy held up his beer bottle in a distant toast.

"You deserved much worse." She crossed her legs.

293

"Yeah, I guess I'm lucky you didn't make me cramp up from diarrhea."

"Exactly," Willa said sweetly. Her dark hair was pulled into a ponytail. Tendrils had escaped around her ears and neck making her appear less severe than she had the first time I'd met her.

"You two," Andrew said after he sipped his beer. "So, which one of you headed up which mission?" His eyes darted between me and Jude as he picked a spot to sit next to Mae.

She turned her head and wiggled her eyebrows at me.

"I had yesterday's mission," Jude said. He was across the fire settled between Navi and Casper. "And it looks as if I owe Regan an apology. She was right, there was another person out there. I couldn't see his aura. Even sitting here, it looks more like a mirage shimmering around him. Out there in the bush, it's non-existent."

"Yup." Casper nodded, the ball on the end of his stocking cap wobbled. "I heard you were a real prick to her yesterday over it too."

Jude swallowed. Guilt clogged his throat.

"I was. Regan, I'm sorry. I should've trusted you." He held up his hands.

I smiled tightly and nodded. This would all be over soon. For both of us.

Jude's nostrils flared, picking up my relief.

"So," Doug said, breaking the tension, "You've met Casper and you know Willa and Andrew."

I gave her a small wave. She held up her beer and tipped her chin.

"The one in the suspenders is Ethan and the other fool is Jake."

"Those were some mad dance skills you taught us." Jake removed his baseball hat and flipped it backward. His dark hair poked through the clasp. "But let me show you how a real hoe gets down. Do you mind playing me that first song?"

I opened my phone, connected it to the Bluetooth speakers sitting on the ground next to Navi, and pressed play.

Jake jumped up and embellished the country line dance with some hip-hop moves of his own. Even though the guy was well into his thirties, he could move.

"Come on." He crooked a finger at me, mischief sparkling in his dark eyes.

"No way." I crossed my arms.

"Oh, come on," Ethan prodded, running his fingers over his hipster goatee. He stood up and twined his thumbs under his suspenders and stretched them out. "It's only fair. I'll join you and I just learned the steps today."

I sighed and placed my soda in the drink holder of my chair.

Pretty soon all of us were dancing—some of us sticking to the original moves, others trying, mostly failing, to copy Jake. Mae and Andrew were doing the two step. It seemed as if she'd picked up some skills other than theft while living in Montana.

Jude held his hand out to Navi, and they started copying Andrew and Mae. So, he could continue flirting, but if I did it he still got angry?

I wished Jude's actions didn't bother me. I wished I didn't have a heart. I wished I could be the monster he thought I was. It would be so much easier than pretending to be the nice guy.

After the song ended, I caught Jude by the arm. "Are you ready?"

Chapter 40: Jude

Nobody questioned us as we walked out of camp, but their silence spoke volumes. Regan's friends didn't like me. I couldn't blame them—right now I didn't like myself. Once our bond was broken, I could only hope I would go back to being me. I wasn't perfect, but those imperfections were far easier to deal with before Regan.

I stopped by my tent and grabbed my backpack. I'd thought about leaving it at the lodge so I wouldn't be tempted to sever our bond. Once Mr. Ling *diagnosed* the problem, I was so sure I could mold Regan's darkness, bend it to my will, or force it to yield. It's easier to slay the monster when you know what you're up against. I was wrong.

"Do you have everything we need?" Regan waited outside the tent fussing with the cuffs of her sweatshirt.

"Yeah. Lead the way." I gestured after I stepped out.

Dusky light illuminated the trail along the lakes edge. Water gently lapped on the shore. The distant sun hovered on the edge of the horizon painting the sky in a sorbet of colors and reflecting on the cool sheen of Regan's hair.

I swallowed down the bile crawling up the back of my throat. I wasn't all that worried about performing the ceremony; the medicine man had gone over it with me multiple times. I was scared what would happen to Regan afterward. The twisting, coiling, anger that squeezed my guts, forcing my temper to the surface without my permission would revert back to her and she would, once again, have to bear the burden alone.

I clenched and unclenched my fists and let out a deep breath.

When we came to a small peninsula, Regan stopped. "Do you think this will work?"

"Yes." I cocked my head. "Have you been here before?"

She nodded. "I was here yesterday morning. I couldn't sleep. Right across the lake," she pointed with most of her hand still tucked inside her sweatshirt, "I saw a wolf just like the one we saw together back in Wyoming. Do you think it means something?"

The hairs on my arms and the back of my neck rose. "Yeah. You know it does. What are your thoughts?"

"You know . . ." she licked her lips nervously, "my pet often feels . . . like a wolf. It prowls, it growls, it whines, it paws at the glass. Please tell me this isn't a bad sign. Those stories you gave me about Loki, and, Fenrir, and Ragnarök—it's kind of scaring the shit out of me."

Me too, but I kept my expression calm. "I think what you saw might be your spirit animal."

"But I'm not Native American."

I chuckled. "You may not be from the same tribe I'm from, but you are native to earth and I don't think she cares where you came from. Plus, we're not the only culture that believes in such things."

"I guess," she said, not sounding convinced.

"After we do this," I referred to severing our bond, "you need to ask your spirit animal to reveal its name. I think the stronger the bond you have with it, the better."

Her eyes widened and a shot of fear and refusal

traveled over our connection. Soon, it would be gone, and I knew, to a certain degree, I'd miss it. When we were good, the bond between us was epic, as if we were connected on a deeper level. Experiencing each other's highs and lows, dreams and desires, wants and needs. But with this latest development, it was like one of us threw gasoline on the fire and there was only one way to smother the flames. Cut off its supply line.

I grabbed the arrowhead hanging around my neck and rubbed my finger over the smooth, but sharp stone. The motion helped me think. "I don't know what the wolf represents exactly, but I do know it's powerful. It's my grandpa that's the 'expert'," I air quoted, "not me, but I'll ask him about it when I get home if you want me to."

A small amount of relief trickled through.

"Please."

"Do you think we can still be friends after everything I've put you through?" I asked.

She scoffed with a laugh. "Everything *you've* put me through? All of this is my fault." She circled a finger in front of her. "But I want to clear the air. I may have lied to you about the kiss, but other than that, I've never cheated on you. And as for controlling you, I've only done it that once. Not before and not after. I need you to know that."

I rubbed the back of my neck. "The worst part about it is—I do know. But whatever this thing is, I can't compete with it. I'm afraid if grows worse, I'm going to do something that I can't take back." Admitting to that weakness was difficult. The voice in my head often mocked me because of it. Surprisingly, it was silent for the moment.

"So, friends then?"

"Friends," I agreed. "I wouldn't change anything, Regan—except for this ending. This isn't what I had in mind for us. I know it has to be done. But I don't think it will stop me from loving you." A knot pinched in my throat and my sinuses burned. Once this was over, I had plans to go home. Working for GSS wasn't my dream and soon there would be no reason for me to stay.

Tears pooled in Regan's blue eyes mirroring my pain. "I know. You were my first love." Her chin trembled and she sniffed. "I'm not sure I'll ever feel this way again. But our promise of forever was an illusion and it's kinder to both of us to end this now while there is a chance to salvage our friendship. I can't change who I am to fit the person you needed me to be. The irony is—you taught me that. Now take your own advice. Please?"

The tears building up in my eyes spilled over. I looked up at the sky and prayed for the strength of my people. I was going to need it.

With the back of my sleeve, I wiped away the tears. Once semi composed, I opened my backpack and gathered my things. While Regan wandered the shoreline randomly skipping rocks, I started a fire and unrolled a leather cloth over the rough sand. I set the supplies out in the order I needed. "Whenever you're ready," I called.

She dropped the stone she was holding and turned around. The black cloud of smoke roiled over her head and around her neck like a scarf. Tiny sparkles glittered inside.

I looked away and pointed for her to sit across from me.

She sat down and folded her legs underneath, biting

her bottom lip. "Will this hurt?"

"Yes." The medicine man said it would but because Regan and I had mutually decided to split, it wouldn't kill us.

I lit the bundle of sage on fire and sweet smoke wafted from the tip. The chant the medicine man had taught me was a slow repeating rhythm. I closed my eyes and started to sing.

Soon a calmness enveloped my spirit as if funneling through my pores, saturating my skin in power. The seconds ticked by, and the scent of burning sage changed to sulfur. Regan sneezed and then whimpered. I chanted through my fear. The medicine man said I was not to get distracted by anything. No matter what happened once I started the ceremony, the most important thing was to finish it. If I didn't, Regan and I would be open to momentous spiritual threats. He implied that whatever was attached to her would have free reign. Having experienced just a fraction of what she dealt with, I couldn't imagine setting that creature loose on the world.

A warmth built in my core and heated my skin. It started out pleasant, like being in a sweat lodge but soon turned into a fever of flowing lava rushing to the surface. Rivers of sweat dripped off my nose and chin. Without warning, a razor-sharp knife stabbed into my sternum and split it down the middle. Or at least that's what it felt like.

I stifled a groan and opened my eyes. Between the imaginary break in my ribcage, a substance shimmering like a liquid ribbon snaked from my chest connecting Regan and I together like an umbilical cord. It curled and swayed until it stretched tighter and thinner as if it were trying to rip our hearts out. My hand shook as I held the smoldering bundle of sage under the bridge. It puckered and bubbled in the middle then began to sizzle, smoke rising. The smell of scorching flesh made me gag.

Perspiration shined over Regan's face and her fists were clenched in her lap, her knuckles bone white. A banshee-like wail tore from her lips, and she clutched at her chest.

I wanted to pull the flame away from the cord, but the medicine man's warning echoed in my head.

With a loud pop, the ribbon broke and snapped into my chest. My head slammed back as the pain and heat receded.

When I looked up Regan had her arms wrapped around her body as if trying to hold herself together, red streaks staining her pale cheeks.

I wanted to go to her, to help her deal with the aftermath, but a wave of euphoria hit me like a tsunami. As if all the darkness I was carrying slowly siphoned out of my body and drifted away on the cooling breeze.

A lightness swelled inside my soul filling me with the greatest sense of relief I'd ever known. Instead of jumping for joy, my shoulders curled, and heaving sobs wracked my chest.

At some point Regan got up and knelt behind me enveloping me in a hug with her head on the back of my shoulder. "Are you okay?" she asked.

I nodded and, once the tears stopped, I answered. "I knew the anger I'd been dealing with was bad, but I didn't realize how bad. But now that it's gone . . . How do you manage?"

"With a lot of practice."

"How are you feeling?" I asked.

"Honestly, Jude, except for a broken heart, I feel the

same as before. I think whatever portion you were carrying drifted away before it had time to travel the bond. I'm going to be okay. Are you?"

"I am."

Chapter 41: Regan

I sat up on my cot with my sleeping bag gripped in my fists and sweat clinging to my forehead. Embarrassment bloomed on my cheeks, down my neck, and spread over my chest. My hands covered my face trying to shield me from the dream. *The memory.*

I'd spent many hours denying that I had feelings for Gin. Because I loved Jude and initially, I wanted to repair our relationship. But things had changed and now I was free. Free to no longer tip-toe around my feelings.

Heaving a breath, I checked the time on my phone—it was ten in the morning, but we'd all gone to bed late. Mr. LaCroix gave us permission to sleep in since they had no plans for us today. Cammy and Mae both snored quietly as others began rustling outside of the tents.

"Get them up." Mr. LaCroix's voice hovered outside the tent. It held an urgency I'd never heard.

A minute later Gin said, "Knock, knock," before he started unzipping the tent.

I answered, "Who's there?"

He passed up the perfect opportunity for a joke alerting me that there might be trouble. "Oh, good you're up. Wake Mae and Cammy. There's an issue and we need to get back to the lodge."

"What?"

He waved a hand. "Get them going and I'll tell you later."

After having spent the last couple of nights with them, I learned they were both heavy sleepers and no amount of yelling was likely to disturb them. Reluctantly, I crawled out of my cozy sleeping bag and got dressed.

"Wakey, Wakey." I shook each girl by the shoulder.

Mae and Cammy, neither morning fans, grumbled but complied.

With my pack over my shoulders, I stepped outside. Willa and her team were busy helping break down camp. With their aid, we were done quickly. Ron handed out granola bars, coffee, and orange juice for breakfast before everyone piled into the boats.

Gin grabbed me by my jacket sleeve. "You and I are going to stay back for a minute. That way I can explain the situation without anyone overhearing us."

"Regan, are you coming?" Jude asked. He stood next to the boat with his arms crossed waiting for me.

"I'll be right behind you," I called.

He nodded and gave me a small wave. Even though we were not longer an item, we were bound to worry about each other.

Gin tugged on my arm and led me into the forest.

"What is it?" I asked.

He kept walking at a brisk pace. "Let's give it a minute."

"Well, unless one of them has superpower hearing, I think we're safe." I practically had to run to keep up with him.

"Regan, it's not us I'm worried about."

I scowled. "What's wrong? Is my family okay?" Panic began to hum between my ears. I caught up to him and grabbed his arm to stop him.

"Yes, Regan, your family is safe. For now."

"What's that supposed to mean?"

"Regan." Gin's voice was sharp. I let go of his arm. He'd never used that pitch on me before. "I don't know how you're going to react to what I'm about to tell you. I need to make sure the others are far enough away that you can't accidentally hurt them."

I inhaled sharply. Well, at least he gave me the benefit of the doubt. "So, the further away we are, the sooner you'll tell me what's going on?"

"Yes."

One scenario after another, from bad to worse, propelled me up the mountain. By the time we got to the top, I was winded. Gin, in better shape, gave me a second to catch a breather. I rested my hands on my hips. "You're afraid that I could hurt them, but not you?"

"I'm the only one up for the challenge, Darlin'."

"You're sure I can't hurt you?" I wanted to know what the problem was, but I didn't want to endanger Gin. I couldn't live with myself if I killed someone else I loved.

My gaze dropped to the forest floor, along with my stomach and my self-imposed delusions. *Holy shitballs.* Of all the time to realize I was in love with Gin. Why now? And how was that possible? Jude and I just broke up. I should still be pining for my first love, but I wasn't. Not at all. It's not like I didn't care about him, but the obsessive love I'd once felt was gone.

Gin placed a finger under my chin. A tingle spilled from his touch like a steady burn warming my skin. "No, Regan, you can't hurt me. Not like that." The something I refused to recognize was no longer hidden in the depths of his emerald eyes. Or then again, maybe it never was, maybe I had just refused to see it all along.

I shied away, too confused to deal with all the conflicting emotions swirling in my heart.

Disappointment skimmed his features before he swallowed. "But I do need you to prepare for the worst-case scenario. Can you do that? Lock your pet in its cage and hide the key."

I took a couple of deep breaths and visualized my pet secure in its prison. It was pacing around the perimeter as if it knew something catastrophic was about to happen. Unfortunately, the glass box wasn't always the barrier I needed it to be.

"Are you ready?"

I nodded.

Without a preamble, he dove into the deep end. "Regan, your father is alive."

"What?" I'd heard wrong.

"Your father is alive." This time he said it slowly.

Joy like no other blossomed inside my chest making me feel faint. Stars flickered at the periphery of my vision.

"H-h-how?" I reached out and grabbed his arm.

He cocked an eyebrow. "Are you okay?" He stepped closer to hold on to me.

No. "Yes." My pulse whooshed loudly inside my ear like my skull was about to explode from the news. Gin, noticing my distress, gave me a minute to calm down. I nodded, signaling I was ready to hear the rest.

"You see when your dad was hit by the bus, he didn't die. He would've if I hadn't been there. But with my ability to circumvent the brain, I was able to slow his vitals and we had enough time to get him to the hospital."

"Why didn't you tell me this earlier?" As I began to

comprehend what Gin was saying, the golem rose into a tidal wave of curling black smoke and hovered.

"There she is," Gin said with a slight smile. "We didn't tell you because it was touch and go for a few months. His brain was quite swollen, and we weren't sure he was going to make it."

"Why didn't someone tell us?" I whispered, trying to maintain a measure of calm. "He needed us. Maybe we could've helped." The notion that my dad had been lying in a hospital bed, alone and perhaps scared, when his family could've been there for him, fueled a toxic reaction within my heart, my head, and my golem.

"Honestly, I think everyone was scared of your reaction, should you lose him a second time." He paused and blinked calmly before he continued. "It was decided, for your mental health and the safety of others, we should wait and see if he woke up. Did you really want to go through his death twice?"

I could've been by his side, holding his hand, urging him to stay with us. "But he was alive," I said between clenched teeth. I was doing everything in my power to keep my pet under my control. My body tremored from the effort. My mind screamed as if the neural pathways were sizzling like an underground vein of coal.

"Barely. He was in an induced coma for months. But eventually, he woke up." Gin sounded muffled as if he were speaking to me through a long tunnel or underwater.

"And yet, you still didn't tell me he was alive," I whimpered on the verge of defeat. Sweat poured down my spine settling in the waistband of my pants and under my bra strap.

Gin stepped backward out of my grasp, with closed

eyes he bowed his head and took a deep breath. When he looked up emerald flames danced around his pupils making him appear possessed. "Regan, the man who woke up in that bed wasn't Craig. He had amnesia. He still does as far as anyone can tell." His voice was low and controlled but something menacing hovered around him. It was as if I could sense his alter ego even if I couldn't see it.

White light whooshed in and out of my peripheral vision. "So? Don't you think seeing his family might have helped?" I wasn't even sure I said it out loud until he answered.

"It could have. But when he woke up, he was different. Dangerous. It's as if his moral compass was gone, leaving the darkness we both suffer from in control."

A blinding flash exploded inside my head as the golem crashed into the side of its prison. Shards of shattered glass hurled into my brain. Pain ripped through the fabric of my mind. I grabbed the sides of my head and screamed. And screamed. And screamed.

The mountain shook beneath my feet or that could have been just my perception as I fell to the ground on my hands and knees.

I was unaware of how much time had passed when the pain receded one notch at a time and finally subsided to a tolerable level. My pulse battered under my ears and my chest heaved, trying to catch some air. The high I normally got was absent. It always was when my pet broke ranks. But at least this time I was still alive and, as far as I could tell, I didn't need a hospital.

Panic, almost as terrifying as the pain, struck me directly in the sternum.

I brushed the pine needles and dirt from my knees then the palms of my hands as I rose to see if Gin had survived. He was standing where I'd left him with a smile curling his lips that resembled hunger in the most primal way. His pupils were so dilated his eyes were virtually black. For the first time, he looked like the predator he was. And God he was beautiful.

"Are you okay?" I started to rush to his side.

He held a hand out. "Don't," he yelled. His voice was gruff and he was breathing as hard as I was.

"Gin, are you okay?" I wasn't scared of him—I was scared for him.

He lifted his index finger but refused to look at me choosing to stare off to the side.

"Gin," I said gently, "you would never hurt me."

The laugh that rumbled from his chest was like nothing I'd ever heard. It was almost as if his pet was the one laughing, not him. "I'm not worried about hurting you, Regan. I'm more concerned about throwing you down on the ground and making you forget Jude ever existed." He lifted his head and looked straight into my soul. My pet, though exhausted, strained to reach him.

Shit. I'd mistaken a lustful smile for that of actual hunger. Because of my concern for him, I hadn't noticed the pheromones he was tossing around like rice at a wedding. My body, despite my feeble objections and having other things to worry about, responded. Heat flushed up my face and desire, that almost brought me to my knees clenched low in my center urging me to run into his arms and give him exactly what he wanted. I squeezed my eyes shut and turned my head away not wanting him to see how he affected me. Us rolling together in 'the hay' would not solve any of my current problems. No matter what I wished for. I forced my feet to spin and walk away. A moment alone was required in order to control my desire. I was very much afraid if I looked at him again, I'd fail.

I paced between trees, attempting to talk myself out of going back and making him keep his promise. Though there was no denying I was attracted to Gin physically. But it was more than that, I was attracted to him mentally too. He'd once told Tim and Jude that he was my perfect match. More and more, I was beginning to think perhaps he was right. I'd just used all of my powers on him. The first time that happened, I killed my father. Or at least I attempted to. The second time, I'd frozen an entire gymnasium of people, shattered the overhead lights and sent myself to the hospital. But here Gin was, still standing, looking like a twenty-two-year-old God out for vengeance. Or something far more dangerous. Me.

Chapter 42: Gin

With my hands balled into tight fists, I shoved them into the pockets of my jacket and waited for Regan to compose herself. That was a lot of heavy information to throw at her and I wondered how she was going to react. Was she going to hate me? Or no longer trust me? I couldn't blame her if she chose both.

My breath hitched as she walked out of the woods. Beams of sunlight, fractured by the tree branches, spread around her like a halo of light.

She stopped in front of me and asked, "You okay?" She didn't seem angry any longer but there was a wariness about her shoulders that concerned me.

"Yes, ma'am. I'm sorry about that." I could feel my shame flaming over my skin.

A tight smile broke from her face. "No, need. I've been there more than once."

I reached up and swept her long bangs behind her ear. The cravings I'd smothered threatened to reignite as I felt her warm soft skin under my fingertips. "Funny, you're the only one who affects me like that."

Her lashes fluttered as if she didn't know how to respond. She skated around my admission, attempting to direct the conversation elsewhere. Fear gripped my heart as I realized my feelings for her might not be reciprocated. Every time I'd hinted at them, or even when I outright confessed how I felt, she dodged the proverbial bullet.

But I couldn't let go of the notion there was something deeper between the two of us. Her face often contradicted her actions, and she had trouble hiding the desire in her eyes. I wasn't sure if it was because of the connection between our powers or something more profound. If she would only open her heart, I knew together we were destined for a lifetime of happiness. Maybe I was high.

She blinked and stared at a spot behind me as if she didn't want to meet my gaze. "Now that my pet's under control, can you finish telling me about my dad? You said when he woke up, he wasn't himself. That he's dangerous. But so am I." The quality of her voice was empty sounding much like her father.

"Can you promise to keep yourself calm no matter what I say or how I say it? You can't hurt me, but I don't want a repeat performance from you—or me."

She locked her arms behind her back. "My pet has been exercised and well-fed. For now, it's napping."

"Okay, then. Yes, you can be dangerous, but most of the time you choose not to. Craig, it seems, has lost the ability to tell right from wrong. He's detached. More like a true psychopath."

Silver flashed in her eyes, and I waited to see if she could keep her promise. Once she was calm, I continued. "Though in the last few months, Craig seemed to be making some progress. We had plans to reunite the two of you once your powers were stronger and more stable."

"And?"

"We were mistaken. Craig's darkness was never under control. The monster learned to disguise itself in plain sight. With Dr. Gloria's ability to shield other people's powers, we all thought she was safe in a room alone with him. We were wrong. And now she is dead."

Her face creased into confusion then crumpled into anguish. I wanted nothing more than to wrap her in my arms and make the nightmare disappear. But that detour would take the rest of the day and I wasn't sure my advances would be welcome. Especially after I'd lied to her for the last couple of months.

"What? How? Why?"

"Craig killed her."

She set her jaw. "No, he didn't. My dad would never kill someone. Not unless he had to."

Though I didn't want to show her the video, knowing I was about to cause her more pain, it was the only way. I dug my phone out of my pocket with a sigh. "I don't want to show you this but I'm afraid it's the only way you'll believe me."

She reached out for my phone, but I held it back. "You must shut down your emotions Regan. I mean it."

"Okay."

I pressed it into her palm but didn't release it until I commanded, "Lock them up."

Her blue eyes widened, and she nodded before she pressed play.

First, a smile grew from her lips, and then tears pooled. A gambit of emotions—excitement, love, and hope—washed over her beautiful face. I went around behind her and placed my hands on her shoulders as I watched the video with her, so she didn't have to do it alone. Though it upset me almost as much. Dr. Gloria was more than a friend to me, more than a mentor. She was my sounding board, the voice of logic when I ran astray, and my biggest fan. All the things a mother should be. I considered her to be my family. In the blink of an eye, she was gone. A beautiful soul wiped from this earth because of darkness. It had me wishing Regan would've killed him. Or that I wouldn't have saved him.

In the footage, Craig was sitting across from Dr. Gloria with his legs crossed comfortably as if he were having a conversation with a friend. My friend.

"How's your day been?" Dr. Gloria inquired. Her eyes, magnified by her reading glasses, looked guarded. She was behind her desk holding a pencil in her hand jotting down notes.

"Peachy," Craig said, though his tone was detached.

"Did you get a chance to check out those videos of your family I gave you?"

"Yes. I watched them all."

She stopped writing and looked up at him. "And did it help?"

He shrugged. "I still don't remember them. I mean the girl's obviously mine. And I have no reason to believe the other two aren't if my relationship with Sara was as good as it seems from all the information you've shared with me."

"But no real memories or feelings have been triggered?" Dr. Gloria asked.

"No. It's like watching a movie about my doppelganger's life."

"Hmmm, how are the treatments going?"

"The shock therapies? They're electrifying."

"Craig, be serious, now." She removed her glasses and rubbed the bridge of her nose. They hung from a gold chain over her red sweater.

He re-crossed his legs and jiggled his dangling foot

in the air. "Do you still have plans for my lobotomy? I think my brain has had enough abuse."

She glanced up at him. "It's not a lobotomy we've been talking about."

"Your deception of the truth is admirable, but I think I'll pass. I enjoy my brain as is. Thank you." He set his hands over his lap and began picking at the cuticle of his thumb nail with his index finger.

Regan inhaled sharply and I wondered what caused her reaction. Not wanting to interrupt, I didn't say anything and returned my attention to the video.

Dr. Gloria was silent, letting him go on.

Craig rubbed the bottom of his nose with the backs of his fingers and changed the subject. "My two boys? Kennedy and Lincoln, they don't have any powers? Are you sure?"

Relief passed over Dr. Gloria's face and her shoulders relaxed. She was scared of him. Though from this video the reasons why weren't clear. He was acting cold but that wouldn't be proof to Regan that he was a psychopath.

"As far as we know. Only Regan seems to have your gift."

"Yeah, but I've heard enough about her, tell me more about my boys. You said one's in the Air Force and one's in the Army."

"Yes. That's correct." Dr. Gloria tapped her pencil on a pad of paper in front of her.

"Where are they stationed?"

"Off the top of my head, I don't recall."

He huffed a laugh. "You don't remember? Or you refuse to tell me."

Gloria paused to jot down another note before she

looked back up at Craig. "Does it matter?"

A smile twisted his lips, and he cocked a brow over eyes that looked identical to Regan's.

Dr. Gloria sniffed and dabbed her forehead with a tissue before her body stiffened. Craig's steel blue eyes flashed silver.

Regan shuddered. I gripped her shoulders tighter.

Craig got up, pushed his hands into his trouser pockets, and walked over to where the camera was hidden. He leaned down and stared right into the lens, his eyes again glowed like stainless steel in the sunlight. He smiled and winked as if he somehow knew we'd be watching. Abruptly, he spun away and walked back over to where Dr. Gloria sat rigid as if she'd been frozen in place. He patted her on the shoulder comforting her but it was terror that brandished behind her eyes.

He stuck his hand in his pants pocket and pulled out a fist. On Gloria's desk, he set a dozen tiny white pills in front of her. They were stark on the dark wood. A rivulet of sweat ran down her temple until it dripped off her chin splattering the surface. She reached over and swept them off the side of the desk into her palm. Her hand quaked as it fought Craig's control. But in the end, he won. She popped them into her mouth, chased them down her throat with a swig of water, then got up on unsteady feet. She held onto her desk as she walked around the other side where she sat on the couch to slip off her heels. She laid down with her head on the armrest as if she were about to take a nap.

Craig stuffed a throw pillow under her head before crossing her hands over her chest. He scrounged inside the desk and grabbed a ring of keys. With them, he unlocked the cabinet. He fingered through some files.

Finding Regan's and the small one we had on her two brothers, plus a stack more, he tucked them under his arm. Before he left the room, he looked into the camera once again. His smile, though normally vacant, said it all. He won.

Dr. Gloria's eyelids fluttered until finally, they closed for the last time.

Regan looked up at me, tears swimming in her eyes. "Is she really dead?"

Chapter 43: Regan

A slight breeze picked up shimmying through the leaves above, cooling the sweat on my skin. "What are we going to do?" I shook my hands out next to my thighs attempting to combat my rising anxiety as I paced.

Gin seemed as calm as ever with his hands resting in the pockets of his jacket though I knew he and Dr. Gloria were close. "We're going to do nothing. My uncle and Ron are assembling a team as we speak."

"A team for what?"

"To capture Craig, of course."

"You're just going to capture him?" I stopped pacing and clarified.

"At this point, I don't know the exact plan. But Regan, Craig was able to control the man on the other side of the camera. He put him to sleep so he couldn't warn us about what was happening in the room in real time. And that man wasn't even in the same building."

My forehead wrinkled. "Really?"

"Yes. His abilities are far greater than before the accident. We're not even sure to what extent. But can you control someone over a live camera feed?"

My lips dipped into a frown. "I don't know. I never even thought to try."

"Exactly."

"But you don't understand if I could just see him—I know he'd remember. And then maybe he'd be better."

I stepped closer to Gin and grabbed him by both hands looking up into his green eyes searching for signs of deceit. "You have to take me with you. I was his little girl, his fish whisperer. And my brothers were his pride and joy. And my mom—she was the love of his life. Surely, he would remember us if we could see him."

I wasn't sure that he didn't already remember us. My dad had a quirk. A subtle tell that only I knew about and during the video he'd played that card. I used to tease him about it, but I vowed never to give away his secret if he promised to split his poker winnings with me. They were never much considering we only played with pennies.

I couldn't allow GSS to get to him first. They might hurt him. There was no way they would let me near my father if they considered him to be a danger.

My mind whirled, devising escape plans. I was angry at Gin. *So angry.* I trusted him and he'd let me down. My pet was locked in its cage, but it still pushed against the glass searching for signs of weakness. Thankfully, it was exhausted, allowing me to hide my intentions. Because my best defense was to act normal-ish. And a normal girl would beg and plead to rescue her dad.

"Regan, you know that's not possible. At least not yet. Give us some time to figure out what we're dealing with."

"But I can help. I may be the only one that can."

"Yes, that's a reasonable assumption. But I'm scared that if Craig gets ahold of you, he could hurt you."

I scoffed and I spun around, kicking a pinecone out of the way. "He's my dad. He won't hurt me."

"Regan—you don't understand. That's not your

dad. He wouldn't have killed Dr. Gloria. Ever. This person is someone else entirely. And until I have proof he won't hurt you, I don't want you anywhere near him. Give us some time to figure this out. Please?"

"Fine," I spit out. I hoped I hadn't caved too easily alerting him to *my* deception. "But what about my mom and my brothers? If you think I'm not safe, they're definitely not safe."

"From the information we've gathered through our sessions with Craig, I believe he's not interested in Sara. He seemed far more curious about you, but lately, his focus has been on your brothers. During Dr. Gloria's time with him, she did everything possible to help him remember who he is. We all did. And we know so much more about you. Through our conversations, I told him who you are and what you're capable of. And how amazing you are. I believe he saw something on one of the family videos that we may have missed. My guess is, he's going after the twins."

I swallowed the bile creeping up the back of my throat. Powers or no powers, my dad was going after my mom. I'd bet my life on it. Maybe not at first, but soon. And if he was as bad as Gin was insinuating, that made me worry for Barry's safety. He wasn't my dad, but during this last year, I'd grown quite fond of the man.

"Regan." Gin grabbed my hands and warmth like an invisible snake twisted around my arms cloaking me in comfort. I wanted that feeling over my entire body. It surprised me that I could want him so desperately when I was so angry at him.

I snatched my hands away, needing to concentrate on the important things and what my heart wanted wasn't high on the list at the moment—though it disagreed. I crossed them over my shoulders and pressed my face into the crook of my elbow. How could I still feel this way about him after he'd lied to me? Did he have a good reason? I suppose. Was it good enough to keep me in the dark? No.

"Do your brothers have gifts we don't know about?"

Did my brothers have powers? Yes. Lincoln was superhuman fast—or in his opinion, and he had many of them—we were all painfully slow. Kennedy could see tiny glimpses of the immediate future. The catch was that their powers only worked if they were together. We'd assumed it was because they were born mirror twins. Lincoln had situs inversus where his heart and guts were on the opposite side of his body making them a literal mirror image of one another. We'd agreed, as a family, to keep their gifts secret.

Gin stepped forward and rested his hand on my shoulder, his thumbs rubbing over the collar of my shirt. Even though our conversation was of a serious nature, it didn't stop the goosebumps from rising. Did he have any idea how the mere touch of his hand made me feel? The desire was there, oh yes, but it was so much more than that. Though he'd deceived me, I wanted to think he respected me as a person. But his choice to lie validated where I stood in the line of who he trusted. However, I was about to take whatever faith he had in me and flush it down the drain. Two could play the game.

My stomach roiled, my throat seized, and my heart ached. I didn't want to leave him. But he'd given me no other choice. I could no longer trust him. He'd proven that his loyalty was with his uncle. It was understandable, but I was disappointed nonetheless.

"I'll take your silence as a yes. Can you please tell

me what they are?"

I violently shook my head.

"Why not?"

"Because I promised my family, I'd never tell. I don't break my promises."

"I know you don't, Darlin', but I think this situation's a bit different, don't you?"

I about broke every time he called me *Darlin'*. The word was clearly spoken with love. But it wasn't enough. He was loyal to GSS. Not to me. "I'm still not telling you." If I offered that information up too readily, he would suspect I was up to something.

"I understand. But your mother?"

"She's perfectly normal." Though I was starting to question that too. Andrew hinted that my mom had something extra that made her a muse. Plus, when Pamela questioned her about my family, she was able to lie and not get caught. It would also explain why all three of us siblings had gifts.

Ben said he was the only kid in his large family with powers. Mae didn't know because she was adopted. Rory, Navi, and Tim were only children. And then there was Ron. He had a gift but neither of his children did.

"I thought so." He reached up and stroked the side of my cheek with the back of his fingers.

A shiver raced down my spine as I closed my eyes and stepped away. I had trouble thinking straight when he touched me. It made me want to confess my plans and hope that he wouldn't rat me out. Though I had a suspicion his feelings for me would do just that in the name of protection. "I need to call them and warn them."

He hooked his thumbs into the belt loops of his jeans. "We're dispatching a team to protect them right now."

"But they deserve to know."

"You're right they do, but it's a conversation I believe needs to be done face to face. Especially for your mother."

He was right. I couldn't imagine the trauma this would cause her. "Can't I at least call my brothers and warn them?"

"Not just yet. We don't want to spook your father."

"You'd rather just leave them defenseless?" I snapped. My pet snarled.

"Of course not, Regan. I hope you know me better than that by now," Gin admonished me, looking hurt that I would think so little of him. "Your dad left the Anchorage airport at ten o'clock. Only half an hour ago. We have video. It's going to take him another two and a half hours to get to Seattle assuming he's looking for a connection. And at least another three to get to your mother or brothers. That leaves us at least five hours to have teams in place."

With my lips pursed and my nostrils flared, I nodded, though I didn't agree.

"Let's head back to the lodge and from there you and I'll fly to Anchorage. The others have already left."

"Where are they?"

"GSS owns an apartment complex. We'll all be staying there tonight and leaving in the morning."

"I need to go with you, Gin. Even if you keep me away from him. I know him better than you. And it's only fair and you know it," I insisted.

He sighed, sounding resigned. "I'll talk to my uncle."

Chapter 44: Regan

Hours later Gin dropped me off at the apartment complex GSS owned in Anchorage where everyone was staying until further notice.

I went to my apartment and dropped off my things before I found the common area that was shared by everyone. Though I couldn't tell anyone what was going on, I hoped they would provide a distraction until I could implement my plans.

I pulled my legs up on the couch, wrapped my arms around my knees, and stared mindlessly at the TV, waiting for the others to show up. It wouldn't be long since the pizza had just arrived.

Jude walked in the room and sat down next to me, his weight sagging the edge of the leather. "You know Regan, I've been thinking, you could always come home. You don't have to do this."

I opened my mouth to protest but he cut me off. I did have to do this, but I wouldn't tell him why. It wasn't his job to save me anymore.

"I'm saying this as a friend and as someone who—" he paused as if choosing his words, "cares about you."

I wasn't sure what reality Jude was living in, but for the first time in my life, I belonged. He was more of a lone wolf and didn't need people. Once, I'd thought that was my only future. I didn't fight it because the less I was around normal people the less chance I had of hurting someone. Then Mr. LaCroix—the last person on the face of the earth I thought would save the day— offered me a job. That simple twist of fate led me to Tim, Mae, Ben, and even Navi. And of course, Gin too.

The feelings I still had for Jude—the love, the disappointment, the hurt—were still separated into the appropriate boxes inside my head. Compartmentalizing things kept me sane. Eventually, they would have to be dealt with. But the pressure, the obsession, I once had was gone giving me a reprieve. I figured Dr. Gloria could help me with the issue. Then it hit me and sorrow slumped on my shoulders. Dr. Gloria was gone. Another emotion added to the overflowing pile.

I shook away my thoughts and concentrated on the task at hand. "I can't go home. Not right now."

Tim ambled into the kitchen and grabbed a slice of pizza before wandering over to the living room. "Did we give you enough time?" he asked Jude.

Jude nodded and sat back against the couch. His leg pressed into mine as he scooted closer to me. The tingles that normally accompanied his touch were absent.

Tim's eye darted to where our legs met. "Regan, you okay? Jude said there was something wrong."

I turned my head and looked at Jude. *How would he know?*

"What? I've known you for a while, and just because I can't," he tapped his chest, "doesn't mean I can't tell when something is bothering you."

"There is." I fiddled with the sleeve of my sweatshirt then whispered into his ear, "I've been asked to go on a secret mission tomorrow."

The tension in his jaw flexed.

"Will you please keep *this* a secret?" I hinted toward

his previous betrayal to guilt him into keeping his mouth shut.

"Yes," he said quietly.

Mae bounced into the room and snatched two slices out of the box without touching them. They hovered in the air and floated down onto the coffee table. A soda followed shortly after. Her gift was convenient when you wanted something but you didn't want to get up.

"Hey," Ben said, strolling into the room followed by Navi and Cammy. He lifted the lid of the pizza box. His face fell. "Did you guys eat all the pepperoni already?" We all looked at each other and shrugged. Seems as if we did. Ben grumbled and picked a piece of supreme. The girls opted for breadsticks and marinara.

"Are you watching this?" Ben gestured to the TV with his drooping slice.

I shook my head and tossed him the remote. He did some fancy magic and soon they were all playing video games.

Jude scooted even closer to me pretending to make room for the others when in reality there was plenty of space for everyone. He snaked his arm behind me but didn't touch me.

"So, is Rory still mad?" I was curious as to where she was.

"Gin didn't tell you?" Ben folded his pizza and shoved most of it inside his mouth.

"While we were saving Cammy," Mae continued the conversation for Ben since his cheeks were bulging, "Gin flew Rory to Anchorage and sent her back to Ireland."

With a bush plane, it only took thirty minutes to get to Anchorage from the training facility, so he had plenty of time to get there and back before we'd finished our mission. "I wondered where he'd disappeared to while the rest of us were kicking ass. But to be honest, I'm not going to miss the Celt." I mockingly tossed my hair over my shoulder in Rory fashion. Everyone but Navi laughed and shook their heads, un-fondly remembering the action. I glanced at Jude, expecting some sort of reaction since they'd appeared close, but he didn't seem to care. It seemed as if no one did. It was her fault for not practicing her powers. The rest of us had been working our behinds off to get better. Now I needed to pray that I was duplicitous enough to pull the stunt I had planned for tonight.

Between the heat coming from the gas fireplace and my mental exhaustion, at around eight o'clock I started to nod off. I stood up and excused myself. Jude insisted that he escort me to my apartment.

As we wandered down the hall, I asked, "Jude, what's going on?"

"I've been thinking, maybe we could make this work now. I feel so much better after."

When I didn't say anything, he continued.

"Do you have feelings for Gin?"

I turned my head slowly and stared into his dark eyes. "Yes."

He sucked in a breath as if I'd punched him in the gut.

"But it's your fault," I said. Now that Jude wasn't dealing with my darkness, I could be honest with my feelings. And pushing him away would work to my advantage now. If I made him mad enough, he would stop pressing me to go home with him. Jude didn't have my darkness to deal with any more, but the boy still had a temper.

His brows furrowed. "And how's that?"

"I didn't have real feelings for Gin until recently. You were the one who presented him with the opportunity."

He opened his mouth to defend himself.

"No," I snapped, adjusting my position so I faced him. "You asked. Now you're going to listen. Gin kissed me. I stopped him. Then you showed up and accused me of cheating on you. I get it. You caught me sleeping in a room with another guy. But that was *my* worst offense. And to this day," I tapped my finger on his chest, "it still is."

"The fuck?" he said.

"Yeah, I get it—our bond allowed my pet to feed from you. And I've apologized over and over again. And I'm still sorry it happened. But I had a good reason why Gin was in that room with me—you know it. My mental state was in a precarious place. Then you insinuated that I might be cheating on you with multiple guys all because you could *feel it*." I air quoted.

He growled, losing some of his composure. "Man, you have a way of getting under my skin and making me angry like no other person."

That was the goal.

"Then you started flirting with Rory and Navi—I can only assume as retaliation. And then you betrayed my trust and told them I'd killed people after I'd asked you not to tell anyone. I understand you're upset about what I did. But Jude, so am I. Do you think it was easy to kill those men? Do you think I wanted to do it? I didn't, though it needed to be done. But what hurts the most is that you think I'm a monster." I paused and took a breath. "You think I enjoyed it—I didn't, but the golem did. So, am I a monster? Maybe. But your actions are what opened the door for Gin."

Jude stepped back, his shoulders rounded, and looked down at the floor. "I'm sorry. I really am."

"I'm never going to deny that I loved you. But you told me forever. You told me what we had was more permanent than marriage. And at the first hint of trouble, you bailed on me." My voice cracked. "How would *I* ever be able to trust *you* again?"

He took a shaky breath. "I was jealous. So jealous," he whispered and blinked back tears. "I can see the connection the two of you have because of your similarities. I mean even your auras look similar."

"What do you mean? Mine's black. You told me his is green."

"It is, but it sparkles exactly like yours. It was hard to notice at first because the glitter shows up more against your dark background. But the longer I'm around all of you, the more noticeable their auras have become. *Especially* around you. It's like something about you amplifies everyone's colors." He clenched his teeth wanting to hold back.

"You might as well just spit it out, Jude. There's no time like the present. If we are going to manage as friends, we have to clear the air."

He swallowed. "When the two of you are together, your auras start to mingle. They swirl in and around one another. The colors stay separate, but they coil and intertwine like snakes looking for warmth. It doesn't happen with the others. That, along with everything else, made it hard for me to believe the two of you hadn't been together."

"What about our auras? Do you think they ever did the same thing? I could often feel my pet reach out to you both."

His eyes widened and darted around as if he hadn't thought of that before. It was strange having to interpret his emotions without a guide. But I knew him well and it wasn't difficult.

"From the moment I met you, my pet reacted in a very primal way. It's as if it recognized you somehow. It did something similar to Gin, but not as aggressively. When I met you, the golem nearly jumped into your lap and begged for attention. I'm almost positive it loved you even before I did."

"But do you still?"

"No." Not like I once had.

His lips pursed into a sad smile and a barrage of emotions traveled behind his eyes. He nodded.

"Well, I guess that's it then," he said.

"Yup."

With nothing left to say we started walking down the hall until we stopped next to my door. I tapped the keycard against the lock. "I'll see you in the morning."

"Only if you get up early, I've booked a flight home at ten."

"I think that's a good idea."

He turned to walk away.

"Hey, Jude."

He glanced over his shoulder.

"I don't regret a second of our time together. I learned a lot from you and I believe it will help me…" I blinked rapidly trying to dry the tears forming, "stay me."

He held up his hand and waved once over his

shoulder.

Once the door was shut, I leaned against the cold wood and slumped to the floor.

I sniffed as the tears burned the back of my nose before they dripped down my face. In another time and place, I would've let him in on my plan and together we would've saved my father. But everything had changed and I had more important issues to deal with than my regrets about Jude. My father's survival might depend on it. Determined to function, I dried my tears and wiped my running nose with the napkin hiding in the pouch of my hoodie.

I texted Tim to have him stop by my room before he went to bed and then I jumped in the shower. Thirty minutes later Tim was at my door.

"I didn't expect you so soon." I let him in as I finished towel-drying my hair.

"I'd have been here sooner, but we were in a game raid. What do ya need?"

I handed him the envelope. "Will you give this to Gin tomorrow morning? It's imperative that he gets it first thing."

"You're leaving?"

Earlier, Gin had texted me to let me know Mr. LaCroix said that I could accompany them. But only if I agreed to follow all orders. If I failed, I'd be immediately terminated.

I was getting terminated either way, so I made another false promise. I had no intention of following anyone's orders.

My decision to leave would bring me redemption if I was lucky or ruin if I wasn't. But I didn't feel like I had any other choice. My father's reputation, perhaps his life, was on the line. And there wasn't anything I wouldn't do to save him.

"Not for good. I've been asked to join GSS for this next mission."

"Congratulations!" Tim said excitedly then his expression faltered. He pushed up his glasses and scrunched his nose. "Wait. Is that why you're upset? You're going on a mission without Gin?"

"Sort of. I'm sure you'll know soon."

"Hey, Regan. I just want to say, thanks for being my friend."

"I'd be stupid not to be friends with you." I hit him lightly in the arm.

"I'm glad we all found each other." He opened the door.

"Me too." Melancholy washed over me as I waved goodbye. I wasn't psychic and I had no idea what the future held. All I could do was hope this wouldn't be the last time I'd see him.

Chapter 45: Regan

I swiped my bangs behind my ear and refreshed my lip gloss before knocking lightly on Gin's apartment door. I checked the time on my phone. It was shortly before eleven o'clock. He couldn't be sleeping already, could he? As far as I knew, everyone else was still in the common room playing video games. Except for Jude. He'd gone back to his room at the same time I had. Knowing how hard he slept, he wouldn't wake up until the last minute before he had to catch his flight. I planned to be long gone by then.

I knocked a little harder afraid someone would come down the hall and catch me with an overnight bag in my hand.

"Just a minute." Gin drew open the door wearing only a white towel wrapped around his waist. A bead of water ran down his chest. My eyes followed its journey over his rippled abs and v-shaped muscles until it vanished into the cotton.

"My eyes are up here, Darlin,'" Gin teased.

Dang. Every time he used that endearment my body clenched in ways that made my face blush. I smacked him on the arm and darted past him into the room.

"Well, come on in," he said, shutting the door. His apartment was bigger than mine, but other than the size, all the finishes were similar.

His brows creased when he noticed the backpack I

was carrying over one shoulder. "What can I do for you?"

"Go get dressed," I ordered. It was hard to make a coherent thought with him parading around, mostly naked.

He laughed. The sound gave me goosebumps. He turned, the muscles in his back and his snow-leopard tattoo flexing enticingly and disappeared into the bedroom.

The gas fireplace was roaring, though it wasn't that cold outside. The warm light warbled over a sizable drawing of a snow leopard hanging over the sofa.

I cocked my head curiously, slipped my backpack off my shoulder, and started to snoop. On either side of the hearth were built-ins with some knick-knacks and a few pictures. One was of him and his uncle which was taken fairly recently. Gin's hair was shorter but he looked the same. In the other photo, he was younger standing next to a monk in front of a monument of sorts.

"That's Sangpo." Gin returned wearing a pair of plaid pajama bottoms and a t-shirt that clung to his abs and stretched tight over his biceps. He stopped next to me and even though he wasn't touching me, it was as if I could feel his essence wrap around me. Jude had admitted as much and now that I knew it was real, I didn't try to reason the reality away. "He's why I am the way I am."

I smiled, thinking I wanted to thank Sangpo. Because I liked Gin just the way he was even if he was a liar, liar pants on fire.

My expression must've held some worry because Gin's forehead wrinkled. "Regan, are you okay? I thought you'd be happy that my uncle acquiesced to your wishes. For the record, I disagreed with him."

I threw him a dirty look. "Traitor."

"No, I'm merely concerned for your safety."

I propped my hands on my hips. "And you don't think I'm concerned about yours?" If my father was as dangerous as Gin said, I didn't want him or my friends in the line of fire. It was part of the reason I was willing to lose my job. I could only hope that was all I had to sacrifice.

He dismissed my apprehension with a wave of his hand.

"I am happy he's letting me tag along. But—"

"But what?" He stepped closer. The smell of his shampoo and cologne drifted past my nose.

I inhaled deeply and shifted my feet forcing my arms to stay at my sides. "I don't have anyone I can talk to. And I don't want to be alone tonight. Can I stay with you?" The words tumbled out as I stared at the floor.

"Of course, you can. I'm so sorry you can't talk with your friends about what you're going through."

I shrugged and glanced up, meeting his eyes. The flames from the fireplace reflected in their depths. "Honestly, I'd rather talk to you anyway."

A pleased smile rose on his lips accentuating the small cleft in his chin. He'd shaved, leaving his face clean and smooth. I didn't know which look I preferred, the mountain man scruff he'd grown while at the lodge or this. He was gorgeous either way. My fists clenched. The goal was to keep them from reaching up and stroking his skin.

"Why did you lie to me?"

Pain skewed his handsome face. "I didn't want to. Dr. Gloria," he choked on her name, but recovered with a deep breath, "said it would be safer if you were reintroduced to him when he was ready. She believed your joy would overpower your anger. I was outvoted several times. Regan, I was torn between what was right and what was ordered. Will you ever forgive me?"

Now that I wasn't so angry—it's amazing what a few hours of thinking could do—I'd already forgiven him. Mostly. But only because in his shoes, I would've been the asshole who did the same thing. He'd been doing his job. It wasn't hard to conclude what had happened behind the scenes. His uncle, along with Ron and Dr. Gloria, forbade him from telling me that my dad was alive. They claimed it was for my safety and the safety of others. Perhaps they were right to be concerned. Though it was nice to know that Gin didn't agree with them even though he followed the orders.

His phone dinged, breaking the growing tension. With a sigh, he walked away, grabbed it off the dining room table, and texted something in return. I assumed it was his uncle asking what I was doing in his apartment.

Mr. LaCroix owned a security company, so I imagined the hallways were equipped with cameras. And I knew they would be watching me closely since I had a track record of going rouge.

His phone dinged again and he answered it before he set it back on the table face-side down.

He looked up. "Do you want to watch a movie or something?" Per usual, he didn't act uncomfortable, but he almost sounded nervous. I was.

"Uh, yeah, sure." I slipped off my sneakers.

"Are ya planning to escape?"

"Wh-what?" I sputtered and my heart mule-kicked my ribs. I tripped on the edge of the area rug. With lightning-fast reflexes, he caught me before I fell.

"Your outfit," he said, letting go of me and taking a step back. His eyes traveled the length of my black zip-up sweatshirt and leggings, making my skin tingle even though he hadn't touched me.

Why yes, I was.

"You're dressed like a Ninja." He didn't let go of my arm. The heat from his hand penetrated the thick fleece.

"I . . . it's all that was clean." I pulled on the hem of my tank top with my free hand. "I was going to throw a load in tonight but I forgot. It's in the basement, right? I got distracted," I rambled.

"I see." He stared at me with an arched brow looking amused.

"We broke the bond." The words spilled from my lips.

Gin's smile collapsed and he froze. "You did? I thought maybe . . ."

I nodded and bit my lower lip.

As he inhaled, his breath seemed to shake. "I see." He shifted his weight. "You know, you might think this is weird but earlier today, when I said I needed to pick something up, it was for you. I bought you something."

After we flew back to Anchorage, Gin told me he needed to stop by the mall. When I excused myself to use the restroom, he seemed relieved, as if he didn't want me to accompany him wherever he was going. A twinge of jealousy had settled like a thick fog and persisted. I spent the rest of the afternoon wondering if Gin had a girlfriend. And if he did, what was I doing here? It's not like we'd talked much about his personal life. Only mine.

"When I saw it, it reminded me of you. I planned on

giving it to you if you ever completely broke up with him. Luckily for me, I didn't have to hang on to it for long." A twinkle flashed in his eyes before he dug through his backpack and pulled out a velvet box.

He handed it to me. "I hope you like it. Sorry, I didn't have time to wrap it."

My anxiousness turned to hopeful trepidation. I ran my finger over the soft material and opened it. Hanging on a delicate silver chain was a black stone the size of my thumbnail with a rainbow of colors dancing inside. I looked up. "It's beautiful." I pulled it out and held it up to the light. "What is it?"

"A black opal."

My eyes shot open and I carefully laid it back in the box and shut it. "Gin. I can't accept this. It's too much. We've only known each other a short while."

If I included his time in Wyoming, we'd known each other for months but we'd only become good friends in the last month.

He set his hand over mine. "I feel like I've known you my entire life. Please, Regan. When I saw it, I knew I had to get it for you. If you don't take it now, I'll just give it again to you tomorrow. And the next day and the next until you finally accept it. Please?" He opened the box and held the tiny chain in his hand.

I lifted the hair off my neck and turned around. His fingers were cool against my skin. Goosebumps spread from his touch tickling down my spine and arms. I suppressed a shiver.

He came around and adjusted the stone from the front, sending a spark straight down my sternum igniting deep in my core.

"There, it's perfect. You can take it off in the

morning if you want so no one asks about it. I'll understand."

My fingers found the stone resting slightly below the hollow of my throat. I pressed it against my skin then looked up at Gin, meaning to thank him.

Instead, I seized the front of his shirt and drew him down so I could reach his lips.

They were warm and gentle, so different from my dream where he was far more aggressive. My toes curled into the carpet as he positioned his hand behind my head. His tongue parted my lips and explored my mouth. He tasted like mint toothpaste. I pressed my chest against his and moaned as electricity clenched deep inside my core.

He pulled away. My pet whined pathetically. Or maybe I did—I wasn't sure.

"Was that for the necklace or because you . . ."

"Because I like you. A lot," I finished.

"I wasn't sure."

"How is that possible? I wasn't able to hide it from anyone else." Jude knew, but so did Mae, Tim, and Ben.

"Darlin', every time I hinted at my feelings or outright declared them, you changed the subject or somehow pushed me away. So, I wasn't sure."

"Yeah, well, I've been struggling to hide it from you for a while. I told myself it was a silly little crush and if I ignored it, it would go away."

"And has it?"

"No. It just keeps getting worse and worse."

His face relaxed into a smile before he leaned in and kissed me. Again. For real, not just a memory or a dream. His lips gently whispered against mine. I pushed in harder, needing him to kiss me like he had that day, but he refused. His ice-cold control was not giving me an inch.

"Gin, what's wrong?" I pulled back. "You're acting like I'm going to break."

"I need to be careful is all."

"You weren't careful on that mountain top."

"Yeah, well, your defenses were already up. And clearly, I wasn't thinking straight at the time."

I threw my head back and laughed at him. "You think you can hurt me?" I pointed at my chest. "Really?"

"The last girl I kissed like this ended up in the hospital. I refuse to let that happen to you. I'm not willing to chance it."

My pet showed its teeth, displeased with the notion of Gin kissing someone else. It was a possessive little beast. "Don't be stupid Gin," I smiled slyly to soften the blow. "If you couldn't properly erase my memory, and my defenses were practically non-existent by then, what makes you think you're a danger to me now?"

"Well," a beautiful blush pinkened his cheeks, and he stuttered, "Well, ah, the more I let go of control the worse it becomes."

My breath hitched in my throat. "Wait." I clasped both of his hands in mine. "You've never . . ."

His jaw clamped together and he tilted his chin up slightly. The shake of his head was barely noticeable. "Can we leave it at that?" His voice was strained.

Of course, I could. His track record with women was of no consequence to me. But for a twenty-two-year-old man, I could see how he might believe he should be embarrassed. I pressed my hand to his chest. His heart pounded rapidly under my palm. "Yes. But what I won't back down on is how you kiss me. I *need* you to kiss me. Like you did on the mountain."

"I thought that's what I was trying to do."

"No, you were kissing me like I'm fragile. And I'm not. You're going to have to trust me when I tell you that you can't hurt me. But I might like it if you tried."

Chapter 46: Regan

Gin's pupils dilated, masking his emerald irises. His lips crashed into mine while his hands yanked the sweatshirt off my shoulders. His fingers traced my arms in opposite directions until one hand was buried in my hair and the other was pressing my hips tighter to his.

His desire was straining against his thin pajama bottoms, pressing against my stomach. Between my legs throbbed deliciously, almost uncomfortably.

His hand slid underneath my tank top with his fingers wrapping around my waist squeezing hard. The hot skin-on-skin contact weakened my knees.

Not having his level of control, I grabbed the hem of his shirt and shimmied it up his torso until he finally got the hint and stopped kissing me for a second as he removed it. I gazed down and ran the tips of my fingers over the hard ridges. He gasped as his muscles rippled under my touch.

Not able to stop myself, I leaned in and kissed the warm tan skin on his chest. He stopped breathing as I licked, kissed, and softly bit my way down his pecs to his spectacular abs. He stroked the back of my hair as he groaned, then yanked me up and captured my lips between his.

His kisses grew deeper and more impatient as his hands roamed my back, down my waist until one was cupping my ass pressing me tighter against him. I didn't know how much more I could handle. He was driving me wild. Everything inside of me screamed with pleasure and we still had most of our clothes on. Determined to remedy that problem, I reached for the hem of my shirt.

"Regan, Regan, we have to stop." Gin pulled away from the kiss. He was panting hard, and his words did not match the expression in his eyes. His lips were swollen and his hair was messed up in a sexy disarray.

"What?" I snapped as my pet scratched at the side of the glass box and whined.

He chuckled and said, "Easy there, Darlin'."

My eyes narrowed to a sliver at his suggestion. I didn't want to take it easy. I wanted to drag him into his bedroom and dirty the sheets. As bad decisions go—it was probably one of my worst. And the bar, in my case, was quite high. Afraid I would never see him again, I wanted the memory of him forever branded inside of me. From his kisses to everything he had to offer. With him, I could see a viable future. I already loved him, and he'd admitted to having feelings for me, though I wasn't sure if they were anywhere near what I felt for him. He'd seen me at my worst and didn't judge me by that alone. Because he was my perfect match. My true equal.

The thought of leaving him behind was almost too much to bear. If only I could trust his loyalty was mine. But I couldn't. So, I shook off the desire to confess my plan to protect the man I loved more. My dad.

"Regan, I need to do this right. I want to take you on a date. I want to buy you pretty things. I want to sweep you off your feet as you deserve and let the world know we're together."

He was a true Southern gentleman—which I usually appreciated. But not so much at the moment.

"I don't need any of those things, Gin. Just you." I was on the verge of begging.

"And while hearing you say that makes me the happiest man on earth when we do this—I want to be the only man in your life. I'm not willing to share your heart. I know you've broken up with him, but there's no way you're over him. Don't bother trying to lie to me, or yourself for that matter."

I wasn't sure that he was right but I couldn't argue my point on why I wanted this now without giving away my plan.

"Are you okay with that?" He swept the backs of his fingers down my cheek.

"No." I pouted and rested my forehead on his bare chest as I inhaled the scent of his cologne and something masculine, delicious, and solely his.

He lifted my chin with his finger forcing me to look at him.

"Yes," I said, scowling.

"Good. Now I'll take the couch and you can have the bed."

I started to open my mouth.

"Don't argue with me. I will not allow you to sleep on a couch."

My hands snapped to my hips. "That's not what I was going to suggest. It's a king-sized bed. We can share. I promise to be good. I really don't want to be alone."

"You're not going to make this easy on me, are you?" His gaze traveled the length of my frame and lingered on the curve of my breasts before returning to my eyes.

Tingles danced over my skin. "What would be the

fun in that?" I said, though I reluctantly capitulated to his wishes. Disappointed, but not wanting to push him farther than he was comfortable, I grabbed each of us a soda out of his fridge. I unscrewed the cap and pulled one of my anxiety meds out of my pocket. With a measure of guilt—but not enough to stop me—I dropped a single pill in his drink before I handed it to him and dragged him into bed.

I behaved. We only held hands and snuggled while we fell asleep watching a movie.

Once I was certain Gin was out for at least the next four hours—that's how long my pills kept me asleep for—I began to implement my plan.

I grabbed his phone from the bedside table and held it in front of his face. After it unlocked I read through the earlier message from his uncle.

—*What is going on? Why does she have her backpack with her?*—

—*Chill. She's upset. She's staying with me tonight so she doesn't have to be alone. Besides, that makes it easier for me to keep an eye on her.*—

—*Do not let her out of your sight.*—

—*That's the plan. But there's no reason for her to run off now that she's going with us.*—

The messages didn't surprise me or make me angry. In their position, I would've done the same. How could they not think I was going after my dad? They thought by letting me tag along, I wouldn't run. *Suckers.*

They'd given me no choice since they wouldn't supply me with a definitive answer on what they planned on doing to my dad once they found him. I tried coaxing the information out of Gin after my anxiety meds began to kick in. He said their goal was to bring my dad back alive.

"Yeah, but what if he doesn't come willingly?" I prodded.

His words were slurred and he yawned. "We plan to take it one step at a time. We don't want to decide on a course of action before we have all the pertinent information." That was a politician's answer if I ever heard one.

"But what if he poses a danger to innocent bystanders?" I pushed.

Gin's eyes slid to half-mast then he nodded off.

There was no doubt my dad could be dangerous if cornered so it was imperative for me to get to him first.

I tried to mimic Gin's tone as I typed another message to his uncle.

—*Chill. She doesn't want to be caught sneaking out of my room so she's going back to hers. Said something about not being able to sleep and was going to do some laundry. Maybe get a slice of pizza if there is any left.*—

My only hope was that Mr. LaCroix bought my text.

I flipped Gin's phone on silent and set it on the end table next to the bed before sneaking out. By the light of the moon streaming through the kitchen window, I slipped on my shoes sitting on the floor.

I paused with my sweaty hand gripping the knob of the front door. The timing for my plan was crucial, but I couldn't leave without seeing Gin one last time. Anguish swirled in my guts and tears stung the back of my nose. I wasn't sure I'd ever see him again. And if I did, would he be able to forgive me?

Against my instincts, I backtracked and opened the bedroom door leaning on the frame. A nightlight glowed softly over the shape of his spectacular body under the down comforter. I didn't want to leave. I wanted to crawl back into that bed and snuggle into his strong arms with dreams of what our future might hold. Needing to get a closer look at his face, I tip-toed across the wood floor until my steps were softened by the area rug.

I felt like a creeper standing there staring at him admiring his strong jawline, straight nose, and the tiny cleft in his chin. His thick lashes threw faint shadows on his cheekbones and over the small beauty mark under his eye. I bit down on my bottom lip while the tears I'd managed to contain fell over the edge and spilled hot down my cheeks. I loved him. *Damn it, I did.* Even though he lied to me.

The letter I'd left in Tim's care said everything I couldn't. I'd apologized for deceiving Gin and that I hoped he understood my reasonings for leaving. Would he forgive me as readily as I'd forgiven him? I kissed the tips of my fingers and carefully pressed them against his forehead. As if he were a child, a smile ghosted his lips though it disappeared as he drifted deeper. "Goodbye," I whispered before leaving.

I started to shut the bedroom door behind me.

"Where are you going?"

My heart leaped into my throat clogging my ability to breathe. Or scream.

"Regan?"

I turned, scrambling for a convincing story. "I ah . . . uh, I ah . . . didn't want to be caught leaving your room. I thought this was probably a good time."

"What time is it?" he asked sleepily. All he had to do was turn his head to look at the glowing red numbers of the alarm clock sitting on the night table or grab his phone sitting next to it.

"We don't have to be up for a few hours," I said vaguely. It was only one o'clock in the morning, but I needed him to think my timing was reasonable. I had begged to stay the night, I didn't want him to think I was leaving this early to escape. He was perceptive most of the time.

"And you planned on going without giving me a kiss?" He propped himself up on his elbow.

No. "I didn't want to wake you."

"Get your sweet ass over here and kiss me," he growled.

Though my timing was critical, I couldn't deny him without looking suspicious. And with his hair all messy from sleep and his muscular chest on display, I didn't want to deny him anything.

I crawled over the king-sized bed. He grabbed the front of my sweatshirt and pulled me to him. His lips crushed mine. Heat rushed to my skin and a throbbing that was hard to ignore pounded between my legs with every rapid beat of my heart. His hand curled through my hair and yanked my head back giving him access to the sensitive skin on my neck.

Really Gin? Where was this version of you earlier? I don't have time for this.

I couldn't help the half moan, half groan that ripped from my throat as he slid his hand inside my shirt up to my breast.

"I've changed my mind. I don't want to wait. I just don't want to be your rebound," he said between the kisses.

I chuckled at the ridiculous notion. "Gin, you're nobody's rebound. Definitely not mine."

"If you're sure."

Was I sure? In the words of Dougie Mack—absofloggin-loutly. But I didn't have the time.

I sat back on my haunches. "I'm sure about you. But I think you were right earlier. We should take this slow. I don't want there to be anything standing between us."

"Regan, nothing is standing between us. I love you."

I stopped breathing. They were the words I'd longed to hear but . . . "Is that true? Or am I your perfect match because I'm your only match?" Did he only love me because he couldn't have anyone else for fear of killing them?

He threw his head back and laughed. "I already told you, I had a crush on you before you got here. And I've been dreaming about you since the moment we met, long before I knew of your powers. I don't know exactly when I fell in love with you, but I do know that I love you. Don't ever question that."

I started to say something but he pressed his fingers to my lips to shush me. "I think you might love me too. And I don't want to wait. I want you so bad I can hardly stand it." He grabbed my arm and guided my hand under the cover to prove his point. I gasped, he groaned and whispered something quite unexpected and scandalous for the sweet southern boy he pretended to be. The throbbing between my legs detonated leaving me weak with desire. Though I was very keen on taking him up on his offer, I knew it was the drugs I'd slipped him earlier doing the talking. This boy went from zero to one hundred when his control was compromised.

I pressed my forehead against his. "Gin, I love you too, but—"

"No, buts," he groaned. His breathing was ragged. "I have long-term plans for us. I see a future together.

God, Regan, I love you."

Pain and regret twisted my throat. He was going to hate me come morning.

"I love you too, Gin." So much that it made leaving the most painful thing I'd ever experienced, short of killing my dad. My actions were going to break his beautiful, kind, perfect heart as they were currently doing to me. "But we only have a couple of hours before we have to get up and I plan on taking you up on your offer. Two hours doesn't give you nearly enough time to keep that promise. Because *Darlin'* I don't break that easy. Plus, I want to do this when you're the only man in my heart."

He let go of me and flopped back on his pillow rubbing his hands over his face into his hair. He huffed. "Fine. You're right. Just evict him quickly."

His lack of inhibitions was quite charming. If I could make all my wishes come true, I would stay. "Okay. Give me a few days?"

"Regan," he said with a big yawn as his eyes started to droop, "Will you be my girlfriend?"

For someone who seemed so sure of himself and was always able to hide his thoughts, when he was drugged, he was an open book of awkwardness. My heart, already his, fell even further. "Yes, Gin, I most definitely will."

Chapter 47: Regan

With a myriad of emotions swirling, sorrow, regret, and love, I waited until Gin's breathing was deep and even. Because of the drugs, it only took a minute of my time, but I didn't have a second to waste. I positioned the alarm clock away from Gin in case he woke up anytime soon. I checked his phone for messages—Mr. LaCroix had sent him a thumbs-up emoji—then I set it on the TV consul where it was harder to reach.

Running late, I rushed to the front door and peeked out to make sure no one was in the hallway. I went to my room, intending to grab my laundry basket. My original plan had me leaving straight from Gin's room. But knowing they were watching, left me to reevaluate the situation. Seriously, who does laundry while escaping? I checked the time and grimaced. I hoped the car service I'd ordered from Gin's phone would stick around for a few extra minutes. I'd texted that I might be late but if they had another pick-up after me, they probably wouldn't wait.

I forced my feet to walk down the hall, knowing that it would seem weird if I was running. I dropped my laundry off in the basement and went to the kitchen only to discover the little piggies had eaten all the pizza.

Empty-handed, I headed back to my room trusting that the mundane tasks made me seem less suspicious.

Having watched enough crime TV, I left my cell

phone on the coffee table.

Earlier in the evening, I'd prepared some sheets by tying knots in them. With them bundled in my hands, I opened the sliding glass door of the second-story balcony. The security system in the building wasn't meant to keep people prisoners but to keep criminals out.

Close to the side of the building, I tied the sheets to the metal railing and gave them a good yank. I slipped on my backpack and said a little prayer before climbing over the side. The sheets didn't reach the ground so I dropped the last ten feet. The impact stung. I curled my legs and rubbed my shins trying to abate the stabbing pain. When it was tolerable, I army crawled away. The security cameras were set up to ignore anything moving at ground level. Once out of the camera's range, I got up and ran. By the time I'd made it two blocks, I was winded and sweaty but relieved to see the cab had waited.

I opened the back door and jumped in. "The airport please."

Earlier, when Gin had stopped at the mall to pick up the necklace, I'd made the excuse that I had to go to the bathroom. Then I texted him that the closest one was being cleaned and it would take me a few minutes longer because I had to go upstairs.

In reality, I made a teenage girl give me her cell phone. I called my mom's boyfriend at the sheriff's office in Wyoming.

"May I ask who's calling?" the woman who answered the phone said.

"Yes. This is Alice Teigan, Sara's mom." I tried to make my voice sound as if I were in my 70s. "I couldn't remember his cell number and Sara's out." I made the excuse legitimate. It's not like my Grams wouldn't do

exactly that.

"One moment please."

"Alice," Barry's voice sounded concerned, "is everything okay?"

"It's not Alice, it's me."

"Regan? Are you okay?" He started out sounding concerned then his tone changed to worried anger. "What's going on? Have they hurt you?"

"No. But I need you to listen to me—I don't have a lot of time." My dad could almost be there if Wyoming was his final destination. I didn't think it was, but I couldn't take any chances. "My dad isn't dead."

"What?"

"He's not dead. But he's not the same either. He had a serious head injury and the darkness I deal with, well, he may not have control of it."

The jury was still out on that one. In the video, he wasn't himself. Things were off. Plus, he was lying about remembering his family. When he was lying, he would pick at the cuticle of his thumbnail with his index finger. It was his tell.

"Barry, I need you to get them out of there. Now. You have at most two hours. Drain my bank account and disappear. Don't tell me where you're going. Pay the new ranch foreman a month in advance."

My salary at GSS was significant and they'd given me a generous sign-on bonus so there was plenty to go around. Before I'd left for my new job, I'd insisted my Gramps hire someone to help with the ranch and I put Barry on my bank account—just in case. Though he argued with me, I refused to back down. Thankfully, my mom was on the same page.

"Regan," Barry said, "you have to come with us.

I'm not leaving you behind. Besides your mother would kill me."

"Barry, I may be the only person who can stop him if he's gone rogue." I still had hope that I could get my dad back.

"Regan . . ."

"Barry!" I snapped. "I can't do this if I'm worried about them. Please. Keep my momma safe." My voice cracked with pain. "I'm counting on you. Don't go anywhere I'd expect."

"I know how to avoid detection, Regan. I'll take care of them. I promise. But what do I tell her? If she knows your dad's alive, she's never going to leave."

I'd thought long and hard about an excuse that she'd buy. "First, tell Gramps the truth but not Grams."

She was too easy to read, and Gramps had a quiet confidence that made people naturally follow his lead.

"Try telling her one of your co-workers got sick at the last minute and his vacation for four is non-refundable. He offered it to you for half price. The only catch is you have to leave now. If that doesn't work tell her GSS is planning on using them to get me to cooperate. But only use that excuse if absolutely necessary."

"Is that true?"

"No. So far they've been exemplary in their actions."

Though my dad did mention electric shock therapy and a lobotomy in the video Gin showed me so—the jury was still out on them as well.

I continued. "She already thinks poorly of them so this shouldn't be much of a stretch. And don't tell her the truth. Not just yet. In one week, at this exact time," I looked at the clock on the wall, it was 3:05, "I'll call your cell phone so have it on at that exact time. If I don't—stay hidden. Does that sound reasonable?"

"Wow, Regan, you'd make a great cop."

I laughed. At the rate I was going, I'd make a great criminal.

"But yeah," he said, "that sounds solid. I'll plan on hearing from you in one week at 5:05 Mountain time. Until then my phone is going to be off, so you have no way of reaching me. Are you okay with that?"

My phone in my pocket dinged. It was Gin asking where I was. "I don't have a choice. I gotta go. Can you keep them safe?"

"Yes. You have my word."

"Thank you. I know how much you love her and what a bad situation this is putting you in too." Barry was a good man, and I didn't want him hurt, physically or emotionally.

"Don't you worry about us. Just promise me your mom isn't going to lose a daughter too."

"I promise," I said and hung up. I plucked the SIM card out and slipped it into the garbage before I handed the teenager back her phone.

I hurried to meet Gin and texted him an apology for my absence using the excuse that the line in the bathroom was long.

I blinked, clearing the memory playback as the cab stopped in front of the airport gates. I pulled up my hood to shield my face and ran to the front door after erasing any memory he had of me.

I wish.

With my powers, it wasn't hard to get through security. I sauntered up to the PSA pre-check and handed the TSA security guard my driver's license and phone. Though I didn't have a boarding pass, it was easy peasy.

Once inside, I scanned which flights were going where. It didn't take long because Anchorage was a small airport.

Going from gate to gate, I asked the flight attendants if the seats were full even though I'd already chosen my plane. Everything else was a diversion. While Gin might suspect I was headed home, I also had plans to make it look as if my brothers' locations might be my final destination. There was enough time and I had no intentions of making my escape easy on GSS.

Just as the flight I'd selected started to board, I compelled four girls, all similar in size to me, to go to the bathroom at intervals. Inside, with a little help, they switched outfits. I changed out of my all-black clothes and dressed in my colorful spares. I reversed my backpack and stuffed the dirty clothes inside.

"Any of you listen to opera music?" I asked them before I let them go back to their seats.

Expectedly, they all shook their heads.

"Audiobooks?"

Two of them nodded.

Not needing to remind myself of the boys I'd left behind, I picked the one who listened to horror over romance.

Armed with her passcode, I made them flip up the hoods on their sweatshirts before we walked out together.

I joined the line of passengers boarding and made my way to a seat in first class. When a woman stopped in front of me and glared, I *wished* for her to go to a seat in coach. It was necessary for me to get off this plane quickly.

For the next three hours and five minutes, I listened to the horror novel thus learning I didn't like clowns.

Once we arrived in Seattle, I faded into the middle of the crowd and dashed to the bathroom where I threw on my black sweatshirt and reversed my backpack again. Then I borrowed another stranger's phone.

I dialed a memorized number. It rang and rang until he finally answered. "Amy." Lincoln sounded sleepy. "This has got to stop. I told you I wasn't interested in a relationship from the beginning. Just because you don't believe me or you want a different outcome doesn't give you the right to harass me. This has got to stop."

"Linc, are you kidding me?" He was a notorious ladies' man.

"Regan?" he perked up like he didn't know for sure who it was.

I tried calling Kennedy first because he was *the responsible one* but he didn't answer, so my second choice was Lincoln. Secretly, he was my favorite. Probably because he was a bigger jerk than I was, which, growing up, meant he often took the focus off my antics. "Whose phone are you calling me from?"

"It's a long story. But I need you to shut up and listen." The timbre of my voice must have been serious enough that my cocky brother, usually full of sarcastic comebacks, kept his comments to himself for once.

"Dad's alive."

"Come again?"

I filled him in on the details the best that I could with my limited time. "And GSS knows that you have powers. They don't know what they are or that the two of you need to be together for them to work."

"Regan!" Linc snapped.

"What? I didn't tell them. But after the fiasco that Dad caused, Gin guessed. Denying was pointless. Do with it what you choose. Tell them. Don't tell them. For what it's worth, I think GSS is reputable. They've been nothing but good to me." Of course, I'd yet to tell them no.

"Then why did you dash if they were willing to let you tag along? That doesn't make sense."

"Because they think dad might be dangerous and I want to prove that he isn't first before they get here."

"Are you sure he isn't?"

"No. Not positive. But I owe it to Dad to try."

"Agreed."

I didn't think Kennedy would've capitulated so easily. He was the type to put my safety above Dad's. Linc and I often saw eye to eye when the rest of our family disagreed with us. I didn't know if that made me feel better about the situation or stupid. Either way, I'd made my decision and wasn't backing out now.

"I need you to call Kennedy and let him know what's going on. I'm sure you guys will have your hands full soon. Oh, and if Pamela's there, you'll know her by the big teeth, she can tell if you're lying. So, block your thoughts if you're able."

I was hoping he was like me and Pamela couldn't get through. Linc was a pretty convincing liar. Plus, all of his organs were reversed. I didn't know if that would help or not.

"Look, I gotta go. I'll contact you when I can."

"Take care of yourself, little bit," he said. His nickname for me brought tears to my eyes. I wiped them away and implemented the next phase of my plan.

Chapter 48: Gin

My eyes opened at the insistent knock on the front door of my apartment. I glanced at the clock sitting on the end table and wondered why the alarm on my phone hadn't gone off. Did I leave it in the kitchen?

A smile ticked up the corner of my lip as I remembered who'd been in bed beside me. And though she was no longer there, I had no problem recalling the way her necklace rested just above the swell of her breasts and the moments that passed between us directly before she excused herself from my apartment. She didn't want to be caught leaving in the morning. Not that I would've minded. Especially now that she'd agreed to be my girlfriend. My smile grew bigger and happiness filled the void inside my chest. I'd heard rumors that when you found the one—you'd know it. And I knew it.

I pushed down the covers and threw my legs over the side of the bed. The knocking on my front door grew louder.

"Yeah, give me a second," I said as I yawned. Though I was awake, my head felt cloudy as if I'd been drinking yet I didn't have a hangover.

I threw on my tank-top and walked barefoot by the TV stand. My phone was lying face down on the surface. I picked it up to find not only was on it on silent, but my alarm had been disabled. I didn't remember doing either. With it clasped in my hand, I hurried to the front door.

Tim stood outside, dressed in silk pajamas and swanky house shoes, holding out an envelope. "Regan asked me to give this to you first thing in the morning. She didn't give me an exact time." He shrugged.

I grabbed it out of his hand and motioned for him to come in. While he took a seat at the kitchen table, I pulled my strongest coffee from the cupboard and started a pot. Once it finished, I handed Tim a cup. "Cream? Sugar?" I asked.

"Please," he said.

I set them on the table and sat down with my hands curled around the warmth of the mug. Steam swirled.

"Are you gonna open it? It seemed urgent." He stirred a massive amount of sugar into his coffee and finished it off with a heathy dollop of cream.

"Oh, alright." I was going to wait until he left before I opened it. But upon his insistence, I ripped the seal and unfolded a short letter. My stomach rolled while I read her words.

Dear Gin,

I know you're going to be mad and I'm sorry for deceiving you. But you couldn't guarantee my father's safety. And he's the one man I love more than you. So, I've gone to find him. I hope someday you can forgive me—remember I've already forgiven you for lying to me. So, don't hold the grudge forever, okay?

I love you,
Regan

The emotional upheaval going on inside was almost too much to process. She loved me, but she'd left me. A surge of fear overrode all other feelings. A sheen of sweat began to rise to the surface of my skin. I gripped the letter in my hand and looked up at Tim. "Where is she?"

"I don't know. She said she was going on a mission. She didn't tell me what it was, mate."

"Fuck!" I stood up.

Tim's eyes widened. "Dude, what is it? I've never heard you cuss before."

"Regan's gone to find her dad." My fists clenched. I'd told my uncle and Dr. Gloria that omission was going to get us in trouble.

"What?" Tim said. "Who? Her dad's dead."

"Wake up the others and go get dressed. Meet me in the common room," I ordered without answering his questions. I'd inform them all together so I didn't have to explain things twice.

I hurried to my bedroom while searching the messages on my phone. The last few texts to my uncle weren't mine. Anguish twisted in the hollow of my throat, making it hard to breathe. This was my fault—if I would've just told her about her father in the beginning. Instead, I'd hidden the information, proving my loyalty was to the company, forcing her to go out on her own.

I swiped through my car service app, and found the rideshare she'd ordered to the airport at 2 in the morning. Panic hummed below the surface of my skin. She had a six-hour head start. She could already be in Craig's grasp. And he knew Regan's powers were the equivalent of rocket booster to someone like him. Dr. Gloria had written in her notes that Craig wasn't fond of humans— as if he didn't think he belonged to the same species as the rest of us. She also mentioned that he may have an obsessive desire to repopulate the earth with our kind.

Though he didn't want total annihilation for the human race, he was looking for subjugation. And with Regan by his side, his desires for destruction weren't impossible. I didn't think he would be able to recruit her, she had a good moral compass, especially with powers like hers. But I wasn't positive. He was her father and—according to her—he was the only man she loved more than me. I had to find her.

I brushed my teeth, and then threw on clothes as I called my uncle.

"Is everything okay?" he answered. I didn't call him often.

"No. Regan took off."

"What?" he yelled.

"She's gone. I think she gave me something to make me sleep. She snuck out in the middle of the night to go find her dad." It was the only explanation on why I felt so groggy.

"Shit! Do any of her friends know anything?"

"I'm about to find out." I slipped on my shoes sitting by the front door.

"Good. I'll call her brothers and see if they know anything. Then I'll set up a meeting point for all of us."

With my wallet and phone tucked into the back pockets of my jeans and my keys in my hand, I raced to the common area of the apartment building.

Tim and Mae stood together whispering.

"Where are the others?" I demanded.

"I woke them up," Tim said. "They should be here soon."

Without waiting for them, I filled Mae and Tim in on the situation, figuring they could pass the information on to Navi and Ben.

"What about Jude? Did you wake him up?" I asked.

Tim's face fell. "Oh, I forgot about him."

"Come on." I headed down the hall toward Jude's room. Navi and Ben fell in line when they saw us.

Tim knocked loudly on Jude's door.

When he answered a couple of minutes later, I asked, "Do you know where she's gone to?"

"Who?" He propped his elbow above his head on the door frame as if trying to make himself larger. It didn't matter to me that he was slightly taller and wider. He was of no threat to me, at least not physically.

"Regan, you idiot," Mae said.

Jude threw her a dirty look. "Why would I know? We broke up."

"You did?" Tim said.

Jude didn't bother answering. "What is this about?" He looked at the time on his phone. "I have a plane to catch."

"Regan's missing!" Mae shouted.

"No . . . no," Jude paused as his eyes darted to me and narrowed.

His hesitation gave him away. "So, you do know where she is," I said.

He shook his head. "No, I don't."

"If you have any idea where she's gone, you need to tell me. Her father is dangerous and if she gets to him first, I'm worried what will happen to her. And you should be too. You've felt the darkness she deals with, now imagine what's going to happen if her dad gets a hold of her."

Jude cocked his head and crossed his arms over his chest. "What are you talking about?"

Tim shoved in front of me and Mae. "Her dad, he's

alive. Really!"

Air rushed from Jude's chest and he blinked a few times. Then fear passed behind his eyes as if he realized her dad might be a danger to her.

"You need to tell me where she is," I snarled.

He swept his fingers through his hair and gripped the back of his neck. "Oh. God. I can't."

I knew they'd broken their bond, but Jude still had tracking abilities. Or at least he said that he did. "You'd better, or you might not make it out of here alive." He wouldn't be the first person I'd killed.

Navi grabbed my arm and tried pulling me away. She shuddered and released me as if she'd been burned. I looked down at her. "It's not wise to touch me at the moment. Are you okay?"

She nodded but her eyes were wide and her normally dark skin looked a bit greenish. Once certain she was alright, I met Jude's stare.

"No," Jude said again. "I can't. I don't know where she's at. She didn't tell me and we severed the bond between us."

I took a step forward and Jude retreated a step back.

Mae, not making the same mistake as Navi, grabbed my T-shirt and tried holding me.

"I'm not going to kill him," I said to her. "We might need him." Admitting that out loud about gutted me.

He rolled his shoulder back, standing tall, "You're right. If we get close enough, I can still track her. And besides, I know Regan better than any of you and I'm not leaving until we've found her. I'll cancel my flight."

I inhaled and exhaled before I nodded. "I suppose you're right. But know this, I'm not letting you stay for any other reason than I love her, and her safety is my priority."

Chapter 49: Regan

I sighed in relief as the traffic began to thin out. Having done most of my driving in Alaska and Wyoming, the I-5 in Seattle was a true nightmare. Thankfully, the directions on my borrowed phone were good and the car I'd borrowed—yes that's what we're calling it, I had plans to return both items—was comfortable to drive. I finally was able to relax as I exited the interstate toward Deception Pass.

When my dad told Dr. Gloria he didn't appreciate her deception and he'd take a pass on a lobotomy, all I heard was they wanted to remove part of his brain in a barbaric procedure. It wasn't until he began to pick at his thumb cuticle with his index finger did I realize he was leaving me a trail. Deception Pass.

As soon as GSS discovered that I was missing, they'd come looking for me. Even if my dad wanted to find my mom, Wyoming was too obvious. He needed to pick somewhere only I'd know to look for him. For years, he'd talked about taking me to Whidbey Island where he'd grown up. Deception Pass State Park was where he fell in love with the outdoors. He said one day he'd take the family there. Not in my wildest dreams did I imagine this scenario. That sentiment was becoming more common by the day.

Once I'd arrived in Seattle, I found a plane to Wyoming and made another girl on that flight play bait and switch by trading clothes. I changed into her obnoxiously bright outfit before I boarded a flight for Great Falls Montana where Kennedy was stationed in the Airforce.

But I didn't stay on the plane either. I made a flight attendant give me her spare uniform and I changed in the congested bathroom. Then, dressed as an employee, I'd walked off the plane and borrowed a rental car.

Almost to the bridge, my pet lifted its head and looked around before it started pawing on the glass. I slowed the car down worried that the distraction might cause me to crash. I pulled over on the edge of someone's driveway to see what the problem was.

A small cabin-like house was nestled back in the trees. In the yard was a sign that looked as if it had been painted by a couple of kids. The letters were crooked and some backward but the message was clear. *Welcome to Washington.*

Just as I was about to pull back onto the road, my pet howled. I slapped my hands over my ears but it didn't mitigate the noise. Then from beyond the trees a black wolf trotted and stopped directly under the hand-painted sign and sat down.

I rubbed my eyes sure I was hallucinating this time. There were no wolves in Washington this close to the coast. Plus, I hadn't gotten much sleep.

I blinked hard, but when I looked again it was still there. It glanced up at the sign, then back at me. *Washington.*

"Washington?" Yeah, I know where I'm at.

My pet barked, the sound low and rumbling, not quite like a dog but similar. The actual wolf stood up, wagged its fluffy tail, and darted back into the forest like a silent ghost.

"Wait. Washington? That your name?" I smiled. Another president in the family seemed fitting. It was going to take a while for me to get used to such formality or I was going to have to find a nickname. Because seriously, that was a mouthful.

I sat there for a few minutes to make sure I wasn't hallucinating. Stranger things had happened to me, and I wasn't above questioning my sanity. Once fairly certain I was stable, I pulled out of the driveway and drove across the bridge, feeling better than I had in a long time. My pet and I were on a first name basis, Jude was headed home to live the life he desired, Gin and I were apparently an item—that was if he remembered in the morning. For now, my mom, grandparents, and Barry were safe, and I was almost positive I was about to find my dad.

Giddiness vibrated under my skin. The thought of seeing my dad brought tears of joy to my eyes. He'd been my everything. We were peas in a pod. While my mom and brothers didn't care for the outdoors, my dad and I couldn't get enough. He took me on my first camping trip when I was five. I remembered my mom was a basket case before we left and pleasantly surprised when we returned alive and healthy. After that, she stopped worrying, realizing that my dad was capable of taking care of me. We camped, we fished, we hunted—God I missed him.

Light flickered off the gentle waves of Skagit Bay. Rocky outcroppings covered in evergreens jutted into the deep teal waters. The quiet hum of the road beneath my tires and the scenery calmed the excitement and apprehension itching under my skin.

Though I didn't know the exact address, I did know the name of the road since it was named after my family. At a slight bend in the narrow side street, I caught a view I recognized from some old photos and pulled into the nearest driveway.

After my grandparents had died in the house fire, my dad had sold the property and joined the Airforce. Now, in the same spot a behemoth abode, squared and boxy, sat back from the cliff overlooking the ocean. Growing up here must have been peaceful until disaster had struck, leaving my dad alone with bad memories.

I stepped out of the car. Anxiety jolted my chest. I rubbed the tender spot on my sternum. What if my dad was here? And worse—what if I was wrong and he wasn't?

With one hesitant foot in front of the other, I walked up the cobblestones to the modern front door. My hand shook as I knocked.

I glanced at the security camera overhead and thought *what the heck?* If someone called the cops, it's not like I couldn't wish my way out. I grabbed the door latch and pressed my thumb down. It opened into a foyer with marble tiles and a tall ceiling. Light from the cylindrical chandelier cast a warm glow over the room. I hollered inside, "Hello? Anyone home?"

My heart thumped loudly, masking the sound of my feet as I walked over the threshold into a stranger's house to wander around. My eyes scanned the area, looking for signs that my dad was here, or at least had been here at one point, but there was nothing obvious like a bag lying around or shoes at the front door.

The kitchen was an understated combination of marble, wood, and elegant lighting allowing the view to steal the show. Everything was quiet except for the hum of the fridge.

My adrenaline was rushing, making me a bit queasy, so I searched the cabinets for a glass. I used the fancy fridge with the ice maker to get some water.

With the cold drink clutched in my hand, I meandered through the dining room to the living room and paused to check out the pictures on the wall. It started with two gentlemen somewhere in their mid-twenties getting married and progressed to family photos with one child, then two, then three. The most current picture was of them with their three adult-ish children.

"Baby girl," I heard from behind. The glass slipped out of my hand and hurtled to the polished wood floors. Shards flew everywhere. My nerve endings flared, and I stopped breathing momentarily.

I slowly turned around. My pet snarled and its hackles raised. My stomach shot to my throat and twisted with multiple emotions. Fear. Suspicion. Joy. Love. I landed on the last one and held tight.

He looked the same, standing there on the outside deck next to a wall of windows with the breeze tussling his light brown hair. He pulled the accordion doors open further letting in the humid air perfumed with seaweed and salt water.

"Daddy?" My voice sounded like a scared child.

He nodded and held out his hands. "Baby girl."

I ignored my pet's warning and dove into his arms. I buried my head into his chest. He smelled the same as always, like the fancy cologne my mom bought for him. Sobs racked my body.

"Oh, my little fish whisperer, everything's going to be okay. I'm here now." He patted the back of my head.

"I knew you'd come for Mom," I said between sobs.

When I finished crying, well mostly, Dad pushed me away to look me in the eyes. The skin between his brows wrinkled. "Little mouse, what makes you think I'm here for your mother?"

I stepped out of his grasp. "You're not?"

"Of course not."

"Then what are you doing here?"

"I left those clues for you. Gin told me you were smart, but I had to find out for myself just how resourceful you could be. You know me better than anyone. Especially now. However, I'm curious as to why Sara's not answering her phone. I talked to the hired hand and he said your mom, your grandparents, and her new boyfriend left in a hurry. Something about last-minute vacation plans."

I tilted my head. He didn't even sound jealous that my mom had a new boyfriend. Though my dad had never been the type. It was a good thing with a wife who garnered a lot of attention. But her having a new boyfriend and him not sounding upset seemed unreasonable.

"I'm assuming that has something to do with you?" he said.

I decided honesty was the best policy. I always had a hard time lying to my dad—it's like he could tell. Now I wondered if that was one of his gifts. And if so, it was probably even stronger than before.

"Yeah. They showed me the video where you killed Dr. Gloria. I don't know your intentions. And I wanted to protect them if you weren't . . . you."

He shook his head. "Gloria's not dead."

"Yes, she is."

"I didn't give her enough pills to kill her. Only enough to sleep for a while."

I lifted my hands in front of me, flaring my fingers while shrugging.

"Shit." He paced and stabbed his fingers through his hair. It was longer than how he'd worn it in the military. "Wait." He stopped to look at me with disbelief. "Are you sure she's dead? Or did you only see the video and someone told you she died?"

I nodded.

"Then what makes you think they aren't the ones lying to you?"

My jaw dropped open in shock. I hadn't considered that angle.

He waved his hand in the air. "Well, if she is dead, my intention was never to kill her. Only to escape."

"But why?"

"Pfft," he huffed. "So many reasons. They were using electric shock therapy to *help me.* And mentioned a procedure called psychosurgery. I may not be the same person I was, but there's no need to cut out part of my brain."

I'd heard my dad mention something like that on the video, but I didn't think he was being serious.

"Truthfully, what made me run was, I wanted to see you. They insisted you weren't ready. But I think it's me they're scared of."

"Why?"

"Because my powers are," he paused and lifted an eyebrow, "substantial. And don't take offense, because of my age, I'm not as susceptible to suggestions as you are. Though I must say, I'm impressed you got away so quickly. That tells me you have a mind of your own. Gin did mention that. He speaks quite fondly of you."

Heat bloomed on my cheeks. The feelings were mutual. At least they were until probably an hour ago. "So, what are we going to do? Should I find Mom?"

"No." He shook his head. "They're not wrong when they told you I've changed. When I woke up, I didn't remember anything. And sometimes I'm not sure if I do remember, or if the memories I have are the videos and pictures they showed me. You know Gin can replace memories?"

I nodded. He could erase them too, but I didn't mention that. Gin's secrets weren't mine to tell.

"They were very thorough in educating me on my life before this. Though at times, I think I feel things coming back to me,'" he pressed his fingers to his temple, "but right now I'm still trying to figure it out."

"What does that mean for Mom?"

He inhaled and studied the pictures of the other family hanging on the wall. "I can tell from all the information they've given me, I loved her deeply. But those feelings are no longer there."

"They might be if you just tried," I insisted.

"You're right. They might. But your mom sounds happy. Does she really need to relive all of this if my feelings are never reciprocated?" He stopped and looked at me. "And honestly, I think it's better this way."

I scowled.

"No, kiddo, think about it—you and I are dangerous. Because of our abilities, our loved ones can be used against us should we disobey orders. You know this to be true."

I did. It was the reason I willingly went to work for GSS. *Keep your friends close, and your enemies closer.*

Though from my experiences, GSS didn't seem to be my enemy. And Gin certainly wasn't. Then again, I'd yet to defy them until now.

"According to Gin, your mom's doing well and Barry sounds like a good man."

He was a good man, but I wasn't willing to let go of the idea that my family could be mended.

Dad reached out to touch my shoulder. "Kiddo, I can see your wheels turning. But you know I'm right. Your mom and her parents are safer without us around. You just said your goal was to keep them safe. The best way to do that is to stay away from them."

"And what about Kennedy and Lincoln?"

"Do they have powers?" He picked at his thumbnail with his index finger. He was lying to me—he knew they had powers and this was my test. Could I be trusted?

"You don't remember?" I asked.

"I don't and nothing they showed me led me to believe they were special like you."

"They do. Compared to me, their powers are limited and they have to be together in order for them to work."

"Ah, I see." He rubbed his hand over his whiskers. "What can they do?"

"Linc is really fast and Kennedy's a little bit psychic, I guess. The last time I saw them, as far as I knew, they were normal. All I know is what Mom told me and she wasn't very forthcoming."

If my dad had any memories of my mom, he would know that to be true. Her evasive tactics were impressive.

"I see. Well, we'll deal with that when the time comes. For now, we need to get out of here. They're bound to figure out the clues I left for you eventually."

Chapter 50: Gin

While sitting at the conference table at Malmstrom Air Force Base in Great Falls, Montana, I folded my hands together and studied Kennedy and Lincoln as they watched the video of their dad killing Dr. Gloria. The twins glanced at each other in the exact spot where Regan had tensed when she'd watched it.

I waited until they were done. "What?" I asked.

Kennedy slid my phone across the surface. They both said at the same time, "Deception Pass."

It sounded familiar but I couldn't pin down the location.

Kennedy continued, "For years our parents talked about taking all of us there on a family trip so we could see where our dad grew up. For Regan's graduation, we were all supposed to go together." They threw me matching expressions that said *that plan was shot to hell.*"

It was eerie enough that they were identical to the point that I couldn't differentiate the two and it was even creepier when their facial expressions were precisely timed. Both had tightly cropped blonde hair and the same piercing blue eyes as their mother. Thankfully, Kennedy was wearing a button-down shirt and Lincoln was in a T-shirt with an anarchy symbol printed on it. From what I knew about them, it summed up their personalities.

"Regan's been gone ten hours and Craig longer than

that. I don't suppose you'd have any idea if that is his final destination?" I questioned.

Once we found out Regan was missing, my uncle had us on a private plane headed to Great Falls where Kennedy was stationed. At the same time, he had Lincoln flown in from Fayetteville, North Carolina to meet us. Once we gathered, Lincoln admitted that he'd heard from his sister and her plan was to intercept their father to keep us from killing him.

Though we had no intention of harming Craig, I hadn't been able to guarantee his safety to Regan. I would've been lying to her, and I'd already done enough of that. Our plan was to capture him, but plans don't always go accordingly.

"I doubt it," Kennedy said. "He's not stupid. He'd know the minute we saw the video, we'd figure it out."

Lincoln sat back with his arms crossed. "Honestly, I think you'd have a better idea of what his plans were. You've spent more time with him this year than we have."

His accusation was not lost. I responded with a nod. Like Regan, they had a right to be mad. Though the twins didn't seem as surprised by their dad's actions as she did. "You're right. But while he was here, he was detached and non-interactive as much as he could be."

We'd already given them Dr. Gloria's files to read before they watched the video.

"I will say this." Kennedy scratched his chin. "Regan was a bit blinded by Dad at times. We're five years older and our childhood was slightly different from hers. It's not like our dad's a bad guy or anything. But by the time she came along, he had his quirks under control. From what I've gathered from Mom, in the early years, they struggled. She said he, like Regan, suffered from some strange compulsions. He liked to stir the pot, so to speak. He could influence people's emotions, and in the beginning, he preferred to create havoc. But with time, and her influence, he learned how to control his urges and explore them in other ways. I think the accident broke the dam our mom was holding back."

"Ken," Lincoln warned.

"No," he snapped at his brother. "This is *little bit* we're talking about. And Dad, at least the dad we buried, would want us to save her."

Lincoln stared down at the table, his jaw muscles working under his skin. "You're right," he mumbled.

Kennedy shifted his attention back to me. "We think our mom has a gift too. Matter of fact, we used to tease her."

I cocked my head.

"Her gift is hidden in plain sight. I think our mom and Tim have a lot in common."

That would explain the many inconsistencies I'd come across while dealing with Sara. She was able to lie to Pam without being caught, but Willa's pee powers worked on her, and I'd been able to alter her memories of the day we questioned Regan. Both Willa and I were much stronger than Pamela.

"We always used to joke that she could make a gay man straight. Beautiful people often get their way and nobody questions it. But we think she would have the same gift even if she were ugly. Or a fourteen-year-old boy who hadn't hit puberty." Kennedy glanced Tim's way.

My lips thinned into a hard line. He was probably right. I could only imagine that Sara was beautiful her entire life. Irritation flared my nostrils. How could I miss all the signs? From Sara's powers, the bread crumbs Craig had left behind, and Regan setting me up while she made her escape. "Do you think your mom would be any help capturing your dad?"

Both of them shook their heads in tandem. "No. Not after what we've seen and read in those files. That man's not our dad," Kennedy said. "Plus, with how much she still loves him . . ." Lincoln looked away as if he knew the truth but didn't want to admit it. Kennedy tapped the table. "Now, how are we going to get our sister home safely?"

"Well, there are a few things I'd like to go over with you before we finalize a plan. Your dad—".

"Craig," Kennedy interrupted.

"Yes. Sorry. Craig stole Regan's file on the way out. Yours too, but our information on the two of you is limited. Your sister's file is much more in-depth. The problem is, while she was here, I was testing a hypothesis."

Lincoln's face twisted with anger. I held up a finger. "She was aware I was testing a theory. She just didn't know what it was, that way there was less chance of skewing the results. I had planned to tell Regan what the outcome was today, but she left and I didn't have a chance." And because of that, she was in far more danger than she was aware of. "Regan's powers act as a catalyst for others. Being around her makes their powers stronger. She isn't aware. Craig is. His powers were formidable to begin with. And with Regan at his side, he'll be unstoppable."

Lincoln shifted uncomfortably in his seat. "I guess this is the spot where we should mention . . ." He looked

Alex Gordon

at his brother. Kennedy nodded. "Our powers don't work unless we're in the near vicinity of one another."

I rubbed my hand over my chin. "Interesting." This family was full of surprises. "I wonder if the two of you act as a catalyst for others as well?"

They shrugged. "I doubt it. Otherwise wouldn't have Craig noticed it years ago?"

"How often did he use his powers while you were in his presence?"

"Not often," Kennedy said. "We were his family. He didn't need to."

"Exactly. Navi, can you come here please?"

She shuffled over. "Yeah?" Her eyes nervously darted toward the twins.

"I need you to go stand between the two of them and rest your hands on their shoulders." Her dark eyes widened as if I'd asked her to marry one of them. "They won't bite."

"I might," Lincoln said, smiling flirtatiously.

Navi's eyes grew even wider.

"I'm just kidding. We won't hurt you, I promise." He quirked a finger to urge her forward.

She gulped hard then stepped up between the twins before hesitantly resting her hands on their shoulders. Kennedy reached up and patted her hand attempting to soothe her fear. Her cheeks reddened.

"Okay. I want you to teleport them both through the wall."

She vehemently shook her head.

"What's the worst that can happen?" I asked, wanting the twins to be prepared.

"I'll knock us all out."

"No worries," Kennedy said. "We have thick skulls.

I promise."

"I'm going to let you in on a little secret," I explained that the twin's powers acted as a booster. I hoped I was right.

Her lips squashed together as she nodded, visibly contemplating her situation. She didn't want to do as I'd asked, but she was a people pleaser. She closed her eyes and took a deep breath before vanishing along with the twins. On the other side of the wall, she squealed with success. When she ran back into the room, her frightened eyes had changed to excitement. "I haven't been able to do that yet!"

I cocked a brow at the brothers. They exchanged wide-eyed glances. I was right.

Chapter 51: Regan

Dad glanced at the big clock hanging on the wall over the family photos of complete strangers. "We need to get going. It looks as if they have a daughter around your age. Why don't you find her room and pack yourself some clothes?"

"But . . . but they're not mine."

"I have a feeling her closet is well stocked. She won't miss them. I don't want to stop. Okay?"

"Okay." I trekked up the staircase and peeked inside doors until I found a room with soft yellow décor and a youthful feminine touch. The afternoon sun reflected off a full-sized mirror attached to the closet door. My hair was gross and the flight attendant's uniform I was still wearing was uncomfortable. I stripped down, leaving the clothes on the floor and found the attached bathroom. I wanted to take my time to enjoy the luxuries this room afforded but my dad was anxious to leave. I quickly showered and wrapped a fluffy white towel around my head and one around my body. I hurried to the walk-in closet before perusing through rows and drawers of beautiful clothes—far more expensive than anything I'd ever owned. Though mortified by my actions, I found some underwear that had the tags still on them. I gasped when I saw the price. Who knew underwear could cost that much? After pulling on an outfit, I selected some clothes and tossed them into a carry-on suitcase with a designer label before I stole some supplies from her bathroom. I headed back down the hall.

A faint rustling caught my attention. I stuck my head inside an office to find my dad opening a safe that was buried in the wall behind a painting.

I walked over to the desk. The screensaver darted around the computer and the faint scent of coffee, from the cup sitting next to the mouse pad, drifted in the air. Curiously, it was black as death. Like me, my dad usually used copious amount of creamer. It was just another sign that he wasn't the same man.

"What are you doing?"

"It's less suspicious if we have cash. Though we can make people give us things for free, the less of a footprint we leave behind the better."

I wasn't even that okay taking the girl's clothes, let alone stealing this family's money.

"That's not right," I said.

His head snapped toward me, and he pinned me down with a hard stare. "The two gentlemen that bought this property got it for a steal after my grandparents died. I was young and I just wanted it gone, hoping the memories would go with it. So, please excuse me if I don't feel bad," he said snidely and turned back to what he was doing.

Whoa.

Jogging down the stairs, I went out to the car and waited for him. This new, less likeable, version of my dad was going to take some time to get used to.

"Where are we going?" I asked when he slid into the driver's seat.

He set two sodas in the drink holder and buckled his seatbelt before pulling out of the yard. "We'll head south for now."

As soon as he turned onto the highway, he stepped on the gas and sped away.

GSS's concerns were starting to creep up on me. My dad wasn't being completely honest. Though, if he didn't mean to kill Dr. Gloria, he hadn't done anything violent enough to warrant him being a target. And what if GSS had lied to me? What if Dr. Gloria wasn't dead? Then they were using her as an excuse to target my dad. There was only one way to find out.

My plan was to act as normal with my dad as possible until I could figure out the truth. "At some point, I need to call Gin. Maybe I can get them to back off."

"I think that's a good idea," he said, surprising me. "When we stop for gas, we'll switch cars and take someone's cell phone."

Look at us, all Bonnie and Clyde—the thought was disturbing. I rested my face in the palms of my hands. But I held out hope that our spree wouldn't be one of violence. That was a line I wasn't willing to cross.

"For now, get some sleep, kiddo. You look beat." He reached over and messed up my hair. The gesture was so familiar it gave me a glimpse of normalcy allowing my anxiety to take a back seat. At least for the moment.

I closed my eyes and later woke up as we pulled behind a black sports car with dual exhausts parked next to the city sidewalk. Red, white, and blue decorations hung from the streetlamps just starting to glow against the dusky sky. American flags waved gently outside most of the businesses. I couldn't believe only a month had passed. It seemed like a lifetime ago that I'd arrived back in Alaska with hopes of learning how to control my powers.

Dad handed me the keys to the rental car. "You're up. Make a trade but make sure he doesn't remember a thing."

A gentleman, about thirty years old, was strolling down the sidewalk fumbling for his keys inside the pocket of his wool pea coat. Once he found them, he hit the button to unlock the door. It beeped.

If that guy had an emotional connection to his car, it wasn't going to be easy. He'd give it to me, but erasing memories didn't come naturally. But my pet, not having had a snack all day was eager to try.

I got out of the vehicle and said in my best flirty voice, "Hey, nice car."

He gave me the once over and replied, "Thanks, ya wanna go for a spin?"

"Absofloggin-loutly. But only if I can drive." I batted my lashes and I held out my hand for the keys.

He stopped and paused. "Can you drive a stick?"

"Let's find out, shall we?" I licked my bottom lip before I bit down.

He shrugged and tossed me his keys all on his own accord. *Fool.* I jingled them in the air. "But sorry, you're not coming with me."

His eyes narrowed, not sure if I was teasing or serious.

I opened the glass box and a coil of smoke slid down the side infusing me with power.

I wish. His expression lost its suspicion and his eyes glazed over. I grabbed his wrist while staring at him. *Forget we were ever here.* I pressed the keys to the rental into his hand and said, "This is your car. You have plans to trade it in and buy something sportier this weekend."

I kind of felt bad because the minute he got into his

glove box for his registration, he'd figure out the car wasn't his. But not bad enough to stop me from stealing his car.

Dad grabbed my suitcase and I hit the tailgate button to pop it open.

A woman wearing a power suit and red stilettoes with matching lipstick walked out of the restaurant across the street.

"Hey," I shouted, "Can I borrow your cell phone?"

Running across the road, I took it from her. Then all memory of me was erased from her mind. It wasn't as hard to do on regular people as it once was.

I jumped in the passenger seat of the sports car. It was immaculate inside and smelled like leather, a new car, and cologne. I snooped through the glove compartment finding a box of condoms and a bag of weed. Looks like we'd interrupted one heck of a party.

Once we were out of the city, I asked, "Can I call him?" Dad nodded. "Can I *not* put it on speakerphone?"

He hesitated, then nodded again. "You and Gin, huh?"

My face began to flush.

"I thought he said you had a boyfriend? Jude, was it?"

My mouth dropped open. This was not a conversation I wanted to have.

"Good for you," he said, "You leveled up."

I glanced his way. "What?"

"Jude's gifts are cool, but Gin—now there's someone worth your time. Don't worry we're hardwired to surround ourselves with power."

Thinking back, Jude did say he didn't have that much trouble with my darkness initially. It was after Gin had kissed me that things got really bad for him. He said that's when the nagging voice in his head turned sentient, whispering horrible things about me; I was a lying, cheating, whore, and a killer that couldn't be trusted. The voice didn't let up even after we'd broken up. *Shit.* I leaned forward and rested my face in my hands. It only stopped after we'd severed our bond.

Did I even have a choice in the matter, or had my pet decided for me? Had it tossed Jude aside the minute it found someone stronger? The notion that it had that much influence made my stomach heave. I swallowed hard to keep the bile where it belonged. Not capable of dealing with another problem, especially one that wasn't a pressing matter, I tucked it away for safe keeping.

"No offense, I really don't want to talk about it with *my dad*," I said. I couldn't even hide the horror in my tone.

He chuckled. He looked like himself, he sounded like himself, but still, there was something off. The subtleties of his new personality weren't exactly an upgrade. He was short-tempered and a thief, keeping my pet on high alert. Though it had finally calmed down and stopped growling. Now it was giving my dad a constant side-eye as if it were watching him but never looking directly at him.

"Understandable," he said, attempting not to laugh, "but after you're finished talking, we're pulling over and you can drive. I'm tired."

Excitement lit up my face. I was itching to see what this baby could do, knowing that my dad could divert the cops at any time he wished.

I inhaled a long breath, my fingers hovering over the phone, and dialed Gin's number. Tiny butterfly wings tickled the lining of my stomach and fluttered inside my chest. I had no idea what I was going to say or how mad he was going to be.

"Yes," Gin snapped impatiently as if he wasn't used to getting calls from strange numbers.

"Gin," I said.

"Oh, God! Regan! Are you okay?" His words, normally slow and calm, raced out.

"I'm fine. Everything's good."

"Where are you?"

"That's not important."

"You're not alone?" he inquired. His cadence went back to normal as if he'd gotten control of his surprise and he was carefully choosing every word.

"No. I'm with my dad. And you're wrong about him."

"Regan," Gin said my name like a warning, "are you on speakerphone?"

"No."

"Are you lying to me?" Though his demeanor was now composed, he sounded suspicious.

I swallowed. "No," I said defensively.

"But he's next to you?"

"Yes."

"He killed Dr. Gloria."

"If that's true, it wasn't his intent. He only meant to sedate her."

He huffed out an irritated laugh and said like I was stupid, "Regan, he gave her half a bottle."

I was silent for a few seconds. "How do I know you're not the one lying to me?"

"You don't," he said softly. "I could text you her death certificate, but there's no way you'd be able to tell if it was forged. I could send you her notes on Craig and you'd be horrified. But you'd never know if they were faked or not. I'm asking you to trust me Darlin'."

My toes curled. "Why should I trust you? You lied to me."

The silence on the other end hung between us. "I didn't lie, I just didn't tell you. And I wish I could go back and rectify my mistake. But I'm not lying now. You saw the video, she's dead. He killed her." Even over the phone, his pain was clear.

The two were close and her death was bound to be difficult for him. Though I wasn't sure he could be trusted, I wished I could be there, instead of here.

"Dad, why did you make her take so many?" I held the phone away from my face so Gin could hear his answer.

"I asked her once what would happen if I took a dozen pills, she said it would make me sleep, but it sure as hell wouldn't kill me. She told me, if that was my plan, I could find easier ways to accomplish it."

That didn't sound like Dr. Gloria to me, but how would I know how she behaved with my dad? I only had one video to go by, and she didn't seem fond of him.

My dad glanced in the rearview mirror. "I assumed a few pills wouldn't kill her. My intent was to sedate her so I could get away. I wanted to see my daughter and you guys flat refused."

I put the phone back up to my ear. "See?" I said.

"I hope you realize, he's the one lying," Gin said. "Not that I'm not grateful to hear your voice, and the others will be happy you're alive. Jude's out of his mind with worry and completely torn up that he severed your bond and now he can't find you."

Familiar with Gin's inclination toward privacy, with that comment, I knew he was alone even if I wasn't. "Jude will be fine," I said. As of yet, I wasn't feeling that sad that we'd severed the bond. Because having some privacy to process feelings without a voyeur, was truly a relief and I was thankful our connection was gone.

A few beats of silence lingered over the line until he said, "And you're still okay with the decision the two of you made?"

For the first time in our conversation, Gin sounded scared. My breath hitched in my chest and I had to hold back the emotion attempting to break free. "Yes. He's never going to be okay with my life choices."

"Well, Darlin', I'm starting to question them myself."

Despite the insult, I couldn't help but laugh. "I understand that my dad isn't the same person that he was, but I don't think he's who you're making him out to be either. I'm asking you to give me some time."

"You know I can't do that Regan. Your father's dangerous and deep down in your heart, you know that I'm right."

Maybe, but I wasn't giving up on him until I was certain. "I don't know that you are." I looked over at my dad. "I only called to let you know that I'm safe," I said ready to hang up.

"Regan," Gin yelled.

My dad's head snapped sideways and he mouthed, "You okay?"

I pressed my lips into a line and nodded. I whispered to Gin, letting him know I was still on the line, "Yes?"

"Was any of that stuff between us real? Are we still . . . Or was I just a distraction so you could escape?"

I wanted to lie to him. I wanted to tell him I used him purely for my gain. It would be safer for him if my father didn't know that I had feelings for Gin. But I couldn't. Besides, with the way Dad was eyeing me, that ship had sailed. So, I told Gin the truth. "Though I'm afraid I'll never be able to trust you again, my feelings are real." Or at least I hoped the feelings were mine and not just my pet's.

Over the line, I could hear him sigh with relief.

"And I can only imagine one scenario where that would change." I altered my tone and growled, "So, help me God, if you hurt my dad, we're finished."

I hung up and tossed the phone out the window and along with it a small piece of my heart.

Chapter 52: Regan

Outside the window of our ritzy hotel room, flashes of rainbow colors lit up the blackened sky. The firework explosions were muted by the thick glass.

I didn't feel like there was much to celebrate. I missed my friends, and my dad wasn't the same kind of fun that he used to be.

I turned back to the TV and flipped through channels as I sat on the couch. Ours was a suite decorated in cool tones and had two bedrooms, a living room, a dining room, and a shared bathroom. "Dad, you're obviously up to something. Do you want to fill me in? Or do you enjoy keeping me in the dark?"

While my dad claimed to have no destination or plans, I suspected he was lying. At the moment we were in southern California, L.A. or Hollywood, or wherever we were now. When I wasn't driving, I was sleeping so it was easy to miss a city or two along the way.

Without answering me, he dried his hair and tossed the towel on the floor after he was done. Some things never changed. My dad was a bit of a disaster. My mom always said he was as messy as us kids.

Someone knocked on the door, interrupting my interrogation. It was room service. A guy rolled a cart inside carrying dinner. My dad handed him a tip before he left. This would be the first actual meal besides fast food and gas station snacks we'd had in the last twenty-some hours that it took us to get here.

Again, I wasn't sure if here was the destination or if perhaps we were headed to Mexico. My dad had been cagey and elusive with his information. On the drive, he kept quizzing me. He wanted to know the intricacies of my powers and what the other students and instructors were capable of. I even told him about Rory and that she'd been sent home because she was a dud. I was honest to a point—my skill at omitting the important details was much sneakier than it had been last year.

"This Rory girl—you clashed?" My dad had asked.

"You could say that."

"So, you didn't spend much time around her?"

"As little as humanly possible."

"Interesting. Were there any other students that were sent home?"

"Nope."

Curious about my dad's abilities as well, I grilled him too. It only seemed fair. When he said he could control masses of people without much trouble, I scoffed as if I didn't believe him. I could only do it if I was angry. To prove it, when we pulled over for gas at a busy truck stop along the way, he made everyone exit the building on his command. A cruel smile lifted his lips reminding me of my pet right before I released it. Around fifty people, and two long haul truckers that were using the shower facilities, walked outside—all because my dad commanded it.

While he demonstrated his abilities, my pet backed into the corner of its cage with its hackles raised and growled, the sound rumbled between my ears. It didn't like my dad, that much was clear. It seemed frightened of him. But by the time my dad finished, my pet, though still trembling, had calmed down. It had practically laid on its back with its feet in the air as if it submitted to my dad's power. It had never shown me the same kind of respect. To be honest, it irked me.

Once the truckers were no longer under my dad's influence, their heads swiveled around wondering why the hell they were standing in the parking lot bare-naked and dripping wet. People stared and pointed. Mothers shielded their kids' eyes and hurried back to their vehicles carrying their purchases close to their chests. A couple of men shouted at the truckers to leave. Once they overcame their temporary shock, they scuttled back inside the building, their ample bellies and other things flopping with every step.

I couldn't help but chuckle. I'd never tried anything similar unless I was beyond angry, and I wasn't sure that I'd succeed. Though I knew Gin had plans for me to try, we hadn't gotten there yet, and now, because I left, we never would.

Knowing it was pointless to dwell on what could've been, I turned my attention back to my dad. I continued with my latest interrogation. "So, what's it going to be? Are you going to tell me what we're doing?" I grabbed my dinner off the hotel cart and set it on my lap as I plopped down on the couch. I picked up a French fry to dip it in ranch sauce. I was doing my best not to form an opinion on my dad too early. He wasn't the same person and I needed to give *this* Craig a shot.

He sat down with his burger at the small table next to the window. "I'm torn. I'm not sure you're going to be willing to help me."

I cocked a brow. "Help you what?"

"To change the world, of course," he said before he

took a huge bite of his burger. A pickle squished out the other end and fell with a splat onto his plate.

I laughed. "Don't set your goals too high," I teased, waving a fry in the air. "No, really, what is it we're doing?"

"I just told you. I don't think GSS uses our powers for the greater good. Sure, they do small things that benefit the individual, but what are they doing to solve the world's problems?"

He couldn't be serious. I swallowed and took a drink before answering. "I'm not sure it's their job to fix the world. I think the only way to fix it is to start over." I wasn't big into politics, but I was smart enough to know neither party in America was really out to help the people. It seemed to me as if they spent most of their time arguing with each other and not accomplishing anything for the average American.

"Why not? And if not them, then who?"

"I don't have the answers, Dad." This conversation was stupid and pointless.

"What if I do?"

"Enlighten me." I rolled my eyes so he could see.

"Together, I believe you and I can change the world. We'll make this planet a better place for everyone."

"You're funny," I said drily, thinking he was still joking. When he didn't respond, I wiped my lips with my napkin and looked at him. "Are you for real?"

"Yes. I fear that with the way this world is headed, there'll be nothing left for future generations."

"How would you know? I thought you forgot everything."

"I have traumatic amnesia. But I know how the world works and I can function in everyday life normally. And as my brain heals, the other things will get clearer. Having you around seems to be helping. My memories are surfacing sporadically. Plus, I've been watching the news and you might be surprised, but I can still read. From what I can tell—it's only gotten worse in the last year."

"I'm glad your memories are coming back. But don't you think you should focus on getting better first? Trying to change the world seems a little far-fetched in your condition. Besides, why do you care?" I set my plate on the coffee table.

"Because, despite the fact I don't recall everything, I do love you and your brothers and I want a world where my grandchildren can grow up safely."

He sounded like a political advertisement. Next, he'd ask for my vote. I sneered. I was never having kids knowing that my genetic defect could be passed on. "I don't buy it," I said, shaking my head.

"What? That I want to help the world?"

I nodded.

"You're hurting my feelings."

"Pfftt." I didn't believe him. I'd yet to see any true feelings. Sure, he'd called me kiddo, baby girl, and his little fish whisperer but we hadn't had a single conversation on where our next fishing trip would be, what I planned on studying in college, or how mom spoiled the twins because they were her favorite. Dad would always deny it but then he'd wink and tell me I was his favorite. This altruistic schtick was questionable, to say the least. I might've believed him if I were dealing with my dad, but this was Craig 2.0 and I didn't buy it for a second.

He studied my face long and hard before he raised

his hands in the air. "Okay. I can see you're not convinced. What's it going to take for you to trust me?"

I shrugged. Trust wasn't high on my list.

"Well, let me start here. At one point, while I was in a coma, so were you. It was the first thing I remember feeling," he patted the spot over his heart, "anything. Before it was dark and lonely. Then the darkness receded and I found you, hovering in a rainbow of colors, in the heavens or somewhere in between. You were about to give up and pass on to the other side. The pain that caused me was unbearable. I realize I'm not the person I was, but I am your dad. I always will be and our connection is strong. Strong enough that I was able to find you in the vast emptiness I was lingering in. As I felt you drifting away, I told you *'my baby girl doesn't back down. She never gives up.'* Do you remember?"

I stopped breathing momentarily and I nodded, too shocked to actually answer. I remembered every detail as if it had happened yesterday. What it was like there, what Dad said, what Jude did to save me. All of it. And I'd never told *anyone* what I'd experienced. The only way he could know is if he was there too.

"Kiddo, you're destined for greatness. I knew it then. I know it now. At the time, I thought you were going to have to do it alone and I told you I'd be there when you finished changing the world. But I think the Gods have another plan in mind."

"You mean God."

He shrugged. "That's what I said. Now that I'm here, come on baby girl, let's do this together."

Tears sprung from my eyes and flooded down my cheeks. My jaw trembled while my chest quaked. I'd thought he was dead at the time, but he wasn't. He was there for me then, and he was here for me now. I'd been skeptical because he was different. But Jude's grandpa once told me *different wasn't always bad, just different.* I had to give my dad the benefit of the doubt.

I bit down on my lip and nodded. "Okay, Daddy," my voice trembled, "let's change the world."

A smile bloomed on his face crinkling his silver blue eyes. "There's my girl."

"But how do we start?"

"I have a couple of ideas."

"And if the goal is to save the world . . ." The vastness of the problem was overwhelming and quite honestly, ridiculous, in my opinion. But, he was my dad. And I loved him more than anyone in the world. If this was what it took for me to get him back, count me in. "Couldn't we use all the help we can get? I know people."

He chuckled. "Matter of fact, we could. Why don't you give me a few weeks to think some things through? Together, we can brainstorm, and then we'll give Gin a call to see if GSS is willing to work with us. Does that sound like a good plan?"

Relief, excitement, and hope twisted in my throat. I couldn't even squeak out *a yes* so, I nodded. With the back of my sleeve, I dried the tears from my cheeks. I had no idea how we were going to save the world. I didn't even know what we were saving it from. But it didn't matter. I really didn't care. The thought that soon I'd be reunited with my friends—and Gin—left my heart racing.

Only a month ago, though it seemed like a lifetime, Mr. LaCroix had warned me, *Regan, your powers, in the wrong hands, could topple governments. Destroy worlds even.*

But what if, with my powers in the right hands, all of us together could save the world?

A word about the author...

Alex Gordon is a bit of a wanderer, having lived in Washington, Montana, Germany, Alaska, and Tennessee where she currently resides with her husband and two rescued German shepherds. When not writing, you can probably find her hiking, or if she's lucky—fishing, though she's not opposed to camping out on the couch with dessert and binging murder mysteries.

alexgordonauthor.com

Thank you for purchasing
this publication of The Wild Rose Press, Inc.

For questions or more information
contact us at
info@thewildrosepress.com.

The Wild Rose Press, Inc.
www.thewildrosepress.com